THE SPRING MAIDEN

THE CARTOGRAPHER'S WAR
BOOK ONE

ALLISON ANDERSON

OLIVERHEBERBOOKS

Cover Design by Cauldron Press

Published by Oliver-Heber Books

0 9 8 7 6 5 4 3 2 1

For Dad.

This is all your fault.

Winter
Autumn
Faerie
Summer
Spring
The Isles of Aigean
The Mist
To the Continent
Speculo
Olympia
Talaria
Olympia
Tauros
Eleusion
Delphine

PROLOGUE

DRESSES AND SHADOWS

"Save me, Angelica!" Penny Barclay gasped, squeezing through the tight crowd of well-dressed courtiers around her. "I don't think I can dance another set."

With no sparks of romance, no feelings of love blossoming like she wished they might, Penny had spent the entire night waltzing down her dance card— all while her mother sat watching. Any time Penny caught a glimpse of Lady Dominique Barclay's sparkling jade gown, she would catch those similarly green eyes on her. Perhaps *she* was driving the flickers of romance away with her steely stare.

Mother always insisted love was a fool's errand. A trap. A trick. A lie.

But Penny yearned for it anyway.

"Penny!" Angelica Hermen shouted, breaking away from the gaggle of potential partners. With Angelica's dark ringlets piled atop her head and her warm, brown skin glowing with excitement, it was easy to see why the gentlemen flocked to her.

Penny grabbed her best friend's hands. "This is exhausting

and not a single man has survived Mother's glare." Mother was known as "the Domineering Duchess" for a reason.

Angelica looked about. "I'm sure no one will blame you for taking a rest. If you make a run for it now, you may be able to skip this dance with no one the wiser. The cotillion is a doozy anyway. I'll waylay any potential dance partners and give you a break. I'm sure your mother will appreciate not having to skewer anyone for five minutes as well." Angelica winked.

"You're a gem. I couldn't have survived this night without you."

"Dearest Penny, this night is yours and I know you will seize it with a glowing green fist!"

Penny hugged her friend with a laugh and eased her way through the crowd, seeking a drink and perhaps somewhere to cool off. She spotted a table laden with a variety of fruit juices and iced water. After picking out a cup, she scooted toward the large windows at the back of the ballroom.

Penny pressed a heated cheek to the soothing chill the windowpanes offered. On the other side of the barrier lay a flowering garden full of spring blooms. Iris, crocus, tulip, and lilac all spread in thick bunches, perfectly trimmed— except where it looked like someone had trampled a large bed of white daffodils. Penny's fingers tightened around her glass. How could someone be so careless? Especially in such a beautiful garden.

Not ten feet away, a door stood sentry, leading out onto a dimly lit patio that gave entry into the gardens. She looked around until she spotted Mother speaking enthusiastically with another lord, likely unaware that Penny was even off the dance floor. By the way Mother's hands fluttered through the air, it likely pertained to the harvest. It would be a warm day in Winter if she ever found Mother speaking about anything but the business.

"It'll take two seconds to peek and then I'll be right back," Penny muttered, setting her half-finished drink on a nearby table. She hurried to the door and stepped out into the night. A shiver worked its way down her spine as she left the safety of those lit halls.

Penny crouched at the edge of the flowerbed. "What kind of person does this to flowers?" Her nostrils flared as she pinched the stem of a bent flower between her fingers to stand tall. Her free hand settled in the soil next to the plant.

Green light permeated her palms.

Penny closed her eyes and reached out to the plants with her mind. Magic swept over the small bed of flowers. Stems thickened. Ripped leaves knitted back together. Creased petals straightened. One after the other, the flowers regained their original splendor, some even growing stronger than they were before.

Penny stood and brushed the dirt from her palm. "Much better."

A shout pierced the tranquil air.

Her skirts tangled her legs as she whirled toward the moonlit garden. A man wearing the same colors as the servants inside the castle crashed through flower beds as he raced parallel to the white castle wall. Fear sat plain on his pale face as he took a backwards glance. A dark shadow followed immediately behind.

The two ran out of sight. No one else stood in the garden. Would anyone even hear her if she yelled? If she went back into the ballroom and stirred up a fuss, Mother would likely make her leave the ball. But she couldn't allow the servant to come to harm.

She followed. They were in a garden, a place where she reigned. She would do everything in her power to keep innocent people safe. It would be fine. Her slippers crunched across the pebbled pathways, the frantic steps of the chased man easily guiding her. A large hedge maze came into view. The servant darted toward the entrance, and a shadowed form slammed him into a bed of violets resting beneath an oak tree.

Red flared across Penny's vision as she thrust glowing palms toward the wrestling forms.

Roots from the great oak whipped out from the ground and separated the fighters. They squirmed in their new confines, but Penny's hold only tightened as more roots pinned their arms and legs to their sides and hoisted them into the air.

She strode toward her dangling quarry. "Doesn't anyone hold an ounce of respect for flowers anymore?"

"Excuse me?" A deep, incredulous voice came from one of the hanging bundles.

The green of Penny's palms lit the faces of the two men now under her supervision. The servant still bucked, his face straining. The other owned the deep voice— and a pair of seething amber eyes.

And his eyes weren't the only thing that caught her attention. Two pale, pointed ears stood out against his inky black hair. He was ellylon fae, at least half if not full. There were many in Olympia with fae blood in their ancestry, but not many as closely descended as this man.

His brows furrowed and Penny realized she'd been staring.

"What?" she asked belatedly.

He frowned. "I'm trying to apprehend a trespassing rebel on castle grounds, and you're concerned about blossoms?"

Rebel? She turned to her other captive. Mother had spoken about some insurrections since the Tyrant King's death a few years ago, but she didn't expect the rebels bold enough to infiltrate the castle. She cringed as the servant squirmed, vitriol spewing from his tongue.

"Filthy gifted scum!" he spluttered.

Perhaps he wasn't so innocent.

Amber Eyes blew out a breath. "Thank you for assisting in the capture of the rebel. If you could release me, I will fetch more of my men to take him into custody." He glared at the cursing rebel. "A young lady should not be subject to such company."

Penny held back a snort. Young lady? He only looked a few years older than Penny herself. She dropped Amber Eyes from the oak tree's grasp.

He studied the bindings Penny had procured. Once he seemed to deem them suitable, turned and began circling around them.

Penny fidgeted, smoothing imaginary wrinkles from her gown. She loved the way the moonlight shimmered over the embroidered outlines of colorful leaves and flowers— the only color added to the customary white dress. The small piece of rebellion buoyed her spirits. "I suppose I should apologize," she muttered under her breath.

Amber Eyes turned back to give her a flat look.

Her buoyed spirits faltered. *Curse fae hearing.* She sighed while her magic pieced the garden back together before following after him. "If I'd known the man was a rebel, I wouldn't have intervened. I simply saw a servant being chased and wanted to help."

Amber Eyes shifted, his piercing gaze cutting through the shadows around them. "There is no real need to apologize. I should be thanking you for helping me." His eyes flicked to hers for only a moment before returning to the scene around them. "I don't know how many more flower beds would have met their untimely demise had you not come along."

Penny opened her mouth, a sharp retort on her tongue, but a high-pitched whistle from Amber Eyes cut her off. Too late, she clamped her hands over her ears.

"There you are." Amber Eyes crouched as an odd-looking mass of gray fur bounded into view.

Penny's jaw dropped, her frustrations toward the rude fae forgotten. "Is that a three headed dog?"

Moonlight shone over the sleek, gray coat dotted with black and white spots. Three heads bobbed up and down as Amber Eyes reached out to pet each one.

Curiosity piqued, she stepped toward them. "Is it a he or a she? Why three heads? Was it bred this way?"

Amber Eyes' attention stayed riveted toward her face, expression unreadable, before he seemed to realize her questions warranted a response. "He was a mistake. I was working on a project when my brother's dog came in and knocked over a bottle of multiplying agent and drank a bit off the floor. She's fine, but her litter came out mutated. Spot's the only pup who made it and we still don't fully understand why he did."

The low timbre of his voice cascaded over Penny as he told his short tale. Now that he wasn't snapping at her, the sound was soothing. She wanted to ask him to keep talking.

Spot looked over at her and timidly sniffed at the edges of her dress with one head. Slowly, each head perused the rest of her. It only took a few moments before all three were nudging her for attention.

Penny stilled. "Spot? You named your very unique, one of a kind, beautiful dog, *Spot*?"

Amber Eyes looked at her, a crease between his dark brows. "I thought it a fine name, considering his spots."

The dog demanded Penny's attention. One head licked Penny's right palm. Another sniffed her dress. The last placed his head beneath her other hand, demanding to be petted. She laughed as the one sniffing her dress came up to be pet by the hand being licked.

"I don't have enough hands!" she exclaimed as she tried to pet each one.

Amber Eyes' lips curved into a shining smile.

The whole world came to a standstill.

The smile brightened everything around them. Colors became more vibrant and the moonlight seemed to highlight every lovely line of his face. Penny swore she would never forget that smile. It would become the smile all other smiles would be compared to from then on. She smiled back, not able to help herself.

Heat suffused her cheeks. "Please excuse me. We've not been properly introduced and here I am keeping you and your faithful companion from your evening." She offered an elegant curtsy. "I'm Penelope Barclay, though everyone calls me Penny. While I now know Spot's name, I don't believe I caught yours." She offered a hand.

Callused fingers met hers. A bolt of lightning ran up her arm and down to her toes from where their hands touched. She nearly yanked her hand from his. He leaned over her fingers, his lips a hair's breadth away. Penny couldn't suck air into her lungs. A hair's breadth was a mile.

He slowly released her. Had it actually been slow or had time just ceased to make any sense? Penny blinked. *What just happened?* Heat zipped through every particle of her body.

His touch finally left hers. "It is a pleasure to meet you, Lady Penelope. My name is—"

"Penny!" Mother's frantic voice called. Penny spun away from her companion. Mother came around the corner a moment later. "Praise the Goddess! I have been looking everywhere for you."

"I'm sorry, Mother, I was just—" She turned to Amber Eyes and Spot, only to find the indent their feet left in the grass.

1

CUTTINGS AND CONTENTION

Dearest Penny,

Can you believe it's been a full year since our debut when I met Devan? I can't believe the time has gone so quickly. Now, I'm married, honeymooning in Faerie, and you are getting set to take over your family's business. Look how far we've come!

Thank you again for the wonderful wedding gift. I can't tell you how many times I've used the stationery kit since you gifted it to us. Devan has likely used it more than I have, though none of his letters have been anywhere near as fun as mine.

We reached port in Summer two days ago. The beaches in Olympia don't even compare. The water is so clear you can see the fish swimming dozens of *feet below. I even saw a pink dolphin! Devan laughed when I told him and said to wait until we go to the Isles next year.*

Everyone has been working tirelessly. Father's still trying to get the Court in Winter to agree to his proposals, but they've been silent. Hopefully, being here will help open some doors. However, after seeing the dolphins, I am inclined to wait as long as the Winter Court wants.

The only thing that could have made the journey more enjoyable was if I could have had you with me. Someday. Anyways, good luck with planting. I know how much you enjoy this season—especially with your birthday being this week! I know you think marital bliss has fogged my brain, but I could never forget my best friend's special day. I hope you enjoy your present. I saw it at market yesterday and knew it was meant to be.

Your Kindhearted Friend,
Angelica

Penny sat at her haphazard desk in the barn, holding Angelica's coded letter to her chest alongside the leather bracelet studded with pieces of sea glass. The green of the glass shined the exact shade of Penny's eyes.

Had it really been a year? The scene played so fresh in her mind. The ball. The gowns. Her friend.

The pair of amber eyes.

That voice still followed her everywhere. Flashes of dark

hair or spotted dogs always turned her head. She hadn't seen him again in the year that had followed their chance meeting, but she still caught herself looking for him everywhere.

She took in a deep breath, letting in all of her wants and desires. She allowed a single imagining of what her life would be like if Mother wasn't so uncompromising about her leaving the duchy as little as possible. Imagined what it would be like if she could travel the entirety of the kingdom whenever it suited her rather than the few times Mother deemed it unavoidable. Only taking trips to the neighboring noble houses did not count in Penny's book. How different she would do things if she were the one who decided which course her life took. Or who she let into it. She held all of the feelings and wishes in that breath.

Then she let the breath go, sending her desires with it.

Penny set the parcel down and picked up the list of workers assigned to their northernmost field. The numbers didn't add up. She was three workers short for the next two weeks. She gathered up her papers, putting her bracelet and Angelica's letter in one of the many pockets of her apron, and walked out of the barn.

"Mornin' to ya m'lady!"

Penny turned and found Aaron, their field master, sitting atop his horse. As the two got closer, Aaron swung nimbly from his saddle for a man of his stout stature and walked beside his mount the rest of the way to Penny.

"Ah, Aaron, just the man I needed to see." Penny held up the papers in her hand. "I noticed some discrepancies on the list for the north field. Perhaps you can help me find where my workers went?" She handed the field master the lists.

Aaron rubbed a hand through his thinning, gray hair and shuffled through the papers. His horse came up to Penny and nosed her cheek. Penny scratched the mare between the ears and reached into one of her many pockets. She withdrew an envelope and dumped the contents of the pouch into her hand. She separated three tiny, tear shaped seeds from the others and deposited the majority of them back into their envelope. With the tip of her finger, she dug a small hole in the dirt between her feet and dropped the three seeds into the earth. Using her water flask, she sprinkled a little water over the soil. She covered the damp spot with her hands and then allowed her Goddess-given gift to feed the growth of the tiny seeds.

Gaia's presence within the earth connected with her magic. The feeling of reassurance as well as the drain on her spirit was a familiar one. For a few carrots, it only took a sliver of energy from her, helping grow her own magical stamina. Every bit of magic she gave back to the Goddess gave her a wider breadth of ability. Within seconds, two tufts of green popped out of the ground. Penny smiled. When her magic first manifested, it had taken her a full minute and a rest afterward to sprout this many plants. Now she could do a field in as long as it took to walk the span of it without a break.

She yanked the stems out of the soil to reveal the purple roots underneath.

"If you keep feedin' my horse them carrots she's gonna start thinkin' you like 'er more than I do."

Penny offered his horse the treats. "I have to make sure *all* of our workers are well taken care of."

The gruff man snorted and ruffled the horse's mane. "This ol' girl's bin spoilt rotten since you and the duchess had the stable rebuilt. I can't get 'er lazy hide out of there without a handful of oats e'ry mornin'." Aaron let out a chuckle and handed the papers back to Penny. "Looks like you drew the short straw. We've been five workers down since the fire last week. The boys are still coughin' and I told 'em you wouldn't want 'em back 'til they was good to work. You also gotta add Benny's leg still healing from the fire earlier in the year."

"No, you're right," nodded Penny. "I don't want them working until we're sure they're well enough to work." She tucked the papers into one of her pockets. "Is there anyone from town we can ask to help out for a week or two? The cuttings need to go in this week and half of the field isn't set up for irrigation."

Aaron smiled. "I posted in town two days ago and got five men comin' in before the end of next week. I didn't put 'em on the list 'cause I didn't know names, but when they get 'ere I'll send 'em yer way and you can tell 'em what they need to do to get that field on track."

Penny released the tension in her shoulders. "I should have known you had it all taken care of. Thank you, Aaron."

"'Tis an honor, m'lady." He hoisted himself onto his horse. "Yer mother has me at Hook Field if you need me. They was havin' troubles with the canal and I'm meetin' with Alfie 'bout it." He gave Penny a wink to which she let go of a small laugh. Putting the field master in spitting range of the water mage usually ended in disaster. With a hearty laugh of his own, Aaron nudged his steed with his heels and the two set off toward what was likely to be an eventful day.

With that thought, Penny crested the next hill and saw the family lands spread out in every direction. Barclay Manor sat atop the next hill over— a beacon of strength watching over the growth of the family's legacy. The red brick of the building shone bright in the morning light, contrasted by the large trees on the grounds around it. The canal sparkled as it wove around the orchards and spread through the hills. Alfie had certainly been earning his keep. The water mage kept the canal in pristine shape.

A tune stuck in her head as she walked, one she heard in

the village two nights ago during the spring festival. Her hum rang through the air as she kicked a solid black pebble down the road. She was lucky she had even heard the song. She'd met with Aaron that night on the outskirts of the tiny village Mother's field hands resided in. Penny regretted that she hadn't been able to attend the festival that year. Mother had always tried to take her to celebrate her birthday. They had loved going when she was younger, but with her duties rapidly building up on the farm within the last couple of years, she hadn't been able to participate in the festivities this year.

A solid kick sent the pebble into some weeds along the edge of a field. She took a fortifying breath. It was good. Mother had finally given her some responsibility, something to do besides sit at the manor all day twiddling her thumbs. She would give up a few parties if it meant she was able to actually make some decisions. She'd nearly wept when Mother had put her in charge of the farm hands' schedules last year.

Her musings carried her to her destination where she found a few workers already digging out trenches for the water and a wagon sitting on the side of the road. She strode over to the wagon and lifted the cloth laying over the precious cargo within. The pomegranate tree cuttings all looked healthy and ready to plant, bundled in wet burlap like sleeping infants. She returned the cloth covering the plants and joined in the work.

Penny directed each worker as they prepared the ground and dug the holes for the trees. With wooden markers in hand, she plotted out what type of pomegranate went to which spot on the field so she could grow the roots into the appropriate squares. Her magic easily took over.

Each row came and went as she remained connected to the earth around her. The magic of her ancestors mixed with the Goddess's in the soil. Their blood, sweat, and tears called out to her gift, helping her nourish the plants. Mother always told her their gifts were strongest here because of the amount of magic the family put into this ground. Generation after generation of Barclays all labored to feed this soil, all with their own unique gifts of growth. Stories ran through her memory of great-grandmothers and grandfathers that could raise an entire field in a day after a flood. Aunts and uncles who had the ability to create new kinds of fruit by fusing seeds of different kinds. One had built walls of thorns during the war with the fae. Another was said to have raised a forest to give lumber to build towns. Amazing feats had been made through the beautiful gifts the Goddess had given her family.

Mother regularly talked about how much magic the land had lost. Great miracles of magic weren't heard of anymore because the land was losing its gift, the magic fading from the earth. It was moments like these however, when she could almost hear the echoes of her ancestors in the ground, that she was closest to the Goddess that had given everything life.

Workers labored around her, all of them with sweat on their backs and determined looks on their faces. By midday, Penny could see each of them had a thick coating of dust painting their faces.

One of the workers whistled, loud enough to reach the end of the field where Penny stood, and gestured for all of them to gather at the wagon for lunch. Penny set the cutting she had in her hand beside the small handcart next to her and joined the others. A few sheets were pulled out of the rear of the cart and spread over the packed earth around the cart. Rolls, dried fruit, and hard cheeses were passed around. Penny put her water flask to her mouth and took a greedy gulp before biting into the roll one of the workers put in her hand.

In such close quarters, she couldn't help overhearing the chatter of those around her. It wasn't unusual for the workers to overlook her presence. They all wore the same clothing and she worked alongside them often enough they seemed to forget she wasn't just another worker. She tried to keep to herself and always attempted to give the employees the privacy they deserved, but in some cases it was rather difficult.

"I'm telling you," said one of the men on the other side of the cart, "this group is paying twice what we get here just to go to a few meetings and travel around telling everyone about them. I wouldn't mind making a little more gold just for wandering around."

Penny had a hard time not looking up from the food in her lap.

"The Barclays treat us good and fair," hissed one of the older workers. The voice belonged to Gerard, one of Aaron's kin. "Sounds like these people would be payin' fool's gold to me."

Penny leaned down to peek at them under the cart. The first speaker was a newer hire, a man a few years Penny's senior. He had already been in a few altercations with some of the other workers. Mother had been keeping a close eye on him.

He huffed. "It's not true. My friend got sworn into the group and told me the money's good. If that isn't enough, the message they're spreading will be cause enough for me." He leaned, but his whisper could be heard over the quieting chatter around them. "They're telling everyone the princes are a sham and that magic ought to be taken out of the picture. This group doesn't like the way the fae have been coming over to Olympia, especially after the Faerie Wars. Now that we have so much magic on the throne, they are worried about crafty fae coming back in and taking over again. Being Sireadh, I thought you might be interested."

The Faerie Wars? Two hundred years had passed since the High Queen, who now sat on the throne, had pulled all of the immortal fae behind the Mist at the end of the Wars. It wasn't until the Tyrant King's deposition by his sons that any kind of alliance had come from either side. Crown Prince Dion had worked hard with both the water folk on the Isles as well as the fair folk to come together as allies instead of maintaining a relationship as fallen gods and freed slaves. While history told how difficult it was for humans under fae rule, the three princes were doing all they could to bridge the divide and find peace with their neighbors. Penny shifted closer to the conversation. It didn't make sense that there were people who were rallying against the magical lands once again. Not when they hadn't had much contact until the Tyrant King had opened relations and Crown Prince Dion had signed the accords.

Gerard straightened. "Those princes are the best Goddess-sent gift this country has seen in ages. Sireadh or no, I won't be speakin' against them." He waved the traces of assumption away. "Don't you be preachin' that kind of garbage here, Martin. We're loyal to the Crown in these parts."

"The crown doesn't even have a king to wear it!" one of the other workers cut in. "It's been over four years since the old king died and we still don't even have a rightful ruler."

"Perhaps this group is right," said another. "More and more fae keep showing up on our land. Who's to say they won't want to go back to the way things used to be?"

Penny frowned. Mother sat on the Crown's Council. From what she'd shared with Penny, the accords between Faerie and the Isles of Aigean were very specific about this never happening. There would be a devastating war if one of those kingdoms decided they wanted to return to the time before the Faerie Wars. The accords were common knowledge. Why would these men believe something like that could ever happen again?

"Magic has no place in this world," said another.

"It was bad enough the king had such an obsession with magical women. We wouldn't be in this situation if he could have simply bedded bronties."

Heat flared to Penny's cheeks, though from the crass comment or her indignation, she didn't know. While Mother regularly complained about the Crown Prince's ridiculousness, Penny still knew the three princes were doing everything in their power to help this kingdom. While the three of them may have not shared the same mother and had been born all from magical heritages— mage, Aigean, and fae respectively— it still rankled her that there were people who didn't respect their positions simply because of what they were rather than who they were. Even if they were bronties, those without magic, it wouldn't change how they ruled over the kingdom.

"Having mages is bad enough without adding fair folk to the mix."

Penny stood, reaching the end of her patience. "That is quite enough!"

Every head turned in her direction. Guilt riddled faces peeked between righteous indignation.

Martin scrambled onto his feet. "We're speaking the truth. You can't keep us from our beliefs."

"Treasonous talk will not be tolerated at any time on this land. Your group is spreading something that will hurt many people. That kind of thing is not all right and will not be allowed to grow on Barclay soil."

"They are already here!" he snapped. "This group has funds and men. You can't stop them, only join them or fall when they have finally put this kingdom on the correct path."

Penny didn't even think twice before the words left her mouth. "You're dismissed."

Martin's eyes widened in horror and his eyes flicked around the group before returning his gaze to her. "You... you don't mean it." His voice came out slightly wobbled and he hunched his shoulders to hide the furious blush creeping up his face. "I wasn't doing anything wrong."

She gave him a stern look, still not allowing herself to glance at the audience around them. "I am not in the habit of saying things I do not mean. You're dismissed. Pack up your things and leave. You are not welcome on my family's lands any longer."

"You can't!" He clenched his hands and took a step toward her. "I didn't do anything wrong!"

She held a hand to one of her pockets and three of the other men stood between them, including Gerard.

"I will not allow treasonous talk on this farm. If you have such a problem with magic and those that have been gifted with it, this job is not the right fit for you. Get off my orchard."

A few of the other workers applauded. Some that had joined in Martin's tirade shied away from him.

Martin's face purpled with rage as he found no allies amongst his fellow workers. He pointed at Penny threateningly, thrusting his finger toward her as one would a knife. "You'll regret this."

Penny simply remained standing there, not willing to take the threat seriously and certainly not backing down.

With an outraged huff, Martin scooped his water skin off the ground and turned on his heel. Penny's eyes stayed fixed on the man until he was well out of sight.

She turned to address the group. "Lady Barclay and I will not tolerate such talk on this farm. If you have the same feelings as Martin, report to the barn for your week's pay at sundown and you will have until the end of tomorrow to pack your things and leave. I will not allow treason to sow itself into the work we are doing here." A few nods met her glare.

Penny gathered herself and walked back to the cart she'd

been working from. Martin's voice continued to ring in her ears. A chill slid down her spine as she placed cuttings in the ground. Her eyes lingered on the horizon where the rebel sympathizer had disappeared.

You will regret this.

She looked about at the others with their faces still hardened toward one another.

I pray that I won't.

2

MOTHERS AND DAUGHTERS

"You cannot just fire people, Penny." Mother's words echoed around her room while Philomina, Mother's lady's maid, set pins into her hair. The reddish-brown hairs weaving through the coiffure looked vibrant complemented by the chocolate-brown dinner dress.

Penny pinched the bridge of her nose and leaned against the door frame of Mother's dressing room. Her own maid, Sissy, had finished helping her get ready for their dinner at the Hermen's before Penny had come into Mother's rooms. "I couldn't let a rebel sympathizer walk around spouting treason to every person he came across." She crossed her arms over her chest. "I made sure he got his wages."

"That's not the point." Mother fiddled with a gold earring. "We're down too many workers because of these blasted fires and three workers left because you didn't keep tighter control of a situation. It should have been handled more tactfully. Everyone will simply blame this dismissal on the raging of an emotional woman rather than a rational business owner. He may go spread word of your conduct and we won't be able to find workers to help in time for the harvest."

"I wouldn't want anyone who believed anything that came out of that man's mouth on my farm."

"When you run things, you can make those kinds of decisions." Mother stood and turned toward her. "Until then, it is not your job to decide who we let go. Your job is to simply make sure everyone is in their proper place."

Penny let out a long breath. "You know, I can do more than babysit adults."

"Then prove it." The words cut into Penny far deeper than Mother's sharp look did.

How could she prove it to Mother? What exactly was she supposed to prove? Penny had been overseeing the workers for an entire year now and this was the first time there had been any sort of issue. Why was Mother so against her having any kind of control?

Philomina finished with Mother's hair and went into the closet to fetch a cloak.

Mother turned from her vanity. "I need you to understand how important our image is. We are two of the only businesswomen of the noble class in a kingdom run by a government consisting of mostly men. Every decision we make is scrutinized under a magnifying glass. There will always be people waiting for us to make a mistake just so they can use it against us. Our actions need to be dictated by our heads instead of our hearts."

Philomina brought out a pair of evening shoes and placed them on the floor by Mother's skirts. Mother's eyes never left Penny's as she slipped her feet inside. "I understand what that boy said could have been harmful, but there are ways of handling a situation like that instead of throwing him out on his rump in front of his peers. A man's wounded pride is not something to underestimate."

They walked out of Mother's room and met the steward, Rich, by the front door. Philomina and Rich accompanied them out to the carriage. Rich handed Mother letter after letter, reading off the names of the senders. "Lady Gilbert. Mrs. Cyril. Mr. Dawson—"

Mother passed an unopened envelope back to him. "You can throw that one in the trash heap."

"Who's Mr. Dawson?" Penny asked. She was certain his name was not on the list of business associates.

Rich looked over his shoulder, warning in his eyes.

Mother didn't even turn her head. "A man trying to take something that is not his."

Philomina gave Penny an exasperated look behind Mother's back. The two servants only ever gave Penny those expressions when a single topic came up.

Courtship.

Rich helped Mother into the carriage and Philomina's hand alighted on Penny's shoulder. "Someday, a man is going to catch your eye and there will be nothing Her Grace can do about it. Love isn't something that can be walled off forever."

Penny wrapped her fingers around Philomina's and gave them a squeeze. "Thank you, Philo, but I don't see how anything will get past the hawk-eyed Lady Barclay."

Rich held out a hand and helped Penny into the seat across from Mother. Stacks of unopened letters already lay on the seat next to her. Penny settled into her seat and latched her attention out the window. It was going to be a long three hours.

Their carriage pulled up to the home of the Hermen family—Angelica's family. The carriage door opened, and a chill breeze carried the faint scent of the gardens, lilacs and hyacinths beginning to bloom.

Lord Stone Hermen himself met them at the front step. His large frame nearly filled the space of the open doorway. He gave a low bow to each of them before turning to Mother. "Your Grace, I'm so glad you and Lady Penny were able to come for dinner."

"As are we," she answered politely. "We have much to discuss and I'm grateful for the chance to speak face to face."

A butler took their cloaks and they followed Lord Hermen to the dining room. "Patricia has been looking forward to the evening all month. It was a good excuse to make the boys take real baths. They've been working our newest team of oxen for the past several weeks. Samson and Andrew are very proud of the large manure pile they've gathered up."

He laughed at the twin looks of disgust passed between Mother and Penny. While manure was important for some of the crops, neither of them loved the work it took to spread the rank fertilizer over the fields. The only good thing about manure days was the long soak in the bath afterward.

They came into the ornate dining room and were met with the rest of the Hermen family. Lady Patricia Hermen sat at the foot of the table next to their youngest child, Little Myrtle, and the seven boys spread out after that. Each looked exactly the same with their mops of brown curls and mischievous brown eyes. They ranged from fifteen to seven with a set of triplets somewhere in the middle. Penny never could remember which boy was which.

She sat beside the tallest, who had to be Samson. He had a book in his lap that he kept surreptitiously glancing down at.

Penny couldn't make out the words. She leaned toward him as the *patsas* soup was served.

"What are you reading?"

His eyes flicked from his mother to Penny. A blush marked his embarrassment. "Mother has us studying Faerie War history." He closed the book gently to show her the title. *Battles of the Faerie War: Volume One* flashed in gold leaf on the brown leather cover. The gilded words brought back memories of sitting at Mother's side, reading her own copy of their history with the Fae. According to the records, the wars had been devastating. But in the end, humans had come out victorious. The High King and his horde had been overthrown.

Samson slid the book under his chair. "She threatened us with a test tomorrow if we didn't behave this evening. I'm preparing for the inevitable."

The Hermen home was the only high standing home beside Penny's that instructed their own children's lessons. Lady Hermen taught them herself, never hiring a nurse or governess. Lord Hermen was Minister of Trade for the entire kingdom— which was why Angelica and her husband were taking their honeymoon in Faerie to help negotiate on his behalf. Their view on family dynamics was one of the reasons Mother worked with Lord Hermen so well. Family came first.

Penny chuckled and dipped her spoon into the savory beef soup in front of her. "At least you have an exciting subject to study quickly. My mother only ever threatened me with mathematics tests." She took a sip of the herby dish and almost hummed. The first time she had heard of the soup she had nearly gagged at the mention of the ingredients. Her complaints about cows' feet had quickly dissipated once Mother had made her eat it.

Samson picked up his spoon. "I would take mathematics any day. I can't stand staring at stuffy old books."

"Perhaps if I'm ever punished with another test, we can swap."

"Aren't you finished with most of your lessons by now?"

"Yes, but if our mothers are anything alike, you know she wouldn't hesitate to use such torture if I did something she didn't like."

Samson smiled.

The dinner progressed comfortably, the rest of the Hermen family talking and joking with one another. The spirit of the house was as warm and lively as the food. Fried cheese, lemon chicken with potatoes, and dessert custards came and went in front of every person. By the end of it all, Little Myrtle, the youngest of the Hermen children, was fast asleep in her mother's arms. Penny refrained from rubbing her eyes. She didn't want to return to her somewhat empty house after a night like this.

Lord Hermen stood from his seat. "Boys, we've got quite a bit of work awaiting us in the morning. Best head off to bed."

All seven boys groaned and began shuffling from the room. Penny returned each "goodnight" offered until Samson was the last one in the room.

"Samson, my boy," Lord Hermen called, "you should probably join us. It will be good to let you see how this is done."

Samson grinned until Lady Hermen snagged the book from behind his back. He opened his mouth to protest, but his mother simply smiled. "At least I caught you with a textbook. Alexander snuck in an adventure novel." She patted another book sitting on the table beside her.

"Come along," Lord Hermen called. Samson skipped to his side and Lord Hermen slapped a hand on his shoulder.

Lord Hermen led them through the house and into the large study near the back. A large tortoise shell hung above the roaring fireplace. Penny took a long inhale of the musky scent of leather soaked into every fiber of the room.

Lord Hermen gestured to the chairs nearest his desk and sat in the large, cowhide chair on the other side. Along with his trade, Lord Hermen also ran one of the largest cow herds in the kingdom, the livestock bred to pull carts all over the land. "We've got three mounds piling up for fertilizer, Lady Barclay, and more from Mr. Gilbert's ranch coming within the next couple days. We should have the shipments over to you by the week's end."

"Excellent. I've brought the arranged payment, but the fertilizer wasn't the main reason I asked to meet."

Penny straightened in her chair. What other reason could Mother possibly have?

Lord Hermen looked just as surprised. "What are we here to discuss then?"

Mother took in a deep breath. "We've been running short on workers in the fields. We've had a few accidents within the last couple of months and have had to let go of some of the workers. I came here to see if you've had the same struggle or if it were possible that I could borrow a few of your workers for the summer."

Penny settled in her chair. It wasn't uncommon for Lord Hermen and Mother to assist one another in their businesses. Everyone in Eleusion worked together to help the kingdom prosper.

But Lord Hermen frowned. He turned to Samson sitting in a chair to the side of the desk. "Tell them what happened on your trade last week."

All eyes turned to Samson as he took a deep breath. "There were bandits along our route. Six men attacked our wagons headed toward Tauros with supplies for this season's wine. They took a full wagon of cork and paper."

"Bandits?" Penny shared a look of shock with Mother.

"It wasn't the first case either." Lord Hermen ran a hand down his face. "We've lost a dozen shipments of iron within the last month, not a trace of them left. The bandits are being discrete, but we noticed, and I had the watches on the wagons doubled. It was because of the increase that Samson here saw anything. I don't usually send the boys out, but Samson volunteered."

"Now you're just as understaffed as we are," Mother remarked.

Lord Hermen nodded apologetically. "Seems we can't hire any locals either. Most of the other business owners out here are having the same problem. Eleusia and the closer towns are swamped with available jobs, but no one is taking them."

"Why not?" Penny asked.

"Seems someone is raking in all of the workers with good pay. Every man I asked on the street if he was looking for work said he wouldn't trade anything for the gold he was getting."

The words brought back an echo of the conversation she'd overheard Martin directing. She turned to find Mother's eyes already on hers. They spoke at the same time.

"Rebels."

3

FABRIC AND FRIENDS

Dearest Penny,

Your last letter was rather vague. What could you have possibly done to upset your mother? You're the fiercest rule follower I know! Even the great Duchess of Eleusion cannot help but see what a strong, capable woman you've become.

On a less depressing note, Devan and I were invited to tour the Summer Palace. My first fae palace. Can you believe it? We go next week and I've been hunting the markets for the perfect ensemble. What should one wear to represent the Minister of Trade in a foreign kingdom?

We are going for a ride through the Farraige Gaineamh tomorrow night. Trade caravans travel over the dunes into Spring. Devan was able to hire a transport to take us to the halfway point so we can see about contributing to their trade routes. There will be so much to see and we will be riding MAGIC CARPETS! I squealed like a little girl when Devan told me. I can't wait!

Oh Penny, being married these past months have been a dream. Devan is the most amazing person I know. Some things have been hard, but there is nothing like having someone you trust at your side.

It's really too bad you never got the name of that fellow from the ball. Before you ask, no I have not revealed any of what you told me to anyone. Your secret flash of romance is safe with me. From how you described him though, he likely would've been the only man to withstand the Duchess as a mother-in-law. Perhaps there's still a chance of tracking him down. Not every horrible thing your mother preaches about romance is true.

Your Very Fashionable Friend,
Angelica

P.S. I can feel your blush from Faerie!

PENNY'S HEART GALLOPED UP HER THROAT JUST DOWN THE HALLWAY outside her own room. The window beside her framed the night fading under the first touch of sunlight, but it wasn't enough to scare away the prickle of unease slithering up Penny's spine in the dark.

Mother said her fear had been far worse when she was younger. Both Mother and Philomina had spent nights in her room after a nightmare, soothing her back to sleep. Penny had no cause to blame, only the shadows that coated the walls.

"Penny."

She jumped, her skirt spinning as she whirled toward the sound of Mother's voice. She pressed a hand to her racing heart. "You scared me." She blinked. The sleek riding gown was not what she had expected to see Mother wearing. "I thought you were meeting with Aaron this morning." Mother met with the field master in the middle of every week, but never wore such an outfit to do so.

"Change of plans. Since you were able to get the north field back on schedule and Hook Field was finished over the weekend, I thought we could take a day and go into Eleusia. I need a new riding hat since I ruined mine last week." Mother's favorite riding hat careening into the canal on their ride last week flashed through Penny's mind. By the time they'd retrieved it from the water, the beige fabric had fallen beyond repair.

"I would love to join you," she said, gears in her head spinning. "I need to look for a new bridle for Meli. I read the weather mages were holding off the rains until next week. It should be a perfect ride into town."

"I agree," Mother replied. "Now, go get into your riding habit and make sure to pack an extra outfit to put in your saddlebag. We won't take the carriage today so we can try out our wares before bringing them home."

Penny skipped back into her room and rang for her maid. She never needed help getting into her work clothes in the morning, but her riding attire needed a little more attention than she could give it on her own. She reawakened the magelights scattered all around her bedroom. A few dimmed only seconds after. They would need to be traded to the light mages for more.

Penny's personal maid came in without a knock, rubbing her red rimmed, hazel eyes and attempting to stifle a yawn as she walked toward Penny's dressing room.

Penny chuckled as she followed her maid's dragging feet across the carpets decorating the floor. "Sissy, haven't you learned to go to bed at a proper hour yet?"

Sissy let out an indignant snort. "We can't all be morning glories like you and Papa, my lady." She walked into the large closet in Penny's dressing room and immediately turned back to her mistress. Sheepishly she asked, "What did you need me to get out?"

Penny laughed and sent her in after her riding clothes. Sissy was a wonderful maid... after the sun was fully up over the horizon and she'd eaten a proper breakfast. She had not inherited Aaron's ability to rise before the sun.

Sissy brought out a dark green jacket with a cream chemisette to wear underneath. Penny untied her work clothes as Sissy grabbed her boots, hat, and gloves from their places in the closet. They worked quickly to get Penny into her riding habit. Once dressed, Penny sat in her small chair at the vanity to allow Sissy to style her hair into something more fashionable. Sissy unbraided Penny's thick, reddish-brown hair and pinned it up into her hat. With the quick outfit switch finished, she sent Sissy back to bed and left to meet Mother at the door.

Mother waited for Penny in the hallway, her outfit looking sharp and pristine in the glow of the morning light. The beige always looked stunning on Mother, accentuating the rich color of her skin. They made a fashionable pair as they walked to the stables where their horses and their stablehand waited for them.

Rides with Mother were always a joy. Mother always seemed to enjoy the breeze in her hair and the exhilaration of the ride as much as Penny. They didn't often let the horses run wild, but when they did, they streaked like stars across the sky with Penny and Mother grinning ear to ear. It was one of the only unladylike things Penny ever saw Mother wholeheartedly enjoy, and it made Penny love it all the more. It was the one thing they did together that rarely turned into work.

Excepting today.

Mother pulled her mount to the side of Penny's. "It's very upsetting, what's going on over at the Hermen's. We have talk of rebels on every side of the duchy now."

Penny's shoulders sagged. "I don't understand how a rebel group was able to infiltrate so much of our land. What do you think it means?"

"I can't blame them for targeting us," Mother replied, brushing right over Penny's question. Penny hated when she did that. "We have one of the most prosperous hubs of trade in the kingdom farthest from the capital and Faerie. It makes the most sense to me."

But it still didn't to Penny. "You would think they would want to be closer to the people they're trying to eradicate. Based on what you've told me, the rebellion hasn't been a concern anywhere else. Wouldn't they want to lie low and attack from within?"

Mother shrugged. "I suppose we'll never know."

The road to Eleusia, the large river town on the outskirts of their small duchy, started receiving its early morning traffic. As it was nearly over half a day's ride to the city, Penny kept Meli at a sedate walk behind Mother and watched the other travelers. Shepherds and cow-herders guided their charges to other pastures while traders and merchants were taking their wares to and from the other towns in this part of the kingdom. Penny took in a deep breath, savoring the buzzing air.

The Duchy of Eleusion was nothing as grand or vast as some of the other lands the lords and ladies of Olympia had charge over, but it was one of the most important. With its small dock along the river Iarann and all of the land cultivating crops and animals, it was considered one of the largest trade hubs in the kingdom— though you couldn't tell by the size of it. Mother claimed it a rather small city when compared to the others scattered throughout Olympia. From the sheer size of the capital Penny remembered, it was likely true.

Penny's legs ached by the time they reached the inn's stable. It took a few stretches on her feet before the soreness eased. She retrieved her small satchel from her saddle bag and slung it over her shoulder. When she turned toward the door, she saw Mother waiting for her. Penny stepped to her side and they walked onto the large market street.

Everyone seemed to be making good use of the weather. The long cobbled road teemed with people, buyers and sellers alike. Artisans called out to the patrons on the street and attempted to sell their wares. Penny found herself surprised as she watched a few of the merchants use magecraft to showcase special items, proclaiming them to have many magical properties.

Few mages lived in the Duchy of Eleusion. For fifty years after the Faerie Wars, those with magic or anything like it were hunted down, even though there were many that had helped win the war for the humans. But fear overshadowed that. Mages were put to death and even some of the nomadic Sireadh tribes had gone into hiding, their quiet ways disconcerting to those plagued by memories of the fae. But time helped heal much of those wounds. Now, the town of Eleusia was one of the largest cities left mostly occupied by magicless bronties. While Penny had never actually been to any other major town besides the capital, she'd learned that the men and women living in Mother's duchy were the least magical people in Olympia. Penny guessed it was because farms and food don't require much magic and Mother was never one to turn away strong, hardworking people.

Penny followed Mother as she ambled through the crowd, in no rush to get to their destination, but also not stopping to purchase anything on the street. Mother easily broke through the traffic, a root seeking her water. Penny kept a firm grip on her satchel as she was jostled by those passing by.

They walked up the street to the boxy, coral-colored shop on the corner of the market. As Mother entered, the little bell above the door jingled and the middle-aged woman Penny associated with the shop came out of the back, followed by a large man carrying bolts of fabric.

"Lady Barclay, what a pleasant surprise," Claudia said, her voice warm enough to match the sunlight outside her shop. She gestured for the man to put the satins and chiffons down on the tabletop along the edge of the room. She stepped up to take Mother's coat.

As the two chatted about the latest fashion and the destruction of Mother's hat, Penny perused the shop. While the building was small, the array of available fabrics and styles made it feel gigantic. Beautiful silks, brocades, and velvets adorned every wall and dresses of the most popular style stood in the window for all to admire as they walked past. Penny never understood why Claudia lived in such a small town when she was one of the most sought after seamstresses in Olympia.

The one time Penny had said as much, Claudia had responded, "When one is a master of their craft, the people most deserving of their masterpieces will flock to them."

Penny looked through the ribbon selection and picked out a couple of colors to bring home for her and Sissy. The young maid had a special fondness for ribbons, one Penny had never quite understood, but happily indulged when she could.

She placed the ribbons on the counter next to some of the things Mother had already set aside to go on her new hat. Mother loved this shop because she could come in for anything, considering the owner worked with some of the most talented fabric mages in the kingdom.

"Claudia, I think I would like the emerald velvet as an accent. What do you think?" Mother held the fabric out to the woman to inspect.

Claudia tapped her chin with one of her delicate fingers. "I could have someone spell it not to take up much dirt, but I don't know that it would complement the veil. What about this suede I have over here?" The women traversed the many fabrics and Claudia used her internal map to find exactly what Mother was looking for. Though Penny knew Claudia was not a mage, the entire shop still hummed with a different kind of magic.

Penny made her way to the shop windows where Claudia displayed some of her finished pieces. Three dresses stood in the window, looking out onto the streets filled with life they wouldn't be a part of unless someone took them off of their stand. Penny pulled off her gloves to gently stroke the soft fabrics with helpless fingers.

She joined their vigil at the window and stared out. The rattle of horses and carts spilled through the thin glass. The sunlight banished the shadows and Eleusia danced in its glow. People moved to and fro, laughing, scowling, yelling, muttering, skipping, striding. Living. Making their own choices, living their own lives—

Except for the man glaring at her from across the street.

Penny's gloveless hands sparked green.

Martin.

She took a single step away from the window, away from him. His anger sliced through her. Mother's rebukes from this week salted the wounds. She took a deep breath and swung back around toward the voices behind her.

"Mother—" Her eyes returned to the window.

"What is it, Penny?"

Penny's shoulders fell. In the split second she'd looked away, he had disappeared.

"Nothing."

After Mother finished selecting everything they would need for the new hat, Claudia shooed them out of the shop to find lunch while she worked. It never took the woman long to create a masterpiece and she said it would be ready for them that evening.

They walked the short distance back to the inn where they stayed whenever they had business in town. The stables were the best in the area and the horses were always taken such good care of. The innkeeper was a wonderful host and his place of work was always immaculately clean. Penny wouldn't have been surprised if he had bwachod— the little fae, likely brownies or pixies— under his care.

They walked into the main room and took a seat at one of the many tables. A serving girl appeared, practically out of thin air, and welcomed them to the inn. Once she took their order, she whisked back to the kitchen.

Mother's fingers drummed on the table. "I think the new hat will suit my jacket much better than the old one did."

"I liked what you and Claudia chose for the lining inside. The green was very vibrant and gave such a splash of color."

They continued to chat— about the planting, the weather, the new clothing styles of the season— until the girl returned with their food. Penny tucked into the chowder and bread and leaned in her chair contentedly after she finished.

Mother grabbed a small notebook from one of her many jacket pockets and jotted down a few notes. "Aaron told me we are to take in a few hires from outside the village. After the episode with the man you hastily fired" —*will she ever let it go?* — "I am worried about letting in more men. Do you think we should be?"

Martin's angry face flashed in her mind. She wiped the image from her thoughts. "I don't. The workers we do have are completely loyal to you and I don't believe they would tolerate any more nonsense."

"I am glad to hear it. I'd hate to think what would happen if we had a bunch of rebels running about through our pomegranates."

The picture Mother painted brought a twitch to Penny's lips. "You worry too much. You know Aaron would never allow anyone who intended harm near the crop."

"Well, you can never be too careful. Men wear masks, as we can easily see given the young man you evicted. We can never truly know what they intend. All they care about is themselves and they will do anything to get what they want."

"The men and women we have under our charge are good workers and I do not foresee any problems with new hires," Penny stated. Thinking they really needed a subject change. "Aaron said you had trouble at Hook Field."

Mother went on to describe the incident at the canal. With Mother's attention diverted, Penny's mind wandered. The anger in Martin's eyes and his last words still sent a chill down her spine. She'd never seen such biased hate before. How could someone feel so vehemently about the rulers of their own kingdom? She recalled the tales Mother had told her about when the Tyrant King had ruled. Everyone had been afraid of his wrath, worried he would consume the entire continent in war and blood. She could still remember the day, over four years ago, when Mother had been summoned by the Crown

Prince to attend the funeral of the king. Mother had cried tears of joy and worry as she'd packed.

"—what do you think?" Mother's voice cut through her deep thoughts.

"I'm sorry mother, what did you say?"

Mother raised a brow. "I was curious to know if you would like to go to the saddle shop first or if you would like to head over to the apothecary with me. Philomina's supply has run low on Faerie Yarrow extract."

"I'd love to join you. We can head over to buy the bridle on the way to Claudia's. The place I'd like to purchase it from is down the market a handful of shops from her."

Mother stood to settle their bill and ask for the horses to be readied. Penny joined her as she set out for the street. The walkways were a bit lazy after the rush of the afternoon, passersby less chatty and the children tucked into the shade of the houses to avoid the glaring sunshine.

Mother walked around to the stables where the stablehand on duty held both of their horses ready. Penny's gaze swept down the street. A crowd of men walked down the road, laughing with one another on their way to find their own lunch or to find a moment's rest in the heat of the day. Their path met a small opening, leading to a blacksmith's yard. Martin stood there, his eyes already on her.

Penny blinked and he disappeared in the passing crowd. She looked around the street, but there wasn't a trace of him.

Mother called from where she stood by the stables.

Penny shook herself. "I must be seeing things."

4

HERBS AND HANDS

PENNY HOMED IN ON THE LOPSIDED APOTHECARY THE MOMENT THEY turned onto the street. The small hut sat crookedly in the middle of the tiny square that made up the entirety of the magic quarter in Eleusion. The owner of this particular place of business was of fae descent, and the woman could always find plants other people had a hard time getting their hands on.

Penny and Mother tied their horses to the post outside the rundown building and Penny followed Mother to the warped door. Pieces of colored glass hung from the slanted roof outside the building, casting splashes of color on the otherwise plain outer walls. Through the dingy windows, a variety of jars, books, and dried herbs sat near the windowsill. Mother placed her gloved hand on the handle and attempted to push open the door. After a few tries, she gave up and rapped her knuckles against the sturdy wood.

Penny jumped when she heard shuffling and the sound of many bolts being unlocked from the other side. When the door finally burst open, the tall, willowy woman Penny always associated with the place sagged against the doorframe. Farrah had to be older than Mother, considering all of the stories Penny heard, but she didn't look or act much older than Penny herself. She wore a rag of a dress and Penny could see her toes peeking out from under the hem. A spot of brown smeared across the fair skin of her forehead and a blush of exertion saturated her cheeks.

"Great galloping pumpkins! I thought I saw you two coming tomorrow," cried Farrah with her lilting accent, her white blonde braid swinging as she shook her head. "I need to purchase some new bones for Nonnie. They've been reading wrong since solstice. Come in! Come in!" She waved them into the shop.

Penny stepped into the cluttered front room, taking in the stockpile Farrah had accumulated. While the layout never changed, the items to purchase regularly did. Herbs of every variety hung from the rafters and jars containing all kinds of ingredients lined the overstocked shelves. There were drawers in front of the wide counter, housing stones and other minerals to help with magecraft. Tapestries, paintings, and sculptures cluttered every available space not taken up by bones, sticks, or bags.

Farrah swung around the large counter to stand in front of a wall of branches, mirrors, and other large items that didn't fit anywhere else on the walls around them. The door leading to what Penny could only guess was more cluttered storage space stood behind the counter as well. She wasn't certain, however, since Farrah never let anyone back there.

"Have you ladies been drinking that tea I recommended last time you were here?" Farrah asked as she grabbed a pink stone the size of her arm and began to polish it with a cloth hanging from her apron. "My mama says it should be just the thing to get that magic going."

Mother had been perusing the jars of roots when she

turned toward the shopkeeper. “Yes, I think it’s helped speed up the rate of growth immensely. Penny finished a field last week in half the time she would have last year.”

Farrah winked one of her dark brown eyes in Penny’s direction. The blush on Penny’s cheeks, caused by Mother’s praise, grew even warmer.

“I knew it would help. I’d be happy to send some more with you today in addition to whatever else you came for.”

“Yes, that would be wonderful. More importantly, I’m in desperate need of some yarrow if you have any on hand,” Mother said, a small smile on her lips. Mother always seemed more at peace when they walked through this shop. Magic and plant-life seeped through its walls, more than enough to put Mother at ease.

With a short salute and another wink, Farrah slipped into the back room. Penny could hear a couple of loud bangs— and a few choice words Mother would never utter— as the shop owner worked.

Penny’s eyes wandered until a beautiful tapestry hanging in the window display caught her eye. Her feet eagerly moved toward the woven fabric. The vibrant colors loomed into what had to be a map of Faerie, the land split into the four different regions— Spring, Summer, Autumn, and Winter —and the woods teeming with magical creatures. There was no writing anywhere she could decipher, but she didn’t need words to understand the beauty of the piece. Penny saw armored dragons, fierce griffins, grotesque trolls, and sneaky goblins hiding in the shadows of trees and mountains. She saw every other kind of fae as well. Ellylon frolicking in beautiful, flower-filled meadows alongside glittering streams. Bwachod disappeared in the shadows of the trees, leaving only small footprints in their wake. Even the gwyllion and their haggard appearance looked enticing. The tapestry made Faerie look like a dream and Penny found herself caught up in it. As a child, she had loved to pretend she was any number of the fae creatures and read every book Barclay Manor's library held about them.

"I knew that would catch your eye, my friend," said Farrah from behind her. Penny had become used to the spry fae popping up in places, but it still made her jump.

"It's beautiful," Penny whispered, not yet willing to take her eye off the threaded masterpiece.

"My father acquired it for me last week from a brownie who used to work in the Spring King's household. They redecorated a couple decades ago and the brownie had snagged it for her own house, but she said it didn't match her new furnishings and sold it at market. With the rewritten alliance Prince Dion created, there has been tons of attic space freed up on that side of the Mist." Farrah laughed.

The tapestry must have been made before the Faerie Wars. The Mist bordering Faerie from Olympia wasn't featured on this map. No image of the nightmarish Gray Man stalked the Mist as it did on so many of the maps Penny had seen. She'd never been far enough north to see it in person, but she'd heard enough stories. It was said the Gray Man dwelled in the Mist and threw out the people— fae and human alike— that tried to go through the border. But only after the Mist had its way with them. Only those invited by the Faerie High Council or the High Queen could cross the border safely.

The wisp of a woman returned to the counter to finish helping Mother with the order. Penny continued to gaze at the small map, trying to soak up each woven fiber into her memory. *I likely won't see anything like this again.*

Penny finally turned away when Mother announced it time for them to leave. Farrah came around the counter and swept Penny up in a hug.

"Don't you ever lose that spirit of adventure," Farrah whispered in her ear, "and come see me more often." The fae took Penny and held her at arm's length. Penny nodded and Farrah gave her a toothy grin as she released her.

Mother waved goodbye as she made her way to the door and Penny followed back out to the horses. The sun cast its light over the roofs of the city, the colors of its last rays lighting up the sky in an array of pinks and oranges.

A breeze blew over Penny's skin, a small reprieve after the heat of the day. She stopped beside Meli when a sheet of paper curled around her boot. She peeled it off, ready to throw it in a waste bin, when a pair of lively eyes met hers. The missing poster featured the face of a little fae boy.

Penny held it out to Mother. "Were we aware of this?"

Mother's eyes saddened when she saw what Penny held. "Yes. He's been missing for months. I can't imagine what his family is going through."

"Months?" She straightened the paper and saw the original posting date. He'd been missing since before solstice. Her chest ached for the family who had received no answers. She folded the piece of paper and tucked it into her satchel.

Mother mounted her gelding, Wheaton. Penny followed to stand beside the horse.

"Mother," Penny began, trying to think of the best words to put her at ease, "would it be all right if I accompany you to Claudia's and then head over to the saddle shop for Meli's bridle on my own?"

Mother's lips turned down and her brow creased. Penny put on her most serious expression, doing her best to express that she could take care of herself. The decision solidified in Mother's eyes and she nodded her head.

"I think you should be fine on your own, but don't worry about going all the way to Claudia's with me, seeing as we will pass the saddle shop on the way."

Penny nearly squealed. She caught herself before she got carried away and glided as genteelly as she was able over to mount her own horse.

As the two began to ride back through town, Mother turned. "You have your packets with you?"

Penny patted the satchel strapped across her torso. "Of course. I would never leave home without them."

"Good, good. I still hope you never have need of them, but if you do, do not hesitate. I won't have my daughter being kidnapped, or taken down a dark alley, or who knows what else! If any man you do not recognize approaches you, run toward the shop and don't look back. You do anything you can to get away from anyone who would harm you, do you hear me?"

"Yes, Mother. Of course I will," Penny said, her voice placating.

Mother gave a sharp nod and guided her horse in front of Penny's as the traffic in the road grew more cramped. Mother surveyed the crowd, likely keeping a lookout for any passerby with malicious intent.

Mother's warning slowly faded from her ears. Her eyes never tired of seeing so many people and all of the cultures that came with them. She soaked in the array of colors painted across the houses. Cheerful blues and greens contrasting with the more subtle tans and grays. She spotted a handful of flowerbeds lined with budding flowers, some even with a few blooms this early in the year. Smoke puffed through the thatched roofs and out of chimneys. The warm glow from the fires chased shadows out the windows and onto the street.

Children ran around their mothers' feet as the wives greeted their husbands coming home from wherever their work took them that day. Old couples sat on their porches, watching the sea of people pass by and offering smiles or waves to anyone they recognized. A young couple, what looked to be a fae girl and a human boy, sat on a bench by the road, sharing words of adoration, Penny guessed, by the blushes blooming across their smiling cheeks.

As they came to a stop in front of the saddle shop, Mother brought her horse alongside Penny's before she could dismount. "You won't be long in the shop, will you? I don't want you out in the dark."

"Mother, I assure you, I'll complete my business here as quickly as I am able and will be at your side before you even remember I'm gone."

Mother looked over at the shop then back and gave a swift nod before nudging her horse in the direction of Claudia's shop.

Penny waited until she was sure Mother couldn't see when she grinned. She quickly dismounted and tied Meli to the post outside the small building she was about to enter. She walked through the door of the shop with the smile still spread across her face.

Penny walked out of the shop with a new bridle and half of her pocket money well spent.

The sun sank below the hills outside of town. Penny was glad to see the lamplighters walking from post to post, lighting the wicks in the small lamps along the road. This city had not converted to magelight as a lot of the other major towns were. Penny had heard many of the people here wanted to keep to the old ways and so the town continued to be lit by firelight rather than magic. She shook her head at the foolishness. The resources used to make candles and lanterns, plus the time it took to light them every day, was a waste in her eyes.

Meli's hooves tapped a smooth beat along the cobblestones, matching the lazy hum of the crickets in the dark. Penny found herself dragging her feet as they made their way down the street. She tried not to resent Mother's strict rules. They kept her safe. In moments like this, however, Penny imagined herself as someone whose life didn't come with as many restraints. She dreamed that she could be a normal seventeen-year-old, that she didn't have a busy mother, or a gift that affected so many lives.

Meli bumped her in the back with her snout, distracting Penny from her musings. She chuckled and patted her neck. The horse then snorted in her hair and pushed Penny to move a bit faster.

Penny grabbed Meli's bridle, looking for anything that would be bothering her. "What has gotten into you?"

Meli shook her head and Penny caught sight of three men watching them. She flicked her eyes down the street to where Claudia's shop stood, the glow from the lights inside shining out, beckoning her to move faster. She pulled Meli's reins, her steps at a fast clip.

Her fingers fumbled with the clasp holding the flap of her bag. She finally unlatched it and reached inside, ready to take hold of one of the envelopes, as rough hands wrapped around her arms and ripped Meli's reins from her hand. Large fingers smelling of dead fish smothered her shout for help as her body was lifted and carried into a dark alleyway. Meli's scream sent ice down her spine. Penny thrashed more in the arms holding her off the ground.

Her mind froze and whirled in a constant cyclone. She screamed and screamed, but no sound escaped through the fingers clamped over her mouth.

Sweet Gaia, I'm going to die.

Penny squirmed as the men ran from the light of the major street. Their gruff voices snapped at each other to keep her still as they snuck through back alleys.

"Don't let go of her leg!"

"Wily mage tried to bite me!"

"Take her bag, but be careful. We don't know what kind of nasty tricks she's got in there."

She recognized the voice. A growl replaced her scream.

Martin.

His eyes met hers with a leer. The weight of her bag disappeared as someone cut the strap. A rough scrap of fabric was shoved into her mouth and wrapped around her head, effectively gagging her. Thick ropes encircled her arms and legs, tightening uncomfortably as the men knotted them in place.

The four men carried her through the maze of the harbor town. Penny couldn't tell where they were. She'd lost sight of Meli the moment they dragged her away, but the sound of the horse's screams still rang in her ears. Tears pricked the corners of her eyes and she was sure the entire kingdom could hear the sound of her racing heart. *You do anything you can to get away from anyone who would harm you,* Mother's voice repeated over and over. She thrashed more and one of the men wrenched her arm to the point she screamed through the gag. The tears in her eyes fell to the ground, leaving behind the barest trail of her capture.

They swept past the backs of houses, inns, shops, and businesses. Whenever the group came across anyone else in the alleyway, the men walked right past without even a backwards glance. The fight in her dampened. No one was going to help her.

"The Cartographer's going to be thrilled when he sees the catch we're bringing in," said a voice to her left.

The Cartographer? Tears streamed down her face as they continued to walk down the dark alley. The smell of fish grew stronger the farther they went, telling her they were getting closer to the docks on the river. *If I end up on a boat I will never get home.* Her thrashing renewed, but her energy was waning. More tears fell from her eyes.

"I think he will be less than thrilled when he finds out you lost your bounty," a voice boomed, coming from every direction around them. The sound resonated through Penny's body, making the hair on her arms stand on end.

All of the men skidded to a stop. Penny glanced around to find the owner of the voice, not quite believing her own ears. Vague familiarity cleared her panicked mind, but the shadows of the men around her blocked anyone from view.

"Who's there?" one of the kidnappers called.

Penny let her head fall back and looked up. Her heart stopped when she saw the man appearing in the windowsill above them and his eyes trained directly on her face.

Amber eyes.

5

MAGIC AND MAYHEM

Penny's erratic heartbeat increased upon hearing the rumbling voice and seeing those eyes. She didn't understand why he was here, now, after she'd only met him the one time, but she could trust him to help her.

Amber Eyes leapt down from the rooftop. The gag in her mouth muted her gasp as he landed on his feet in the alleyway. The men holding her jumped, their bodies giving way to their fear.

"Who are you?" one of the men asked in a strangled tone. Their hands tightened on her limbs. She pulled against their bone crushing grips. Perhaps Amber Eyes was the distraction she needed. Her eyes met his, trying to convey her thoughts.

"I am but a humble servant, helping a lady in need," he said, gaze not breaking from Penny's for an instant. His hood concealed his dark hair and the tips of his ears, but Penny would never have forgotten that face. He held a sword loosely in one hand, as if it were simply an extension of his arm, and a small dagger in the other.

The two men holding Penny's legs dropped them to the

ground with a thud. Tears of pain swirled with those of fear and frustration. The men left holding her arms jostled her into an unbalanced stance since her legs were tied together so securely.

The criminals crept closer to their new target. The steel of the daggers in their hands gleamed in the faint moonlight. Penny's eyes widened as they charged, only to watch Amber Eyes move so swiftly he seemed to disappear and reappear behind them. He glided through the darkness as he evaded and disarmed the two kidnappers trying to kill him.

One of the men holding Penny up by her arms turned to Martin holding the other. "Keep hold of this one," he said, shaking Penny hard enough to make her lose her footing. "This is taking too long." He let go of Penny's arm, unsheathed the sword at his hip, and stalked toward the fray.

Penny glanced out of the corner of her eye. Martin's clothing hung on him, disheveled and dirty, just like the rest of him. He looked much worse than when he'd left her field only a week or so ago. Perhaps Mother had been right. She should've handled his situation better.

The small pang of sympathy fled the instant she heard a clash of steel further down the alley. She looked over at the hand not holding her by the arm and saw Martin held her satchel. Looking for any chance to escape, she closed her eyes and reached with her magic for the small seeds in her bag. The gloves encasing her hands hid the glow of her magic from everyone in the vicinity. The seeds sprouted and reached out a couple of roots, but without any water nearby, they wouldn't grow more than an inch.

A shout sounded from the other end of the alleyway, breaking her concentration. One of her kidnappers got up from the ground with a growl and thrust his sword toward Amber Eyes. The fae twirled out of the way just before the tip of the blade could cut his cloak. Penny breathed a sigh of relief.

With her feet tied, she had no chance of running, but hopefully Amber Eyes could take care of these awful kidnappers and come to her aid. *Great Goddess above, please let us get out of here alive.*

He rendered one unconscious and tore a blade out of another's hands. Even Penny, with her limited experience, could tell Amber Eyes was skilled in the art of hand-to-hand combat. He danced where the other men stumbled, the night as his partner. It seemed as if the very shadows around them aided him in subduing the evil men surrounding him.

The man with the large sword turned back to Martin. "Take her to the boat!"

Penny screamed through the gag when he swung her over his shoulder as he would a sack of potatoes. She looked up to see her would-be hero staring right at her, eyes blazing, as the other men kept him from her.

A grunt escaped her as Martin's shoulder dug into her stomach every time he took a jogging step. Tears ran in rivulets down her face as she grappled with the ropes around her wrists and ankles. He kept on through the short alleyways. The sound of water slapping against wooden docks made Penny's eyes gush. *If he gets me on that boat, I'll never escape.* And she needed to escape. It would be easier to contain her on a boat, and she would likely have no access to anything her powers could influence. She would be at the mercy of these horrid men. The Goddess only knew what they planned to do with her. The gleam in Martin's eyes promised only pain.

Penny bucked in a final act of desperation, the sound of her imminent doom driving her. Martin squawked and Penny's bag went flying out of his hand as he grappled to get a hold on her. The satchel sailed through the air to plop right into a muddy puddle of water, gleaming in a ray of moonlight. Penny, seizing the much prayed for opportunity, reached out with her mind to the seeds and felt the moment they heeded her commands.

Martin screamed as the vines of the blackberry plants wrapped around his ankles, effectively knocking both him and Penny to the ground. Penny closed her eyes as she hit the ground and the breath left her body, but she kept hold of her connection to the plants as Martin continued to cry out. The long, thorny vines overtook him. While the thorns on the plant were sharp, the barbs were not poisonous and were not long enough to cause any serious damage. They were the perfect tool to help Penny in her need for escape.

She opened her eyes and rolled over to see the man had been encased up to his neck in vines. His breathing grew frantic as he cursed her over and over. His eyes continued to widen as he took in the large bed of plants he was fully immersed in.

"You stupid witch! When I get out of here, I'm going to—"

Penny inched the vines up his throat. *Hopefully that will keep him quiet.*

Penny stayed laying on the ground. Her unbound hair stuck to her cheeks as she looked around for anything she could use to cut the ropes rubbing her skin raw. She rolled, trying to get her feet under her to at least get away from the horrible man, but the bindings on her ankles made it impossible.

Frustration screamed through her body, manifesting itself in more tears. If she stayed there much longer there was a good chance other terrible men would find her. Martin watched her the entire time, rage seething from his eyes.

Penny worked the bonds behind her back again. The flesh around her wrists burning anytime she moved them. Her cries were muffled by the gag in her mouth as she moved. She made it around one of the buildings in the alleyway, giving her a respite from Martin's gaze, but also taking her further into the darkness she usually did her best to avoid.

Penny's heart galloped and her breathing grew fast as she sat amongst the shadowed garbage littering the cobblestones around her. She didn't know if minutes or hours passed as she sat and allowed the sobs to break free from her chest. Mother's voice echoed in her ears, the warnings of men and their terrible natures playing over and over again, as the shadows slithered over the bare skin of her neck. She'd always believed Mother's stories to be exaggerated, stretched to scare her into following the rules, but now she saw the error of her judgment.

A shadow shifted on the ground near Penny's feet, making her flinch. She scurried to hide herself better in the piles of refuse littered about. The flow of a black cloak swept into the alley.

Realization hit her as he crouched down to her level and began sawing at the cords around her ankles. Tears welled against her lashes as she watched the man she had dreamed about for the last year look her in the eyes once again.

Amber Eyes went around to begin sawing at the rope around her wrists. She hissed as the fibers rubbed against her raw skin.

He stopped. "I'm sorry. It'll sting more before I'm done." He said it more like a question, prompting Penny to nod in acquiescence. He continued and though it hurt severely, Penny did her best to keep the pain to herself.

Once her hands were unbound, she ripped the gag from her mouth and turned to her savior. "How did you find me?" She grimaced. Her whispered words bounced around the wood slatted houses like a shout.

"I was following those men when I saw them take you. I'm

sorry I wasn't able to get to you sooner. Your mount went into a frenzy at your disappearance, and I had to stop her before she hurt anyone."

"Meli!" Penny gasped and grabbed the front of his cloak. "Is she all right? Did they hurt her?"

"Not from what I saw," he replied calmly, though his eyes widened at where her hands clenched his clothing. "She was simply frightened."

She hastily released her grip. "Thank you for helping her. I don't know what I would have done if something happened to her."

Amber Eyes nodded and gave her an understanding smile, just a twitch of his lips. He looked at the scene around them. "I think we should get you off the ground, Lady Penelope."

The sound of her name across his lips crashed into her. *He remembers who I am.*

He held out his hand to help her to her feet. She swayed as the blood rushed through her limbs. He held her until she had regained her equilibrium enough for her to see their surroundings without them spinning.

The rustle of leaves startled Penny and Amber Eyes flicked his attention to where Martin stood just around the corner. "Wait here," he said, and silently strode toward the noise. He disappeared around the corner.

Trash and debris clung to her dress, and she reached down to brush it off. Her heart seized as she noticed how dark the space around her was without his presence. She didn't totally know where she was. A hiccup of a cry escaped. She would have to get to the inn, through the dark, on her own.

With tears freckling her cheeks, she came to the end of the alleyway. She shuddered at the thought of seeing Martin's furious face. Her limbs wouldn't leave the shadow of the alley.

Amber Eyes may have told me to wait, but I have to get out of here. Who knows what other kind of men are running about in the dark? Mother is probably worried sick. And Meli... Penny squared her shoulders. She couldn't stop the tears, but she finally convinced herself to look around the corner.

Her eyes trailed over the long vines of blackberries and found them empty. Penny gasped and swung back around into the alley. Both her captor and her hero were gone.

A weapon. She needed a weapon. She couldn't possibly go running around the streets of Eleusia unarmed if those men were still looking for her. Her eyes landed on a pile of fencing that someone had dumped behind the building she leaned against. She pulled out a long, jagged piece of wood with a sharp end. It wasn't a sword, but at least she wouldn't hurt herself if she had to use it.

She crept once again to the edge of the building and looked back over the piles of vines. A gleam of polished leather caught her attention, and she scurried over to where her satchel sat in the now dried mud. She pulled the pieces of blackberry out and held the bag to her chest along with her short, wooden spear. As quietly as she could, she hurried away from the sound of the river.

Chills shuddered through her as she made her way through the shadows of the town, most of the buildings decorated with unlit windows and broken windowpanes. She'd never been to this part of Eleusia, Mother always having stuck to the main roads with her. She walked past mountains of garbage and heaps of broken buildings. One pile looked like it consisted of solely dead fish. Penny gagged as she walked past. All manner of vermin skittered over her boots as she walked and Penny had to hold back multiple screams. She nearly stepped on a large rat, which finally made her squeal and bolt down the alley.

The light of the main streets called to her as she traversed the shadows. She caught pinpricks through the buildings as she walked, but she swallowed her fear and continued straight to where she believed the inn to be.

At last, she came out onto a side street where the light of a tavern glowed out onto the packed earth of the road. Boisterous voices bellowed out a song and she saw two men grappling with a third as they hoisted him out of the building. Penny didn't stay long enough for any of them to see her. Mother had warned her about what men did when they had been deep in their cups. Soon, she was running through the shadows of the city as fast as her tired feet could carry her.

Penny recognized buildings she ran past. She wasn't close to the inn, but she was close to the magic quarter. Her feet led her right up to Farrah's door where she began pounding only to feel the door open beneath her fist.

"Penny!" Mother's voice rang. "Thank the Goddess!"

Penny's knees buckled and she fell into Mother's arms.

6

BROTHERS AND SISTERS

Dearest Penny,

KIDNAPPED?! You were kidnapped?!

I know you said you were only a little scuffed up, but what about your heart? It is no small thing to have your safety violated in such a way. You are so brave. If there is anything I can do, I will. My soul aches knowing you are in such a state and don't you deny that you are. You are the sister of my heart and I know you, Penny Barclay.

Just after I sent the letter flaunting all of my fun and fancy at prancing around Summer, I get a letter saying my dearest friend in the entire world was captured by a group of rebels and was in mortal peril. How ridiculous you must have thought me when you received my illegible brag-

gings. If I'd received your letter but a day earlier I would have ripped it to shreds and wrote a much more appropriate one. I'm sorry if my not knowing caused you any suffering.

What can I do, Penny? Can I tell you the Goddess has a plan for you? Would it be cruel to say that perhaps this thing happened for a very important reason? I can't say for certain what it could be, but I pray something good will come out of it just the same.

And I won't mention what a coincidence it was that your mystery man showed up just when we were talking about him. Nope. I won't.

I love you. You are a part of me and I can't imagine living in a world without you. I will thank the Goddess every night that you are safe.

Your Heartbroken and Loving Friend,

Angelica

"*Vile men slapped a knee*

When she was their detainee.

Penny, Penny,

She was a pretty lass.

The men were rather crass

As they put their hands upon her—"

"Paulo."

"What? I was going to end it with '*arm and were to do her harm.*' Get your mind out of the gutter, Diana."

Diana threw the pillow in her hands at her brother's face, eliciting a screech from the very put together marquess and his lyre. Penny giggled, not able to help herself. She swept her skirt covered knees up onto the cushion she'd laid on the ground beneath her. Diana reached to grab another pillow from the arsenal she'd collected from around the room.

"You really are the worst songwriter ever to grace this earth," said Diana as she flicked her long, red braid back over her shoulder. She settled a new pillow onto her lap.

"You wound me, little sister." Paulo pretended to swoon and almost toppled over the back of the settee. The strings of his lyre screeched in protest as he wrapped his arm around the instrument to keep it from falling.

"I can't believe we're born from the same parents. I'm almost certain you're adopted and Mater has not had the heart to tell you yet."

"Diana hates to share
Paulo does not care
For he has all the flare
And poor Diana's not the heir—"

Diana groaned into the ammunition she had set in her lap.

Penny turned to Paulo. "That one was terrible."

Paulo plucked a dissonant note and raised his face to the ceiling. "Great Goddess," he cried, "why must I be surrounded by women with no ear for the masterpieces I create?" He turned back, shaking a finger at both of them. "You will both rue the day I become famous for my musical talent rather than my magical one."

Penny laughed again as Diana glared across the parlor at Paulo. The fierce redhead looked quite menacing in her hunting clothes, the brown pants and green shirt, which made it easier to blend into the forest. Penny couldn't recall ever seeing Diana in anything but men's clothing and couldn't picture her in a dress for all the world.

"I'm glad the bailiff was able to apprehend the rebels,"

Diana said, turning back to Penny. "I'm especially impressed by your mother's thinking with the blackberry plants. I bet it was quite a show to watch the man squirm."

A shudder swept through Penny. She and Mother had gone to report the incident to the bailiff of Eleusia only to find the man hauling Penny's kidnappers out of a wagon. They'd been able to apprehend them just after Mother had reported Penny had gone missing. It hadn't taken long for them to find all four men tied up in the middle of a main road. The bailiff had told them it had to be the work of one of the Crown's spies, those under the command of Olympia's youngest prince, also known as the Lord of the Underworld.

The three princes weren't only irregular in their parentage, but also in the way they put themselves before the kingdom. Mother often had much to say on the topic, but not much power to change it. Crown Prince Dion would inherit the throne as soon as he married, but he worked together with his brothers and the Crown's Council to run the kingdom for the time being. The second prince, Prince Evan, was in charge of Olympia's navy. Having been born half mer, he had skill in the water unparalleled by any other and also had the ability to walk on land. The third prince, the Lord of the Underworld, ran the kingdom's spy network. He was the most mysterious of the three brothers. Most didn't even know his actual name, choosing to only call him by his moniker. Penny had heard the name once, but couldn't remember what it was. Mother only ever referred to him as "the youngest prince."

Penny's eyes flicked back and forth over the shadows in the corners of the room. While she was glad the Lord of the Underworld was looking out for their kingdom, her guts remained an anxious knot inside of her.

"Now Diana," Paulo interrupted, "we're not here to rehash a terrible occurrence in our friend Penny's life, but to provide an excellent distraction from the so-called incident. Put Bloodthirsty Diana away." He gave Penny an exasperated look and shook his head as if to say *do you see what I have to deal with?*

She gave him a shaky smile. It had been a relief to receive word the day before that they were coming. The last two weeks since the abduction had been... dark. Penny could still feel the puffy skin under her eyes every time she blinked. Mother had been in hysterics when Penny had arrived at Farrah's shop. Once Farrah deemed Penny mostly unharmed, Mother had called for a carriage and had whisked them home. Penny hadn't been allowed back onto the fields since. Sleep continued to elude her, childhood fears of the dark rearing their ugly head. While the raw skin of her wrists had healed, the wounds in her heart remained raw. Penny had certainly been in want for some distraction and the twins were the perfect company.

"Well, since we are trying to find something to laugh at, why don't you tell Penny about what Lord Hermen pulled with the cows last week."

"Oh!" exclaimed Paulo as he practically leapt from his spot on the couch. "The weasel got me again! He tried to tell me he couldn't sell my cows because they had some kind of disease—"

"Back-walker's disease," supplied Diana as she began picking her nails with a knife.

"Yes, *back-walker's disease*, and said all of my cattle would have to be sold at half price. I told him he'd have to show me proof. So, I met him at the pasture, and he had one of my workers show me this cow walking backward. Backward! He told me it's bad luck and no one will buy them for full price. I stood there, speechless, until both of the men started laughing at me and I realized I'd been pranked. They'd trained the beast to do it. I don't know how your mother deals with that man, and I certainly don't understand how he made it to be Minister of Trade."

"You can't be that surprised he's targeting you. You did try to kiss Angelica at that party when you knew she'd already been promised to Devan," said Penny.

"Oh, sweet Angelica. That bore of a man does not deserve such a beautiful—" The embroidered pillow smashing into his face cut him off with an *oof.*

"For someone who can see the future, you sure get hit in the face by pillows quite often," Diana snapped.

"Penny," Paulo said from behind the pillow, "would you please tell my obnoxious twin that if she continues to insult me I shall marry her off to the next gentleman who comes calling?"

Diana gave out an unladylike squawk and hugged the pillow she had poised to throw back to her chest.

"We all know what an empty threat that is," said Penny. "If you were really willing to, you would have married her off to Lord Alfred when he offered that enormous bride price."

"Yes, and I've regretted not taking him up on his offer ever since!"

Diana threw her hands up in the air. "It's not my fault the man has the brain of a cockroach and can't take a good joke."

"Covering yourself in mud and attempting to convince his crew the boat was being stalked by a river monster is not a good joke or proper courting etiquette," said her brother as he strummed a few chords.

"See, there's the making of a good song..." said Diana and then began to sing. While Paulo was the self-proclaimed musician, Diana's harmonic tones were nothing to scoff at.

"Lord Alfred looks like a gaping fish
And would offer Paulo his wish
Of seeing his glorious sister

Married to a prosperous mister
For a large pile of silver and gold.
But his sister was brave and bold
And scared off the fishy looking lord.
For on his ship she went aboard
And scared the daylights out of all
That would have caused her fall."

Diana stood and ended her ballad with a flourishing bow. She looked up at her audience as if waiting for an applause.

Penny grimaced. "Let's just agree neither of you are meant to be songwriters."

Paulo slumped back in his chair with his arms folded and his face in an exaggerated pout.

Diana flopped back into her chair. "Don't look so melancholy, Paulo. At least you're a man and can actually be a songwriter if you so wish. Whereas I have to use you as a foothold to do anything I want."

Paulo resumed his usual smirk. "Well at least I'm a very dashing foothold, right Penny?"

Penny held back a snort. "Oh, yes. Very dashing."

Diana just rolled her eyes at her brother and turned back to Penny. "So, any lords come vying for your hand as of late?"

The repressed snort erupted. "Didn't you see the line of waiting suitors streaming from the door when you pulled up? It's been exhausting trying to fight them all off."

Paulo gasped in delight. "Penny, that was the most sarcastic thing I've ever heard come out of your mouth. Diana, look! We're rubbing off on her."

Penny quirked a brow. "I don't know where you've been if that's the most sarcastic thing you've heard me say."

"I think it's more the fact that we saw a break in your perfect daughter facade that caught us off guard," Diana replied.

Penny straightened said facade. “I don’t have time for suitors anyway. We have too much going on to have to add getting to know if a man is worthy of my time.”

“Well, I think you’ll be in for a bit of a shock then,” said Paulo quietly. Penny’s head snapped up and she saw the color change in his eyes. The forget-me-not blue matching his sister’s took on the pearlescent sheen. Paulo’s magic had a much subtler tell than her own.

Penny opened her mouth, but Diana straightened and whispered, “Incoming.”

Penny scrambled into an actual chair while Paulo threw pillows back to Diana. The three positioned themselves in a more austere fashion just as the parlor door opened and Mother swept into the room.

“Lord MacGregor, a pleasure to see you,” Mother said as Paulo stood and folded into a perfect bow.

“The pleasure is mine, Your Grace,” answered Paulo as he straightened. His courtly smile had replaced his mischievous grin. “You’re looking radiant as always.”

Mother nodded graciously and glided toward Diana who stood and gave a small curtsy that looked more like a bow.

“Diana, it’s always lovely to see you,” Mother greeted with sparkling eyes.

“As it is to see you, Dominique.”

Penny smiled at the familiarity between the two. It wasn’t often Mother allowed such things. While Diana may have been a bit unorthodox when it came to being a proper lady, Penny was glad Mother had always encouraged the wily redhead to be who she was. She watched as Diana and Mother talked back and forth as if they were old friends, though Diana was only two years Penny’s senior.

Paulo rubbed at his temples. His oracular power often left him with massive headaches. The cost of magic always affected everyone physically. Penny was lucky she only received an energy drain. She'd heard of many mages with a cost high enough not to use magic at all. Paulo's was difficult too because he didn't have control over when the visions came, only that the aches were worse the longer he went without seeing anything of the future.

A knock on the door brought her back to the parlor and announced tea. A maid walked in with a cart full of biscuits and cakes followed by another girl toting a silver tray, which she set on the table in front of them. Barclay Manor's tall steward, Rich, came in bearing a few documents for Mother. The quiet man leaned down to whisper a few words in Mother's ear, not a thin gray hair out of place. Penny tried to hear what he said, but only heard the incoherent rasp of his voice. Rich left and the maids followed just after him. Penny began fiddling with the teapot and cups on the tray as she prepared tea for each person.

Mother quickly glanced over the papers Rich had brought. She set them aside once she received her cup of Farrah's blend of herbal tea— the same one Penny poured for herself.

"Lord MacGregor, how goes the wool industry this year?" Mother asked, turning to her less favorite twin.

"We expect to sell quite well this year," began Paulo after he took a gulp of his chamomile. *Hopefully it will help with his headache.* "The weather mages are projecting high winter storms coming in from Faerie. I should be able to start selling more to the fabric mages earlier since the fae have begun to come to market on this side of the Mist. My cousin, who runs the daily operations, expects a rush when the storms start to move into our borders in the early fall."

"Yes, I heard as much. Penny and I have been doing our best to move up the harvest timetable to avoid the frost. The pomegranates are hardy enough to survive a bit of cold, but they never sell as well."

"Perhaps not as fresh fruit, but they still make decent wine. As Prince Dion and his brothers will be celebrating their fifth year in power at winter solstice, I'm sure there will be plenty of celebrations with cups to fill. I know Lord Abrams has been working his winery overtime in preparation."

"Five years and still no king." Mother shook her head. "That boy needs to get married and secure the throne before someone comes along and takes it. We need a true king, one with an heir and a few spares if we can get them."

"I agree, Your Grace."

Diana sank back into her chair, her teacup balanced precariously on the saucer in her hand as she said, "I can't blame Lady Carnation for dragging her feet for as long as she has. I wouldn't want to be married to a playboy either."

Mother's lips pinched together, her green eyes squinting as she said, "I would have to agree with you, Diana. If she were smart, she would run the other way and let one of the other insipid girls have him."

Paulo laughed and then exclaimed, "The woman is smart! She's waiting until she has Dion wrapped around her finger before she becomes queen. She's as shrewd as our old court tutor, that one."

Penny gazed down at the cup in her hands. "I bet it is so hard to be betrothed to someone you know you can't fully trust with your heart. When I marry, it will be to a man I know I can trust with not just my heart, but every part of me."

She looked up to see an array of expressions ranging from slight disgust to absolute abhorrence.

"How many romance novels have you read this week?" Paulo asked with a tea cake halted halfway to his mouth.

"You know you have a long time to prepare for that," Mother said, her face as white as a ghost.

"Yes, why trust a man when you are already to inherit your family's title?" Diana asked, siding with Mother, as she licked pink icing off of her fingers. "Then you don't have to worry about them holding you back from doing what you want when you want."

Penny painted a smile on her face, even if it didn't reach her eyes. "From the looks on your faces you would think I just announced I am running away to join the Sireadh. We all know I am in no rush to be married."

"Thank the Goddess for that," Mother said, smoothing out her light green skirt.

"Yes," said Diana. "What are men compared to farms and pomegranates?"

"Indeed," Mother agreed.

The three started on the next topic as if Penny's words were a passing lark and she would move on as easily as their conversation had. But was that all her life was ever to be? Farms and pomegranates? She looked to Mother, the great Duchess Barclay who could do anything and everything on her own. Was that all Penny had to look forward to?

Loneliness settled in her chest. If only she had Paulo's gift. Maybe the future wouldn't look so bleak.

7

AMBER AND FLAMES

The MacGregor twins planned to stay the night and travel back home the following morning. Penny cherished the evenings they stayed for dinner. The large table never felt as lonely with the two siblings keeping the conversation light, their stories always leaving laughter in their wake.

Penny's spirit hummed more cheerfully than it had in the days following her abduction. The dark circles she kept seeing under her eyes in the mirror had lessened and her heart didn't try to stop working every time someone came around a corner. Well, at least some of the time. She'd nearly screamed when she'd bumped into Rich in the hallway on her way to bed. She slipped under her sheets with a light heart, having, at most, a sliver of fear of shadowed alleyways.

Sissy wished her a good night as she put out all but the light on Penny's bedside table and went to find her own bed. The shadows the maid left in her wake didn't yet hold sneering faces.

Penny found her eyelids growing heavier as she attempted to read the novel in her hands. Paulo had given it to her when he had arrived. Even though he claimed Mater had sent it to her, she knew he'd bought it. He secretly indulged her love of romance novels even as he swore he would rather die than touch one. He always picked the best ones, and she couldn't wait to see what he had selected for her this time.

However, after reading the same paragraph twice, she decided it was high time she put the book aside. She set it on the small table by her bed and put out the magelight. She immediately tucked the small stone under her pillow.

As soon as she nestled down under her blankets, her mind drifted into the dream she had recently found herself in more and more.

"Is that a three-headed dog?"

Moonlight shone over the sleek, gray coat dotted with black and white spots. Three heads bobbed up and down as Amber Eyes reached out to pet each one.

Curiosity piqued, she stepped toward them. "Is it a he or a she? Can it be both? Why three heads? Was it bred this way?"

Amber Eyes' attention was riveted toward her face. His features had regained their sharpness in her mind's eye since the incident. His short hair, broadcasting the point of his ears, always surprised Penny, and no longer just because of the fashions of Olympian men. Since she'd seen him last, she had come into contact with even more of the fae and they usually had hair flowing down past their waists. His face held less of the blur it had taken on previously. The only thing that remained unchanged was the intensity of his eyes. Those had never dulled.

"He was a mistake. I was working on a project when my brother's dog came in and knocked over a bottle of multiplying agent and drank a bit off the floor. She's fine, but her litter came out mutated. Spot was the only pup to make it and we still don't fully understand why he did."

Spot looked over at her and timidly sniffed at the edges of her dress with one head while the other two remained appraising her. Slowly, each head perused the rest of her. It only took a few moments before all three were asking for pets.

Penny stilled. "Spot? You named your very unique, one of a kind, beautiful dog, Spot*?"*

Somewhere in her consciousness, she understood it was a dream. The dream regularly changed depending on what was really going on in the waking world. Once, Mother had caught sight of the both of them and locked her in a tall tower of the castle. She'd believed Penny had fallen in love with him and was afraid the pomegranates wouldn't make it through the year. Penny had laughed at that one. Last week, Amber Eyes saved her from being abducted once again and had valiantly fought the shadowy figure her dreams had named The Cartographer.

Amber Eyes looked at her, a crease forming between his dark brows. His gaze snapped to the building behind her and then he crouched down and began shaking her, his mouth forming words Penny couldn't understand until she heard him say, in a voice not unlike Sissy's, "*Fire*!"

Her eyes flashed open and she saw Sissy standing over her.

"What's going on?" Penny asked groggily.

"There's a fire!" Sissy cried as she ran into Penny's closet. "Papa just showed up at the house and told the doorman a fire started in the wheat fields not half an hour ago. It's headed toward the pomegranates."

Penny threw the covers off her body and jumped out of bed. Sissy emerged from the closet, Penny's work clothes in hand. The moment after Penny slipped on her boots, she raced out her bedroom door and flew through the rousing manor.

She ran straight to the stable to find Mother already atop Wheaton and a stable hand holding Meli's reins. Penny mounted and the two women were off in a flash toward the glow coming from the direction of the fire.

Penny crested the hill on Meli's back, the glow on the horizon illuminating the dirt road in front of her. Mother rode alongside her and they both came to a complete stop in view of the destruction of the winter wheat fields. Acres of charred earth stretched out before them.

Mother urged Wheaton toward the flames still licking across the fields, reaching their fiery claws out toward the mature pomegranate orchards in the field over. Penny followed as they came up to the line of workers slinging buckets of water over the plants yet to be touched by the scorching heat of the fire. The two of them rode to the water wagon and found Aaron there with his horse hitched to the front.

"Thank the Goddess," he moaned when he saw them. "It's headed toward Peartree Field and it's gettin' too hot to do anythin' 'bout it without cookin' the hands too."

Without another word, Mother rode toward the fire. Penny took off behind her. When they got as close to the roaring flames as the horses would allow, they dismounted and sent the beasts running back to safety.

A line of white hot flame bordered the field. Thousands of rows had burned to ash and the fire had a scarce few acres between it and the line of leafy trees. If the flames reached the branches they wouldn't be stopped before they ruined the entire orchard.

"Grab my hand," Mother urged, sweat already running down the sides of her face.

Penny immediately grasped her hand and they knelt on the ground. Their hands took on their iridescent glow, the grassy green of Penny's gift and the more olive green of Mother's intermingling. They placed their free hands on the ground and instantly connected with the earth around them. With the added power, Penny could sense the plants almost a half mile in each direction.

"Penny, I need you to cut the wheat while I try to move the trees," Mother rasped in her ear.

Penny immediately drew the wheat not yet touched by flame back down into the ground, shrinking the roots and shriveling the stalks before the fire could get its greedy fill. Each stalk, each branching root shrunk down into the soil. Some of the flames grew too close and caught on the plants still reaching toward the sky. The raging inferno moved quicker than the speed with which Penny could bring the stalks down.

"Penny, you have to get them down before the flames get ahead of us."

Penny pushed her magic further in response to Mother's firm, but pleading voice. The speed of reversal increased, but she did not know if it would be enough. Mother's energy was waning and her own followed shortly behind. Mother had never demanded so much of her.

Slowly, but surely, the wheat came down and the path of the fire was blocked from the trees. Mother released Penny's feverish hand. With the tether removed, Penny slumped face first onto the ground.

She lay there for a moment, listening as feet came running up behind them on the road. She should get up. Letting the men and women under her charge see her in such a state was not appropriate. But she could not find the strength to lift a pinky.

Mother's tired voice called from beside her. Though she couldn't quite understand the words, the tone said she was getting things in order. Penny drifted.

The sound of Mother's voice had moved farther away and a gentle hand shook her awake.

"Lady Penelope, can I help you back to your horse?"

Penny peeked through her eyelids and saw a pair of ash covered boots settled just to the side of her. Her body protested as she moved her limbs. With a groan, she pushed herself up to find a man she didn't recognize. Her eyes widened.

He couldn't be more than a few years older than herself. His shoulder length hair had lost its color in the ash floating through the air and coating him head to toe. His broad shoulders stretched the fabric of his shirt, but he wasn't so large to look intimidating, only strong. He had a kind look on his face and his eyebrows were drawn slightly in concern, but none of these things held Penny's attention for longer than a second.

What made her stare, what made her heart beat erratically, was the color of his eyes— his amber eyes.

Penny scrunched her eyelids shut and opened them again, not quite believing what she was seeing. But no matter how many times she blinked, the image remained the same.

"Lady Penelope?" the owner of the eyes asked.

Penny shook herself slightly and looked around, not quite remembering where she was. The drain on her gift left her sore, like any other overworked muscle would, and her head groggy. Her eyes drifted back to him as she tried to figure out what he was doing here.

"Who are you?"

His lips twitched. "My name is Lou. I was just hired as a farmhand a few weeks ago. We hadn't had the pleasure meeting yet and I apologize for the state of my first impression." He gestured toward his ash covered clothing with a curve in his lips.

Her mind cleared. Aaron had said he had been in the process of hiring more men before her trip to Eleusia. "You certainly arrived at an interesting time. Thank you for the work you obviously put forth based on the *state* you are in."

Lou gave a small chuckle and gestured toward her own clothing. "At least I'm not alone in that, Lady Penelope."

She groaned at the ruined condition of her skirts. Her eyes once again latched onto his. "Who told you to call me that?"

His brows drew together in confusion. "What?"

"'Penelope.' No one calls me Penelope."

"Isn't it your name?"

Penny stood, no longer enjoying having a conversation from the dusty ground. Her bones creaked. Lou shot out a hand to steady her when she swayed, but Penny waved him off. "Yes it is, but I find it to be a mouthful and have always preferred to be called Penny."

"I apologize if I've made you uncomfortable," he replied. His face seemed more thoughtful than repentant. "I suppose 'Lady Penelope' just stuck with me."

Penny looked him over once again. Recognition flared strongly within her, but the man standing before her was not Amber Eyes. The sole similarities between the two were the very unique color of their eyes and the way her heart beat strangely in their presence. Eye color could be easily explained, however, blond hair and rounded ears could not. Still, the feeling churned within her as she glanced away from him.

Penny held on to her footing, finally able to take in the scene around her. Dawn had broken over the horizon and cast its rays over the weary faces around her. Mother stood in front of the water wagon, pointing toward piles of burnt wheat still glowing with heat. The field had an empty half-ring around the fire where she'd been able to pull the plants back down into the ground. The crescent of churned dirt was only about one hundred feet wide, but it had been enough to allow the workers to get ahead and prevent the flames from taking over the orchard. Mother had practically walked the trees another fifty feet away from the smoldering field. The trunks bunched together like scared children huddled close to one another in fear.

Tears gathered in Penny's eyes. So much grain, so much food, gone in a single night. Acres of charred earth stretched out before her, blackened beyond repair. Tears slipped down her cheeks as she walked toward Mother, Lou following closely behind.

"Oh good. I'm sorry I left you laying on the ground, my dear, but I knew you wouldn't want to move after how hard you pushed yourself." Mother wiped her face on her sleeve, which did nothing but smear more ash across her forehead.

Penny came up next to Mother alongside the cart. She went to wipe the evidence of her tears off of her face with her own sleeve, but when she brought it close and watched flakes of soot fall to her feet, she thought better of it.

"Do we know what happened?"

Mother shook her head. Her expression had never looked so disturbed. "Everyone I've talked to cannot say they even know where it started. I'll be sending a bird to an investigator today. Three fires in as many months is not natural."

Fires were certainly a fear to have when dealing with large amounts of crops, but they were an uncommon occurrence. The first fire had been two months after Winter Solstice. One of the winter crops of barley had been drying and it had looked like lightning. The second had been at one of the sheds, the fire that had injured some of the farmhands. But three?

Penny studied Mother's face as she felt the blood leave her own. A sinking feeling settling in her gut. "You think someone did this on purpose."

Mother nodded. "It's the only thing I can think of. While fires themselves are not unnatural, they are usually drawn to brittle plants and dry weather, not recently watered, green crops. The flames certainly shouldn't have burned half as well either."

Penny mulled over Mother's words as she once again looked at the devastation around them. Her thoughts stalled. "What if..."

"What if?"

Their green eyes met. "What if the rebels have been targeting us for longer than we realized? What if my abduction wasn't the first problem we've had with this group?"

Mother turned to her daughter, clarity and rage clashing in her eyes. "Someone set that fire, Penny... and it was someone with magic."

8

FIENDS AND FUTURES

Mother's figure paced back and forth in front of the large fireplace warming the study. Her brows furrowed as the investigator gave his initial report. It had been five days since the fire, but Penny swore she could still smell the smoke in her hair.

"You were right to call on me, Your Grace. All three of the fires' points of origin showed evidence of magical activity," the middle-aged man stated, his deep voice echoing in the large room. He held a small notebook in one hand while he ran his other over his bald head, which reflected the fire's glow. "If my readings are correct, I believe your instigator is in fact someone with a fire charm— or at least someone wanting it to look that way."

Mr. Cooper had arrived just that morning. Penny hadn't ever heard his name until they called for him, but what she learned after the fact turned out to be quite impressive. The man held the reputation of a uniquely talented investigator, the best in the region because of the mage gift he was born with. Where most people— fae, bronty, waterfolk, or mage—

could sense magic to some degree, this man had the ability to see it tangibly and sometimes even manipulate it.

Mother turned to Mr. Cooper. “Were you able to find a trail?”

Mr. Cooper’s lips twitched into a slight grimace. “Unfortunately, I did not. It isn’t uncommon with these kinds of investigations to find the perpetrators in possession of a masking charm. While I can see the residual magic left from the fire, the creator left no trace.”

Mother’s face pinched in disappointment, but she wouldn’t give voice to her feelings. Instead, she eased her features back into a look of determination.

“Well, Mr. Cooper, what is to be done?”

The large man gave a heaving sigh, leaning back in his chair beside Penny’s. “There may not be much more I can do here, Your Grace. I would recommend heightening your fields’ security and posting a reward in the major towns in the vicinity. Someone may have heard something and may be more willing to talk if there’s some incentive. I’ll continue to question the townspeople in the area and I’m going to head over to Eleusia in two days to see what I can stir up there. Your suspicions about the men who attempted to take your daughter as the same group that has also been targeting your crop is highly likely.”

The image of leering grins flashed through Penny’s mind. “Is the evidence so sure?”

“It’s certainly not concrete, but I wouldn’t be surprised,” the man said. He turned to her with a face of solemnity. “You come to find, my lady, coincidences are much rarer than you believe them to be.”

Mr. Cooper and Mother continued to iron out details, but Penny didn’t catch much. Mr. Cooper’s words resonated in her. Someone was targeting her lands, targeting her. This

Cartographer was trying to wreak havoc on her duchy. But why?

She needed to do *something.*

She jumped when the ox of a man stood from his seat. Her fingers clawed at the arm of her chair. Mr. Cooper towered over her. Her breath stuck in her throat until the man turned to collect his hat and coat from where Rich had placed them on the rack. He bid them goodnight and left the study to find his guest room in the manor.

Her fingers relaxed and her body sank back into the cushions. That had been the third time this week she'd reacted so viscerally to a man. *I'm fine. I'm fine. I'm fine.* Her hand shook as she smoothed out her skirt. The echoes of the gruesome rebels faded from her head.

Mother let out an uncharacteristic huff and slumped into the chair Mr. Cooper had vacated. She glared into the flames, as if the fire was at fault for the mess they had to deal with.

Penny set a slightly less shaky hand on Mother's arm. "What are we going to do?"

Mother remained quiet and Penny wasn't sure if she was going to answer. As Penny opened her mouth to repeat herself, Mother spoke.

"I don't know." Mother pinched the bridge of her nose and then looked over at the grandfather clock standing sentinel over the room. "I think we will have to figure it out in the morning. I'll need to come up with a more extensive list of people who could wish us harm in case it isn't rebels."

Penny stood and walked to the desk to study the field assignments for the next week. She sighed. "We're going to have to make plans for a more permanent watch. I know Aaron assigned a group for this coming week, but I'll make sure to have him write up a schedule for the rest of the month." Penny shook her head as she squinted at the papers in the low light of the fire. "We may have to hire more men or ask for assistance from our neighbors. Since the MacGregor's haven't left yet, we might as well ask them in the morning." Penny could not have been more grateful that Paulo and Diana had decided to stay at Barclay Manor to help. After they woke up to the house bustling around the night of the incident, they said it was imperative they remain and help with the clean up.

Mother stood from her place by the fire and joined Penny by the desk. "I had hoped we wouldn't have to call in favors, but it seems you are right. I'll write to Lord Hermen in the morning as well. I know he's still short workers, but perhaps we can come to some kind of arrangement."

Penny rubbed the back of her neck, the tension of the day catching up to her in her exhausted state. "What about the burnt fields?"

Mother studied her daughter for a moment. Penny could see Mother deliberate over the question. She must have found what she was looking for because she leaned over and took Penny's hands.

"Penny, I think you are going to have replant those on your own. I have to report to the capital tomorrow, the new session of court opens the following week and I need to report on what has happened here before the palace is swamped with courtiers. You're just going to have to do it."

Penny was rendered almost speechless. "You're leaving me to do the full one hundred acres?" she stuttered out. "Without you?"

Mother frowned. "Unfortunately. I would much rather be here to take care of it, but there's nothing else to be done." She released Penny's hands and turned back toward the desk.

Of course. It wasn't that she trusted Penny to do it. It was that she didn't have a choice in the matter. Penny's shoulders slumped.

"Now, you have two weeks until the rains are sent from the weather mages at the coast, and I'll hopefully be back the week after. It'll be difficult, but hopefully you can get most of it done before I get back."

Anger stirred in Penny's chest. She could easily replace the grain. She'd been working hard to hone her skills. She opened her mouth to say just that, but Mother continued on.

"Besides, I think it's high time I give you a chance to prove you can take over this land when the Goddess decides I'm done being its caretaker."

How had Mother not seen the efforts she made to do just that? Penny worked just as hard as everyone else on their lands. Her fists clenched.

But maybe I can finally prove something to her. Penny took a deep breath and swallowed her pride. At least she was allowing Penny the chance, even if there was begrudging in her tone. Penny sighed. "Mother, don't say that. You have a great many years left as matron of this work and I won't listen to any kind of talk saying otherwise."

Mother laughed aloud. "I don't think my untimely demise will come anytime soon, but we should be prepared nonetheless. Especially with these brutes attempting to ruin all of our hard work."

Penny shook her head. Mother was right. They had more to worry about than just Penny's hurt feelings. They began to go over the number of workers they had, attempting to devise a plan for the foreseeable future.

Penny attempted to stifle her fifth yawn when Mother officially declared it time the two of them left the work for the morning. With bleary eyes, Penny walked out of the study. Her steps had turned into more of a trudge than was ladylike, but she couldn't find the energy to care. She worked her way down the hallway to the staircase when she heard laughter coming from the drawing room. Curious, she made her way over to peek through the door and saw her two friends sitting by the fire, their profiles silhouetted by the flames. With a smile, she swung the door open and glided in.

She watched the two continue chatting quietly as she made her way through the room. Diana wore a clean tunic and pants with her knee-high riding boots propped on the table in front of her. Paulo was wearing a fashionable dinner coat and slacks, his pants tucked into his polished boots which gleamed in the fire's glow.

"There you are," Diana said when Penny caught her eye.

Paulo turned with a large smile as he watched Penny sit on the sofa next to him. "Long day?"

"You could certainly say that," Penny replied. "What are you two still doing up?"

"Making bets," Diana responded, mischief glittering in her eyes.

"Bets? On what?"

"My visions of the future, of course," said Paulo, his hands flaring dramatically. "Diana and I always bet— when I have a good one— whether or not it will truly come to pass and how long until it becomes the present."

Penny turned to Diana. "How do you know what to bet? You don't see them."

"You're right, but Paulo loves the challenge enough that he shows them to me."

Penny's head swiveled to Paulo on the sofa beside her. His lips smirked at Penny's obvious shock. "You can share your visions with others?"

"Yes. It's a more recent development. Like when you and your mother combine your gifts or when married mages share theirs, I can show my visions with anyone I have an emotional connection with as long as we are touching. It helps quite a lot when I need to present one of my visions to the court. With Diana or Mater as my second witness, they have no room to doubt my words."

Diana's voice piped in. "It used to just be impressions of feelings in the visions. Then, it was smells or sounds, but now it's an actual picture along with words."

"I haven't mastered it. I see real events and Diana only receives blurry copies when I share them, but I always tell her the truth so it's a fair bet."

"By the Goddess!" Penny gasped. "That's amazing!" The cobwebs of exhaustion swept away. "What a gift to be able to share. I can't believe you never told me before now."

Paulo puffed his chest out. "I'm told my grandfather was the only one in the last hundred years to perform such a feat. It's a great honor to be able to emulate him in such a way."

"Yes, yes." Diana waved her hand as if to cast off the smoke of Paulo's pride. "All hail the mighty fortune teller."

"Oh Diana, don't pout. It's unbecoming for a lady of your station," Paulo teased.

"Anything interesting in your recent visions?" Penny asked, attempting to waylay the fight she saw coming.

"My visions are always interesting." Paulo settled back into the cushions like a satisfied cat.

Diana rolled her eyes.

"Have there been any recently that you've had to send to the capital?" Penny knew his gift as an oracle was important to the prosperity of the kingdom. When he had a vision holding something of value to the country, he always reported it to the Crown.

Paulo rolled his eyes. "Nothing of great consequence lately. More for the gossip vine than anything else. There has been nothing of value to the kingdom in quite a bit."

"So what were you betting on?"

The twins shared a glance. Penny swore they spoke telepathically anytime they did so.

"Boring stuff."

"Prince Evan's new horse."

"The first frost."

"What color Lady Carnation wears at the Opening Ball this year."

"Who gets the stag at summer solstice."

"All right, all right." Penny held up her hands to ward off the twins' ridiculous list. "You don't actually have to tell me."

The twins both chuckled as Penny stifled another yawn.

"It seems to be time for bed," Paulo said, standing from his seat to light one of the candles on the mantle.

Diana and Penny both stood to follow as he walked out of the drawing room. Penny turned toward Diana. "Are you heading out soon?"

Diana looked up at her brother as they followed him down the hallway. "Yes. We just got word from our steward that Paulo is needed back at home before he has to return to court. We leave tomorrow."

"Tomorrow?" Penny parroted. She had expected them to leave soon but hoped it wouldn't be for a few more days. It seemed everyone was leaving her.

Diana smiled down at her. Penny took note of their height difference for the hundredth time since their friendship began. "I know you always want us to stay longer."

Diana patted Penny on the back when all three stopped in the dark hallway leading to the guest wing. The light in Paulo's hand cast their shadows upon the walls around them.

"We would stay forever if we could," Paulo said smiling, "but I think Mater would have our heads. She so dislikes being stuck in the house all the time without someone to order around besides the servants." He grinned at his twin as she shoved him to the side. The flame on his candle wobbled but didn't go out.

Penny's answering chuckle turned into another yawn and she bid the twins goodnight. She pulled a small magelight out of the pocket of her dress, and with little pressure from her fingers, lit the path toward her rooms. When she turned down the hall to her own rooms, she gazed out the window. The stars glittered across the open sky. The shadows of the pomegranate trees textured the hills.

Tonight didn't hold the shadows of the past like it had in nights before. Tonight held the promises of tomorrow. She would prove herself. She would show Mother that she deserved the Barclay name. This was her chance and there was nothing that would stand in her way of success.

9

SMILES AND LIES

Dearest Penny,

What on Gaia's green earth is going on back home? Father's last letter reported multiple thefts around Eleusia, businesses shutting down, and more fires at Barclay Manor. This is insane! Devan and I have talked of little else since we received word.

What does your mother think about all of this? I'm sure she is absolutely livid. Father said court opens in a few weeks. I hope she goes in there, magic blazing, and knocks some heads. The Council deserves a good rattling.

Winter finally sent a representative. It was so strange. The fair folk in Summer acted as if the delegation had a plague. Apparently, the Night Court and the Day Court don't mingle very often. Autumn and Winter's darker magic seem to put off those with the light magic. I didn't see anything wrong with it. The ambassador was very kind, but firm that Winter would not join talks of any trade agreements until they had an established ruler once again. Father made it clear he wanted us here until Winter agreed. Seems we will be in Faerie for a while.

So if we aren't ever to bring up Amber Irises or whatever you call him in your head, is there anyone else we CAN talk about? Being married has subjected me to the reality of true love. Now I feel everyone needs to experience marital bliss. You have to have something! I'll even take a cute farmhand flirtation if you have one. It's my sole goal in life to prove your mother wrong.

Your Overly Romantic Friend,
Angelica

PENNY'S HAND SHIELDED HER EYES FROM THE GLARING SUN AS SHE watched the workers cover a field with manure shipped from Lord Hermen. He was kind enough to always age the muck enough to not hurt the plants when Penny and Mother rapidly grew their crops. The manure would help the production of the wheat since so many of the nutrients the plants needed had been burned in the fire. She continued to watch the progress throughout the day, giving out orders when needed and mixing the fertilizer in herself at times. The pungent smell made her eyes water. When they completed one field, she moved on to another.

One hundred and ten acres in total had burned and needed

replanting before the rains were sent within the next week. If they had any hope of allowing the plants to settle into the dirt before then, they had to get all the new seed planted within the next three days. Penny wiped her brow. It was going to be a long few days.

Lord Hermen and Paulo were a Goddess-send and would be lending out thirty men and women between the two of them for the repair and safeguarding of the new crop. The workers would be there the next day if the roads remained clear. Twenty of her own workers spread across the fields around her and somehow she always knew where a certain pair of eyes were.

Penny caught herself throughout the day looking for a tuft of blond hair or a set of broad shoulders. Lou was one of the best workers on the field and all of the people around them knew it. Penny witnessed him quietly listening to someone when he stopped for water. He comfortably helped direct a cart when they needed the manure moved. The men seemed to enjoy his quiet strength and the women continued to bat eyelashes his way.

Penny was glad to find how well liked he was. As Mother had kept her sequestered in the house after their trip to Eleusia, she hadn't yet been able to work with the men Aaron had hired. Mother said they'd gone through an extensive interview between herself and Aaron. Penny didn't envy them.

The sweat coating her limbs and the sharp smell of the warming manure foretold lunchtime. Aaron called everyone to the wagons.

"Lady Penny!" He waved her over to him.

Penny's eyes strayed to Lou as he sat beside the other workers. *Later.* She met the field master. "Good afternoon, Aaron."

"It's certainly lookin' good," he remarked, nodding his head toward the fields. "Mighty good work y'all been doin'."

"Thank you. Was there something specific you called me over for?"

"Yes'm. I've gotta few watch schedules that need approvin' and a handful of field layouts to check and sign."

Penny worked with Aaron, praying they would be done before everyone finished eating. She just wanted a moment to eat her food— or so she told herself. She brushed off her disappointment when she finished right as the other workers packed up their meal. With an apple and a meat pie in hand, she marched back into the field. There were more important things to worry about.

The work was laborious, but the weather stayed mild as she worked the ground. A soft breeze continued to buoy up her aching muscles. Penny regularly broke away from her task as workers from other fields sent messages needing a response or she was required to send orders to other fields. Maybe Mother did trust her with a few things.

Penny looked around as the sun sank lower over the horizon and watched as a few of the workers began to drag their shovels back to the tool cart. She looked around for a head of blond hair as she stepped toward the cart.

"What are you looking for, Lady Penelope?"

Penny spun to find Lou just behind her. "By the Goddess, you scared me."

Lou winced and his cheeks reddened slightly. "I apologize. I didn't mean to frighten you, my lady."

The tension fled her shoulders. "No apology necessary. I should've heard you coming up behind me."

Lou gave a small smile in response as he rubbed the back of his neck with his hand. "Were you looking for something?"

Penny's face heated when she realized he had caught her

looking for *him*. She turned away, hoping he wouldn't see. "No, no. I was just looking over what we've accomplished today. I'm really hoping everything goes smoothly tomorrow when we start planting."

He nodded and looked over the fields intently. "It's too bad there isn't a more efficient way to get the seed planted."

She looked at him, stunned. "What?"

His deep brow furrowed further as he thought, not even glancing Penny's way. "Like using a weather mage to spread the seed or an earth mage to bury them. You wouldn't need half as many workers."

Penny's brows rose. "I'm sorry, are you an expert in farming?"

Lou shook his head, his gold hair brushing the tops of his shoulders. "Not at all. It just seems like there may be a better way to do it."

She set her hands on her hips. "I'll have you know, the Barclays have been growing these crops since before the Faerie Wars. We do the things we do for a reason. We didn't become the most prosperous farming community in the kingdom because we're morons."

She huffed and turned away from him, leaving him without another glance. Mother's words of ignorant men giving her business advice ran on a loop in her head. Penny had heard it more often than not at any societal events they'd attended. *Blasted men and their foolish ideas.*

All of the other workers had left the field and were now loading onto the carts. Penny stood at the end of the line and clambered into the back of one. Lou came up behind her and they ended up together in the cart of tools which allowed two people to ride on the back and two at the front to direct the horses.

"Lady Penelope."

Penny glared at the worker seated next to her. If he kept up his unsolicited advice, Penny might shove him off the back of the cart.

His head tilted, the edge of his jaw sharpening in the fading light. "I'm sorry if my words caused you offense. My mind sometimes gets carried away with ideas and the way I presented them may have offended you. It wasn't my intention."

Penny nodded and tucked an errant hair behind an ear. "Thank you for your apology."

He nodded back and turned his attention to the road.

The hurt in her chest eased. *So maybe he's not so bad. It wouldn't hurt to at least get to know him a little better.*

She took a deep breath. "Are you enjoying work as a field hand?" As soon as the words left her lips, she wanted to slap herself. *What kind of interesting question was that?*

Lou's eyes lit up. "Surprisingly, yes. This is actually the first time I have done something like this, and I find it to be quite relaxing."

Penny's eyebrows lifted. "You call this relaxing? What were you doing before?"

"I used to be an apprentice of sorts. The mentor I was training under disappeared right after the king died and everything was a little chaotic. I've been working for my family since then. When I heard Lady Barclay was looking for workers, I knew I'd found what I needed."

Penny shifted as the cart rolled over a hole in the road. "Why did you need to stop working with your family?"

He shrugged. "I haven't really stopped. Everyone else is simply busy with other things and I thought I could use another job for a little while. It's more of a break from the capital, if anything."

Penny's ears perked. "You lived in the capital?"

Lou winced but covered it with a smile. “Yes. All of the members of my family work in the capital, though I like to travel a lot more than they do.”

“Wow,” Penny sighed. “I would think it’s a lot more exciting there than it is out here.”

“Exciting isn’t the word I would use.” He chuckled. “Exhausting is more like it.”

Penny frowned. “I’ve only been to the capital once, but I found it more than thrilling to see such diversity and culture. It’s such a wonder compared to what you can find out here.”

Lou looked around at the fields as they bounced on the back of the wagon. “I would have to disagree with you there. This is much more of a wonder.”

Penny followed his gaze. In the faint light of the coming night, the orchards glowed with life. They had a few other fields with wheat or barley that Mother sold to Mr. Gilbert and the towns around them, but the majority of their lands were covered in the leafy boughs of pomegranate trees. The sounds of crickets and cicadas chirruped in the air and the stars peeked through the curtain of daylight as the sun waved its final goodbye for the evening.

Perhaps it was a bit of a wonder.

They rode the cart back up to the barn and put away the tools. The two women that had driven the cart waved in farewell and walked arm in arm toward their respective houses in the village. One held a lantern to light their way and the one without it laughed at something the lantern-holder said.

Lou came to stand next to Penny. They watched the workers safely walk down the road. Penny’s skin prickled slightly as the breeze blew across the back of her neck, but she welcomed the feeling after working so long in the sun.

When the two women’s forms disappeared, Lou turned toward Penny. “Your family’s land is magnificent.”

Penny raised a brow. “Why do you say that?”

His gaze roved over the moonlit landscape around them. “I’ve never been anywhere in this kingdom where two unmarried women can walk home from working all day and make it to their beds safely without thought. In all honesty, I’ve never seen land worked by women.” He turned his eyes on Penny. “I’ve also never met a noble woman whose title was her own and not her husband’s. I’ve certainly never seen any noble women laboring alongside their workers either. This place has a freeing magic to it that makes you hope the traditions that have bound us in the past are loosening and that we can create a world where everyone is free to be who they wish.”

“Around a lot of nobility are you?” Even though the words were light, Penny’s heart soared. Mother’s title was an oddity at court, and their duchy worked differently than other lands in the kingdom. Most titles fell to a male heir, no matter their birth order. The Barclay name and all its holdings always fell to the heir with the strongest magic over plants. Their magic kept food on Olympian tables, which was more important than if the lands were run by a duke or duchess. Mother had inherited the title from her father and Penny would inherit it after her.

He rubbed the back of his neck. “Not many, but you see enough of them in the capital.”

She chuckled. “It was a joke.” She returned her gaze to the fields. “But really, we know and respect each one of our workers and we would never ask them to do something we ourselves weren’t willing to do. Everyone who lives within my mother’s duchy matters.”

She let out a small sigh. “Everyone was appalled that there were men in our duchy willing to kidnap me.” The news of her abduction had reached the edges of Mother’s lands and she expected even Lou to know what had befallen her.

Lou nodded gravely.

"I expect my mother rode up to the capital in a blaze of her own after the fire as well. She has made sure to give everyone who lives here their own path to freedom from strife, and in return, those living under her dominion help our work to feed and support the other lands around us." Penny's heart swelled. She loved this place. For all of the feelings of confinement it sometimes caused her, she couldn't help feeling a deep attachment to it as well.

Lou smiled. "It's good to see someone passionate about the people they have a responsibility to protect. It gives me hope for this kingdom."

They stood silently on the threshold of the barn as the stars began to light the sky. Penny's thoughts whirled like a cyclone as they remained in place, neither ready to leave but both knowing it was getting late. *Sweet Gaia, I'm ruining this. Angelica's going to throw a fit when I tell her.*

After a few more moments, Lou shifted next to her. "I should leave you to your evening, Lady Penelope." He nodded to her and took a step toward the night.

"Where are you staying?" She winced. *Impertinent much?*

"I've been staying with Master Aaron in the village for the past few weeks. He and his wife are wonderful people."

Penny couldn't help but grin. "Ada is the best. I know she'll take good care of you."

Lou smiled, a true smile, back at Penny and her heartbeat picked up. *He's beautiful.* She couldn't stop the blush that stained her cheeks. Her focus rushed back as Lou spoke again.

"Yes, Mistress Ada has a giving heart. It's truly a testament to your lands that such people live here. It takes a certain kind of master to encourage charity in the people they have charge over."

No words could break through the crash of pleasure his words gave her. *He likes the way we run things. He's impressed by us— by me.* A hoot called down from the top of the barn, startling Penny. They both looked up to watch a barn owl swoop down from the edge of the building's thatched roof.

"Well then, I will take my leave," said Lou. "Thank you for your conversation, Lady Penelope."

Penny cleared her throat. "Yes, I— I'll be seeing you tomorrow... on the fields again." She fidgeted then offered her hand for him to shake. *Perhaps if I act like I know what I'm doing he won't think I'm a bumbling fool.*

Lou chuckled. However, instead of shaking it as she had intended, he grasped it and bowed over it fluidly.

"Until tomorrow." He turned and walked in the direction of the village.

Penny stood there, speechless, until the heat finally cooled to a manageable temperature and her nerve endings had ceased firing. She rubbed her palms over her flaming cheeks.

Just wait until Angelica hears about this.

10

GRAIN AND FEET

Penny's eyes slowly opened to darkness surrounding her. She shut them an instant later as cold crept through her and she had to take a few deep breaths before she could look into the shadows again.

She rolled in her large, warm bed and looked over to the window. No light leaked through the gaps in the fabric, telling her it wasn't quite dawn yet. She'd had a hard time going to sleep last night after her conversation with Lou, but no exhaustion lingered.

Today was planting day.

Hopping out of bed with a magelight, she thrust her feet into slippers and ran over to her closet where her newest set of work clothes hung on a hook by the door. She put on her brown dress but had a hard time tying the apron on, her fingers fumbling in her haste to get outside. She slipped into her boots and practically flew through the door before she remembered to grab her hat off of the rack.

Penny strode quickly down the hallway. The night sky still glittered with stars out the windows as she breezed past. She made it to the stairs and had the childish urge to slide down the banister, but thought better of it and walked quickly down the steps. Penny marched to the kitchen, the smell of baking bread greeting her.

"A little early for you isn't it, Lady Penny?" Cook asked.

Penny followed her nose straight to the warm oven full of rolls. She closed her eyes to inhale another strong sniff of the yeasty aroma and let out a contented sigh. Not opening her eyes, she said, "The dead would wake from their slumber for one last bite of your delicious creations if they knew what a treasure you were."

She heard the pleased laugh behind her and turned toward Cook's rosy face. "You are such a little flatterer, my lady."

Penny balked in mock offense. "Flattery is a novel term for what I would call worship."

Cook giggled again and shooed Penny from the oven. "Go on and grab your breakfast. There are some *lalagites* over there that I pulled out not ten minutes ago."

Penny dashed over to the counter and found the flat cakes under a small towel with a small jar of honey sitting beside them. Penny wolfed down a number of the small cakes, some even sprinkled with crumbles of goat cheese. She licked her fingers clean of the honey, ran over to give Cook a peck on the cheek, and raced out the door.

Penny's boots drummed a beat on the packed earth. The rhythm was lively and matched the song she hummed as she waltzed down to the fields. The sky lightened with dawn and the birds sang from the trees around her. She couldn't imagine a more perfect setting to start her day.

Though, if she got to show off her magic with a certain blond employee in attendance, it might get even better.

Penny made it to the first field being planted that day and found Aaron and Lou riding up in a wagon pulled by Aaron's mare. Aaron drove the cart up to her and hopped down. Lou followed just behind.

"Mornin', m'lady," Aaron jovially greeted.

Penny pulled on every ounce of confidence she had. She would not stumble in front of Lou. "Good morning, Aaron. Lou. I assume that's the seed you've got behind you." *Mother would have said something much more intelligent than 'I assume that's the seed.'* By the Goddess, would she always act like a silly girl in front of this boy? Why was he any different than the rest of them?

His golden gaze and warm smile answered that question.

"Yes, m'lady," Aaron said. "I had one of the boys run water in the ditches through the night. Should be plenty of moisture for you to work with."

Penny cast her eyes about and took a deep breath of crisp, stabilizing air. "I'm pleased with how well everything's gone so far. Let's see what today brings."

The three of them unloaded bags of grain around the fields, giving the workers easy access when they came in. Penny's arms tired as she hauled the heavy canvas bags out of the back of the cart and deposited them on the ground. By the time they'd hit every field, there was a thin film of sweat covering her brow. She grinned.

The field workers trickled in as they parked the cart off one of the paths. Aaron clambered onto the wagon behind his horse and rode off to collect another load of seed with Lou bouncing beside him. *They'll be back.*

Penny immediately assigned tasks to the men and women as they came in, using a handcart as a makeshift desk. She started workers at the farthest field then worked her way back toward the middle field where she stood. Once she had a full head count of the twenty-five workers assigned to these fields, she tucked the small field grid papers in her apron pocket and left to make her rounds.

Penny could never sit in one place for long. Striding along the dirt paths around the fields, she grabbed a bag of seed herself and planted it with her own hands. She continued to watch the field hands and answered questions other workers from around the farm brought to her attention throughout the morning. Aaron and Lou rode back with the rest of the seed before everyone took a small break for lunch. Once the bags were placed at the appropriate fields, Aaron rode back to where Penny stood and someone grabbed the lunch tarp out of the back.

"Forgive the delay, m'lady," Aaron said. "Had a couple boys needing some help on another field before we could bring the seed."

"No need to apologize," Penny said, waving it off as she looked down at the pile of documents needing attention. "I expected you to be rather busy today."

Aaron thanked her and walked off to grab his own lunch. Penny grabbed her field papers back out of her pocket and began counting off fields. A throat cleared behind her and she jumped. Penny spun to find Lou holding out a cloth with bread and cheese as well as a water skin. The pounding in her heart eased. *It's just Lou.* Relief settled in her chest.

"I thought you might like some lunch before all of it was devoured," he said, a smile playing on his lips.

Penny looked over at the tarp and saw the lunch basket nearly empty. She tucked her papers away and took the offering from Lou's hands. Their fingers brushed as she gathered the cloth. The brief touch shot a bolt of lightning up her arm. Penny watched Lou's smile fade and his eyes grow intense with something she couldn't put a name to.

"Thank you," she said, not taking her eyes from his.

Lou's smile returned. "My pleasure." He didn't look away.

Penny's cheeks flamed and she watched Lou's eyes grow wide and a slight blush creep over his cheeks. His eyes darted around as he cleared his throat and shuffled his feet. Penny looked down at the ground, attempting to not make the air between them any more strained, but failing. *Could I be any more awkward around him?*

Before the air grew too tormenting, Lou straightened and looked over at the bags of grain by the closest field. "So how does wheat growing go exactly? Is it much like pomegranates?"

A bellowing chortle came out from behind him, and they turned to see Aaron walking up to them. "'Is it much like pomegranates?' he says. Ha!" Aaron threw his head back with a laugh as he came to a stop beside them.

Lou threw a questioning look between Aaron and herself. "I suppose I will take that as a *no.*"

"You'd be right to," Aaron said, slapping a hand on Lou's shoulder. He stood a good six inches above Aaron, making the older man look quite short. Lou must have been around a foot taller than Penny herself. *Angelica's perfect mix: tall, dark, and handsome.*

Penny shook her head before her thoughts swept her away. "Aaron, don't tease him." She turned back to Lou. "Do you know how long it takes for wheat to naturally grow from seed to harvest?"

"I'd guess only a season or so," he responded.

Penny called up her best tutoring face. "Winter wheat, like what we are planting here, is usually planted at the end of the year and harvested the next summer. The roots dig a few feet into the ground, making the entirety of the plant about as tall as Aaron." She gestured toward the field master who did his best to stand straight. "Pomegranates, however, don't begin to fruit until about two or three years after a cutting is planted. It takes more of my gift to grow a pomegranate cutting just as it would take more time. Naturally, its root system is also shallow, but the way we account for that is by growing the roots together in squares, allowing the trees to help one another in bad weather conditions."

Lou nodded. "Your powers have to follow the rules nature has ordered. Same as with any other mage, the nature of your medium changes. It makes sense that it would take more effort."

"It does. The magic also takes away from the pomegranates' natural progression. We tinker a bit with a few things— root systems, branch thickness, and what have you— but if we mess with the proper order, the pomegranates come out bad. They are more susceptible to disease and will rot before they ripen. Some won't ripen at all. It would be the same as helping a chick out of its shell. They aren't as strong and usually die early. Everything has its season, just as Gaia ordered it."

He looked out to the fields they had worked. "I'm interested to see how it works."

Penny smiled. "Come along then."

Penny beckoned them in the direction of the farthest field, now completely planted and the field hands already off on their next assignment. Her eyes roved over the field. Her boots met the edge of the worked ground and she began her inspection. The dirt looked dry, but when Penny crouched down to grab some of the soil, the layer underneath parted softly with moisture. There was plenty of water to work with. She counted hundreds of little rows of mounded dirt ready for their debut.

Penny sat on the path next to a corner of the field and began to untie her laces. Another set of boots came into view next to her.

"What are you doing?" Lou asked.

"Taking my boots off." She set her first boot off to the side to free her hands to slide her sock off of her foot. She wiggled her toes when her skin met the fresh air.

"Do I need to take my boots off as well if I follow you into the field?"

Penny looked up to see his face serious and devoid of any sarcasm. She laughed aloud as she untied her other boot. "Of course not. While my hands may be the ones that glow, my feet work just as well."

"I didn't know you needed to touch the ground."

"I don't, not really. I simply have more control over the plants when I do. I have to get this crop to a certain height rather than to full flowering since it isn't the right time to harvest. We want the flowers and the grain to come in their own time. Once the wheat grain begins to grow, my mother takes over nurturing until harvest."

Penny tugged off her other sock and handed her boots to Aaron, trusting he knew what to do with them. She stepped over the small ditch separating the field from the road. The moment her foot touched the softer soil, her work began.

Penny closed her eyes and felt the thousands of little seeds laid out before her. The sensation wasn't nearly as poignant as when she'd worked alongside Mother during the fire, but she was still amazed by how much she could feel. She started with the seeds closest to her and began walking. She didn't need to open her eyes as she allowed the seeds to show her where to step and when. The new stalks brushed against her skirt as she walked. The fresh smell of growth tickled her nose and filled her lungs with life. Penny felt the roots digging down into the ground, following their instincts and the promise of more water.

Penny finished the field and opened her eyes. Leafy stalks stood to her waist, their long bodies flowing in waves as the breeze swept through, leading them in a dance only they knew the tune to.

Penny smiled to herself. Her brow had a small layer of sweat, but the magic still pulsed strongly inside her. She turned and almost ran into a solid wall of flesh. She stumbled backward and nearly fell when two hands whipped out to grab her shoulders.

“My apologies, my lady. I got too close.” Lou’s voice rumbled through his arms and into hers. He let go once she regained her balance, but the warmth of his hands lingered.

Penny mumbled about him not needing to apologize, her breathing fast, but his attention was taken once more by the field she’d just finished.

“That was magnificent.” Lou’s voice held the quality of an eager child witnessing their first snowfall.

The tips of Penny’s ears warmed at the compliment and washed away the shock of his presence. “Thank you. However, by the time we’re done, I think you’ll be tired of watching me work. It gets rather monotonous.”

“I don’t know if I believe that.”

The heat in her cheeks expanded all the way to her hairline and she ducked her head. She grappled with herself over his words. *Does he just like the magic or is there possibly more to it than that?*

Once she’d regained her composure, she led him toward the next field. She began her work without ceremony and finished this one more quickly than the last. On the fifth field, she started to work up quite a sweat. Her limbs quivered and soul-deep exhaustion settled in, but she was going to prove to Mother that she could handle something like this.

Lou continued walking behind her. Having someone with her boosted her resolve and she kept moving. When they reached the seventh— and last field— Lou stepped off the path and began to remove his own boots.

"What are you doing?" Penny asked, eyes widening.

"I want to feel it."

"Feel what?"

"The magic."

Her groggy mind halted in astonishment. "You can feel magic?"

Lou looked up at her with a smirk from where he was untying his second boot. "Yes. It's not so uncommon in bronties, you know?" He stood from his spot on the ground and looked at his bare feet then back at his boots. His features turned astonished, as if he was actually shocked he'd just removed his shoes.

Penny closed her eyes once more and began her trek through the field. The skin of her back slicked with sweat, but she couldn't stop. She rooted herself down into the earth and almost stopped dead. The magic under her feet called to Lou... to *his* magic.

She nearly stumbled as she followed the pull, and saw— in the way that she saw the plants— his gift reaching out to caress hers. An immense power called to the ground beneath their feet. The magic of the earth seemed to give reverence to his and attempted to follow him as he walked. If he didn't walk right behind her, she might have followed him too.

They continued on through the field in silence. Lou's steps behind her were so hushed the only way she could tell he was still there was through the call of his magic. Her thoughts twisted this way and that. It didn't seem as if he realized she saw what his magic did. Honestly, it still shocked her that she could see it, that her magic was capable of such a thing and that she'd caught him in his lie. He said he was a bronty. Could he be a rogue mage? Could he work for The Cartographer? Was he the one who burned down the fields? She began to feel the sweat more acutely with him following just behind her.

"So," she began, wanting to distract herself from her thoughts but wanting to uncover whatever he was hiding, "are you so interested in farming that you had to follow me out? I figured a thing like wheat planting wouldn't be so exciting to one who's done as much traveling as you have."

Penny heard Lou's quiet chuckle just behind her. She remained on task as he replied, "I'm simply a man who wants to learn as much as he can about the world around him."

"Oh?" she asked. "What value would working on a farm give you?"

"Actually, more than you'd think. It gives perspective to the minds of the people living here. I enjoy experiencing the same things as those who live and toil around me. Back home, I don't have much opportunity to work alongside people like those you have under your employ."

Penny frowned. "Is your work in the capital so different?"

She couldn't see his face, but she thought she heard thoughtfulness in his voice when he replied, "More than I wish it was. I have responsibilities and people relying on me that I find myself forgetting as I haul bags of seed or help water rows. It's soothing out here. I've certainly been more distracted than I ever am at home. The capital is full of distractions— many of the magical sort. It's nice to be out here without bits of magic flying about all over the place. Makes everything feel more real."

He doesn't like magic? Even as a mage? Penny continued on, pretending not to run a fine comb over every word he spoke. Acting like she wasn't trying to find the holes in his lie. "What kind of work do you do exactly?"

Lou remained quiet longer than he should have. "This and that. Sometimes I work together on a team or go off to find something to do on my own. Since I've been old enough to be out from under my father's thumb, I've been working."

Penny grew quiet as they continued to walk, ruminating on his words in her head as she worked with the earth under her feet. *What does any of that even mean?* When she resumed asking him questions, he remained vague and redirected the conversation. It was hard to keep track of the facts— if there were any.

They reached the end of the field. Penny opened her eyes and found the sky glittering with starlight. She looked around and found Aaron hitching his horse to the wagon. All of the other workers seemed to have already headed home.

Penny turned to study Lou who was looking over the fields as she had. Could this man simply be a mage hiding his gift? Or was there something much more sinister happening right under her nose?

She clapped her hands. "Well, it's time to go. Got lots to do and all that." She turned to walk down the road toward the house. She needed to figure out how she was going to discover what his intentions were and why he had lied about being bronty. If he didn't like magic, he could be suppressing his gift and working alongside the rebels anyway.

Lou looked at her quizzically. "Aren't you going to ride back on the wagon with us?"

She looked back at where Aaron stood waiting for them. *Right.* "Of course." She trudged toward the cart and slumped into the back. Aaron smacked Lou on the back and gave Penny a large grin as they set off toward the manor to take her home.

Her eyelids drooped, her magic completely spent. Her limbs were jelly and her thoughts turned to mush. She would figure out what to do about Lou tomorrow.

After she drank a gallon of Farrah's tea.

11

REBELS AND BLACKMAIL

Dearest Penny,

Why must we live with all four seasons in Olympia? Having a blissful summer everyday is glorious. You should see my skin. I'm almost as dark as Father!

Cute farmhand hit it right on the nose then? Ha! Devan nearly spilled his tea all over the table when I cackled at your description of LOU, The Adorable, Steamy, Amber Eyed Hunk of Sweetness. Who knew your type would be golden eyed men? I've seen several of Father's employees with that color of eyes. If this one doesn't work out, I'll get you in touch with another.

I'm so glad you finally got a break from The Warden. I know you hate when I call her that, but your mother can be such a killjoy. I bet she *would be fuming at you making advances on a man. You deserve it! Everyone deserves a good flirtation, even those who have no prior experience.*

Here's some tips:

1. Eye contact is everything.

2. Make sure he knows who is in charge.

3. Be clear with what you want. Men do not take hints well so you have to be specific.

Actually, all of that sounds like things your mother would say about a business transaction. Shake that off.

The most important thing is doing what feels natural and allow your heart to guide you. If it is meant to be, it will all come naturally.

There, that sounds less like what the Dower Duchess would say.

Best of luck in your romantic advances. I'll be cheering for you!

Your Most Supportive Friend and Confidante,

Angelica

A RUMBLE ROARED IN THE DISTANCE AS PENNY SCRATCHED HER QUILL along the parchment in front of her. With a flourish, she signed her name and set the letter to Diana and Paulo atop her reply to Angelica on Mother's desk. The twins' letter had come that day in the form of the most bedraggled, but well paid, messenger she'd ever seen. They'd sent the letter when Mother had arrived in the capital and their questions had expressed their excitement for Penny's temporary independence.

Droplets pattered against the window as Penny stood and walked toward the study's fireplace. It had taken her much longer than it should have to compose the two letters. Her feet began to tread in time with the rain.

Who is Lou? How do I go about finding more information about him? Is he a spy for The Cartographer? What would his purpose be?

She couldn't see what he would gain by working on the farm. No more complaints had come from the other workers about people preaching rebellion. However, most of the field hands liked Lou. Would they even come to her if they thought he was a problem? Or had he flattered them all into thinking he was one of them? What would Mother do in a situation like this? *She'd probably call the townsmen to throw him out.*

But Penny couldn't force herself to do it. He intrigued her— more than he should— and a hint of something told her not to be hasty.

Penny looked over at the clock standing sentinel in the room as it called the midnight hour, followed shortly by the ring of thunder. She rubbed at the spot on her forehead where an ache was building and crouched down to shuffle the coals in the fireplace with an iron poker.

When the light finally went out, she stood to leave the room. She remained rooted to her spot for a few more minutes, attempting not to allow the shadows to creep into her skin. She then sat down on one of the chairs by the hearth out of pure spite.

It had been more of a problem since Mother and the twins had left. It crept up on her in the late hours of the night and she heard the sounds of the river in her dreams. Jeering voices whispered to her through the curtains of her bed and followed her through the halls of the unlit manor all hours of the night. She could never tell Mother. She'd never allow her near any dark corners if she knew Penny was having problems with the dark again. Mother was stern, but when it came to Penny, she could be suffocating.

When she was seven, she had broken her arm climbing a tree behind their house. She'd hoped to see the edges of Olympia, which she'd not realized were too far for her young eyes to see. She'd been nearly all the way back down when Mother had called her name from across the small meadow near the tree. Penny had slipped and fallen the rest of the way down, landing on her arm. She'd done her best to not let the pain show, but she remembered the panic in Mother's voice and the tears that had flowed down her small cheeks in response. Mother had scolded her soundly after the doctor set the bone, but had then immediately put her to bed and kept her there as if she had come down with a plague. Penny had lasted until the next morning before she had snuck out onto the fields to play with the pomegranate blossoms, her healing arm swinging in its sling.

Just as with her broken arm, Penny wouldn't allow the shadows to best her. She would not fear that which she knew ought not to be feared. She needed to move past this.

However, her fear spiked when a bolt of lightning shot the shadow of the silhouette crouched in the window against the wall.

She gasped and peeked around the back of the chair. Her heart pounded in her ears as the lock clicked and the pane moved upward. Sweat beaded across her brow as a hand reached in from the outside and hoisted the silhouette of a man onto the sill.

She screamed when the body turned to face her.

The shadow jumped and the green of Penny's gift lit up the space in front of her. Her magic reached for the ivy hanging in the corner of the study. She didn't wait to see if the vines held back the intruder before leaping from her chair. A crash sounded behind her just as she reached the door. She turned the knob but a body slammed into her, ramming her into the door instead of allowing her to escape through it. She opened her mouth to scream again, but was cut off by a hand coming over her mouth. She wrestled the arms holding her to the door. A crackle of magic surrounded the man and fear rushed through her limbs.

"Please, Lady Penelope! Let me explain."

She stilled at the sound of his voice, but then began thrashing once again. She knew it. He was a spy! He was here to kidnap her. He was going to take her right out of her home with none the wiser.

Tears welled up in her eyes and in an act of desperation, she bit his hand. Lou spun them around so his back was to the door and released her into the room.

She took in another breath to scream.

"I'm not here to hurt you, I swear!" he rasped, hands out placatingly.

The sincerity in his voice shut off her shout. For some inexplicable reason, she believed him. Everything in her head told her not to, but deep down there was this innate sense that told her his words were the truth.

A rapid knock sounded and Penny mistook it for the pounding in her blood until the handle of the door jiggled as someone tried to get in. "Lady Penny? Are you all right in there?" Sissy's voice came muffled through the thick wood of the door.

Penny's eyes never left Lou's so it was easy to see him mouth *I will explain.* Penny didn't know what would happen if she allowed her maid to enter. He could kill Sissy just for seeing him here.

"Everything's fine," she heard herself call. Her voice sounded far calmer than she would have expected. She glared at Lou and went to the door. She pulled on the handle and he moved enough for her to see her maid illuminated by magelight.

"Are you sure? I thought I heard something fall and images of you being crushed under the large clock in there flashed through my mind." Penny would have smiled at her maid's vivid imagination if it wasn't for the intruder standing beside her.

"No fallen clocks in here. I will be out in a little bit." She went to close the door, but paused. "If I don't come down in half an hour, make sure to come and fetch me." Now she could at least have someone looking for her if she disappeared.

Sissy nodded. "If you're sure. I will stoke the fire in your rooms." She turned and with a few echoing steps down the hallway, Sissy disappeared.

Penny shut the door to meet the honey-eyed man who had broken into Mother's study like a thief in the night. They stood there, both still as stone, and stared at one another. Neither willing to take their eyes from the other. Neither willing to break the silence.

Fine. Penny straightened and pulled a small magelight out of the pocket of her dress.

At the movement, Lou let out a breath. "I swear to you, I have no intent to cause you any harm," he repeated.

Penny glared. "Yet you stand here in my mother's study after breaking in through the window. Why on Gaia's green earth should I believe a word that comes out of your mouth?" *How could I have thought I had any feelings growing for you?*

He spoke as if she were a spooked horse. "I swear I did not come here to hurt you."

"Then why are you in here? Who are you?"

"I'm someone of little consequence. I was just sent to look for information."

"What does this *information* look like?" she hissed. "Crop rotations? Harvest numbers? Trade accounts? If not, then you've walked into the wrong study."

One of his golden eyebrows lifted as he gazed at her. "I'm not here for information about your family's farm. I'm here for the information regarding the rebels." His grin flashed threateningly in the moonlight, but Penny couldn't find it in herself to be intimidated. A laugh burst out of her mouth before she clamped a hand over her lips.

"You... you think we're in league with the rebels?" Penny put a hand to her chest and laughed harder. Was he insane?

It was several seconds before he responded. "I wouldn't go so far as to insinuate that you are involved, but I would not put it past the duchess of the place where the rebellion has a foothold. I'm here to find any information I can and will use any means necessary to retrieve it."

Mother was a suspect? Who suspected her? Penny shook herself and plopped back into the chair she had vacated, searching within herself for the surety she should have felt. "Well, what are you waiting for?" She gestured to the room around them. "By all means, have a look around. I promise your search will end fruitlessly." Penny knew this office like the back of her hand. She swallowed. "My mother and I have nothing to do with any rebellion and certainly will not associate with the likes of The Cartographer."

Lou physically jolted. "How do you know that name?"

She gave him an irritated look. "I was literally kidnapped by his minions. It's not hard to overhear things when they are carrying you through dark alleyways with nothing but the splash of the river or the creak of barges as the only other noise." She realized her hands were shaking and she clenched them in her skirts. "How do *you* know that name?"

Lou frowned, concern and pity swirling in his gaze. Her

eyes couldn't hold his for long with a look like that. It made her feel ridiculous.

"They say you escaped on your own," he whispered. "How did you manage it?"

Penny had told no one what had actually happened that night. How the man from her past had swept in to free her just to leave her in the dark once again. She didn't raise her eyes to his as she spoke. "I used the seeds in my pouch to free myself and ran to a friend's house. Someone must have seen the men because next thing I knew, they were already in the bailiff's custody. You still haven't answered my question."

The squeak of wet boot was the only warning she had before Lou sat in the chair beside hers. Mother would be livid if she saw the wet farmhand dripping on her chair. She looked over to find him studying her intently.

"What?" she snapped.

"I want to tell you, Lady Penelope, but I can't decide if I trust you."

"Well get in line."

The sparkle of humor in his eye ruined his thoughtful expression. "I think the fact that you've allowed me this much consideration after breaking into your home is sign enough that you are someone with good instincts. Someone who won't share secrets. If I'm being completely honest, I could use the help I think you might be able to provide."

Penny simply stared at him until he came to the conclusion on his own. If he wanted to spill his secrets to her, it was his choice. She would not help him along.

He remained silent for a few moments more before he whispered, "I work for The Crown and have come looking for evidence of the leader of the rebellion."

Penny tried to hold in the shock, but some must have slipped through because Lou smiled. He was suggesting

Mother was involved in the rebellion— could possibly be its leader? Penny looked at him closely and a seed of doubt settled in her chest. Did he know something she didn't? If he did work for the Crown, did his presence here indicate they had evidence against them? The thought of Mother being involved with the rebellion was... ludicrous. Penny shook her head. Wasn't it? After all, Mother generally avoided letting Penny out of her sight— excepting the night she was taken.

"The Crown?" she asked dumbly. "As in *The* Crown. The Crown Prince? The Navy General? The Lord of the Underworld? Those crowns?"

"Yes, Lady Penelope. I take orders from the youngest prince who receives them from the Crown Prince and the Council."

Penny fell back into her chair. "I thought you were a rebel."

His eyes narrowed. "I am not, nor will I ever be."

Penny could do nothing but grin at the severity of his tone. "I'm glad to hear it. If you'd confessed to being one, I would have expedited your departure from our lands in the infamous Barclay fashion."

"You would have chased me out with plants?"

"You seem surprised," she remarked. "Don't underestimate the world Gaia has given us. It is often in the most unlikely of places where you find wells of strength and ferocity." She gave him a fierce grin. "Even roses have thorns."

Lou did his best to hide it, but as Penny said the words she saw appreciation and bemusement in his eyes. She meant those words with every fiber of her being. Many people passed over the Barclays for being fragile women with no skills for running business in a man's world. Even wives of successful businessmen regularly commented on how a woman's place in the home was either in a parlor or at a dining room table rather than the office. The Ladies Barclay had always proven every one of the naysayers wrong. The shock that always crossed their faces was one of Penny's delights.

And just now, she had the desire to see it again.

"So," Penny continued, the best impression of Mother she could muster on her face, "what are we to do now?"

"What do you mean?"

"Well, I now know that the Crown has a spy in my duchy. I know that this spy is here to take care of a rebellion that, within my mother's right, should be taken care of by the guardian of these lands. I know the alias of the man who is giving the Crown grief and what some of his men look like. I also know, considering that I haven't learned of it from my mother— who stands on the Crown Prince's council— that the princes are attempting to keep the growth of this rebellion a secret."

His bemused expression vanished.

A smirk settled on her lips. "Since that is the case, it would be very unfortunate if word got to my mother in the capital that the Crown Prince is attempting to eradicate them without her knowledge and that a spy was sent to sniff out her loyalties. I bet your job would get very messy if you had to get into all the logistics with my mother and her famous stubbornness. We all know she would want to do things her own way— brash and brutal. Your superiors would berate you for not accomplishing your task the way they ordered. You'd likely be shipped off toward the next piece of grunt work they had come up.

"So, Lou, if that's even your name," she leaned toward him, her grin bared, "what are *we* going to do about them?"

12

SPIES AND BARGAINS

Penny's heart pounded against her rib cage.

This spy could call her bluff at any moment. Penny would never truly get in the way of the Crown's work. She was loyal to the Crown Prince, no matter if Mother said he was a "devious youth with no self control." While she'd only ever seen him at her debut, the similarities between Prince Dion and his father ended at their similar looks and rumored admiration of beautiful women. He and his brothers had saved this kingdom thrice over with their deposition of the last king and signing the truce with the fae and the water folk. Penny remembered what Eleusion had been like under his reign. The poor districts in Eleusia and the surrounding towns looked a thousand times better than they had back then. The reforms put into place by Crown Prince Dion and the Council— while still ongoing— had done much to counteract the poverty that had stricken the kingdom through The Tyrant King's rule.

Penny would do whatever it took to prove her loyalty. But what if they knew something she didn't? This rebellion bubbling up in Eleusion made little sense— and Mother's attitude as of late only less so.

It didn't matter. Even if Mother was just acting strangely, she couldn't let this chance slip away. She couldn't allow the opportunity to take back what those men stole from her pass by. She wouldn't live the rest of her life shrinking away from dark corners. Great Gaia, she was a Barclay! She would face her fears head on and demolish them in whatever way she could. This was her chance to take a modicum of control over her life.

She recalled Angelica's last letter.

1. Eye contact is everything.

2. Make sure he knows who is in charge.

3. Be clear with what you want. Men do not take hints well so you have to be specific.

Just because the advice was given in regards to flirting didn't mean Penny couldn't use them to get what she needed. Angelica was right when she said Mother would use these tactics. Penny lifted her chin and raised a brow she knew looked just like Mother's. She'd practiced it in the mirror enough.

Lou's shock melted into a calculated furrow of his brow complemented by the large frown on his lips that drew Penny's gaze. "I cannot allow an untrained citizen to become involved in an operation to track down a rebellion," his voice lowered to below a whisper, "which is supposed to be kept secret."

Penny leaned back in her chair once again, doing her best to look nonchalant as her heart rate spiked. "I think you'll find that it would be much easier to include me. I can provide resources a man skulking in the shadows cannot obtain easily and my name carries sway in this part of the country, maybe more than the Crown Prince's. My snooping around would be seen as protecting my own interests whereas yours would cause too much attention." She took tally on her fingers. "I have access to private records and shipping information from Eleusia. I have the bailiff of the town and the constables of the surrounding villages being paid from my mother's coffers, and know every one of their mothers, wives, and daughters. You'd be surprised what men will do when their wives grab hold of their ear and what information will pass over private dinner tables. I'll give it all to you... if you allow me to accompany you."

Lou's head was already shaking in denial. "You have no training. I have more than enough operatives on this mission as well as contacts in the surrounding areas. I won't endanger a member of nobility, let alone *a lady,* to accommodate the fantasies of a girl wishing to play spy."

Green flickered at the edge of her vision. Penny clenched her hands in her skirts to hide the obvious glow of her anger. "*Fantasies?*" she hissed. "You think I want to do this for the thrill? That I'm simply in it for the ride? Is that a request you get often from the ladies you surround yourself with at home? What a fine stock of women you keep for company. Unfortunately for you, there are no such women here."

Penny stood from the chair, holding her hands where he could see them and allowing the green glow to cast away what shadows the magelight couldn't scatter. "I will help you and you will allow me to. I have a right as heir to make sure the people of my lands remain safe from the evils of others, especially those who wish to do harm to so many. You are on Barclay land and Barclays will get the justice they deserve with or without your aid."

Penny's eyes remained locked with Lou's, neither yielding under the emerald light of her magic. Her breaths came short and hard as the strain of exhaustion aggravated the ache in her head. She didn't let go of her magic.

At last, he nodded. "All right, Lady Penelope. I will take up your offer. However," he held up a hand as she opened her mouth to speak, "I have a few stipulations."

Penny nearly sagged in relief, but sat back in her chair neatly as the magic in her hands faded into her skin. She blinked several times to adjust to the lack of light.

Lou leaned toward her. "First, and foremost, I will not allow you to accompany me on missions determined to be extremely dangerous. You have no prior training or experience and in most situations, I can't afford to be worried about you while also trying to accomplish my mission."

He waited and she bobbed her head. "I understand. I don't want to be a problem, but I will be accompanying you on missions deemed potentially harmless."

Lou chuckled darkly. "*Harmless* is not a word used in this line of work." He held up two fingers. "Secondly, I will ask for your full scope of information but will maintain the right to keep mine to myself. I have secrets I've sworn not to divulge and doing so could put you in great danger. I will not reveal them or anything else I deem unnecessary to the mission."

Penny mulled over his words as she studied his face. He could try to wiggle his way out of giving her any information by declaring it too dangerous and leave her floundering in ignorance. His eyes remained on her and she could see the glimmer of honesty there. He may be a spy, but he seemed a decent enough man.

"All right, but if I find you are keeping anything vital from me, you will find yourself in a rather uncomfortable situation."

He let out a breath. "Lastly, if I give you an order, you must respect and follow it. I'm the one with experience and you will answer to me while we are in the field no matter if you are the heir to these lands or not."

Penny couldn't help but grin and held out her hand. "I accept your terms."

Sparks spread through her arm and into her chest the moment his skin came into contact with hers. She nearly jumped back from the reaction.

"Sheesh, what kind of mage are you?"

Lou startled. "You know I'm a mage?"

She wanted to snort. "I saw your gift the other day on the fields when your powers reached out to mine." Though, the experience still made her heart pound. It was unlike anything she'd ever experienced before.

He once again sat back in his chair. "I had no idea. You hid your suspicion well."

Penny raised an eyebrow. "What would you have done if I had called you out right there on the field?" She shook her head. "I couldn't let you suspect that I knew. I could've been putting the lives of my workers at risk. It was better that I found a way to confront you alone or at least somewhere you could do the least amount of damage. I've been up the last few nights trying to figure it out, but you came to me first."

A small smile crept over his face. "I never came to confront you. I knew you could have never been a part of it. I didn't know where your mother's loyalties lie, so I came to find out."

Penny looked him straight in the eye. "My mother is loyal to this kingdom and those who live in it, same as me. We would never support anything that put the lives of our people in danger or the prosperity of our land in jeopardy. The Crown Prince will find no quarrel with us... that is, unless he brings one to our doorstep. Only then will he find himself on the opposing side of House Barclay."

Lou held her gaze, his eyes nearly glowing in return. "I will not doubt it again."

She leaned back in her chair. "So, where do we begin?"

13

THUNDER AND SIRENS

The large map rolled out over the long dining room table as the sky thundered outside. Penny grabbed a silver candlestick from the mantle to hold down one corner of the parchment while Lou fetched a heavy vase sitting on a decorative table to hold down another. Both of them met in the middle of the table to view the whole of the Duchy of Eleusion scrawled on the thick parchment before them.

"It's rather impressive," said Lou, "all mapped out like this."

It was. Mother religiously updated the colossal map with population growth and detailed building layouts. She took great pains to ensure she was aware of what was happening in her duchy. Having rebels integrate themselves into their lands without Mother's knowledge was more than shocking.

Lou leaned over the map, his eyes roving over every inch. He took notes on a scrap of paper in tight, straight script with a quill he said was charmed to never run out of ink. Penny spied no ink pot in his satchel and she had yet to see the pen run dry. *That must come in handy.*

His gaze caught on a spot on the map. "What is that?" He pointed to a small sketch of buildings, a little ways off from Eleusia, marked *Despoina.*

"A new settlement that popped up before winter solstice. Mostly farmers and people not wishing to live in the busier towns, but needing to stay close for employment."

"It looks rather large for something so new," he said, his voice skeptical.

"It's certainly flourished in the short time since its establishment. It even has a profitable inn on the main road."

He looked over at her. "Have you been recently?"

Penny shook her head and Lou returned his attention to the map. She'd gone once with Mother when Despoina's occupancy had grown enough to petition to be an actual village. Mother had brought her along so she could learn what the process entailed, but Penny hadn't returned since.

"I think we should take a look. It's suspicious that it was built right when word of the rebellion reached the ears in the capital."

Penny held back an excited grin. "I can go?"

Lou continued to look down at the map as he nodded. "It ought to be safe enough." He picked up his quill and began scratching notes down again. He glanced over at her. "You'll have to wear a disguise of course. We don't want the villagers to recognize you."

Penny fingered the sleeve of the light green house dress she wore. It certainly wouldn't do to go on a covert reconnaissance mission in satin. Her work dress should be a suitable enough disguise.

They ironed out the details of their travel and planned to go the next morning. With the rain, there was little they could do on the land and Mother still held the reins in regards to the regular running of the estate. It would be nice to not have to sit in the house all day.

Penny led Lou out the back stairway least used by the servants because it led to the cook's garden outside and Cook had her own door.

Lou stopped at the door. "I apologize again for frightening you. I hope that through our new arrangement I can regain your trust."

He left without waiting for a reply. Penny stood there for a few moments before turning back to her own rooms. He wanted her trust?

Hours later, Penny lay awake in her bed, her mind running through possible scenarios of how the next day would go. She rolled around under her covers, anticipation driving her to fidget. She finally sat back up after a while and lit the magelight on her bedside table. The yellow light cast large shadows over her room. All of them were familiar.

She grabbed the book sitting next to the magelight and immersed herself in another world. Paulo really did know what she liked. She devoured any tales of valiant knights winning maidens fair. Stories of clever dragons and tricky fae always intrigued her. She secretly had a major soft spot for the misunderstood villains as well.

The book in her hands had just been published by her favorite author, Collista Seda. Mrs. Seda wrote epic stories of romance, intrigue, and heroic deeds. The particular book Penny was reading was about a fae woman and a nobleman who were desperately in love and were separated as he was called to fight in a terrible war. The woman remained faithful to the valiant lord, even though the people around her schemed to make her marry any one of the many suitors that came knocking at her door.

Penny reached the part where the maiden was caught

sabotaging one of the tasks she had given a suitor, when a loud *boom* rattled the walls of her room. The sound was followed by the swish of rain off the roof of the manor. Perhaps it was time to put the book down. Penny set it aside and turned off the magelight once more. Thoughts of an amber-eyed nobleman racing to rescue a fair maiden from certain doom whirled around her until sleep took hold.

Penny used the stirrups to lift her in the saddle as Lou led the way from his own mount in front of her. Her eyes roved over the land, taking in all of the sights and sounds as they rode through unfamiliar territory. While Despoina was rather close to Eleusia, they had taken a path that wound up through the hills outside the city in order to reach the settlement. Penny could feel the soft breeze from the coast as it ruffled her hair and could smell the salt it cradled in its current.

Meli nickered as Lou brought his gelding— borrowed from the manor's stable— to a stop in order for Penny to catch up. His eyes scanned her as they came alongside him and his mount. He didn't focus on her in a way that made Penny uncomfortable. It was as if he were checking for chinks in a suit of armor rather than the way a man usually appraises a woman. He must have found nothing noteworthy because he nudged his horse in the direction of the village and took out a few pieces of paper from his saddlebag. He thumbed through them for a moment. He returned them to their place in his bag and turned back to Penny before she could even guess at what he had written on them.

"We should reach the village in half an hour or so. If you

have any qualms about what we are about to embark on, now is the time to say so."

Penny's gut clenched slightly as the reality of her situation settled. This had the potential to be dangerous. Penny turned the tightness in her core into a flame. She could do this. It was for her people. It was for herself.

Penny met Lou's expectant gaze. "I will not turn back now. I'll see this through to the end." A glimmer of something shone in his eyes for a moment before he turned away from her. Perhaps pride? Camaraderie?

They rode the horses side by side as they came into view of the town. Penny could feel the temperature drop slowly and the air charge with the storm they were expecting later in the day. Apparently, the work of the Crown wouldn't be cowed by something so trivial as the weather. The thought made her smirk and she glanced at the sky behind her to see large, black clouds forming on the horizon. Lou looked in the same direction, his eyebrows drawn together.

"I hope the storm passes quickly. I wouldn't like to be stuck here for long." He turned back toward the village and urged his horse into a trot. Penny prayed they would be inside the inn before lightning struck.

They rode their horses swiftly into the village as the first drops of rain hit the top of her head. They guided their mounts up to the small inn just as a sheet of rain began pounding the dirt down the road. Lou urged Penny to race under the cover of the inn's overhanging roof as he took the horses around to the stable. By the time Lou returned, puddles were forming in the road and Lou was drenched.

The two of them burst inside the building as a loud thunderclap shook the walls of the establishment. About two dozen men were seated in various places around the common room and a handful of women walked around with trays. Penny stuck close as Lou led her to a seat at the back with the stub of a candle sitting in a glass jar. Penny could tell their seating was a strategic placing as they could see both the front door and the door to the kitchen from where they sat.

Lou waved one of the girls over.

"What can I do for you, handsome?"

Lou gestured between Penny and himself. "We will have whatever your cook is serving and a jug of water."

The serving girl didn't even look Penny's way as she batted her lashes and flipped a thick, black braid over her shoulder. "Let me know if there's anything else I can do for you. With weather like this, you might be stuck here a while."

Penny could do nothing but blink as the girl's swaying hips wove through the other customers. Did that kind of thing actually work? She'd seen other girls use such things to garner a man's attention, but Penny just wanted to laugh.

Apparently the posturing was in vain because Lou didn't even give her a second glance.

Penny settled into her seat. "So, what now?"

"Now, we sit."

"Sit?" She sat back up. "You mean just sit here and do nothing?"

"Yes." He raised a sardonic eyebrow. "It shouldn't be too hard for you, right?"

Penny sat back in her chair and grumbled, "Farmers must make for lousy spies."

"You can certainly give it up at any time. I won't hold it against you."

She narrowed her eyes. "You're just trying to get rid of me."

"Is it that obvious?"

Her glare sharpened.

Lou's lips twitched into a small smile just as the serving girl returned with their water. The girl made sure to touch

Lou's hand when she passed him his cup. It was fascinating to watch such calculation in the girl's movements. The server made short work of setting Penny's clay mug down in front of her, all without glancing her way and flounced away as a different patron asked for another round.

Penny laughed.

Lou looked at her, but she waved off his questioning expression.

She soaked in the atmosphere of the dining area. A few farmers sat at a table, nursing mugs of watered wine. At another circle of chairs, she watched a young man grimace as the man next to him, who Penny guessed was his father, slapped him on the back and laughed with a couple of other men seated at their table. Her gaze caught on the blue skirt of one of the serving girls coming out of the kitchen with a tray piled high with food, the girl's face plastered with a smile that looked more haggard than happy.

Penny was so caught up in the life swirling around her that she didn't notice their waitress sidle up to their table with bowls of chowder until her food was unceremoniously plopped before her. A piece of potato sloshed onto the table and the girl drifted away.

Penny shrugged and eagerly dug into the food. Potatoes and corn floated through the thick chowder. Chopped green onions sprinkled the top and pieces of cheese stuck to the sides of the bowl. The steam warmed her cheeks and curled through the damp air. It was all forgotten when Lou pulled out a small piece of parchment stuck under his bowl. Lou glanced around the room and Penny mimicked, searching for anyone who was looking in their direction. No one even flicked eyes their way. Lou unfolded the parchment then lit the corner of it with the candle sitting on the table. The flame was a breath from his fingers when he dropped it into his untouched bowl of chowder and got up from the table.

"This trip just got more interesting." A dark look settled into a frown of irritation. "I believe we have a secret admirer, Lady Penelope."

Penny hesitated before she stood and followed him out of the inn. She opened her mouth to ask where they were headed as the stables came into view. The rainfall had lessened, but a slow drizzle still managed to seep into her clothing on the walk between the two buildings. Penny swept wet tendrils of hair away from her face and attempted to push her humidity-induced frizz back into its braid as they stepped under the covered stable.

Lou walked past a few of the stalls and stopped. Though she only had view of his back— his gold hair dripping water onto the floor in a puddle around his boots— it was obvious he was waiting for something. The building was quaint and she saw both their horses in stalls next to one another. Across from them stood another horse, but the rest of the stalls were empty.

Penny heard a deep inhale from Lou before he asked, in a low voice, "What are you doing here?"

Penny looked at him incredulously. Just as she was about to answer, a musical voice flowed through the air.

"Men. Always thinking they can leave the women at home to play house while they go on the real adventures."

A woman came out from behind the unfamiliar horse. Penny felt her jaw drop, but couldn't seem to catch it. The woman had the grace of a willow as she sauntered out of the stall. She wore a simple blue dress with a brown apron, but it could have been made of silk and lace with the way it moved with her steps. Her sculpted eyebrows arched in question at Lou. Her full lips formed a sensual smirk.

The woman had to be some kind of goddess.

Lou folded his arms over his chest. "When I asked you to stay in place I expected you to take it as an order," Lou replied, his voice light, but sharpness underlined his tone.

The woman laughed, flicking a wave of wine-red hair over her shoulder.

Penny involuntarily took a step closer. The sound was something out of a dream. Penny almost added her own laugh, a smile breaking across her face.

Both Lou and the woman turned in her direction. Penny could see Lou out of the corner of her eye, but her point of focus remained on the vision in front of her.

"By the Goddess, Rissa, put your charm back on."

The woman, Rissa, laughed again— which Penny did join in— and reached into one of her saddlebags. She grabbed a thin cord of leather from which hung a small shell. Rissa slid it over her head and the moment the white shell rested on her chest, the fog over Penny's mind lifted. Her body went taut.

"What on earth?"

Rissa sauntered over and took Penny's face between her smooth hands. The vibrant color of her sea green eyes snagged Penny's attention, but didn't pull her into another trance. "Sorry, darling. My little bauble is always such a nuisance when I ride and I took it off when I rode in on Meridian." She pointed back to the horse behind her.

Penny looked into the gorgeous woman's face. She had never been self-conscious of her appearance before, but this stunning woman made Penny's practical work clothes seem as if she were wearing moth-eaten potato sacks with her hair resembling a ferret's nest.

"Rissa." Lou's voice lowered in almost a whisper as he stood next to the two women. "Explain."

Rissa let go of Penny's face with a sigh. Her lips turned

into a petulant pout. "A girl gets lonely all up at the capital by herself. I was twiddling my thumbs up there waiting for you. Would you believe me if I told you I just wanted to see you?"

Penny's stomach did a little flip as she stared at the two people in front of her. Rissa had been waiting for Lou in the capital. *They must be together.* Her mind was a tumult of emotions as she came to the realization, though she didn't know why. She shook herself inwardly. *It's certainly none of my business.*

"Rissa, you know I don't need to explain myself to you," continued Lou. "However, you certainly need to explain yourself to me. You have a *job* you are supposed to be doing."

Rissa sighed dramatically. "Yes, a boring job babysitting all of the simpering women and grabby men while you get to gallivant around looking for rebels. Not that you'll find any here. I've been looking around since this morning and the single thing this hole is guilty of is not having a proper inn." Her head whipped back to Penny. "Wait, who is this? You're not taking in the rabble again are you?"

Penny's cheeks burned and her fists clenched in her skirt.

Before she could utter a word, Lou stepped closer. "Apologize, Rissa. You just referred to Lady Penelope Barclay as *rabble*."

Rissa's eyes widened in shock. "*This* is Penelope Barclay?" She turned her attention back to Penny and swept into a curtsy. "I sincerely apologize, Miss Barclay. I had no intention of insulting you. Our friend here has a habit of bringing in new recruits to our— um, *cause* and I assumed you were another victim of his charity."

Lou raised his face to the rafters of the stable and closed his eyes. He groaned as he dragged his hand down his face in exasperation. It was the first time she had seen him show so much emotion. It would have made her laugh if they were in different circumstances.

Penny turned back to the woman in front of her. She placed her hands on the mostly dry skirt at her hips. Time to put on the Duchess of Eleusion face. "Yes, I am Penelope Barclay. Who are you?"

"Pardon my lack of decorum," said Rissa. "My name is Amarissa Delmar. My friends call me Rissa. I work with our friend here."

Penny froze. Rissa was a spy. Her odd emotional turmoil vanished as she whirled on Lou. "There are *women* in the prince's spy network?"

Rissa laughed heartily, her voice still sounding like a bell—though not as resonating as before.

Lou glared at her.

He shifted to look at Penny. "Yes, Lady Penelope, there are women who work in our organization. Though, at the moment, I'm questioning why the Lord of the Underworld recruited this one."

"You know exactly why the prince added me to the roster," she said as she rubbed a finger over the shell of her necklace.

Penny's eyes followed the movement. "What is that? If you don't mind me asking."

Rissa's lips quirked into a smile. "Are you acquainted with many water folk, Lady Penelope?"

"Not as many as I'd like, I'll admit."

"You're still likely familiar with the regular sort. Mermaids and mermen, selkies, sea hags. I am a much rarer kind of water folk."

Penny's mouth dropped open a fraction as Rissa's words clicked. She was beginning to feel like a fish herself. "You're a siren."

Rissa spread her arms and bowed. "In the flesh."

"Rissa was one of the first of the water folk to come to land after the accords were signed," explained Lou. "As she has the ability to take on a naturally human appearance, she made a life for herself above the sea when Prince Dion presented the tri-kingdom treaty. We found her singing the money out of sailors' pockets in Olympia's harbor quarter and knew we needed her. She now lives in the palace as one of Lady Carnation's companions, but her main position consists of espionage and acting as liaison to our weapons expert."

Rissa folded into a bow once again. "Thank you for the raving review," she said as she brought herself back up. "I can always count on you to make a girl feel special."

"Are there many women in your organization?" Penny asked.

Rissa counted on her fingers as Lou replied, "We have a handful of them. They are incredible operatives and fantastic people. Most don't suspect women as spies and the prince has certainly used it to his advantage."

"Yes, the work is tough," added Rissa, "but once you learn, you simply can't give it up."

The youngest prince had women working for him. Women who had control over their own lives. Women who were fierce and on as equal footing as any other person. Wasn't that what Mother always preached about? That Barclays were special because the women were just as good as the men? Why shouldn't there be other places, places where Penny could explore such a world without the restraints Mother shackled her with?

Penny looked between the two of them before bursting out, "I want to do it."

Rissa grinned brightly.

Lou looked as if she were speaking another language. "Do what?"

"Learn to be a spy. I want to be able to help the kingdom."

Lou looked at her in horror, his mouth opening and closing. *Now who looks like a fish?*

Rissa slapped him on the arm playfully. "Well, aren't you going to train her?"

Lou's eye flicked back and forth between Penny and Rissa before turning his attention solely on Penny. His cheeks were dusted with a faint blush. "Lady Penelope, not to say you aren't a very talented person, but I don't think the work of a spy should be added to your repertoire. It wouldn't be proper conduct for a lady of your station, and it would take away from your work."

"Now would be the perfect time for me to get involved. There are rebels running amok. If they burn down the rest of my orchards, there won't be work for me to do."

"She has a point," chimed Rissa.

Lou glared. "You aren't helping."

Rissa pretended to lock her lips and throw away the key.

"You already agreed that I could work with you. Wouldn't this qualify as that?"

"Exchanging information and training you to wield a weapon are two very different things."

"I would take training very seriously."

Lou shook his head. "That is not the issue. We don't know how much time we have to train, and I wouldn't want you thinking that your small bit of knowledge would be enough to allow you to do things on your own."

Penny scowled. "Do I look like one who does things on a whim?"

He raised a brow at her. "You did just ask to be trained in spy work because you found out another woman was working with me."

Penny bit the inside of her cheek to keep her sharp remark

to herself. She wanted to be in a position to help her people. She wanted to be someone she could be proud of. If she didn't do something, she would have to wait until she was ancient before Mother would ever give her any control over her life. By then, it could be too late.

In all honesty, becoming a spy sounded like exactly what she needed.

"How about this?" Penny asked, coming to a rather good solution. "You take me under your wing. Train me to defend myself against the villains we'll be up against. Teach me all of the secret handshakes or whatever it is you use to communicate. Whatever you can teach me during the duration of your time here is all I'll require. I won't become one of your operatives, but I would like to have some kind of training. I won't be a liability to this mission. And I swear once you leave, I won't try to go off on my own unless you tell me I've done well enough to do so."

Lou stared at her. A battle swirled in the depths of his amber eyes. His face remained impassive, but no one could deny the riot of emotions in his gaze.

Rissa watched Lou, the smile still curving her red lips. When Lou looked over at her, she shrugged. "It's a good idea. Besides, when would you get an opportunity like this?"

Lou turned back to Penny, his hands clasped behind his back and she felt herself straighten in response to his commanding posture.

"All right, Lady Penelope. I will grant you the opportunity to train. We start tomorrow, an hour before dawn."

Penny barely contained her relief. She looked directly into his eyes and said, "I will not be late."

"Well," Rissa purred, "this was quite the unexpected surprise. Though I am pleased." Her smile resembled that of a cat when it finally caught the mouse.

"Don't you have somewhere to be?" Lou grumbled.

"I suppose I'll return to my post," Rissa replied, her eyes rolling and shoulders slumping in mock disappointment as she walked back to her horse.

"Tell Heff I am going to need some new daggers," he called after her.

"Who's Heff?" asked Penny excitedly. "Is he another operative?"

Rissa's tinkling laugh glided into Penny's ears as the siren grabbed the reins of her saddled horse. "My husband a spy! It would be a warm day in Winter before you ever saw that man out of his smithy." Her laugh grew as she led her horse out of the stall.

Lou chuckled and the last bit of tension fled from Penny's shoulders. They both stood at the door to the stable and watched Rissa's vibrant red hair disappear into the rain.

"We should head back to the manor." Lou turned toward the horses. "We'll need to find a good place to train."

Penny came up next to Meli. She smiled. "I know just the place."

"Excellent," Lou said, pulling out that small stack of papers. "Since I trust Rissa to know there isn't much here, we will simply have to sit at the inn and hope something drops in our laps. Perhaps we'll get lucky." He shuffled the papers around for a moment longer then tucked them back out of view.

But not before Penny saw her own name in ink.

14

BUMPS AND BRUISES

Dearest Penny,

A SPY????

I'm glad to have our coded letter system because I would've strangled you if I had to go all the way home to find out you were a spy. Have you met any others? Did Lou mention the other members of the prince's network? Honestly, I want to race home and join you. Though, I don't know how Father would feel about that. We've got enough here to keep us busy.

The Winter delegation left yesterday. It was disappointing not to come away with an agreement, but I was able to get some information. Winter's ambassador, the one who came with the delegation, is actually married to the High Queen's cousin. When we asked why there was no ruler in Winter, she simply said that there will be... in time. Why must these fae be so vague about everything? I know full fae can't lie, but why can't they at least be straightforward?

Back to the good stuff. So this Lou is much more fascinating than we gave him credit for. A nice face and an intelligent mind. My, my, Penny, you've certainly caught quite a fish. I hope you're able to use training to get a little closer to him. Physical contact is such a good way to liven the tension. And you get to see him exercise. The glisten of sweat, the swollen muscles, it's enough to make a girl swoon. I can't tell you how many times I have snuck in to watch Devan go through combat practice in the training yard. Such a good show! You are going to love this!

I want every delicious detail.

Your Very Wise Friend,

Angelica

PENNY HIT THE GROUND FOR THE FIFTEENTH TIME THAT MORNING.

So much for livening up the tension. It'd been five days and Penny had barely touched him.

Lou held his hands behind his back once again. "As an operative, you should be prepared to face unexpected situations. They should never catch you off guard, and you should be able to counteract them." He held out his hand to help Penny off the ground. Once she stood on her own two feet, he crouched into position. "Let's begin again. *Ullmhu.*"

Before Penny could even spread her feet apart in reaction to his call, Lou was already moving. He called, "*Chul na lamh.*" She raised her arm to block a jab to her head.

At least she got it right that time.

As he moved, he called out the positions of *Cumadh.* Penny had to wrack her brain to remember what form he called for her to use. More often than not, she landed on the ground without remembering how her body was supposed to respond.

Lou herded her around the clearing as she struggled to defend against his onslaught. There had always been a small piece of land behind the manor left to grow wild. The small lot had been set aside for magical exercises or experiments. It was most used by the younger Barclay family members to break in their powers— the perfect place to meet for Penny's new training.

A small clearing sat in the middle and large cottonwood trees circled the space. The ring of trees butted up against the canal where Penny remembered spending summer evenings listening to crickets debut their symphonies. The crickets were now silent under the barked commands of her trainer.

When she believed him to be in one place, he would be in another. He moved swiftly as shadow and quietly as death. No wonder why Angelica loved watching Devan. Witnessing the strength, the grace of Lou's steps— he was entrancing.

Her own footsteps drummed the earth as he pushed her defenses over and over. It didn't take long for her body to begin protesting the exercise. Her footfalls increased their volume as she tromped through sloppy forms. If he was deathly grace incarnate, she was bumbling awkwardness.

"Again," Lou called over and over.

As the sun broke over the hills of Mother's land, Lou ended their session. Penny hunched over gasping and watched as Lou wiped the dust from his pants. He meandered to his bag sitting by his magelight and took a sip of water from his water skin. There wasn't a hint of "glistening sweat" on him.

Penny closed her eyes as a wave of pure exhaustion swept over her. She prayed the magelights around them didn't highlight her flushed face. Her clothing stuck uncomfortably to her skin and sweat soaked into the fabric of her dress. She was accustomed to hard work, but muscles she didn't know she owned trembled as she thought about walking back to the manor. Her job as Mother's heir was easy compared to this.

Lou turned back in her direction. "We may have to think about a different training sched— Lady Penelope, are you all right?"

Penny groaned from her spot on the ground. She couldn't come up with a reply that wouldn't make her sound weak or unwilling. She was pathetic. Her body quaked as she moved toward the manor. She just had to make it to Sissy. Then she could take a hot bath and drink some warm tea. She'd be good as new.

"I'm fine." She cringed. The hoarseness in her voice didn't encourage confidence.

Lou walked over and picked up her magelight. "We have much to work on. With how well you've picked up on my movements, I don't believe it will take long to get you to a place where you can at least break free from trouble."

Maybe if she distracted him, he wouldn't see just how miserable she was. "Where did you learn to do that, those forms?" Penny asked from her spot on the ground. "Are they something the youngest prince taught you?"

Lou tossed the magelight to her. It landed unceremoniously in her lap. Great Goddess, she couldn't even move to catch it.

"The last spymaster taught me the *cumadh*."

"You mean, you worked with the spymaster before the Lord of the Underworld? The Tyrant King's man?"

"Yes."

Mother had told her of the dead king's spymaster. The Tyrant King and his spymaster were men spoken of in dark corners and under hushed breaths nowadays. The man had been a merciless brute. Like the Lord of the Underworld, not many saw the old spymaster's face, but he left his signature of pain and blood everywhere he went. There were stories whispered about the way the spymaster killed anyone who opposed the old king. Tales of torture and murder. The rumor of his death was that the princes killed him alongside the king. His body had been discovered with a dagger in his chest.

She fought the urge to stay on the ground and dredged up enough strength to stand. "Pardon my saying so, but you don't seem old enough to have worked under him. How old were you when you began working in the king's service?"

"My father handed me over to the spymaster when I was seven."

"You were a *child*?" Penny screeched. Her hands clamped over her mouth as her words echoed through the trees.

Lou swung around, eyes wide. With a grave voice he said, "Yes, I was a child. However, the spymaster was more a parent to me than those who shared my blood."

Penny could not formulate an answer before he turned back around.

Lou was a complete mystery to her. To be a child and have your father hand you over to one of the most ruthless men in the kingdom should have been horrifying. She couldn't imagine what his father must have been capable of if Lou was grateful to be in the spymaster's care.

But he was kind. He always helped those around him. He never belittled anyone or caused problems. Even in his work on the wheat fields, everything he had done seemed genuine. Based on his upbringing, he should have turned into a monster.

Yet here he was.

"What about your mother?" she asked. "Did she have nothing to say on the matter?"

Every mother Penny knew would have raved about the injustice of a child being put through that. Honestly, Mother likely would have taken things into her own hands and fled with her children from such a horrible situation.

Lou turned his face back to her as he said, "I don't know who my mother is. I showed up at my father's home before I was walking and have not heard a word of her since."

Penny closed her eyes, shoulders sagging further. "I'm sorry. I shouldn't have asked."

Lou shrugged and stepped toward the edge of the clearing. "How would you have known? Besides, I can't miss what I never had."

Penny's thoughts shifted to her own father, a man she'd never known. While Lou's father was a terrible man and he never knew his mother, Penny's situation was opposite. She couldn't place when she had stopped asking Mother about her father, but she had. Mother had never offered up any explanations about his whereabouts, only that he was gone, and she wasn't. It had never struck Penny until that moment, but after her conversation with Lou, she was curious as to how different her life would be if she'd had a father to help raise her.

That subject was never spoken of. Penny could remember being curious about her father when she was younger, but Mother had forbidden any discussion of him for reasons Penny still didn't know. Not that it mattered. Penny didn't have any recollection of the man.

"Lady Penelope," Lou called as she began shuffling toward

the trees. "You should have told me the training was too much. I would have ended earlier if I had realized. I'm used to training operatives, not sensible ladies of nobility. Perhaps this really wasn't the best idea."

Penny shook her head. She couldn't stop now. "No," she breathed. "I want to learn. I want to do it." Her voice strengthened as she spoke. "My weaknesses must be overcome, and we only have a short while to do it. My mother returns in ten days. We don't have time for me to take it slow." Besides, working so hard left no room for the dark to torment her after her head hit the pillow at night and she was able to spend time with the puzzle of a man in front of her.

She stopped to give Lou her best no-nonsense face. She needed to do this not only because it would help her people, but also to prove to herself that she wasn't fragile. She needed to know that the next time someone tried to take her, she had a few weapons at her disposal. She needed control.

"I still don't like this idea. Training could take months. It might do more harm than good."

"I need whatever training you can give me, Lou. This is my land. I have a right to help the people here, but I need your help to do it."

Lou looked at her gravely. Penny held his gaze until he finally nodded his head. She let out the breath she hadn't known she was holding.

"All right, Lady Penelope. We'll continue the regimen. As I was going to say, we'll need to figure out a new schedule as your mother will be returning. I assume you will want to continue to be a part of my operation." He said the last part more like a question than a statement, though by the look in his eyes Penny knew he already guessed her answer.

Penny took a step toward him, her legs protesting harshly. "Yes. I'd like to continue," she stated firmly. "Our most concerning challenges will be training and getting time to follow leads off of the farm. I've been thinking and I believe Aaron could help with the latter, but I don't know about the former. My mother rises before we begin our lessons and goes to bed much later than anyone I know. During daylight hours, I'm at her beck and call. I have no idea how we will find the time."

"You know," said Lou, "I might have an idea."

15
CHAOS AND DANCING

Dearest Penny,

All right, so perhaps actually being involved in the training itself isn't a good opportunity to flirt. I apologize for not thinking that all the way through.

Don't try to back out. This is your chance! You can finally feel what it's like to have your heart pound and your insides flutter just at the sight of another person. Love is worth it.

These past months with Devan have been a dream. I'm so glad Father hired him a few years ago. He is someone I can always count on, who I know loves me and all of my silliness. I know you want it too. I've seen it in your eyes.

Perhaps there is something else you can do to

encourage his regard? We need to figure out what he likes. He can't only like being a spy.

You'll get this figured out, Penny. There isn't anything you've failed at when you've put your mind to it. Well, except that whole thing about getting your mother to loosen up a bit.

We are headed to Spring in two weeks now that the Winter delegation has left. Father said there's been some trouble with the trade routes that way, so we've been sent to scout it out. Devan is ever the stalwart employee.

I will miss the beautiful scenery of Summer, but I can't wait to get a view of the Spring Palace. It's in the trees. TREES, Penny! I will do my best to send a sketch when we get situated. I am so excited!

Your Happily Married Friend,
Angelica

THE PARCHMENT IN PENNY'S HAND FLUTTERED IN THE EARLY MORNING breeze. Mother's handwriting swirled over every inch of the page. Directives and grievances abounded.

Mother had yet to meet with the princes. She'd met with every single member of the council as they came into the city. No one had any idea about the rebels congregating in Eleusion. No one knew what was going on. The princes were being as elusive as the information Mother sought. It seemed they'd been avoiding her. Penny smirked.

She stepped into the clearing and found Lou already

working by the glow of magelight. The man moved fluidly from one motion to another, never once opening his eyes. There was a kind of magic sown around the space as arms came forward to meet only air and feet slid through the tall grass.

"Would you care to join me?" Lou's invitation floated quietly between them. His eyelids never parted, but it was likely he'd felt her presence before she had even broken through the trees.

Penny's cheeks burned. He'd caught her ogling. "I've received word from my mother."

Lou dropped his hands and opened his eyes. "Nothing bad I hope."

Penny shook her head and waved the paper in her hands. "It seems she will be extending her stay in the capital."

His head tilted to the side. "Is that good or bad?"

"Good for us, bad for the princes." She straightened the letter. "Well, good for us besides the dinner party I have to attend tomorrow."

"Dinner party?"

She nodded. "Mother and I have been invited to visit Lord and Lady Discordia. Apparently, their daughter is hosting a small ball— again. We don't usually attend, but Mother insists we go this time."

Lou shook his head. "Clarice Kali is the strangest girl."

"You know her then?"

"Unfortunately," he grumbled. "My work keeps me out of the way in the capital most of the time, but there is no avoiding running into Miss Clarice at least a few times every season. She's everywhere." He shuddered.

Penny laughed. "I've only ever had the opportunity to be in the same room as her twice and that was more than enough."

"I guess we'll just have to make the most out of it then."

"What does that mean?"

Lou grinned. "How would you like to go on your first reconnaissance mission?"

Penny's head nearly hit the ceiling when Lou opened the door to the carriage.

Sissy startled and looked at her in concern. Her maid had come as chaperone on the trip through the two duchies it took to get to Discordia. If she kept jumping every time she saw Lou's face, the two-day ride was going to be long.

"We've stopped to water the horses and figured you ladies would like to stretch your legs."

Sissy still watched Penny with narrowed eyes. It would not do for Sissy to see through her. No one could know about who Lou really was.

"Thank you." She made her way out into the open air. The smell of early spring flowers and trees eased Penny's thoughts.

The edge of Eleusion laid just over the next rise. The rolling hills of home were about to shift into more forest covered terrain. The trees spoke to her when she passed under their leafy bows. They whispered to her magic, calling on it to look and see. Penny stood on tiptoe but couldn't catch sight of the tops of the trees over the hill.

Discordia lay right between Barclay Manor and Olympia's capital, thick forests making up most of the lands a two-day ride from each. She only had two days to wait until she could perform her first mission. They were only half a day into their journey and the anticipation was already driving her mad.

When she'd seen Lou sitting atop the carriage this morning, she'd stumbled into Sissy. This mission was really happening. Her hands hadn't stopped fidgeting in the carriage, her mind unfocused. Anytime Sissy spoke, Penny had to ask twice what she'd said. Sissy's confused looks had evolved into plain suspicion an hour before they stopped.

"I'm so grateful to be out of the carriage," Sissy groaned. "My back couldn't take much more."

Penny nudged her sixteen-year-old— a whole year younger than herself— maid with her elbow. "Being so old must be difficult."

"Watching you squirm the entire ride was exhausting. I don't know how you aren't sore."

Penny did not look over her shoulder at the spy secretly accompanying them. "I suppose I'm nervous about this party."

"You, nervous about a party?" Sissy laughed. "I've only ever seen you jumping for joy anytime we've gone to anything like this. I don't think that is the case whatsoever."

"Why not?"

Sissy pulled on Penny's arm and turned them back in the direction of the carriage. Lou stood just to the side, checking the trunks on the back.

"I think someone is twitter-pated and doesn't know how to talk to a certain, very handsome farm boy."

Tension fled Penny's shoulders, but she couldn't swallow. Lou turned back to them, a light smile on his face. A choked laugh pushed through her lips. "Is that what you think?"

"Considering you haven't taken your eyes off him since we turned around? Yes, that's what I think."

Penny pulled her eyes away from Lou. Sissy's knowing smirk sent her cheeks flaming. It wasn't like that between her and Lou at all. Right? Convincing Sissy of that would be difficult if Penny didn't know for sure. She'd been attracted to him in the beginning. He was kind, smart, knowledgeable. That had been obvious before he'd revealed himself to be a spy. Her feelings had changed with that information. He wasn't someone to try out flirting with anymore. They spent way too much time with him throwing her into the dirt for him to find her attractive. He went off on grand adventures and made his own decisions. While his life hadn't been easy, it was his.

Penny rubbed the heel of her palm against her chest. Not only did Penny have Mother's exact looks, but apparently was to inherit her exact life as well. She never doubted her place, but why couldn't she choose her own way of doing things?

Was her attraction to Lou simply a symptom of her desire to live her own life? Her gaze returned to him.

Or was it more than that?

Discordia Park sat filled to the brim with guests. Finding Mother in the throng remained impossible after having looked for twenty minutes. One would think "the buffet" to be a good meeting place, but when the party featured six different buffet tables it made things rather difficult.

Hundreds of attendees crammed into the dimly lit ballroom. The chandelier overhead held hundreds of candles aloft, Discordia Park having been warded to smother any large amounts of magic on the premises. The darkened windows at the back showed the smattering of stars glimmering over the orchestra arranged in front of the glass. Men and women flitted about, moving from one crowd to the next. *Probably trading whatever bit of gossip Clarice gave them on their way through the door.*

Luckily, Penny had been able to circumvent that particular host by coming in a side door. The other guests hadn't been as lucky. While Penny knew there wouldn't be any water folk, she spotted a group of fae leaning against a wall, their colorful hair vibrant against the dark wood of the room. Each of them eyed every brunette head of curls in the room with wariness.

Penny kept moving, her eyes homing in on every spot of green in the room. Mother could be anywhere.

"Oh, Lady Penny!" sang a grating voice.

Curses. "Clarice," she said, turning toward the mound of tulle headed in her direction, "how wonderful to see you."

Clarice brought the sea of bright pink up against Penny's skirts. "Isn't it wonderful catching up with old friends? I was sad I didn't see you enter with your mother, but the duchess said you'd be here."

"You've seen my mother?"

"Of course! I was shocked to see her come in. I nearly swooned when she said you would be arriving after her."

Penny held her courtly smile in place by sheer force. "Do you happen to know where she is now?"

"Sadly, no. But perhaps I can help you look."

Penny darted back a step before Clarice could latch an arm around hers. "Great. I'll go this way and you go that way. I think I saw Lord Calvert walking that way as well."

The girl spun, looking for the owner of the name Penny had thrown out on the spot. "Harry's here?"

Penny escaped the small girl by the skin of her teeth. Luckily, she'd watched Angelica use similar tactics on the young ladies at other social events before. If anyone knew how to navigate the dangerous waters of proper society, Angelica did. A small pang of loneliness stuck between Penny's ribs. Hopefully, there would be another one of Angelica's letters waiting for her when she got home.

She wove through the crowd, now doing her best to avoid the giant, pink puffball hopping all over the place. *Clarice really is something else.*

Finally, pine green chiffon peeked through a group of

polished nobles. Penny pushed herself through the press of bodies and made her way to Mother's side. She straightened her wheat-colored dress. Flowers formed by intricate beading faded from the bodice into the skirt. The sheer sleeves and light fabric of the dress made the heat of the room more bearable. Especially in this stuffy crowd.

"Your Grace, you really should consider taking up a winery of your own," drawled one nobleman. "Lord Abram is monopolizing the industry. May be a good business venture to try your hand at." The nobleman tossed back the dregs of the glass in his hand. From the smell, Penny guessed it to be from an Abram collection. *What a coincidence.*

"I have no mind to do such a thing," Mother replied. "Lord Abram and I work quite well together. As long as he gives me a fair cut of the profits, I'm more than happy to continue our partnership." Without looking in her direction, Mother wove an arm through Penny's. "If you'll excuse us." She withdrew them from the group.

"What was all that about?" Penny asked.

Mother frowned. "More pompous males giving unwarranted business advice."

"Oh, your favorite."

Mother squeezed Penny's arm. "When you take over running the duchy, don't let bigoted bird brains tell you how to run our business."

"I swear to not allow any bigoted bird brains *near* our business."

Mother smiled. "I'm glad you made it tonight. After you've made it most of the way through your dance card, I'd like to have a moment alone."

Penny pulled out the dance card from the reticule hanging from her wrist. "Only six signed up it looks like."

Mother sniffed. “No, it was full when I got here. I erased the other five signatures that I didn’t want dancing with you.”

“Mother, you can’t erase people from my dance card. What will I say when they come to ask me?”

“You won’t need to say anything. I am the Duchess of Eleusion. I made sure they were told they couldn’t dance with you.”

Penny would have groaned if they had been anywhere else. “You’re being ridiculous. It’s just dancing.”

“Yes, but from what I’ve seen, it’s the dancing that starts it all. It starts out innocent enough, but evolves into tender touches and flirty letters. No, it’s best to separate the wheat from the chaff early before the weevils get in.”

Penny glanced at the names on her dance card. Paulo, Mr. Belson, and a few other names she recognized flashed up at her. “You know, one of these days these young men will be married. Then who will you let me dance with?”

“By then, I’m praying you won’t want to dance anymore.”

Penny bit her lips together.

The small orchestra picked up a waltz and Mr. Belson arrived just in time to save her from making a heated remark. Penny smiled at the serious expression on his face as he bowed to Mother before guiding Penny on to the dance floor.

“It’s good to see you, Mr. Belson.”

He placed a hand on her back and looked up at her. “You as well, Lady Penny.”

Penny stepped in time with the music, following Mr. Belson’s confidant lead. “How is your estate doing? Last time we spoke you said you’d been having issues with poachers.” Mr. Belson didn’t hold a title, but his small bit of land held a piece of forest where a pack of endangered wolves thrived.

“It has been better. Our bailiff apprehended the criminals.”

“I’m glad to hear it. There’s been so much talk of poachers

and thieves lately, I'm glad to hear someone has had some luck getting rid of them."

"How is your duchy?"

"Doing quite well, thank you."

The waltz continued much in the same way. Every dance she'd ever participated in with Mr. Belson had consisted of stilted conversation and simple niceties. Penny didn't have a problem navigating such things, but she wanted to feel something when she danced.

Paulo was the only one she ever enjoyed dancing with. He got her out on the floor for a quadrille, the light steps and swirling movements bringing a skip to her step.

"Too bad we can't dance more than once together per ball. No one here has as light of steps as you do. It's always a relief to my toes when we dance."

Penny laughed. "Maybe you should be looking at better dance partners then."

Paulo shook his head. "Why do you think I have bruised feet? I'm still looking for the perfect partner."

The music kept her feet moving, but her mind stilled on his words. Perhaps she was looking for the perfect partner too.

The dance ended and Paulo accompanied her back to Mother's side. With a bob of his head in farewell he left to find the next girl to squash his toes.

Mother's hand wrapped around Penny's elbow. "Let's find somewhere to talk."

16

DOORS AND WINDOWS

Mother pulled her out of the ostentatious ballroom and found a small sitting room off the main hallway. After she checked the room for other guests, she beckoned Penny inside and shut the doors.

"How are things going back home? Aaron has sent a missive every night I've been gone, but I want to hear it from your mouth."

Mother was nothing if not paranoid. "I'm sure Aaron has given a proper accounting of everything. We were able to get the wheat replanted before the rains. I've checked the cuttings I planted everyday, and nothing has gone amiss. No one has been able to work in the afternoons because of the downpours. Everything is on schedule."

"No more reports of dissenting farm hands? I won't have you firing any more employees."

"Even if they were traitors to the Crown?" It was almost like Mother would have preferred to keep the disloyal workers over the rest. She hadn't even mentioned how well the newer hires were doing.

"It doesn't matter if they are traitors. We are business owners. We must be tactful." Her eyes narrowed. "Why are you asking? You didn't fire anyone, right?"

Penny rolled her eyes. "Of course not, Mother. I've learned my lesson."

"Excellent. We don't need to be angering anyone else."

Penny bit back her retort. Why did she care so much about firing people? And who exactly was she afraid of angering? The workers?

Or was this something more? Penny's stomach twisted. Lou's suspicions that first night he crawled through the window of the study came back to Penny. Mother's peculiar behavior made Penny all the more uneasy.

Mother walked back to the door. "I'm glad to hear about the fields. You did well, even if it took longer than I expected."

Penny's hands flickered but she smothered them in her skirts.

Mother placed her hand back on the door handle. "Are you prepared to reenter the fray?"

Penny took a deep breath. "Actually, I need a moment in the quiet." Her stomach fluttered a bit and her anger dwindled as she thought about the rest of the evening.

Mother gave her a sympathetic smile, obviously not catching the hint of anger in Penny's voice. "I can understand that. I'll wait right down the hallway." The door closed behind her with a click.

Curses. Mother remaining in view might be a problem.

Penny turned back into the room and let out a breath of relief when she spotted a servants' door on the opposite wall. *Hopefully this goes all the way through the house.* The door opened without a sound and she raced through the dimly lit hallway. Green light flickered between her fingers, but no more than that. Lou was right. Their magic dampeners were strong.

Runes and charms decorated most of the walls, painted into the decorative paper and carved into the crown molding. Penny could feel even more pushing her magic down, making it nearly inaccessible. Her ears picked up every squeak of a shoe or whisper of fabric as she climbed up the stairs to the third story, where Lou had told her the main study lay.

A door stood at the top of the staircase. Penny prayed it led to the right place as she twisted the knob. A puff of cool, dry air slipped through the crack in the door as she peered out. Tall shelves of books lined the walls. *Thank the Goddess.*

Penny stepped into the library. The green of her magic lit her steps as she tiptoed across the large room to the opposite side where a pair of polished wooden doors took up half of the wall. She gently pressed down on the handle. A shot of giddiness rushed through her when the door opened. Lou had taught her to pick a lock during their training last night, but it seemed she wouldn't need the newly acquired skill.

She silently shut the door behind her. A wide desk, a pair of bookcases, and a smattering of chairs cast long shadows from the light of her hands. A pair of thick curtains hung behind the desk, blocking all view of the window behind it. Mother would have considered her first step toward the curtains a skip. *There's no need to get excited. You're only opening a window.* Gently, she pulled the curtains aside. Thick panes of what looked like Faerie glass— another magic repellent— filtered the milky moonlight. The window was taller than she was, not that it was much of an accomplishment with her height. Her fingers easily flicked the latch open. The large glass pane swung out with the slightest squeak.

A gloved hand reached over the edge of the sill. Penny's heartbeat quickened. Lou slipped into the study as easily as if he had done it one thousand times. *What is it with this man and climbing through windows?*

His eyes met hers. "Well done, Lady Penelope."

"I only opened a window." She turned away when heat still blossomed on her cheeks.

He opened one of the desk drawers. "A window I would've had a difficult time opening without you."

Penny lifted a paper off of the desk. "Why exactly did you need the window opened?"

"We are looking for a meeting place. I have it on good authority that Discordia was reached out to by The Cartographer's men in the area. I haven't heard whether or not he's decided to join their cause, but I wanted to see what they had to say for themselves."

Penny paused her perusal. "Isn't Lord Discordia rather loyal? Mother says he sides with the Crown Prince on more matters than not."

"Lord Discordia likes to put his fingers in as many pies as he can, stirring any pot as long as it's in his favor." His eyes sparkled with mirth. "Where do you think Miss Clarice gets it from?"

They searched for any mention of The Cartographer. Most of the papers detailed the running of the nobleman's many lands and the estate's holdings. Lord Discordia didn't run a business, like Penny's family always had. Most of the nobility didn't run businesses like them. Most noble families simply ran their lands, taking care of the people under their stewardship and making sure the kingdom's laws were being followed. They served as overseers rather than taking part in the businesses keeping their lands afloat. The Barclays, however, had the very gifts to make their lands prosperous and didn't believe in handing off that duty to anyone else.

Perhaps that was one of the reasons Eleusion was falling to ruin right under Mother's nose. That, or Mother knew more than she was letting on.

Penny's patience frayed. "Lou, my mother will begin to wonder where I've run off to."

Lou didn't stop to look at her as he ran his fingers along the edges of the desk. "Of course. You should return to the—"

Voices echoed from the door leading to the library.

Lou grabbed Penny's hand and pulled her toward the window. With ease belied by his size, he grabbed her waist and swung her onto the sill. Within moments, they were hidden behind the large curtains, pressed against the edges of the open window.

"We have to climb down."

Penny's mind was still caught up in the fact that his arm was wrapped around her waist. "Climb down?"

"Yes. It's too risky to stay here. If anyone finds us in here, we'll have Discordia's guards on us faster than you can sprout a handful of daisies."

The door to the study opened and the voices became clear. "I know there's much better drink in here than what they're serving downstairs," said a male voice.

"Thank goodness, my lord. I can't handle the watered down wine and sweet drinks." Penny recognized this voice as the man who had spoken to Mother about opening a winery. She turned to tell Lou—

Penny's nose was an inch from his. His gaze set her knees wobbling slightly, the amber burning her from the inside out. Their breaths mingled together with the light breeze coming in from behind them. Lou shifted, his mouth moving closer to her face. *He's going to kiss me.* She saw the urge to in the way his eyes flicked to her lips then back to her eyes. Did she want him to?

The men on the other side of the curtain continued their idle chatter. Lou shifted his body closer. Everywhere they made contact Penny's skin sparked. Was kissing appropriate when on a secret mission and a possible enemy was within reach? She was grateful for her light dress or the heat would have overwhelmed her.

His cheek brushed hers. The smell of cedar and leather washed over her. His mouth came to her ear and Penny had to strangle down a gasp. He was so close. She'd never been this close to a man before. Mother would kill her.

"Lady Penelope," he said, his voice no more than a breath.

Penny could barely nod.

"I need you to wrap your arms around my neck."

Sweet Gaia, he wanted her to do *what*?

"I need you to hold onto me so I can use the rope to climb out the window. We have to get out before we get caught."

Penny blinked. Several times. *Climb out the window.* Great Goddess, she was an idiot.

He took hold over her hands and brought them around his neck. His face remained brushing against hers. "Now my next request will be less easy. You are going to have to wrap your legs around my torso."

Penny started to pull her hands back, but Lou caught them. "Listen, I can't hold you and get us down the rope. You're going to have to hold onto me while I descend. It's a three-story fall and I need to make sure I don't drop us."

Penny's whole body stiffened. He was going to have her hold onto him while he rappelled down the side of the house?

As if reading her mind, he said, "You only have to hold on and I swear we will get to the bottom safely." The voices in the room moved toward the desk. "We have to do it now."

He spun around, still holding her arms, and pulled her onto his back as she wrapped each leg around his torso. It would be far worse for both of them to get caught rather than them breaking bones in the grass below. At least if they fell, Penny might be able to cushion the blow.

Lou hoisted them out the large window, his feet braced on the sill and his hands grasping the rope. Penny clung to him as he took a slow step down the wall. She squeezed her eyes shut and buried her face in his back as he took another. Steadily, he descended.

Three steps.

Four steps.

Five.

Six.

Penny's muscles protested her tight coil around his body. Her breaths came out frantic and she couldn't open her eyes.

Then Lou's foot slipped.

A squeak slipped from her throat and rang out into the night. Lou's body stiffened. They didn't move as they waited to see if anyone would come to investigate.

"Are you all right?" Lou whispered as he resumed their descent.

Penny nodded against his back.

He resumed their descent. "The squeal would say otherwise."

Penny's eyes shot opened. She shut them just as fast. *Great, not only am I an idiot, but a coward as well.*

She held tight, fear and mortification roiling within her. Lou stopped moving once again and Penny tightened her hold.

"Lady Penelope." Her name was a laugh caught up in a whisper. "You can let go now."

Penny's grip on him tightened further, causing him to stumble, before she realized what he said. She opened her eyes and blinked at the ground beneath Lou's boots. She nearly toppled to her rear in her haste to put her feet on solid ground.

Lou turned around, an odd combination of concern and excitement on his face. "That wasn't so bad was it?"

The urge to shake him eclipsed her embarrassment. “Next time, you hold on to me while I get to climb down the rope.”

His smile brushed away any resentment she clung to. “We’ll have to try it out one of these days.” He beckoned her along the wall toward the front of the house.

Penny’s brows rose. “You’re in a pleasant mood for someone who didn’t get what he was looking for.”

He lifted a hand, his first two fingers holding a slip of parchment between them. “Didn’t I?”

17

ECHOES AND MEMORIES

THE SWISH OF MELI'S TAIL DID LITTLE TO CALM PENNY'S RACING heart.

Eleusia shone brightly as the sun finished its descent into the horizon. Penny's eyes flicked back and forth as buildings sprung up along the road and people milled about alongside them. Her spine stiffened as they passed a small tavern and a group of men burst out, already heavily intoxicated. Meli's ears flattened in displeasure. Penny tried to shake out the tension hunching her shoulders.

Lou led the way through the traffic. The small slip of paper he'd found tucked in a crevice in Lord Discordia's desk contained the location of two orientation meetings run by The Cartographer's men. One was in Discordia. The other in Eleusia. When Lou had told her the name of the inn, anger had flared within her. She didn't recognize the name. This was her family's land and Penny found herself quite inadequate as its heir.

As they came into the market, Lou took a side street leading away from the more commercial part of town. They passed fewer and fewer businesses as their horses' clomping steps on the cobblestones turned into dull thuds in the packed dirt. The residences grew closer and closer together and became less and less stable. Garbage piled up against the buildings. The rush of water babbled over the hustle and bustle of the street. Her heart shot up into her throat.

Eyes shied away from her horse as they passed. Penny tried to breathe evenly, but the smell of rotting fish and waste assaulted her and brought tears to her eyes. Alleyways grew familiar as they rode through the dark town and the sound of rough men's laughter echoed in her ears. Even her cloak could not block the cold descending on her.

Penny didn't notice Lou had stopped until Meli came up alongside his gelding. Penny's eyes locked with his and Lou gave her a concerned look.

He dismounted and came to her side. "Is everything all right, Lady Penelope?"

Penny gave him a shaky nod. Lou could likely hear the thumping of her heart against her ribcage. She wanted to be all right— needed to be all right. She despised feeling like she could never walk down a crowded street, that she couldn't turn a corner without being accosted by wicked men. She loathed the way the shadows sent slivers of terror down her spine like they had in her youth. Even at home, she kept being spooked by farm hands popping up out of nowhere when she had known most of those men her entire life.

She needed to get back in control of herself and this was the time to do it.

Penny took a centering breath and dismounted. Lou grabbed Meli's reins and tied them to the post alongside his own horse. Penny's eyes finally took in the looming inn they were standing outside. Three stories high, it towered over the buildings around it.

The large door stood open and hushed voices came whispering out its mouth. The building creaked as a breeze swept through the small square. The glow of lamplight filtered out of the crusty windows like demonic eyes.

Penny's entire being revolted against going inside. Lou offered his arm and led Penny into the gaping maw of the decrepit beast.

Upon entering, Penny noted the sheer volume of people seated in whatever space they could fill. She saw young men sitting in the rafters above the main room and nearly gasped at the sight of multiple children milling about on the floor.

Lou led her through the crowd to a pair of empty seats in the front, near the large fireplace warming the room. They sat next to a couple who couldn't be older than themselves.

"Good evening," said Lou. "Saving these chairs for anyone?"

The other man chuckled and swung an arm over the young woman next to him. "No, they're all yours."

Lou gave his thanks and pulled Penny down alongside him. "We've never been to one of these meetings before." He offered his hand to the other man. "I'm Pluto," he tilted his head in Penny's direction, "and this is my wife, Corey."

Penny reined in her surprise. Lou hadn't mentioned using alternative names and they had certainly not decided to pretend to be husband and wife. Penny would have words with Lou after this meeting— no matter that his improvisation caused warmth to spread through her limbs.

The man shook Lou's proffered hand. "Good to meet you, Pluto." The man laughed. "Unfortunate name. I'm Nate and this is my fiancée, Cecile. This is the second meeting we've been to, but it's nothing to get worried over. The man just talks and will take the names of those interested at the end."

Lou looked between Nate and Cecile. "Are you two interested?"

Nate chuckled and Cecile gave a timid smile. "We don't know yet. Cecile's father is a big supporter, but there seems to be a whole lot of anger going into these things. Most folks here are just tired of living the way they have and are looking for a change. I think they hope these people can give them that."

Penny's gut twisted. There were people living in poverty thanks to the rule of the Tyrant King. The Tyrant King had been called as such for a reason. His temper and his gluttony knew no bounds. The taxes had been horrendous and if his desires weren't met, he would send his loyal spymaster to make sure the people felt his anger. The king would have consumed the entire kingdom if his mouth had been big enough. Mother had always done her best to provide aid to those that lived in their duchy, but sometimes there was little she could do to help those under her charge besides make sure they had work and food on their tables. Penny remembered their duchy had been hit the hardest with taxes because of its prosperity, the ramifications of which they were still dealing with.

Things had certainly improved over the last five years. The princes and the Council had brought the kingdom back from the brink of ruin. Mother had begun all sorts of projects within the city; building warehouses to provide work, cleaning projects for the river, even outsourcing some of the grain milling to other mills in order to get more revenue flowing. Life was slowly getting better under the rule of the three princes, but it seemed some couldn't let go of the pains of the past and believed quick change was the only way to get what they wanted.

Lou's curious eyes met with hers as a man stood and called for everyone's attention. The mountain of a man stood a head taller than those in the room and bore a long sword in the scabbard at his waist. It wasn't uncommon for someone to wear a sword, most men being part of their town's militia or one of the Crown's garrisons stationed nearby. But this man didn't hold himself in the way of a guard or a soldier. He looked ready for a fight.

"Good evening, old friends and new friends. My name is Hyatt and I am here to give each of you that which you seek. Many of you have lived under the fist of oppression for too long, tucked into squalor and hopelessness, while those tainted with 'Gaia's gifts' have feasted and reveled in their riches. The power hungry magicals of this world have passed you by your whole life, but no more. We are at the cusp of a new dawn, an age where the gifted *give* to those of us who deserve it."

As the man continued to speak, Penny looked at the faces around her. Most held the haggard, wary gazes of men and women surviving this world. To them, this man's words probably sounded like a dream come true.

Penny had never wanted for anything in her life. Mother always ensured their peace and prosperity. Her soul pricked as she saw the threadbare gowns and patched up pants of the little children around them. How many were to wake up tomorrow without the hope of peace?

Mothers and fathers held little ones close and tucked sleepy heads under their chins. How many of them feared for the lives of their children?

"The Cartographer needs men and women like you who are willing to do what it takes to see so-called *bronties* at the helm of this great country. Our cause wishes to paint a new kind of world, one where the pure of spirit are no longer oppressed, but are the ones who hold the reins of those who would use us for their own gain."

Penny flinched at the cheers of the people around her. Her eyes flicked over the fiery looks of the men and the haughty looks of the women sitting in their laps. Greed and retribution gleamed in too many eyes. These were the people who would willingly burn hundreds of acres of grain because it was grown by mage hands. Grain that would feed these little ones and provide livelihoods for others. These were angry people who didn't know where to point the heat of their grief.

"For too long we've been trodden on by the spit-polished shoes of those with magic. Too long we have been living in the filth of oppression. Now is the time to act! The Cartographer is ready. Are you?"

Another cheer rang through the inn— cut off by the sound of an unnatural wind shaking the building. The gusts extinguished the lamps and stirred the flames in the fireplace into a roaring inferno.

A loud voice called from outside, amplified by the air rushing through the open windows. "In the name of the Duchess of Eleusion, you are under arrest for conspiring against the Crown of Olympia and inciting rebellion. Come out peacefully and no one will be harmed."

Peace was the last thing on these people's minds. Mothers grabbed their children and men charged out the front door. Penny heard the clashes of steel and the cries of the fallen as Lou grabbed her hand and pulled her out the back of the inn.

Men in the greens and black standards of the bailiff of Eleusia gathered those streaming out. Since Eleusia didn't have much military presence due to Mother's insistence they needed the land for food instead of soldiers, the bailiff of Eleusion was the only law enforcement Eleusia had. Penny's eyes remained rooted on them as they rounded up the children and the cries of their mothers rang in her ears. The image was disrupted as Lou used the crowd to block the men from grabbing hold of them and darted through the throng. They made their way into a tight alley leading out of the square. Penny's heart raced faster than her steps. Lou had to keep her from tripping over pieces of debris littering the ground. The shouts of men and the cries of children echoed after them.

Penny's hands lit up. Her gaze swung back and forth over the ramshackle buildings they passed. The glow of her hands hardly illuminated the ground before them, but she still attempted to smother the light in her skirts. She didn't want to get caught out here by any rebels running around.

Lou stopped to look around a corner.

Penny gasped. "What are we to do about the horses?"

Lou turned his head and gave her a reassuring smile, though it did little to calm her. He turned back and pulled her into another alleyway without a word.

They continued on this path for several minutes before coming to a large crossroad. Lou took a turn that Penny hoped would lead them back around the square only to come skidding to a stop at the sight of the rebel who had spoken at the inn.

Hyatt.

The large man's countenance turned dark as his eyes landed on Penny and Lou's joined hands. He pointed a thick finger in their direction, rage rippling over his features. "Mage."

Lou pulled Penny behind him. Two daggers appeared in his hands as Hyatt slid the sword from the scabbard at his side.

"You will not touch her," Lou said, voice sharp as the steel in his hands.

"How are you going to stop me, boy? That girl is an abomination and deserves to be put down."

Lou replied with the swipe of his dagger.

The two men fought on the small road as Penny stood

rooted to the spot. It was as if her limbs were tied once again. Terror crashed through her as the ring of blades echoed in her ears. Hyatt swung his sword at Lou's head. Lou ducked and swiped at the rebel's gut with his dagger. Hyatt turned and threw a punch with his free hand, hitting Lou in the shoulder. The grunts of the men fighting brought darkness creeping into her vision. Her knees shook as Lou dodged another swing of Hyatt's sword. Hyatt readjusted and his fist met the flesh of Lou's arm.

One of Lou's blades skidded across the packed earth and stopped at Penny's feet. Penny looked down in a daze and retrieved the dagger. The blade shone in the light of the moon and Penny couldn't help but admire the craftsmanship even as her thoughts slugged through her head.

"Penelope, run!"

Penny's head snapped up at Lou's shout and her heart skittered as she saw him barely sidestep a thrust from his opponent. Clarity settled and Penny immediately dropped the blade to thrust her hand into the satchel at her side. A pouch of seeds and a small water skin were in her hands a moment later.

Penny splashed the water onto the ground and threw the seeds into the mud. She shut her eyes and connected to the life on the ground. Her hands glowed brighter as large vines thrust themselves out of the water and sped in the direction of the fight. Penny directed the trailing plants to avoid Lou's magic and instead cling to the man who would cause them harm.

The plants obeyed.

She heard the man bellow in rage and opened her eyes to see the vines reach out their spiny limbs toward him. Hyatt swung his sword like a scythe as the plants did their best to capture him. The enraged man swung wildly at Lou. He was able to stab Hyatt in the side. A roar rang through the alley as Lou lost hold of his weapon. The man turned and thrust his sword at Lou once again before turning and running full speed at Penny.

Penny shut her eyes. The vines followed in Hyatt's wake, but couldn't catch him as he came upon her. Her eyes opened just as the man swung his sword high over his head. Penny's magic shuddered.

With a flash of gold between them, Lou thrust the dagger — which had been sitting at her feet— into the rebel's chest. Hyatt's eyes went wide. Lou pushed the dying man back.

His body fell to the earth in a silent heap.

18

DEATHS AND GIFTS

PENNY'S STOMACH HEAVED ONTO THE ALLEY FLOOR.

She'd never watched a man die. She'd never seen someone's life disappear in a flash of cold steel and desperation. She gagged again.

After a few minutes, she wiped the bile from her chin and turned from where she knelt on the ground. Her tear-filled eyes watched Lou walk over and take the sword from the limp hand that had seemed so fearsome moments before.

Lou came up to Penny and offered her his own hand. "We should probably get moving before anyone comes upon us."

It was nearly impossible to place her hand in his.

Hands that had killed a man.

Hands that had saved her.

Lou pulled her up off the ground. She wavered and he wrapped an arm around her waist to keep her steady.

"It's always difficult to watch someone's life disappear before your eyes," Lou whispered as he guided her back toward what she hoped was the inn. "It never gets easier, and it always damages a piece of your soul. I would have spared him if I could. I hope you know that."

Penny nodded her head, but the well of tears overflowed at his words. As someone who watched life blossom before her every day, it was devastating to see how easily it could be wiped out. As they walked, Penny couldn't help but think about everything leading up to that moment. Martin's words. Her kidnapping. The fires. The angry faces of the people in the inn.

"I just don't understand it," she confessed in a hushed tone. "How can people be so angry about something no one could ever change? You can't choose what kind of people others are born as. Why are they so convinced it's something that needs to be controlled?"

Lou continued to lead her through the twists and turns for a few moments. She nearly gave up hoping for an answer before she heard him relinquish a sigh.

"Your mother is guardian over the lands farthest from Faerie. Eleusion has quite the status of housing the highest bronty population of any of the other noble houses in the kingdom. Most of the citizens in your duchy had likely never seen a member of the fair folk before Prince Dion wrote up the treaty with the High Queen."

He led her around a corner and pulled her closer to him to avoid a pile of refuse before continuing. "Imagine their surprise when full-blooded fae began to flood the river in Eleusia or walk in from the highway to sell their wares at market. Creatures out of bedtime stories walking in broad daylight among them. Even before the new treaty, there was always opposition in regards to those with any sort of magic."

Penny nodded. Just after the Faerie Wars, mages were put to death when they grew into their powers. Any relations between humans and fae were seen as heresy and the guilty party burned at the stake. It had been a long time since the land had seen anything like what their ancestors did to those people. Penny felt the frown crease her face. Unfortunately, deep-rooted prejudices outlasted the grave.

Penny walked quietly beside him. As heir, she often thought about what kind of lives the people within their duchy led. There were always concerns with their welfare in the back of her mind. She wanted people to be happy with where they lived, to have food on their table and warm fire in their hearths. But what if it wasn't actually enough? What if there were some things she couldn't fix? It wasn't like she could go back in time and stop the fae from enslaving humankind.

Penny thought of Farrah with her obvious fae heritage. She'd never learned how the female came to be in Eleusia. Penny had known her since she was small, even before the alliance between the High Queen and Olympia's ruling family. She had never noticed that Farrah was the only fae she'd ever seen residing in Eleusia up until a few years ago.

Shame pained her as she realized how naive she must seem. She'd thought she knew her people. She'd worked side by side with them. Talked with them. Knew some of their names. Yet, she wasn't one of them. She was raised by a mother with magic who taught her about all of the lands and kingdoms surrounding them. She was among the gifted members of the nobility. Magic was something to be revered in her house, not shut away.

But Mother had shut *her* away. Penny let out a long breath through her nose. Mother always talked about the evils of men, but never about the evils of *man*. Their conversations were invariably about how men could hurt her for being a woman. Penny shook her head. But she hadn't been abducted or nearly killed because she was female.

Penny looked up to study Lou. Her resolve to help him with

his mission deepened. She *needed* to help him root out the villains in Mother's lands. Not solely because of the pain they had caused her or because of her desire to take some measure of control over her life, but because of the pain they would bring if they were left to stir up the people to hate.

They walked back into the square where they found their horses still tied to the post near the inn. No trace of rebellion marked the empty street. Two or three of the bailiff's men stood at the door of the inn, but after a few words between Lou and one of the bailiff's men, they were able to leave.

Penny looked back over her shoulder at the man Lou had spoken to. "Why were they so accommodating? You would think they would question why we had horses near the inn."

"How do you think I know so much about what goes on in the kingdom?" He gave her a mischievous grin. "Having members of local law enforcement in your pocket gets you information you would have a difficult time acquiring otherwise."

"You've bribed my mother's men?"

"Is it really a bribe when I was paying them before you were?"

Penny would've laughed if it had been any other night.

Stars glimmered in the late hour and Penny shuddered as the cold whipped through her hair. They led their mounts onto the main road and Lou slowed his horse to ride beside her. The steel pommel of the sword he had taken from the dead rebel glared out from his saddlebag. Penny's eyes shifted from the silver of the blade to the gold of Lou's sober gaze.

"Lady Penelope, I'm sorry for the danger I put you in tonight. If I'd known about the bailiff's men I wouldn't have allowed you to accompany me." Confusion settled on his features. "The order must have come in when we were inside the inn. I have no idea who found the meeting place, but I'm more shocked to hear that your mother ordered the arrests. It's almost like she knew beforehand."

Penny's brows furrowed and she looked down at Meli's mane. She'd forgotten the bailiff's men said they were under orders from Mother. "Perhaps she found out while she was in the capital and sent an order ahead of her. She went to Olympia not only for court, but to petition the council to look into the fires on our lands. Someone must have given her information about the rebel uprising here and she wrote to the bailiff to take care of it before she arrives home tomorrow."

"Perhaps you're right."

She met Lou's eyes. "I'm sorry if it's ruined your plans."

Lou shrugged. "I knew we couldn't keep it from her forever. I figured as soon as she left for the capital she would find out. That's one of the reasons you found me in her study. I needed to make sure I had the facts straight before her return. However, I hadn't anticipated her getting word to the men in Eleusia. I had operatives waiting to intercept any messages from her in case such a thing was to happen. I don't know how one snuck past."

Mother did have a way of making sure she had control over every situation. There really wasn't much Mother didn't know.

Well, besides this cursed rebellion apparently.

Her smile dimmed. Seeing the faces of those people tonight hurt her in ways she'd never felt before. She hated seeing the weary faces of those people, of thinking that they didn't have what they needed to provide for their families. Perhaps Mother didn't have as much control as she believed she did.

Penny turned her attention back to the man beside her. "Thank you, Lou, for opening my eyes." The reality of her situation became hard to swallow. "I really don't know what goes on in the lives of the people around me. I felt like I knew everyone because I worked with some of them, but the small amount of people I work with doesn't speak for the whole of the people whose lives depend on me."

The scenes of her abduction and of the recruiting rebel flashed through her mind. Those men didn't look like people who had lived in hardship. They looked like men who believed they were entitled to everything they hadn't been given and the world could burn until they either got it or there was nothing but ash left.

"I want to rid this place of the anger that has been festering. I want to train with you so that I may be in a better position to help my people. I want to become someone they can turn to in times of struggle and know that I'll give them aid. Do you think I can? Will you help me?"

Lou's eyes shone in the light of the moon. "Lady Penelope, it has already begun."

They returned to the house just before the curtain of night made way for the sunrise. The stables were dark and Penny dug about her satchel for her magelight. When she pulled it out, a scrap of paper came with it. The face of the young fae boy stared back at her. She hadn't cleaned out her satchel recently. Her fingers squeezed the magelight awake so she could see the page better. It had been weeks since she'd picked this up when Mother had taken her to Eleusia, when she'd nearly been kidnapped.

How did his parents feel about what was going on in the city? Had they left their homes because of what was stirring? Did they even know what was going on around them?

Penny folded the paper and put it back in her bag. It would help remind her of what she was doing all of this for. She unsaddled Meli and put up all of her tack before grabbing a brush hanging from the wall. Penny's eyes caught on the flash of metal from the stall next to her as Lou drew the rebel's sword from his saddlebag.

"Why did you take the man's sword?" Penny asked.

Lou turned to her with a grim smile. "Would you like me to show you?"

Penny set the brush on the door of Meli's stall and walked over to where Lou knelt on the ground. She crouched beside him as he set down his magelight and balanced the sword in both hands. Lou let out a shaky breath as he settled into the straw covering the stable floor.

His voice came out in a reverent tone. "Gaia has seen fit to bestow a large number of gifts on those she deems worthy to hold them. Many have gifts over the weather, fire, light, or heightened senses. There are others who have rarer talents, those of lightning, viewing pieces of the future, mind reading," —he tilted his head toward her— "or instilling life. My talent would also be put under the *uncommon* category."

Penny had never thought to ask again, after their conversation in Mother's study, what his gift was. It wasn't considered rude or anything to ask. Why hadn't she?

He closed his eyes.

Her gaze shifted from his face down to the sword in his hands. Her own eyes widened. Black crawled as dark as ink down the veins in his forearm, making the color of his skin lighten in contrast. The tell of his power made it all the way to his hands still holding the blade in front of him.

He opened his eyes and turned to her, amber glowing in the darkness surrounding them. "Take hold of my arm if you want to see."

Penny struggled to swallow. Her eyes fell on the black lines marring the flesh of his arm as she reached out a shaky hand. She let out a breath as her fingers met the warmth of his skin and fire bloomed in her chest.

The warmth turned ice cold as she then saw what he wanted to show her.

A shadow of the rebel Lou had killed knelt just before them.

A scream burst from Penny's lips. She immediately let go of Lou's arm and threw herself away from the specter. Her eyes landed back on the empty space where the man had just been.

Lou whirled to look at her from his position on the ground. "It's all right, Lady Penelope. He cannot harm you, I swear. It's merely his spirit."

Penny felt her brows lift into her hairline. "You can speak with the dead?"

Lou attempted to give her a reassuring smile and nodded. "This is my mage gift. Using objects or a lock of hair— anything that was connected to them in life— I can speak to the spirits of those who have passed." He turned back to where she knew the image of the man still knelt. "Well, as long as they are willing to talk back that is."

Fear snaked down to her toes. "I've never heard of a gift like that. For something so rare, you would think many would know about you."

Lou's smile turned sad. "Not many know I have this gift. I can only do it every so often. The toll it takes on my heart is high. It was in my father's best interest to make sure no one learned about it."

"Why?"

Lou's mouth twisted into a frown. "He worried about people hounding me to speak to loved ones that had passed or finding out that I could easily find the culprits of murders and assassinations. Only those in my organization know outside of my family."

"Do any of your siblings have gifts? Were both of your parents mages?"

"My brothers both have gifts of their own. My mother was definitely not a mage. We theorize that it must have been inherited from my father who had some mage ancestors, though he was not gifted with any powers himself."

Lou's smile turned into a frown as he glanced back to that not-so-empty space in the stable. "I think we should get to finding out what this man has to say." His expression turned concerned. "You don't have to join me."

Penny did her best to swallow back her terror as she returned to Lou's side. "I can't think of a good reason why I shouldn't join you." She lifted her hand. "Let's see what this man knows."

She grabbed Lou's muscled forearm and turned her gaze to the spirit of the man she'd watched die.

"So, the mage wench has some guts," the rebel leered. "If I were still alive I would have liked to see them spill onto the floor."

Penny's face blanched and she felt the cords of muscle under her hand tighten.

"I'll make you a deal, Hyatt. If you don't speak to her again and you answer all of my questions, I will personally make sure your body receives a burial instead of the pyre most traitors get."

The rebel's eyes glimmered as they glared into Lou's. Penny knew what Lou was offering. Traitors in Olympia didn't receive the sacred ritual of returning their body to the Goddess, but instead were burned in significance of the pain they had caused during their life. Then the Goddess would decide whether to collect their remains or let them float on the wind until they'd served their penance. Lou offered the single bit of peace a dead man could ever ask for.

"You swear it?" the rebel hissed.

Lou nodded.

"All right, little man. What do you want to know?"

"What is your full name?"

"Hyatt Carry."

"Where are you from, Mr. Carry? What was your occupation before you joined The Cartographer?"

"Lived in Eleusia my whole life, right on the docks. Worked as a city watchman until I found The Cartographer's group a year ago."

"Did you ever meet The Cartographer?"

"No."

Lou's arm wilted slightly under Penny's hand. "What was your job?"

"I was a recruiter. I met with folks in their homes or gathering places and told them about The Cartographer's mission to wipe out all of you filthy magicals."

Lou's eyes flashed, but he didn't rise to the bait. "How did you contact your superiors?"

The man took a moment before letting out a reluctant huff. "The post has a box under the name *Prudence Matthews.* That's where we dropped off the lists of volunteers."

"How many others were there?" asked Penny. She attempted not to shrink under the man's attention.

He sniffed derisively. "There were a dozen or so around Eleusia. Couldn't tell you how many everywhere else."

"Everywhere else?" Penny parroted.

The man's mouth split into a gleeful grin. "Oh yeah. There isn't a city in all of Olympia where you won't find one of us."

He turned back to Lou. "The little princes have no idea what's coming for them, and when it hits, they won't be able to stop it no matter what kind of tainted blood they have."

The image of the man disappeared as Lou threw the sword to the ground.

19

POLITICS AND ROOTS

Dearest Penny,

How did your life become so much more exciting than mine all of a sudden? Spies and rebels and handsome men. It has the making of one of your novels!

We leave for Spring tomorrow. I can't decide what I'm going to miss most. The beaches? The dolphins? The markets? It's too hard to choose! Devan says the vendors have been lamenting our departure. Apparently they love gold as much as humans. Who knew?

Father sent a letter detailing the events at court. He said your mother was in quite a state about the rebels in your area. I don't envy those princes one bit.

She gets home soon, right? Are you going to

tell her about your new hobby? You know how she gets when people keep things from her. I still think about when you tried to throw that surprise party for her birthday last year. I think the people in the capital heard her yell "What are you hiding, Penelope Barclay?!" I don't think my father has ever laughed harder than he did when he saw the shock on her face.

Let me know how that little conversation goes. Actually, I'll likely hear it in Spring.

"MY DAUGHTER, A SPY?!"

Ha! I'd pay a king's ransom to see her face then.

Your Very Encouraging and Completely-Trustworthy-with-Your-Secrets Friend,

Angelica

"REBELS. REBELS IN MY OWN TOWN AND THE PRINCES HAD THE GALL to think they could get away with eradicating them without telling me. Can you believe it?" Mother paced back and forth in front of the fire in the study.

Penny's knees cracked as she stood from the chair by the desk. "No, Mother. It was certainly wrong of them to do." The words came out in a drawl as she repeated them for what had to be the fifteenth time since Mother had returned that night.

Lou had returned to Eleusia to take care of the promise he'd made to the rebel. Penny had slept into the afternoon after the events of the night before and was then surprised by Mother's arrival at supper. Mother had immediately begun her rant, only resting from the topic to talk about their work on the orchard.

"I'm glad to see the trees so laden with blossoms this year," Mother remarked as she walked toward the window of the study. "You've done fine work ensuring our yield is high this season. Even the new cuttings are drooping with red flowers."

The farm had turned into a crimson sea. Swarms of bees had already begun dancing through the trees and Penny had received word from the beekeepers in the village that the honey had not been so sweet in years. Even now, she could hear the sound of nocturnal wildlife growing alongside the blooms. She smiled.

"I think we'll have plenty of fruit to send to the capital," Mother continued. "The council has been tasked with preparing for a festival at the end of the year to celebrate the princes' five years of rule." The announcement didn't come as a surprise. Penny was again grateful her work had paid off. They were sure to receive orders for the fruit and wine made from their harvest.

Penny's thoughts whiplashed as Mother changed topics once again. "I'm glad I got word to the bailiff when I did. He reported five— *five* different groups he apprehended. This would've never happened if those three boys playing king had not had the inkling to keep it from me."

"Mother!" Penny exclaimed. "You don't mean that. They have done much for our kingdom in such a short time, and you know it." It was just like Mother to get upset, but Penny didn't realize how deeply she felt.

Mother turned and looked at her daughter with icy eyes. "It was within my right to rid our lands of those warmongers. If I had known. . . If I'd had any idea. . ." Mother dropped into one of the chairs near the fireplace.

Penny sat at Mother's feet. "How could you have known? You can't blame yourself for things out of your control."

Mother sighed. "I should have kept a better eye on my lands. Being in the princes' council has stretched me thinner than I would like. I haven't paid enough attention to the people we have the duty to provide for." Her chin fell to her chest and she looked down into her lap. "I knew our people weren't thriving as well as they should be after the late king passed. I should have taken the opportunity to rally the people together in the beginning, but I didn't. It's my fault this has happened."

Penny shook her head. "Mother, you're one person. You can only do so much alone." Penny stopped and Mother looked up at her hesitation. "If you would give me some more responsibilities, maybe even let me go to the capital—"

"That is out of the question." Mother straightened. "You're still young and have much to learn. You did well with the wheat fields and have taken on more and more responsibilities for the care of our lands these past few months, but you aren't ready to face the other side of our duties." She shook her head. "You're still too young."

"You say that, but I know I'm ready. I can handle more than you think. If you just give me the chance—"

"No, Penny." Mother stood and walked over to her desk. "When you've proven that you can defend yourself from the evils of this world, I will allow you to venture into them."

"How am I supposed to do that if you never give me the chance?"

Mother sliced her hand through the air, effectively cutting off Penny's argument. "I do not have to explain myself to you. I am the duchess of this manor and my word is law. Do you understand?"

Not deigning to answer, Penny turned on her heel and walked out the door.

Midnight. It had to be midnight.

Penny's breaths came in short gasps as she wove through the cottonwood trees. A branch whipped across her face and she let out a grunt as a loose rock nearly caused her to twist an ankle. After the trip to Eleusia, Lou had decided she needed agility training and announced that chasing her through the dark trees around the grove was the best option.

Penny and Mother had been at odds for the two days since their argument. Neither was willing to broach the subject with the other, but the air between them had grown stifling. Penny's relief when she had gotten out of the house to train knocked the tension off her shoulders.

Though she didn't appreciate running blindly about while Lou pointed out everything she did incorrectly.

"Quiet your steps." The low voice next to her ear made her jump and she hit her head on a low hanging branch. "I can hear you from the other side of the grove."

Penny huffed and attempted to follow his orders, but her footfalls only grew louder.

Her thoughts had been a raging cyclone for the last couple of days and the silence of the night only seemed to heighten the whirling emotions. Mother's clear dismissal of Penny's abilities had cut her deeper than anything she'd said before. Penny had hoped the training sessions would give her some clarity, but they simply stoked her frustration and the questions of Mother's loyalties.

"Don't step on the soft dirt. Attempt to step on anything that won't leave a trace and won't make noise."

"You need to measure your breathing," came next. "Your gasping is too noticeable and will actually cause you to tire quicker. Try breathing in through your nose and out through your mouth." He demonstrated as he ran beside her, his breathing completely even and not a hair out of place.

Penny could feel the coating of dirt on her legs as well as the multitude of leaves tangled in her hair. If her fae picture books were anything to go by, she likely resembled a troll.

"You need to avoid the branches. Instead of shoving them to the side, move around them."

Penny closed her eyes for a moment before refocusing on her run. She tried to remind herself that Lou was headed into Eleusia the day after tomorrow and said she could have the night off. He'd received word The Cartographer was still in the area, but his source couldn't pinpoint the rebel leader's location. Lou hoped to snoop out a few of the rebels in the city and dig up more information. While she was disappointed she couldn't accompany him, she looked forward to sleeping like a normal person for once.

Penny stubbed her toe on a rock and withheld a moan. Yes, he was simply doing what she'd asked. He trained her in the way he knew would make her successful as a spy. All of this would benefit her in the long run, would help her reach her goal. It was for the benefit of Mother's duchy— of *her* duchy. The land needed to be purged of this stirring rebellion and her people— be they fae, mage, or otherwise— would succeed and Mother would see just how in control she was.

However, if Lou told her to stop stepping on dirt one more time, she was going to lose it.

He came around her other side, his footsteps completely silent and his arms never brushing against anything. Penny could see the color of his eyes in the speckled moonlight coming through the diamond-shaped leaves above them. *He doesn't even look tired.* No sweat dripped into his eyes. No redness flared across his skin. She was pretty sure she saw his steps carrying a little skip. Penny had to look away before she did something she would regret.

Round and round they went. Penny's lungs heaved with the effort and nausea began to work its way up her abdomen. It was almost like she was a little girl again, getting to know her powers and the price it took to use them. She swallowed down the discomfort as much as she could without the cramp in her side screaming. She would not humiliate herself in front of her trainer again.

Blisters ground against the leather of her boots and the skirts of her sweat-soaked dress continued to tangle in her legs. When she'd asked Lou if she could train in trousers, he had answered "You won't find many situations where you'll have the opportunity to fight in pants."

The temptation to shred the hindering fabric catching on the multitude of flora burned within her.

The run continued to wear on her. However, for a few minutes, Lou stopped commenting on her errors and she felt herself buoyed up slightly by her success. The next moment, the top of Penny's head scrapped across a low-hanging branch and she nearly lost her composure.

"You need to stay aware of your surroundings and become better accustomed to the dark." He looked behind them. "Lady Penelope, you really need to avoid leaving footprints in the dirt."

Red and green flared across her vision.

Penny turned sharply at the sound of Lou's surprised yelp and found him flying straight up into the air.

No... that wasn't right.

Penny's eyes widened. He was being carried up.

A large cottonwood now stood where Lou had taken his last step and the man in question hung from the topmost branches dozens of feet above her head.

The sound of his clearing throat was nearly imperceptible from the distance. "Lady Penelope, could you enlighten me as to *what just happened?*"

At the shock in his voice, Penny couldn't hold in the emotions any longer. A tearful laugh burst from her throat and she fell to her knees. She couldn't help it. Watching him hang at the top of the tree like a wayward kite broke whatever semblance of control she'd been holding onto. The shift from bubbling anger to humor was so startling. Then the physical exertion met the brunt of the cost of her magic and she lost the battle with her stomach. She stayed where she was for a few moments, breathing deeply.

After she felt well enough to move again, she opened her eyes. A blue handkerchief dangled in front of her face. Her mentor stood on the ground once again. She swiped the square of cloth from his fingers and quickly wiped away any sign of her weakness as she hid her burning face from his gaze.

"You continue to surprise me, Lady Penelope."

Penny turned back to Lou, whose eyes fixed on the uppermost branches of the newly sprouted tree. Her brows drew together in confusion.

"Most mages don't have the power to create life," he stated. "If they do, the power comes at a high cost to themselves and their gift. Yet, here you are sprouting fully matured trees out of the ground like you've been doing it since you learned how to walk."

"Most would say I have been."

His eyes met hers. "It's a marvel to be certain and may be

just shy of a miracle." He offered her a hand. Penny carefully took it.

Her weak legs made it difficult to leave her spot on the ground, but she rose to her feet. She would have to sleep through the morning if she wanted to get anything done on the orchards. She craned her neck to look at the tree. Like the others around it, the tree stood at a mature height. The cottonwood would have looked as if it had been there for decades if not for the disturbed soil around its base. She shuffled over to the tree and placed her hands on the trunk. The glow of her magic flickered and she sluggishly connected with the tree.

Her mind's eye took in the complicated system of roots and branches, each reaching for the sustenance the Goddess gave them. Focusing her magic became difficult with her exhaustion, the images coming in vague forms rather than the normally crisp pictures she saw. She blinked her physical eyes a few times in an attempt to dispel the fog, but it couldn't help her with her gift's sight. She'd need to sleep in until noon and drink an entire pot of Farrah's tea to refill her magic by their training tomorrow night. She pushed a little harder, feeling her limbs shake. Her view of the tree remained muddled.

The tree appeared to actually be an offshoot from the one standing beside it. The roots had branched out and sprouted this tree a mere fifteen feet away. In her anger, she'd reached for her gift and the earth had heard her call.

Her hand dropped away from the rough bark. She shouldn't have allowed her temper to get the best of her. Shame roiled in her empty gut. Mother always chided her for allowing her emotions to get the better of her judgment. Her head needed to remain clear and her heart needed to stay calm. She huffed out a chuckle as she recalled why she had gotten worked up. Lou had certainly not deserved her ire.

She turned away from the cottonwood, and found Lou still

watching her, his face relaxed and somewhat expectant. His expression contrasted painfully with the feelings combating within her.

"I'm sorry, Lou." Her voice neared a whisper. "I didn't mean for the tree to take you. I can honestly say, I have no idea what happened..."

Lou's hand lifted to silence her. "Lady Penelope, I think this evening was quite the success."

Penny gaped. "You do?"

"Oh yes." A clever smile stretched across his face and lit his eyes. "Just imagine what we could do if we can train you to use your gift in conjunction with combat. The possibilities are endless. We'll have to begin implementing this at once." Lou glanced toward the horizon. "We still have a bit of time left. Let's see what we can manage to do before your mother rises with the sun." Lou spun toward the clearing and silently stalked through the brush.

Penny stood there, in shock for a moment before she groaned and begrudgingly followed.

20

POLLEN AND PLANTS

POLLINATING HAD TO BE THE MOST TEDIOUS TASK PENNY HAD EVER been given to date.

Not that I've ever been given any exciting tasks.

She grabbed the end of her braid. The red hairs had collected the golden motes. The bees looked much better covered in pollen than she did. The brush in her hand stuck to her fingers. She collected more pollen to fertilize the next tree over. Back and forth, she walked through the trees, brushing pollen along the blossoms her magic told her needed it most.

"M'lady!"

Penny sagged in relief. "Hello, Aaron. Praise the Goddess, I'm so happy to see you."

Aaron sniggered as he came up beside her. "Her Grace decided yer torture is over for the day. Got a fancy guest pulling up the drive in 'bout an hour."

Penny dropped her brush into one of her pockets. She wiped her hands off, the pollen sticking to the cloth of her skirt. She was eager to be done with this in the next few weeks. "Did she say who?"

He shook his head. "Only said yer needed back at the house."

Penny offered her thanks and trekked back out of the field. The sun fell closer to the horizon which meant this mysterious guest was likely staying for dinner. Penny wiped her hands on her skirt.

"Lady Penelope."

Penny's spirit nearly jumped right out of her skin. "Sweet Gaia, Lou! Why do you always sneak up on me like that?"

Lou gave her a considered look. "Apparently we need to work on your awareness. I've been behind you for several seconds."

The eye roll Penny gave him was only slightly tempered. She turned back toward the manor. "I'm sorry, but I have to get back to the house. Was there something you needed?"

"Your unexpected guest won't be here for another hour."

Penny glanced back at him. "How do you know?"

Lou smiled. "I know a lot more than I probably should."

"Do you know who it is?"

Lou caught up to her. "I would hate to ruin the surprise."

"The Honorable Dowager Marchioness of Delphine, the Honorable Marquess of Delphine, and Lady Diana, Your Grace." Rich bowed and left the room, leaving behind the three newcomers.

"I should make up my own title sometime," Diana mused, taking up a chair near the fire. "Being announced after 'their honorablenesses' over there is slightly degrading."

"Dominique, it's been so long." Mater glided into the room and wrapped her arms around Mother. No one could unsettle and ease at the same time like Paulo and Diana's mother could. Mater had the unnatural talent of seeing into people's souls. It wouldn't have come as a surprise to anyone if she had inherited some of her family's oracular gifts.

"Luciana, it is very good to see you, though I don't know why you didn't send a missive ahead." Mother's confusion showed stark on her face.

"My son was insistent we not allow anyone to know we were coming until we'd nearly arrived. He'll not tell me why, but when Paulo insists on something, I tend to listen."

"Except when I say that *bramies* is a disgusting dish," Paulo said. He took a seat on the couch next to Penny. "Okra should not be considered edible."

Mother and Mater sat near the door that adjoined the sitting room to the small formal dining room. The two were quite a contrast. Mother sat upright, her posture perfect and her manner congenial. Mater sat next to her as if she had nowhere else she'd rather be. Mater was at ease wherever she went, obvious by the way she insisted everyone call her *Mater.* A duchess and a marchioness weren't so far apart on the nobility scale, but one wouldn't be able to tell based solely on the two of them.

"So why didn't you send word ahead?" Penny asked the twins.

Paulo's light expression darkened slightly. "It doesn't matter. I made sure it didn't happen."

The chill in his eyes cut off any of Penny's objections. She directed her next question at Diana. "Why did you all decide to come all the way to Barclay Manor? Mother said the season was off to a great start already."

Paulo snorted. "Will you tell her, Diana? Or shall I?"

Diana fiddled with the leather strap holding her braid in place a little too nonchalantly. "You can if you want."

Paulo leaned forward. "Dexter Finton tried to kiss her again and she pummeled him into the ground."

Penny's eyes widened. "You beat up Lord Finton?"

Diana scoffed. "I didn't 'beat him up.' I just showed him what he would get for trying to put women in potentially scandalous situations. If women have to protect their reputations then I'll punch those who try to ruin them."

Paulo swung an arm over the back of the couch. "From what Donnie said, you did more than just punch the man."

"That man is a menace. He deserved much more than what he got."

Mother called dinner before they could take the conversation any further. Their small group strode into the dining room, Paulo accompanying Mater and everyone falling in behind. The smells beckoned Penny into her chair.

Serving spoons clanked against the porcelain.

Mater's voice floated over the steaming dishes. "So Penny, your mother tells me you've been looking after your lands while she's been away. I must say, I'm very impressed." She turned back to Mother. "It must be nice having such a responsible child."

Diana viciously stabbed her stuffed eggplant. "Yes, Paulo is most irresponsible. I don't know how you've put up with him for so long."

Paulo quirked a brow. "I wasn't the one knocking heads with members of the nobility."

Mater's eyes sparkled with mirth. "This time."

The courses came and went as quickly as the MacGregors' stories did. Even Mother laughed during Mater's retellings of Paulo and Diana's great escapes from their nursery.

Mother and Mater sat in the corner of the sitting room after dinner, both with contented smiles. Penny passed a tray of *baklava* to the twins. If only Penny could put Mother at such ease. It would make life much simpler.

Paulo sighed wistfully at the dessert. "It's too bad Jenkins took ill so suddenly. He makes the best pastries this side of the Mist."

The name brought the image of a very fashionable man with thick sideburns and a waxed mustache. Penny's brow furrowed. "Isn't Jenkins your valet? What happened to him?"

"We were set to leave the capital, but the night before we left, Jenkins came down with some sort of stomach illness. We had to leave him in the care of the staff in Olympia while we made our way here."

"Are you without a man then? I'm sure Rich would be more than willing to assist you."

Paulo shook his head. "I was able to procure one before we left. It was a stroke of luck really. Jenkins knew him and he was able to accompany us on short notice. He's a bit young, but he's done a fine enough job." He stretched out one of his pristinely polished boots as if checking for scuffs.

"I'm glad. Poor Jenkins, though."

Paulo stood. "I suppose I should make sure all of my belongings made it into my room."

Diana and Mater stood as well.

"Yes," Mater agreed, "it is getting late. We're hoping to take a trip into Eleusia to see Claudia tomorrow."

Penny glanced at the clock. She glanced at it again. There were only forty-five minutes until midnight. She would be hard pressed to make it to the clearing in time to meet with Lou. He'd threatened to make her run extra laps if she were ever late. It was possible the threat was empty, but after hoisting him up a tree, she didn't want to risk it.

After a rushed "goodnight" to their guests, Penny was the

first to leave the room. Sissy would need to come help her out of her dress before Penny could leave to meet with Lou.

"Sweet Gaia, someone looks eager to get into bed," Sissy remarked after Penny practically jumped onto her bed. "Are you feeling well? It's not like you to want to miss out on spending time with your friends."

Penny slowed her movements. "I'm perfectly well, Sissy. I'm just excited to see everyone tomorrow."

Sissy stirred the coals in the fireplace while her skeptical expression grew. "I'm sure."

Penny kept quiet and nestled down into her blankets. Sissy finished her nightly ministrations and closed the door to her own room behind her with a soft *click*.

Minutes passed before Penny heard no sound through the door separating her room from the maid's. She waited, counting the minutes in her head until she reached five. Silently, she crawled out of bed and readjusted some pillows to give the impression that she was buried in her blankets. It would at least fool Sissy if she peeked her head in later in the night.

Penny tiptoed through her dark room, conscious of the crawling feeling working its way up her back. Her steps made no sound as she slid into her dressing room. She changed into her work clothes quickly and found her cloak, her boots, and her small satchel. She stepped out of her closet and stopped.

Someone stood at her desk, their back to her.

Penny jumped back into the dark closet. The air caught in her lungs, but she suppressed all noise. It couldn't be Lou in her rooms. He should be waiting in the clearing. Paulo wouldn't have come in unannounced, especially with her appearance of sleep.

No other sounds came from the direction of her desk. He may have left. Penny stuck her head out into the larger room.

Before she took a full step out of the closet, something pricked her neck.

Her hand flew up to her throat where something protruded from her skin. She yanked it out and held a small dart between her fingers.

Wait, now she was holding three darts. She tried to blink, but her lids felt heavy as the three darts turned back to one and the edges of her vision grew foggy.

A deep voice cursed, and her eyes shot to where four copies of the man stood by her bed. She couldn't yell. She couldn't scream.

Her legs fell out from beneath her, but darkness smothered every sense before her head hit the floor.

"Hart, you idiot... how you got... you could've killed her!"

The words came muffled, broken, into Penny's consciousness. She only heard the fear and anger plainly in Lou's voice. Something tickled at her face and her magic. She couldn't smell the undertones of lilies that usually marked her room. *Why is everything so dark?*

A new voice came into the conversation. "But I didn't. She's still breathing. I'm sure she'll wake up in no time."

"And what if she doesn't? You had enough poison in that dart to knockout a full-grown man. Penelope Barclay is half that size!"

"And that's why I brought her to you! I figured if she didn't wake up, you would know what to do."

Penny's brows drew together. The muscles in her face awoke with her full range of senses. Her eyelids finally opened.

They were in the clearing. Lou's form crouched protectively

in front of her. From what little she could see of his face, it was obvious he was feeling murderous.

Her eyes slowly wandered over to the other man. He was lanky and tall. Possibly taller than Lou. Brown hair haloed his head in a riot of curls made worse by his pulling at them.

Hart's expression was pleading as he looked at Lou. "I swear, I didn't know she was in there. I watched her room to make sure no one else went in before I did. She was supposed to be— it looked like she was asleep! How was I to know she was going to spring out of the closet?"

Lou stood. His hands clenched by his sides and his steps turned predatory. "I swear, if I didn't— if Rissa wasn't so attached to you, I would rip every single—"

Hart's widened eyes met Penny's. "Oh, praise the Goddess. Look! She's awake."

Lou spun and was holding her up faster than what should have been humanly possible. Penny blinked. Apparently the poison in her system was receding slower than she thought.

The gold of Lou's frantic eyes met hers. "Lady Penelope, are you all right? Does anything hurt?" His fingers gently pressed the skin on her neck and she winced. "Sorry. I hope it looks worse than it is."

Penny's eyes widened. "How does it look?"

"Oh, no worse than a bee sting," came Hart's voice from across the clearing. "Should clear up within the next few days."

"Hart, if you don't shut your mouth this instant I will remove it."

Not a peep came from the newcomer's direction.

Penny pushed a brow up, though it took more effort than usual. "Can someone remove another person's mouth?"

Lou's hostile expression softened just a smidge. "I don't know, but right now I'm tempted to try." A smile tugged at the corner of his mouth. If her limbs had any strength to them, she might have reached out to touch it.

"He poisoned me?"

The thunderous look returned and his hold on her tightened. "Yes, the stupid fool. He claims he was scoping out the house and you spooked him. Unfortunately, he's a shoot first, ask questions later kind of operative."

Her fingers tingled unpleasantly, but the complaint never passed her lips. His arms still held her as softly as his gaze did. Their breaths mingled in the inches between them.

He'd been concerned for her. He'd threatened another person just for hurting her. He wanted her safe. Her chest warmed. If her mind wasn't so muddled, she would have devised a way to get him to kiss her. Right then, she wanted him to. Badly.

His eyes broke away from hers to look behind him. She would have objected if the other person in their clearing hadn't caught her attention.

Hart had moved and was now hanging from one of the thick branches. It was difficult to tell, but he seemed to be assessing the sturdiness of the branch rather than attempting to pass the time.

Odd.

"Get over here and make introductions like a proper gentleman," Lou called to him.

Hart swung off the branch with a flip.

"Show off," muttered Lou.

Penny almost chuckled.

Hart stopped near where Penny still lay partially on the ground and partially in Lou's arms. He gave a flourishing bow and his face came into view. He was much younger than Penny would have guessed, eighteen at the most. Dark freckles smattered his entire face and large brown eyes widened between thick lashes.

"I am so sorry, Lady Penelope. I truly didn't mean for any of this—"

"She likely needs to know who you are before she can accept an apology."

"Oh, right." Hart stuck his hand out and pulled it back again. "I'm Hart Carys." He gave another awkward bow.

"I believe we've met before, Mr. Carys."

Hart bobbed his head. "You'd be right, Lady Penelope, though I'm surprised you remember. We only saw each other for a second."

"I suppose it was a very impressionable second." She gave him what she hoped was a comfortable smile even if at the moment her thoughts rioted. "It would be a very likely assumption that you work with Lou for the Lord of the Underworld."

"You'd be right. I'm the Lord of the Underworld's master sharpshooter."

Penny's brows rose. Her gaze turned to Lou for an answer, but his attention remained on the other spy. "What does a sharpshooter do exactly?"

Hart straightened and pulled a tube from his sleeve. From one of the many pockets on his vest, he withdrew a small dart like the one he'd shot her with. "I shoot stuff. Darts, arrows, pretty much any projectile. Crossbows are my specialty, but I can make anything work. I got to use a trebuchet once—"

"He has a gift, though not any kind a mage could claim. His fae blood heightens his senses and he uses them to make some impossible shots."

The fae blood explained Hart's build. He must have been several generations descended from a full fae though if he hadn't inherited any of the vibrant coloring.

"How did a master sharpshooter come to be in my bedroom in the middle of the night? How did you even get in the house?" After the kidnapping incident and the fires, the house's security had grown impeccable.

"I snuck in as the new valet to Lord MacGregor."

Penny's eyes narrowed. "You wouldn't have had anything to do with Jenkin's stomach illness now, did you?"

A grimace stretched across his face. "Rissa received information and sent me to deliver it. While I didn't have anything to do with Jenkin's illness, I can't say I was unaware of it. I had to get planted in the MacGregors' entourage somehow." He pulled a slip of paper from one of his many pockets and handed it to Lou.

Lou's deft fingers flipped open the folded note. Like Penny's letters to Angelica, the note was in some kind of code to which Penny didn't know the key.

"Do you know where the town of Chthonia is located?" he asked her.

Finally, something she could actually help with. "Yes. It sits right on the border of the duchy, south of the manor. It's quite large." Mother had taken her there a number of times growing up.

"Rissa says it's the rebel's biggest success. They've begun recruiting the townsfolk in droves. Apparently, they've set up a big stage right in the middle of the town square."

Penny looked between both of the men. "When do we leave?"

21

PLATFORMS AND PLATITUDES

The moon shone brightly over Chthonia, but the silver light washed out in the glare of the torches burning in the main square. The gentle crash of the surf beneath the cliffs bordering the town could be heard above the rumble of voices. People streamed through the streets, even as the stars danced above them.

Penny was feeling the full day's ride in her legs as she wove through the town, Lou at her side.

It had been pure luck that Mother had gone with the MacGregors' to Eleusia that morning. Penny had barely gotten out of it by pleading that she couldn't leave during pollination. Mother had looked shocked and— Penny prayed it was more than a fleeting emotion— proud. Paulo had sent word they wouldn't be back until the day after tomorrow. Lou had thought it best to use the time productively.

Penny's cloak covered most of her face, but did little to hinder her view. Bunched, wood and daub houses lined the square as Penny followed Lou through the crowd. A murmuring mob stood assembled at the base of a large platform. A man stood over the crowd gesticulating wildly. The words were incoherent until they made it farther into the crowd.

"What those abominations preach at the capital is hogwash! There is no such thing as *equality* when it comes to those with tarnished souls. Everything comes at a price and those monsters gave up the perfect souls Gaia gave them to be tainted by unnatural powers. They're demons, biding their time until we are complacent enough to be willing slaves again!"

The people in the crowd whispered to one another, each grappling with the man's vitriol. Lou grabbed hold of Penny's wrist and guided her toward the edge of the square. The flickering light of flames cast menacing shadows on the faces around her. Penny pulled her hood farther down.

Lou turned to whisper in her ear. "If this becomes too hostile we'll head back to the horses."

He looked to Penny for a response, but all she could manage was a nod. The resolve on the faces around her weakened her own.

"We cannot let their kind continue to spread across our shores. Even now, a *mage* waits to be crowned king over our fair kingdom. Who's to say he won't use his powers over the weather to bind us to his will? Threaten our livelihoods, our families, our loved ones?" The man gestured toward the crowd around them. "The untainted folk are more vast than those with so-called *gifts*. Bronties are the ones who ought to be in charge. We should be the ones who decide when and where these monsters can use their gifts, not some group of power-hungry devils!"

A large portion of the crowd cheered and threw up their hands in agreement. Penny's insides twisted. It was worse than she'd feared.

She lifted her hood to look at Lou. His face tightened more and more as the man continued his slander. His eyes burned with more than the torchlight as they continued to listen.

"The Cartographer has answered our call, brothers and sisters. He has heard your cries and the cries of those who came before you. *Justice* demands to be served and The Cartographer is here as her right hand. No longer will we be left to clean up the filth left by magic users. No longer will the injustices of the past be left to collect dust while those guilty of doing wrong walk free. No longer will our women and our children be left destitute while those with filth in their blood gorge themselves on the fruits of our labors. It is time for those with power to serve those who need it most. It is time for them to feel the chains of destitution and powerlessness. We will rise, we will fight, and we will be victorious!"

The voices of desperation roared through the square. Penny's heart skittered in her chest at the picture this man painted. She'd never seen people so hungry for the downfall of others. She never realized what real anger, pain, or heartache could do to a person, and what they could in turn be persuaded to do to others. Where would it end? If these people accomplished what they preached, wouldn't the vicious cycle just continue? They couldn't perform the same action over and over again and expect a different result. That would be insanity — and Penny was looking it right in the face.

The rebel opened his arms. "We want to invite all to join with us as we create a new Olympia. All those that have been living in squalor will thrive in the new world we have created."

She was sick of The Cartographer.

She was sick of the lies and the poison these men spread with every word.

"And who is The Cartographer to make such promises?" Her voice came out louder than she had intended, hushing the whispers around them. She met the eyes of the few around her. "How could you possibly trust a man who works in back alleys and won't even give you his real name?"

The whispers started back up, doubt creeping into the few faces around her.

The man looked around, obviously hearing the whispers her words had sparked within the crowd. "The Cartographer isn't simply one man. He is all of us. With him as our guide, we will recreate the maps of this world into something greater, more powerful, than anyone has ever seen!"

Her eyes shifted from face to face, from man to woman, and she could see the glint of desperation and the weariness of hardship in their eyes. Many of the women held children on their hips and sleepy heads tucked under their chins. They deserved a happy life for their children. Her spine straightened. No one should be allowed to use that against them.

But when would it stop? After so many years of persecution under one tyrant, shouldn't they recognize when another has come to fill the gap? Crown Prince Dion and the Crown's Council worked tirelessly to help bring peace to this land, but so far from the capital, these people had yet to see it. It wasn't fair. It wasn't fair that they had to resort to prejudice and hypocrisy to feel like they could better their lives.

And Penny was tired of watching these rebels browbeat them into it.

Lou hissed as she slipped out of his grip. His tutelage had enhanced her agility and she easily wove through the bodies gathered around her. She couldn't stop. Mother would've never even let that man get on the stage. Penny could fix this. These were her people. They were good people.

Penny strode to the side of the platform. Her pulse throbbed and her hands shook as she faced the angry expressions of the rebels. Their thoughts were written there plainly.

Who did she think she was? If this went sideways, they could take her down easily. If she made one wrong move she might never leave this square.

But if she didn't do this, how many of these people would die for a cause they truly didn't want?

She took a deep breath. "You claim The Cartographer is to bring about great change and prosperity for those that have suffered. All I see before me is a man who is repeating the same mistakes made by those who stood on the other side of the line." A few shouts rang out and a small group jostled to the side of the stage. Her heart lodged in her throat as a few of the townsfolk quieted them.

He waved her off. "You obviously don't know what's going on here. Step away from the stage."

Penny gripped the front of her cloak. If they knew who she was, they may be angrier. If Mother found out. . . maybe she could find pride in a daughter who stands up for her people.

"I do know what's going on here. You are trying to turn these people towards violence and hatred because they've been hurt in the past."

"How would a scrap of a girl like you know? You're not old enough to have any experience with hardships."

She pointed toward the crowd behind her. "Tell that to the mothers that hold those children. Tell those small, tired eyes that they don't know hardship. Tell them that because they're young, they are too inexperienced to know right from wrong."

Shouts rang out over the square. The mothers and fathers turned to her side, the rebel's ignorant words turning their anger against him.

Fear left Penny as resolution took hold. She turned to face the crowd now huddled around her. "We are all Gaia's children. All of us have been given our own gifts, talents, and skills. I can't judge a person to be better than another simply because of where they came from or who their parents were. If we're to hold everyone accountable for what their ancestors did, how are we any better than them? When will it be enough? When will the fighting stop? If we believe what this Cartographer preaches, we'll be no better than what we are fighting against."

The crowd's murmurs had grown and many of the women were now looking at her instead of The Cartographer's man. One of the children she noticed played with a charm around his neck. A fae healing charm.

She was as far into this as she could possibly be. If the townspeople were going to turn against her, they would have already. She mounted the steps to the platform and stood opposite the rebel. "I know many of you have been on the receiving end of gifts this man claims are abominations. Eleusion provides more food for our country than any other land and it is because of the magic, because of the family who has been its caretakers for so many generations, that it has continued to thrive. This duchy should take pride in the fact that their Lady has gifts such as hers and provides so much for so many."

"Hear, hear!" shouted a few in the crowd. Others sent scornful looks her way.

"Magic that is only passed down to the Barclays," someone in the crowd called out. "Why should their crops be the only ones that are grown with magic?"

Penny took a step back. Getting on the platform hadn't been a good idea. She wouldn't be able to slip out of the crowd if something went wrong. She should have stuck to the shadows with Lou. Her eyes darted around, looking for his very intimidating figure, but landed on the parting crowd.

An elderly woman shoved her way toward the front. "The young lady is right," she addressed the crowd with a husky voice. "Lady Barclay's done much for this land, along with many others who have been gifted by Gaia. None of us old folk have forgotten when that case of winter sickness swept through twenty years ago and the only thing to stop it were the mages and their healing magic. Most of us wouldn't be standing here if it weren't for their kind."

More of the crowd agreed as the matronly woman came to stand beside Penny.

"We can't forget about the weather mages either," called a man from the back. The crowd parted and the middle-aged man staggered on to the stand beside them. "Our town was on the path to destruction a few years back when that storm came in from the coast. It's because of the mages that it was stopped before it reached the cliffs. Some of them were seriously injured keeping that thing from harming us and the rest of Olympia."

The crowd grew louder as more and more of the townsfolk began swapping stories. Penny's heart warmed as she saw the change ripple across the features of the people before her. Though their thoughts had been hardened by the words of the rebels, their hearts still remember those that had shown them kindness in their adversity.

"Yes, magic has it's uses," hollered the man on the stage, "but if only the evil wield it, only evil will become of it."

"There is good in all of us," Penny retaliated, "mage or bronty or fair folk. We are all children of Gaia and She looks down with love on all of us." She stood at the edge of the platform. "What these men have come to do is turn you away from the path of greatness. Our kingdom is noble. Our Crown Prince has done more honorable deeds in the short time he and his brothers have ruled than their giftless father did his entire life. Do not allow these men to stir you to anger, but remember what great work the rulers of our kingdom have accomplished in the name of freedom from hate."

The crowd turned inward on itself. It was easy to see who believed in the rebel's cause and who didn't. A group of older gentlemen made their way to the front, holding off rebel sympathizers with farming tools and old swords. A few of the townsfolk broke through and joined The Cartographer's men on the stage.

"*You*," the preaching rebel sneered. He shook a vicious finger at her, his face purple with rage. A group of men came and encircled him, brandishing swords toward the crowd. "You are going to regret this."

Penny clenched her hands into fists to stop their shaking and looked down her nose in the best impersonation of Mother she could manage. "No, I don't think I will."

The men down below began thrusting their impromptu weapons and the men fled from the stage. When the majority of the townsfolk sent the rebels and their sympathizers packing, the crowd gave a cheer. Penny's spirit sang along with them. There was goodness in this kingdom.

Standing on tiptoe, she looked over every face in the crowd. Hundreds of eyes looked back, but none in amber. Penny's search stalled when she noticed the tall figure standing at the back of the crowd.

Rich stood between two buildings, the sharp planes of his face gaunt in the firelight.

Penny stepped off of the stage. Why was he there? She had to tell him not to tell Mother. She walked toward where he stood.

A hand settled on her back and she jumped. Lou's amber eyes found hers and she sagged in relief.

"I recognized someone in the crowd. I need to speak with him." She pulled him toward where Rich had been standing.

"What?"

"I saw our steward. He was near the back."

Lou halted their progress. “Lady Penelope, most of the rebels were standing at the back of the crowd.”

Her thoughts stilled. Rich had been standing with the rebels? Penny walked over to the small fountain standing a few paces from them. She stepped up and her gaze landed on the empty wall where Rich had been standing.

Lou pulled her off of the fountain hastily. “Don’t stand where everyone can see you. We don’t know how many more rebels remain in the crowd.”

“It doesn’t matter.” Penny tugged her hood down over her face. “He’s gone.”

“There you are.”

Penny spun to where the voice came from. She had to peek around Lou who had stepped between them. The older woman who had addressed the crowd came and took hold of Penny’s hands without even looking at Lou. “Thank you, miss. The moment I saw those men come into town, I knew they brought nothing but trouble. Your words helped remind those here that we live in good times and the magic folk do more good than harm most days.”

Heat rose into Penny’s cheeks and she squeezed the woman’s hands in her own. She peeked out from under her hood. “I’d never have convinced them to change their minds if you hadn’t spoken up. A stranger telling them what to believe? I would have been just like the man standing here.”

“But you aren’t a stranger are you, Lady Penelope?”

The heat left her face. She choked on the lie before she spoke. “I don’t know what you’re talking about.”

The elderly lady smiled, her crow’s feet growing at the corners of her eyes. “Forgive me, my lady, but you are the spitting image of your mother at this age.” She caressed the end of Penny’s braid dangling out from her hood. “No one else has hair that color nor the intense green of your eyes. I’m sure I wasn't the only one here who realized who you were the moment you stood up to that man." Penny's eyes widened as she looked around the square, at the people still watching her. *Oh dear.* She prayed none of the rebels had recognized her. Who knew what they would do in retaliation?

The woman's hands tightened around Penny's. "Most folk here have lived under the Barclay s for a long time and have great devotion to your family. We certainly made a bad impression of that to your handsome friend here."

Scalding was too light a word to describe the heat that overcame Penny's face. She snatched her hands back from the woman to ward off her words. "Oh it's certainly not— I mean he isn't— Well, yes, he's handsome, but I don't think of him like that. I mean, of course I appreciate handsomeness, but I wouldn't consider him my 'handsome friend.' I mean he *is* handsome and he *is* my friend..." Penny covered her face with her hands. "Oh Sweet Gaia, make it stop," she mumbled through her fingers.

The woman gave a husky laugh and Penny tried to smother the embarrassment from her cheeks with her palms. She finally looked to find the woman smiling, but not at her. Penny turned to find Lou's cheeks with the same pink spreading from ear to ear. His eyes flicked to hers and she turned as fast as she could to avoid meeting his gaze.

"You take care of our girl, you hear? She's one of the greatest treasures this land has to offer. We won't tolerate any harm coming to her."

Penny turned to see Lou give the woman a short bow. His eyes, however, were glued to Penny's. "You have my word."

The words only increased the pounding of Penny's heart. With the grin still on her cheeks, the woman swept back into the crowd, calling for the men to follow the rebels now fading from view.

Penny glanced at Lou, not quite able to meet his eyes again. "I suppose we should be getting back."

Lou straightened and cleared his throat. "Yes, of course." He gallantly offered his arm to her, and she couldn't hold back the deepening blush.

They walked through the waves of people returning to their homes for the night. The dark, angry atmosphere of the town had morphed into something light and liberating. Penny could see it in the way the folks laughed and the lack of aggression in their steps, as if they were happy just to be walking under the stars.

Lou pulled Penny through the last bit of town and out into the dark night. Clouds had gathered over the sky in the short time it took them to walk through town, casting the moon in darkness and blocking the stars from looking down on them. Penny knew the small grove of trees where they had tied up the horses wasn't far, but darkness crept along the ground and up Penny's arms. When they made it to the first section of trees, a rabbit jumped out of the brush, making her jolt.

"You don't need to be afraid. The rebels wouldn't dare touch you out here."

Penny looked up at Lou, the only spot of brightness in view. She couldn't help the small smile. "It's not that." He looked at her quizzically and Penny's eyes narrowed. "What?"

He stopped and turned to face her fully. "Why do you look so afraid?"

Penny swallowed. "Because I am a little afraid, though not of those thugs. I simply don't enjoy the dark."

Lou's eyes widened. "You're afraid of the dark?"

Penny grimaced and looked at her dusty boots. "I know it's a rather juvenile fear, but I've always felt uncomfortable in the dark. It was worse when I was younger, and I thought I had overcome it… until I was taken in Eleusia." She straightened and looked him in the eye. “I promise not to allow it to affect the mission. I can overcome it, it’s just uncomfortable.”

Lou’s expression softened. “Lady Penelope, I would hope to help you through your discomfort rather than simply have you get over it. I may not relate to such a fear, but everyone has their own ghosts.”

“What are you afraid of, Lou?” She asked the question in jest, but discovered a need to know the answer.

A sad smile settled on his lips as his gaze grew intense. “A great many things, Lady Penelope.” He glanced back the way they came. “A great many things.”

22

DUCHESS AND DISCORD

Dearest Penny,

You did WHAT? Where is my Penny that stays at the manor like a perfect doll and doesn't do anything that could potentially upset her mother? Are you ever going to tell her? I would have been absolutely terrified. I'm glad to hear the rebels didn't throw you right off the stage. You're so brave. I'm so proud of you and the woman you've become in the last few months. Who would have thought you would be the one trying to change the world?

You asked for extensive details, so here they are. Spring is a waking dream! A city in the trees, a wonder of architecture and agriculture. The ellylon grow the branches together to create bridges from trunk to trunk. They mold the trunks to form buildings. The palace itself is the biggest tree I've ever seen and they say the Crann Mòr is three times as big. Perhaps we will have to visit when the courts meet with the High Queen at solstice. There are even tiny farms growing on the branches. They grow the strangest looking fruits. I even saw pomegranates the same blue as my sapphire dress. So bizarre!

They have every kind of flora growing everywhere. We saw every kind of plant on our ride into their capital. The fae themselves walk about with flowers in their hair and covering their clothing. The pixies wear the flowers themselves. Oh, Penny, you would be in heaven! I so wish you could see it for yourself.

We will be meeting with some of the fae ambassadors here since Spring is the High Queen's territory. Maybe, we'll even see her! I'll do my best to send more letters. I can't wait to see what the rest of Spring has in store.

Your Very Excited Friend,
Angelica

"What on Gaia's green earth were you possibly thinking?"

Mother's voice neared screeching. Penny hugged her arms across her stomach, hoping to shrink into the small chair before Mother's desk. Rich hadn't returned back to the house. Mother claimed he was on an errand that would take several days. Relief had eased Penny's worries as days had passed and between all of the things he had sent to Mother, not one had mentioned Penny's presence in Chthonia. Perhaps he hadn't recognized her under the hood from so far away.

Penny had been summoned to the study that morning, thinking it was about the harvest, only to find Mother pacing back and forth with a note in hand. From there, Mother had interrogated her about the rebels in Chthonia three nights before, and the truth had spilled from Penny's lips.

"I don't understand why you're so upset," Penny said in a small voice, as if speaking to a spooked horse. "I thought you would approve of me going to defend our people from this rebellion you've been working at such lengths to eradicate." Although, now that Penny thought about it, she hadn't heard Mother actually say what she was doing to get rid of the rebels.

"You know perfectly well why I'm upset, young lady." Mother's glare could have shriveled a great oak. "Anything could have happened to you. *Anything.* I thought after what happened in Eleusia you would understand, but then you go off and do something like this!" She brandished the note in her hand like a sword.

"It's because of what happened in Eleusia that I did it." Penny tried to keep her voice from rising to the same level, tried to keep her temper from rising there too. "I need to do something to stop it from happening again. Helping those townsfolk, exposing the rebels' lies, it helped."

"You think just because you saved one little town that those men are going to disappear? Absolutely not!" Mother slammed the note on the desk and leaned overtop the piles of paperwork scattered across it. "Men like them will always be out there, always waiting to snatch young women like you away from their lives, their families."

"Mother, if we can get rid of the rebels then our people will be safer. Olympia will be safer."

"This isn't about Olympia, this is about *you*. You got it into that fantastical head of yours that facing a group of criminals on your own in the middle of the night was going to prove something. What if they recognized you? Do you know what could have happened?"

"Yes!" Penny's temper snapped and she stood from her chair, mirroring Mother's stance. "I know exactly what could have happened because it already did— and it didn't happen in the middle of the night, under the cloak of darkness. It was on a busy street, with people walking under streetlights. If anyone knows what could happen, it's me. I've seen what lurks in the shadows. Their faces still jeer at me at night, but I knew if I was ever to stop them I had to take a stand. I had to decide to stop being afraid and face the darkness and I did."

"And it could have happened all over again!" Mother's voice rose. "Not only could the rebels retaliate if they knew who you were, but any of the men in that village could have followed you home and taken advantage of the situation in any way they liked."

Penny nearly shrieked, ready to start pulling the hair from her head. How could Mother be more worried about the townspeople she had grown up around than the rebels burning down farmland? "I'm not talking about the men of the village, Mother. I am talking about The Cartographer's men."

"It doesn't matter what men we are talking about. Any number of them could have taken a young woman in the dark of night."

Penny huffed. "I wasn't going to be taken by any of the men from that village. Most of them made sure I was safe on the road home." She wouldn't confess she hadn't been alone. It would be worse if Mother found out she had gone with a man rather than by herself.

Her eyes narrowed at Mother's furious face. "Why are you

so obsessed with seeing men as something evil, a big bad entity with the sole thought of taking advantage of women? Not all men are like that."

"And how would you know?" snapped Mother. "How could you even say that after you were taken?"

"I wasn't taken because I was a woman. I was taken because I was a *mage*. Because I was a Barclay. I was taken because that field worker held a grudge and decided the best way to get revenge was to use the rebels. It had nothing to do with me being female."

"You may think that, but I'm certain your magic was not the only thing on their minds."

Penny's mouth fell open. "How? How can you say such things like you know? I don't understand why every member of the male gender has to be solely thinking about taking advantage of a woman. I know good men. We have good men who work for us. You've never had a problem with me working with a single man under our charge. Why can't others be like them?"

Mother let out a dark laugh. "You think I don't have every one of those men bound before they even take foot on those fields?"

Penny's thoughts came to a screeching halt. "'Bound?' What does that mean?"

Mother sighed. "Every one of our workers agree to a geas. I actually reached out to Farrah and her family to come up with the wording and make the charm for it. Every man on this farm is bound to not cause anyone here any harm. . . especially you."

Penny slumped back into her chair, speechless. A faerie charm. Mother had made those men swear a geas. A binding promise. Magic dictated their actions, not their sense of right or wrong. Had Penny been so easily fooled?

"For how long?" Penny mumbled.

"What?" Mother snapped.

Penny's eyes narrowed. "How long have you been making the workers take an oath? How long have they had their decisions taken from them?"

"I've done it since you were no older than three."

"All this time. Every worker I've ever met has been under your complete control." If Mother had kept something as big as this from her, what else was she hiding?

"You think they're giving up their entire will to me?" Mother nearly snorted. "It's not so dire as that, Penny. They simply lose their will to do us harm."

"And where was that binding when Martin decided to use his connections with the rebels to get back at me?"

Mother sat in her own chair across the desk from Penny. She pinched the bridge of her nose between two fingers, trying to rub away the strain of the conversation. "That was a mistake in the wording, I suppose. They're only under a geas so long as they are hired as workers. The moment you released him from service, you released him from the binding as well. I suppose I should ask Farrah to rework the charm—"

"No." Mother lifted a brow. Penny straightened in her chair. "It's cruel to take away the chance those workers have to prove themselves. If we have to bind the people who we have charge over, we are no better than what The Cartographer says we are."

"Penny, it's not such a harsh request. Those that work for us agree to it willingly." She flicked her hand as if it could swat away Penny's concern. "Besides, I don't discriminate as the rebels do. I make every person who comes to work for us swear the oath, bronty or not."

How could she not see what she was doing? "That doesn't make it right. It's still wrong to bind peoples' wills to your own."

"This is ridiculous, Penny." Mother threw her hands in the air. "I'm simply looking out for everyone here. You cannot expect me to allow people close who would do us harm."

"That's what we have Aaron for. He sees to that and keeps an eye on everything. You've trusted him over any other for all of my life, but you don't trust him to find good people? It needs to stop, Mother. This all needs to stop."

Mother studied Penny. Penny's heart raced in her chest as Mother's eyes narrowed and her lips puckered in disapproval. Penny knew, from the expression alone, Mother would not give it up. Deep roots of injustice simmered through Penny.

"Penny," Mother sighed again, "you're still so young. You haven't had to be part of the world I have lived in."

"And whose fault is that?" Penny snapped as she leaned over the desk toward Mother. "I can't learn if you don't allow me to take a single step out of the duchy. I know there's more to this world than pomegranates and evil men. I want to see it, Mother, and not just from this duchy. I want to experience it for myself."

Mother's eyes contained a thunderhead. "Go ahead. Blame me all you like, but your words only prove that I've made the right decision. You know nothing of what this world is like."

"I've seen more in the last few weeks than I have in my entire life." Penny felt her own storm brewing in her expression. "Being taken, going to that rebel meeting, all of it has helped me see the world for what it really is, and I have yet to find anything so terrible that I must run away and hide. Life isn't meant to be lived within the confines of a single manor."

"You've seen some rebels and now you think you ought to go off adventuring?" If Mother was not a noble lady, Penny believed she would have spat the words in her face. "This isn't one of your silly novels, Penny. There are no white knights. There are no holy quests. There is no such thing as true love.

This world is dark. It's selfish and cruel. Only the ones who take matters into their own hands survive. You're not ready to see the world as I have."

Blood roared in Penny's ears as the two of them stared at one another, breaths ragged and eyes flashing. Mother's rules had always chafed, but now they seared Penny's very soul. Mother's words crushed Penny, more than she ever thought they could.

Penny slowly rose from her chair and turned toward the study's door. Mother wouldn't call her back. She would view Penny leaving as a surrender. It nearly felt like one, but Penny knew when to retreat so she could live to fight another day. If this conversation continued, there would be more harm done than either of them really wanted.

As Penny's fingers wrapped around the doorknob, she turned to speak over her shoulder. "I know you don't believe this world has any good left in it, but I do, and there's nothing that will stop me from trying to prove it to you."

23

STEALTH AND STEEL

Penny peeked her head out her window to make sure no one stood below before unraveling the long length of rope onto the moonlit walkway. She grabbed her sturdy pair of leather gloves and wrapped a length of rope around her waist. Her arms strained as she tugged to make sure the rope was securely fastened to her four-poster bed. She slipped the magelight on the windowsill into her pocket before sliding out into the dark.

Every night after Mother had received word that Penny had gone to Chthonia, someone from the household staff stood sentry outside her door. The first night Penny had tried to leave her rooms before midnight, she'd immediately stopped upon finding one of the maids on a stool in the hall. Mother had nearly exploded when she confronted Penny the next morning.

"After the talk we had yesterday, you think I'm just going to let you walk right out of the house and back into the rebels' arms? Think again. Someone will remain outside your door every night until I can trust you to not run off like a thief in the dark."

When Penny had met up with Lou in the orchard later that

day, she asked him to train her to climb out her window. At first, he was completely against it, but Penny persuaded him to help her.

Now here she was, rappelling down the side of Barclay Manor like a literal thief for the second week in a row. When her feet touched the ground, she pulled the rope to the side of the sill. While the vines growing outside her window weren't sturdy enough to hold her, they did a marvelous job concealing the length of rope against the bricks of the manor.

The manor itself tired her now. Mother put a stop to any talk of rebellion, brushing it under the rug and snapping at Penny anytime she brought it up. Penny couldn't wrap her head around why Mother was acting so strangely.

"I don't understand why you can't just thicken the vines by your window enough to climb down."

Penny only slightly jumped at the voice and she turned to find Lou standing a few steps away. She placed a hand over her erratic heart. "Don't frighten me like that." She took in a gulp of air. "If I use my magic out here, my mother will likely feel it from her room."

Lou looked curiously toward Penny's open window. "How far does her awareness reach?"

Penny tucked her leather gloves in the vines. "Not very far. It's dampened by the stone of the house. If she were on the field, she would feel it a couple of acres away."

"Remarkable." His eyes moved from the wall back to her. "We really should talk about continuing your training."

Not again. Penny moved to walk toward the clearing. "I already told you, I don't care what my mother says. This is something I have to do."

His hand wrapped around her upper arm, halting her steps. "I understand that, but is it worth damaging the relationship you have with her?"

She pulled her arm out of his grasp. "You don't understand."

"I bet I understand more than you think I do."

"No, you don't." She whirled on him. "If it wasn't fighting against rebels, it was always going to be something else. I love my mother, I really do, but she has a tendency to be blinded by her own opinions and paranoia. If I want anything to change, I have to change it myself." There was something going on at Barclay Manor and she was going to get to the bottom of it.

His expression was as guarded as always, but his eyes held the tumult of indecision. She understood his position. It was likely difficult going against someone holding so much authority when you'd trained your whole life to take orders.

He tilted his head toward where she hid her climbing supplies. "Bring the gloves."

Penny cleared her throat and grabbed the gloves out of the tangle of vines. She tucked them into the pocket of her skirt and followed Lou. They walked side by side toward their practice ring, Lou's steps silent and Penny's a little less quiet. Penny waited for Lou to rebuke her, but perhaps she'd improved because he kept any comments to himself.

They came to the clearing where they once again began going through the motions of the *cumadh*. In the weeks following the rebel meeting, Penny had learned three more intricate forms of the martial art as well as some of the offensive maneuvers.

They moved on to sparring where Penny, unfortunately, hadn't improved as much as she would have liked. Lou continued to easily beat her in every round, but Penny had learned a lot. She learned about different muscles and where those muscles had sensitive spots. She learned about nerve points and where to apply pressure to weaken an opponent. They had even begun using thick branches as mock weapons during some of their sparring sessions. Penny would never admit it, but she hated those the most. It was ridiculous the amount of bruises she went home with. They mocked her with her inadequacy.

"Put on the gloves," said Lou. "I think they will help smother your tell."

"My tell?" Penny scrunched her nose.

Lou gave her an odd look. He blinked a few times and shook his head. "Yes, your mage tell. The glow of your hands."

Penny shook her head at herself internally. "Of course." She thrust her hands into the gloves, smothering the light of her gift which allowed her to use it more secretively.

Her favorite piece of training came when Lou allowed her to use her gift in correlation with sparring. Using the plants around her, she was able to see more and process things faster. Branches bent silently away from her as she ran through the trees. Blades of grass straightened to hide her footsteps and moss quieted them. Her ability to influence the flora around her changed the way she saw her training.

When they had first started with her gift, it had been difficult. Her ability to multitask was strained in the initial days and sometimes her mind and magic wore out much faster than her body. She'd needed extra servings of Farrah's tea to compensate for the drain. As the days passed, however, it had become second nature to use her gift the moment she came into contact with the clearing rather than reaching for it every time she wanted to use it. Instead of trudging through the underbr` ush and waiting to walk into low hanging branches, she wove through the trunks as if they were all in an elegant dance and everything around her knew the steps.

When she made her fifth lap around the clearing, she ran back to the center where Lou waited. "You are getting much faster," he commented. "A few more weeks and you'll be running through these trees faster than a rabbit."

Penny grinned. "Using my powers has certainly improved things. I can't believe I never thought to use my gift in such a way. It would have saved me from quite a few headaches." She held up her hands. "And the gloves were a brilliant idea."

"I don't know why I didn't think of them earlier. It was a simple solution and now we can avoid your tell being a beacon to those we are working against."

Penny frowned and looked at her palms. The leather of the gloves was cracked and thinning in places. "Yes. Though I'll likely have to get more with all the rappelling and sparring I will be doing."

Lou remained quiet, causing Penny to look up at him. His face became the image of concern. "You don't think the duchess will lift your house arrest anytime soon?"

Penny sighed and began fiddling with blades of grass with the toe of her boot. "Unfortunately, no. Two weeks and she still doesn't trust me. We've barely spoken a word to one another without there being some kind of disagreement after." The ache that had grown in her chest throbbed at the thought. Tears lined her eyes, but she blinked them back before they fell. "I just don't understand it. We've never been at such odds with one another."

Lou's feet came into view close to her own. "I won't say what your mother is doing is for your own good. I know there's a certain point where people should be responsible for their own actions and I believe you're already there, Lady Penelope." He took a step closer and Penny looked up to meet his understanding gaze. "However, I also know that the people we love may do questionable things when they are trying to protect us from something. I have no idea why my family does some of the things they do, but I know they have good hearts and I know they'll always have my back when I need them."

Penny let out a small breath, her lungs stiff in his proximity. "I know that she loves me. I will never doubt that. I just don't agree with her methods of showing it."

"I think most children have a hard time agreeing with their parents every once in a while." Penny quirked an eyebrow and Lou's eyes widened. "Not saying that I think you are a child, Lady Penelope."

"I would think not since we are somewhat close in age. If you were to call me one, the same could be said about you."

Lou smiled. "I suppose you would be right."

Penny loved his smile. His true smile. It lit up his honey-colored eyes and revealed how young he really was. She didn't get to see it as often as she liked, but when she did it made her insides flip. It was an honest smile, and she needed a little more honesty in her life.

Lou cleared his throat and looked over the treetops. She'd been staring. Her cheeks burned. She glanced away and noticed how far the moon had made it across the sky.

"I should get going." She jerked her thumb in the direction of the house and Lou gave her a small nod. "I'll see you at the west orchard at sunrise, right?"

"Yes, of course. Oh!" Lou jogged over to where a satchel Penny hadn't noticed hung on a branch. "Rissa came through after supper and brought you these." He pulled a large bundle of cloth out of the bag and set it in Penny's hands. She unwrapped the fabric to reveal two small daggers.

The steel glimmered in the shine from Lou's magelight. The double-edged blades met a small cross guard in the shape of curling leaves. The grips were wrapped in a burgundy-dyed leather, making the daggers easy to hold. When Penny's eyes landed on the pommels of the blades she felt her tears creep back up.

"Pomegranates," she breathed.

"It simply couldn't be helped." Lou let out a slight chuckle. "Heff has such a creative mind and when Rissa mentioned who the blades were for, his artistic side took over. He doesn't often get the opportunity to work on something like this for anyone other than his wife. They may look pretty, but I assure you they are very functional. We can begin working with them tomorrow."

Penny dragged her eyes away from the daggers to look at Lou's face. His cheeks flushed slightly and his expression was rather stoic with what Penny had begun calling his "commander face," but Penny could see the glimmer of hope in his eyes.

"I love them," she said in response to that glimmer. "I've never owned anything like these before. Thank you."

Lou's relieved smile grew as radiant as the stars behind him. "You're quite welcome, Lady Penelope. There are also leather sheaths in the cloth, one for a belt and another for the inside of your boot. We can ask Rissa for tips on other sheathes as it will not always be possible to wear a belt or boots. It is best to have a weapon on you if you can help it."

Penny couldn't withhold the urge. With the bundle of cloth in one hand, she threw her arms around her friend. After receiving such a gift, she couldn't think of him as anything less. Lou stiffened, but she didn't let go even as she felt the tears trail down the dust on her cheeks, the salt mingling with the smell of earth and leather emanating from him.

"You have no idea what this means to me," she whispered as he tentatively wrapped his own arms around her. "I'll never be able to express my gratitude to you, Lou. I know that I can trust you to be honest with me and trust you to help me. I know it's probably wrong to say, but I'm glad the rebels came to Eleusia if only because I had the chance to meet you." She pressed her lips to his cheek. "Thank you."

Penny finally released him. His eyes were wide as his hand slowly came to where her lips had touched his skin.

Her face burned and she rewrapped her gift in their cloth. *Did I really just kiss him?* She touched her own lips. Did a peck on the cheek count as a kiss?

After she bid him a hasty goodnight and turned to walk away, she noticed his eyes didn't hold the same happiness his smile did. As she walked, she tried to pinpoint what emotion rested in his gaze. It wasn't until she was back in her room, tucked into her blankets, that she realized what she had seen.

It was sadness.

24

WANTING AND WAITING

Dearest Penny,

He gave you knives? I don't know any man who has given the woman he adores knives, but to each their own I suppose. They are far more useful than flowers that's for sure. And you kissed him! A peck on the cheek is as good as telling him you care about him. It's a good start! I wish I would have been there. I would've painted the scene to give you on your wedding day. I'd name it "An Exchange of Hearts" or something just as corny.

I can't believe your mother found out about your rebel meeting. Wouldn't she have done the same thing? And now she's put you on house arrest. I can't even imagine my father doing something like that. He would just wait for me to dig myself out of whatever hole I dug for myself. He loves all of his children, but he refuses to help us clean up our own messes. Says it teaches us character. Whatever that means.

Spring is still amazing. Their marketplace is gorgeous and has every kind of item you could possibly want. I saw my first satyr as well! It was so strange to see a man with goat legs, but he was so kind when we came upon his booth. The Spring Court has revels every other night, though we haven't gone to any. Devan isn't one for dancing, especially when that dancing becomes involuntary by enchantment.

That's all I can fit in today. We are off to visit the palace gardens. They have a dragonfly garden I'm dying to see.

Your Elated Friend,
Angelica

Dearest Penny,

Your mother has you under guard still? It's been weeks! When do you think she's going to let up? I can't imagine how tiring it's been. I'm sorry the two of you are at such odds. I know that rankles on you.

Though I'm glad you're still making time for the handsome spy who is stealing your heart. Have you received any other gifts? Has he made a move? Tell me. Tell me. Tell me.

How are the rebels? Father mentioned in his last letter that they are popping up in other places now. There have always been people who haven't agreed with the Crown Prince, but I can't imagine an actual rebellion taking hold. I'm beginning to fear for my family. Hopefully, we can come home soon with a big trade agreement. Spring is our best ally so I pray they help us get a foot in with the Night Court.

I found out more about the Night Court. Did you know they are separated from the other courts because of their powers? Summer and Spring have powers that have to do with light and life. The Autumn and Winter fae all work with shadow and darkness. Based on the medium of their gifts, they are separated into the two courts. No wonder the fae in Summer looked at the Winter delegation in such a way. They remain completely separate unless they meet for courtly functions or at the Crann Mòr. It's so interesting to see such similar people at odds.

I'm learning so much here. I'm going to try to talk Devan into going to Autumn near the equinox. Perhaps if we are in the Night Court, we can figure out why Winter is the way it is.

Your Adventuring Friend,

Angelica

Dearest Penny,

It's been two months and still you are trapped in your house? I would be going mad! Is there any end in sight at all? I've been praying that your mother has a change of heart. I know how much being stuck at home grates on you.

I am grateful for Lou. If I can't be there to ease your suffering, I'm glad that someone is. If anything, you can be happy to have all of this alone time with him. Although, I don't think sparring practice counts as a courtship. Maybe it does for spies though? I don't know how to traverse that world. You may have outgrown me. You're going to be a master flirter by the time I get back home.

Ha! What am I saying? I can't even imagine that!

Spring has been... interesting. The High Queen is a bit of a recluse. Apparently, word has spread about the rebel uprising in Olympia and she *has locked down the castle. The people here have grown wary of any humans, though you couldn't really tell unless you'd been here before word came through the Mist.*

It's scary that such a small thing can have such an impact on so many. I spoke with a gnome yesterday that was around during the Faerie Wars. He said the other fae won't want to be anywhere close to another human war. Too many remember the last one.

I hope things get cleared up in Olympia.

Your Slightly Shaken but Still Going Strong Friend,

Angelica

25

BLOSSOMS AND BUSINESS

The clash of steel against steel rang through the clearing.

Penny whirled as Lou's sword came at her from behind. Her dagger caught the edge of his other blade, the muscles in her arms singing with the strain.

Three months. Three months since Mother had put her under lock and key. Mother hadn't allowed Penny away from the orchards within that time. She had also not left the manor on any business as she so often did this time of year. Many of the meetings with merchants and traders were either postponed until closer to harvest or took place at the manor itself. The arrangement made for quite a few chaotic situations as most of the business typically happened in the capital. Penny knew it was because Mother didn't trust her and when she confronted her, Mother always denied it. She was denying many things as of late.

The pomegranate trees were already heavy with fruit and the wheat fields would be ready to harvest in a few short weeks. Penny's workload had lessened as Mother started preparing for the harvests happening within the next few months. It left Penny feeling useless as she paced around the manor in the evenings and Mother continued to work.

These midnight training and planning sessions were the only things keeping her sane. Every night she climbed out her window to run drills in the clearing. Every night her blood hummed and her gift sang as she worked through Lou's instructions. Lou would bring maps and they would go over rebel movements along with the placement of the other spies he worked with. It allowed her to feel in control of the situation while talking plans over with Lou increased her relief that she could still help people.

Lou hit the inside of Penny's wrist with the flat of his sword and knocked the dagger in her hand into the grass a few feet away. She held her remaining dagger aloft as defense against his sword and his own dagger.

The plants around her aided in the fight. Grass grew thick around his feet. Roots from brush and trees snaked out of the ground to create uneven footing or wrap around his limbs. If she could make it into the trees, she could use their branches to fight him as well.

She worked her way toward the ring of thick trunks while defending herself against Lou's onslaught. Using real blades had become quite the challenge for Penny, but Lou had never once drawn blood. Bruises always covered every limb after their sessions, but those were always her own fault.

Lou came at her side. He'd caught her drawing him toward the trees and repositioned to drive her away from them. Penny let out a huff of irritation.

Lou gave her a ferocious grin. "Good try, but you shouldn't have kept watching the tree line."

Penny's mind whirred as she worked up a retort, but Lou knocked his sword against her dagger. As her arm shook with the impact, the pommel of Lou's dagger slammed into her forearm, knocking it sideways. With a twist of his arm, he brought up his hand, taking hers with it, and jabbed the pommel of his sword into the back of her hand. Penny's half formed reply disappeared as her other blade went flying out of her hand, leaving her unarmed.

"Yield," she grumbled, rubbing the sore spot on her hand.

Lou sheathed his sword at his waist as Penny walked to where her two blades hid in the underbrush. "You continue to improve, Lady Penelope. I'm in awe at the progress you've made in the last couple of months."

Penny let out an unladylike snort as she caught sight of one of her daggers and fished it out of the thick grass. "Save the praise for when I actually beat you in one of these exercises." She continued to sift through the brush, looking for the other dagger.

Lou came to her side, holding the missing blade in his hand. She wrapped her hand around, but he held it firmly in his grasp. The corner of his lips turned up. "Don't compare your hard-earned skill to mine. I have over a decade of training, where you have had only a few months. Give yourself the credit that is due." His grip loosened.

Penny pulled the blade from his fingers. "I'll do my best, but since there is no one else to compare myself to out here, I find it very hard not to feel discouraged."

"I assure you, Lady Penelope, you're doing very well considering the amount of time we have been working together. I expect you to progress as far as the other spies have by the end of next year if you keep up this kind of momentum. It's almost like it runs in your veins."

That was something she was worried about. It was odd how a lot of the training reflected many of her lessons from childhood. Discipline and strategy had been at the forefront of Mother's mind, simply put into business practices instead of fighting. But how easy it was for Penny to translate it over. Could Mother do the same? Was she?

The last few months had shown Penny a large portion of Mother's true colors. While she'd viewed Mother's moniker as "The Domineering Duchess" with humor before, she'd only just begun to realize what it actually meant.

If Mother was comfortable binding people to her will, how much farther would she go to see more people bound? Would she be willing to work with a group with plans to shackle those with magic? And what about their leader? Did Mother know this Cartographer? Was this rebellion simply some scheme to gain more control over everyone? Penny didn't have a full picture yet, but if she wanted to stop this, she needed Lou's help.

"Do you think you'll be here to train me until the end of next year?"

The smile fell from Lou's face. He shook his head slowly. "I'm sorry, but it's not likely. I'm to return to Olympia by the equinox, if not before then."

"What? So soon?" She hadn't shared her suspicions about Mother with him. How could she when she didn't have any actual proof? She needed time to figure out how Mother was involved before she brought it to Lou and his contacts in the Underworld.

"I wish I didn't have to."

"I wish you didn't either." She slipped her blades back into their sheathes. "These last few months have been some of the most exciting moments of my life. I feel like I've been living. Like I've actually been doing something besides sit at home all day, waiting for my life to begin. You've helped me seize a slice of freedom, even after my mother tried to take it back from me. You've helped me see that there's more to life than just pomegranates." Her words caught in her throat. "It'll be difficult to go back to normal after this."

Lou gave her a sad smile. "I don't think it will be so hard, Lady Penelope. You have many people here to look after and who will look after you in return."

Penny's shoulders sagged. There may not have been as many as she thought. If she could find evidence Mother was in league with the rebels, she could keep one of the only people she could trust here with her.

Lou bumped his elbow into her side. "We don't need to talk about such things just yet. We have a good six weeks until autumn equinox and I know you'll be very excited to hear what I have in store for tomorrow."

Penny's eyes instantly shot to his. "What's going on tomorrow?"

Lou grinned. "We're going to have a visitor."

"Lord Hermen to see you, my lady."

Mother waved at Rich. "Yes, of course. Let him in."

Penny laid the book she had been reading down on the small table by her chair as Lord Hermen walked into Mother's study.

"Your Grace, you look wonderful as always." Lord Hermen flashed his white teeth at Mother and folded into a gallant bow.

"Lord Hermen, how is Patricia these days?" Mother stood to greet the merchant lord. "I was so sorry to have declined the invitation to call on her when I was in town last."

"My darling wife is perfect as always." He strode into the room as Penny and Mother sat in chairs at the desk. "Our little

Myrtle has certainly been running her mother ragged since she started rampaging this past year. Patricia regularly finds her in the horse pasture which has given everyone in the household one too many heart attacks."

"Sweet Gaia, she's so young to be out with the horses," commented Penny.

Lord Hermen sat in the chair next to hers. "My wife agrees with you, Lady Penny, but we still haven't been able to figure out where little Myrtle gets out of the house." He pinched the bridge of his nose. "It's going to be a long next couple of years with this one."

Penny's smile matched Mother's. This was the first time in weeks they held real smiles on their faces. Her own smile dimmed. Even with the other merchants they had met with, their camaraderie had been strained.

She did her best not to let her thoughts overcome her high spirits as she turned back to the merchant lord. "Lord Hermen, how has business with the fae been going? Angelica's last letter held little of the marital bliss of her previous letters." Penny heard the small hiss only she would be able to pick up come from Mother, but chose to ignore it.

"Angelica and Devan are doing fine," Lord Hermen replied, his face the picture of a proud parent. "I heard back from them just yesterday. They should be making their way to Autumn in the next few days. She still sends her mother raving reviews of her so-called 'marital bliss.'"

Mother cleared her throat. Her expression remained serene, but Penny could see the reproach in her eyes when they connected with Penny's. "I'm happy to hear everyone's doing so well these days."

The two business owners got to work on production numbers and trade routes. Penny's mind stayed with Angelica and her husband.

What would it be like to travel like her friend did? Would Penny ever get to see something so strange and fantastic? Penny thought about Angelica's husband, Devan, whom she'd only formally met at the wedding. The man had worked for Lord Hermen for years before they'd been introduced, and they were engaged within three months after Angelica's debut. It had been a fairytale wedding for Angelica, and her marriage since then had been an adventure Penny would never experience.

Penny imagined herself sailing across the ocean with her husband. The image of that perfect man was muddled. Sometimes the man had hair as dark as night while other times his hair was as gold as the wheat they would be harvesting soon. Either way, the color of her imaginary husband's eyes never differed.

"Penny?"

"Hmm? What?"

Mother and Lord Hermen both stared at her, the former with a look of irritation while the latter smiled in bemusement.

"Lord Hermen asked if we are considering hiring more hands for the harvest this year. The blossom yield has been slightly higher since you took over and he wanted to hear what you thought."

Penny scrambled as she did her best to return to the conversation at hand. Her thoughts snagged as she thought about the workers they did have. She gave a small sigh. "It would probably be best to get a few more helping hands. You never know who might leave before the harvest and we've already had so many issues keeping employees." They had been able to hire a few more after Penny's initial purge of rebellion, but the workload was still stretched thin.

And Lou had six weeks until the equinox. The pomegranates would be picked without him.

"We'll certainly discuss it more after the equinox," Mother stated. "The fruit won't be ripe for a couple more months, but we should have wheat ready to ship before the end of next month. Penny did a remarkable job with the replant after the fire."

"Ah, yes. You brought that up when you were in the capital last. I'm pleased to hear everything turned out well." He gave Penny one of his dazzling smiles. "It's a compliment to your gift, Lady Penny, that you were able to repair such extensive damage."

Penny could do nothing but grin. At least someone had noticed her efforts.

The three of them talked back and forth about the grain distribution and worked their way back to the pomegranate harvest. The hands of the clock spun by as they continued to plan. It grew well past time for supper when they finally had everything set for the next several months.

"You ladies are this kingdom's finest citizens," Lord Hermen remarked as they walked toward the dining room for a late supper. "We wouldn't be half as prosperous if we didn't have the fruits of your labors to trade with the other lands."

"This is our pride and joy," replied Mother. "We would never be happier doing anything else."

Penny prayed that was true.

Penny broke through the trees. Her eyes instantly landed on Lou standing among the tall grass as she jogged into the clearing.

"So," —her heart pounded and her breathing came out

slightly more labored than she would've preferred— "where is our mysterious guest?"

Lou smiled indulgently and nodded his head toward the line of trees she'd just bolted through. Lord Hermen waltzed out of the shadows, his knowing smile mirroring the crescent moon suspended above them.

"Lord Hermen?" She spun back to look at Lou. "Lord Hermen is part of the prince's operation?"

Lord Hermen chuckled. "Who better than the Minister of Trade to have in your spy network? I go all over Olympia and into the countries beyond. My merchant title is the perfect cover for the actual trading I am so qualified in supplementing."

"And what kind of trading is that?" Penny asked.

"Information," Lou supplied. "Lord Hermen is one of the Crown's greatest resources for giving and obtaining information. His network of merchants is one of the largest webs of intelligence on the continent."

"It's been quite the undertaking since the princes reached out to me. I've enjoyed it immensely and I swear my darling Patricia enjoys it more than I do."

"Lady Hermen is in on it too? Does Angelica know?"

Lord Hermen's eyes twinkled. "The youngest prince had Patricia in his pocket two years before he got to me, just before the Tyrant King was killed. Angelica is unaware— and it must remain so— but Devan is one of my staunchest employees. He's the reason they are in Faerie. They're not only there for trade agreements but to make sure we have a good network on the other side of the Mist."

Penny stood, mouth agape as she looked between the two men. She didn't know how she couldn't see it before. The Hermen family would make the perfect spies. Patricia, though not naturally a noblewoman, was one of the highest regarded women in high society. She charmed every noble house she came across with her sharp wit and passion for gossip. Gossip, it seemed, that was filtered by a spy network.

Not to mention Devan...

Penny turned to Lou. "And I can't become a spy because...?"

Lord Hermen's laugh shook the trees.

Lou looked at him with narrowed eyes before turning back to Penny. "I don't think your mother would approve of her daughter leaving the manor for operations that could potentially take months to finish. You Barclays have a very important work here."

Penny frowned, but Lord Hermen cut in before she could allow the words to settle. "Did you receive my message?"

"Yes," replied Lou as Penny's mind returned to the matter at hand. "I wanted to meet with you tonight to hear what you found from your own mouth."

Lord Hermen pulled out a bundle of papers from the inside of his coat. "Here are the receipts from the order as well as the ship's manifest. The shipment will be arriving in Eleusia in three days along with the man orchestrating the drop off." He handed the papers over to Lou. Lou's eyes scanned the documents. He took out his small notebook from the satchel at his hip as well as his magic quill.

"Wait, what is happening in Eleusia?" Penny interjected.

"If these logs are correct," replied Lord Hermen, "a shipment of harmful charms and weapons were purchased by the man we believe to be one of the key players of The Cartographer's group. The boat is supposed to be in Eleusia in three days. If the information I was able to procure is accurate, the man will be distributing the supplies to the rebels in Eleusia as well as in the neighboring towns."

Penny hid her shaking hands in her skirts. "What does that mean for us?"

"It means, Lady Penelope," said Lou, "that I'll be making sure those weapons never get into the hands of the rebels." He handed the documents back to Lord Hermen. "It also means we can get our hands on this rebel leader and finally figure out who this Cartographer really is."

"You'll need more than just yourself," said Lord Hermen.

"I have Hart as well as a handful of other operatives in the area already involved and awaiting further orders. It won't be hard to get a team together. It should only take a few of us to take care of it." Lou began flipping through his notebook.

The words were out of Penny's mouth before she could even think about the repercussions. "I'm going with you."

Lou's eyes snapped to hers. "No, you're not."

"Yes, I am."

Lou snapped his notebook shut and shoved it back into his satchel. "You need to think about this. You've only been training for a handful of months. You aren't qualified for a mission of this scale."

"Didn't you just say recently that I'm doing just as well as some of your other spies."

Lord Hermen chuckled. "You two fight like an old married couple."

Penny turned toward him at the same time as Lou. "Not helping," they said in unison. Lord Hermen's laugh grew.

Penny turned back to Lou, ignoring the frustrating lord. "I don't care what you say or how many very logical arguments you come up with. I am going with you."

26

ROOFTOPS AND RENEGADES

"Sissy, I need to ask you for a favor."

Sissy slowed her brushing of Penny's wavy hair and met her gaze in the mirror. "Would it really be one if I'm paid to do you favors?" Her eyes sparkled with mirth.

Penny's voice came out in a near whisper. "It would be a rather large favor considering if we're caught you'd likely lose your position."

Sissy came around to face Penny. "You mean to say you need me to help you do something without your mother's permission?"

Penny winced. "Yes."

Sissy burst out laughing. "Finally!"

"Finally?"

"I knew you wouldn't last long under house arrest. I've been waiting for you to ask me to cover for you so you could go out again, but it never happened. I'm glad you finally broke."

Penny stared at her maid for a moment. "You guessed this would happen?"

"We all knew it was bound to. Your mother likes to keep

you trapped here, but she's trying to keep a seagull in a chicken coop. We all know you want to fly to higher heights and it's only the obligation to your family that keeps you here." She took Penny's hand in her own. "I know you, Lady Penny. I've been your personal maid for years and I've seen your heart. You're meant to do great things for those who know you. I'll be forever grateful that you chose me as your maid when there were plenty of others who were far more qualified than the daughter of a field master."

Tears pricked Penny's eyes. "Thank you, Sissy." Her heart swelled in her chest. "You have no idea what this means to me."

Sissy wrapped her hands around Penny's shoulders and gave a tight squeeze. "What are good maids for if not helping you discover your rebellious nature?" Penny laughed, as Sissy straightened and put her hands to her hips. "Now, what's this favor you need?"

The hood of Penny's rough-spun cloak scratched against her cheek. Sweat cooled on her brow as a late summer breeze blew over the rooftops. She looked down along the street running before the large warehouse sitting on the edge of the river. Lou and his team had been scouting the building since he had found it the day before.

"Repeat the plan back to me."

Penny turned to give Lou an unamused glare and was met with his look of severity. She huffed out a breath. "I sit here on this roof and wait for you and your men to seize the weapons — and capture the man who brought them here— in whatever mysterious manner you've decided on. I'm to watch for anyone coming into the building and alert you using the warble-sounding bird call you taught me on our way here." It had taken a full, mortifying hour to figure out how to hold her hands in the right position to make the sound. She'd greatly feared she would ruin all of Lou's hard work because she couldn't figure out how to do something so simple.

"And then?"

Penny sighed and leaned against the chimney at her back. "And then I hold this position for the entire hour. I'm not to leave this rooftop for any reason other than my certain demise, even if I hear your men's tortured screams or watch the building collapse on top of you." *Which is a bit dramatic.* "I'll run through the docks then turn in the direction of the magic quarter and stop at the blue house you showed me. If you disappear and don't show up an hour before sunrise, I'm to use the main road and go home."

"I suppose that's sufficient."

Penny huffed. "I feel useless."

Lou smirked at her. "You did say you wanted to come with."

"Yes, to help. Not sit here like a child waiting for my nanny."

"I'm sure you didn't give your nanny half as much trouble," he grumbled out of the side of his mouth.

Penny returned his smirk. "Oh, you'd be surprised. I apparently went through three nannies before my mother decided to raise me herself." Lou looked at her in surprise, but she simply shrugged. "My gift manifested a little earlier than most mages."

Lou's eyes returned to the warehouse with a grave expression. "Mine did too." With a small nod goodbye, Lou leapt from his spot on the roof and landed on the top of the building next to them. He climbed down the wooden slats making up the ramshackle structure and landed on the ground below. At the bottom, three other forms wrapped in dark clothing broke away from her friend as they all made their way to the warehouse. Her eyes kept losing Lou as he seemed to melt into the shadows of the street, but she did see him look up at her one last time before entering the building.

The wait began. Her heart pounded against her ribs as she thought about all that could go wrong. Her eyes remained fastened on the warehouse and noticed the entire building seemed to grow darker. The shadows around it seemed black as tar and crept farther than any of the others on the street. The lack of light glared menacingly at her. Goosebumps worked their way up her arms in light of the darkening facade.

It couldn't have been more than fifteen minutes before three men appeared out of an alleyway at the end of the road. They spoke quietly to one another as they walked, but Penny couldn't make out their words from so far away. All three of them wore nondescript clothing and varied in height and coloring. She could easily make out the swords strapped to their waists and the broad width of their shoulders. Her throat went dry.

The largest of the men stopped before they reached the building and pulled his companions to a halt. His eyes took in the warehouse before widening and darting around toward the other buildings surrounding them. Penny tucked herself on the opposite side of the chimney and did her best to meld into the shadows before he could fully turn toward her. Had he seen one of the others?

After a few moments, she risked the chance to look back onto the street and watched as the men slowly approached the door to the warehouse. She immediately placed her cupped hands to her lips and blew through the small space between her fingers. It took her a few tries, but she emitted the small call to alert Lou to the men's presence.

A few more steps and whispered words passed between the suspects and they split up. The largest man— Penny suspected him to be the leader— sent one running off before walking toward the front door while the other man ran to the back side of the warehouse, disappearing from sight. Penny held her breath as the leader vanished into the building. She slowly began counting the minutes in her head. Five minutes passed. Then ten. Then fifteen.

Just before she counted twenty minutes, a glow came from the direction the other man had run off in.

By the Goddess...

A group of fifteen men strode down the street brandishing all kinds of weapons and each holding aloft a torch. They were led down the street by the man who had left and headed straight for the building.

They knew.

Penny's attention turned back to the warehouse, but there was no movement. No sign of Lou or any of his men. She once again fumbled before she was able to create another bird call.

They should have taken care of the men inside already. They should have easily taken hold of the weapons. What was taking so long?

Where is he?

The shadows in front of the building recoiled from the light of the torches as the men raced into the warehouse. Dread pooled in Penny's stomach. The sound of fighting and destruction rang from the building as light flickered through the small number of windows sitting just below the edge of the roof. The clock in Penny's head ticked closer to the hour mark as the flashes of light and sound continued.

Could she have made a difference if she had gone with

them? Or would she have been one of the voices calling out in pain? Her chest ached as she imagined Lou's face twisted in anguish.

She should have gone with him.

Silhouettes of swords clashing flew up the walls and she could hear the screams of pain from across the street. Clouds of shadow smothered pockets of light. Torches were wielded as much as swords.

She watched with bated breath for the familiar flash of gold, but could make out nothing through the small windows.

Approximately five minutes before the hour, a slip of shadow raced across the roof of the warehouse. A moonbeam caught on the gold of Lou's hair as he ran. Penny's heart jammed in her throat as he jumped the large gap to the structure next door. His body collided with the edge of the building. His hands held to the edge of the roof and Penny nearly cried in relief as he hauled himself onto the roof and disappeared.

But where were the other operatives? The shadows shifted and danced through the torchlight. They diminished and the fire's light within began to grow. Movement at the door caught her eye as a large group of men staggered out of the building just as flames began to lick at the windows. Penny let out a breath as she saw a few shadows unstick from the building and race across the rooftops of other buildings.

She prayed all of them had made it out.

Crawling on all fours, she maneuvered toward the back of the small tenant housing she sat atop. Her rope still hung off the edge and she easily rappelled the building until she stood on the stack of crates leaning beside the back door. Once her feet were on solid ground, she shifted through the shadows around the docks as her mentor had taught her. Her only thought was to get to the blue house to find him.

It was too late to hide when the rebel leader stepped out

from the shadow of the barrels waiting in stacks to be loaded onto one of the boats.

The bulk of him had been diminished when Penny looked at him from the rooftop, for now he seemed as tall as a mountain. The man's rough hands and the smell of cheap wine slammed her into a wall. "I thought I heard a little bird."

Penny stiffened at the sneer in his voice and her body began moving before she realized what she was doing.

With a raise of her boot, she slammed her knee into the man's groin and drew the dagger from her waist. Her foot came down to smash the solid heel of her boot into the top of his foot. A grunt of pain preceded his retreat as he doubled over in front of her. Her dagger came up and she smashed the pommel into the back of his head. With a growl, the brute staggered away and drew his sword. Penny skirted around the man and turned to run down the interweaving docks. A roar of rage and the sounds of pursuit followed quickly on her heels.

Her gloves hid the glow of her hands as she tried to connect with anything growing in the water beneath them. When her magic snagged on growth nearby, something large came from behind and wrapped around her legs. Penny nearly lost the blade in her hands as her head smacked onto the wooden planks beneath her.

Dazed, she swung her blade at the arms wrapped around her legs. She made contact and the rebel leader let out a sharp hiss as his arms loosened.

"Stupid brat! You'll pay for that."

Penny scrambled away and managed to get to her feet. The man jumped up and swung his sword to block her escape. Muscle memory managed to bring one of her daggers in front of her face to block the man's swing.

"Lucky block. Too bad it won't happen again."

Penny didn't respond as he once again thrust the blade in

her direction. Her boots caught on the uneven planks as she avoided the edge of his blade. He maneuvered her into a walled off section of the alley, trapping her. He tucked close and smashed one of her arms into the side of a stacked crate, splintering the wood and sending rivulets of salt beneath them. With a cry of pain, she dropped the dagger in that hand while fending his sword off with the other. He sliced the skin of her calf as she tried to move away from the broken boxes. In the shock of that pain, she fell to her knees.

The man laughed. “I don’t know what they were thinking—”

The man’s eyes filled with the salt Penny had gathered in her free hand. He stumbled back, cursing as he did his best to blink the grit from his eyes. Penny grabbed hold of her other dagger from her boot as the man swung around blindly.

Penny’s heart skittered as he raged. It would only take one wrong step for his sword to completely incapacitate her. He came directly at Penny as she ran to the side of him. He poised his sword over his head, his face purple with fury, as Penny pulled her dagger up in front of her.

One moment, he stood, all of his hate and anger raging in his face.

The next, he fell back with a splash into the river, red blooming across his chest from where the dagger had sunk into his heart. Air passed her lips in ragged breaths as the man’s body bob up and down in the current of the water.

“I guess” —a rasping breath— “you won’t be needing my help then.”

Penny whipped around to find Lou leaning against the end of the dock. Her shoulders sagged in relief as she clenched her jaw to keep back her roiling gut.

“Lady Penelope...” Lou’s voice came out in a near whisper, calling her attention back to him. He turned to look behind him just as something shot out of the shadows and knocked him to the ground. Penny screamed, taking a step toward him, but Lou stood and threw one of the many knives strapped to his waist. The thud of the blade hitting its mark elicited a mixture of horror and relief.

"Are you all right?" she asked. She couldn't see whatever had knocked him off of his feet, but he didn't seem to be looking around for it.

Lou turned to her and breathed, "We need to go. Now."

At the sound of voices growing closer, Penny retrieved the dagger she'd dropped. Lou reached out for Penny's hand and she placed her palm in his. She realized too late that hers was covered in blood, making her nauseous, but Lou didn't seem to notice. In a staggering run, they escaped into the alleyways.

The light of torches trailed behind them. She heard the cries of outrage at the body of their leader floating in the water as Penny and Lou slipped away. The glow of torches continued to chase them as they ran, but after ten minutes of running, Lou stumbled. If it wasn't for the hand Penny shot out to steady him, he would have fallen.

"Lou?" Penny's voice shook as she held him up. "What's wrong? What happened?"

He silently opened up his coat to reveal a broken crossbow bolt sticking out of his abdomen. The stain of blood grew across his shirt and down his pants to drip on the ground. "He made a lucky shot with that crossbow, but I paid the favor in kind."

Penny gasped. This was what had shot at him. She hadn't been able to figure out what had hurt him because it had been stuck in his torso.

She tucked herself under his arm. "It's going to be fine. We're going to get you some help." She hoisted him up and walked as fast as she could with the weight of him draped over her shoulders.

Her mouth went dry at the thought of how much farther they had to go.

The voices grew louder as she hobbled Lou through dark walkways of the large town. Their steps grew more labored as he grew weaker. Her memory of this area was foggy in her fear, and turn after turn, she became more and more disoriented.

At the sound of dozens of boots scuffing the earth, she turned into a completely new alleyway. The beams of torch-light pushed her onward until they reached a dead end.

"No, no, no." Penny's head shook in denial as she looked over every inch of the stone wall in front of her. She walked Lou over to the side and with a grunt, set him against the smooth stone of the building. She returned to the wall to look for hand holds or hidden doors somewhere in the facade but only saw the gleam of glass from high above them. There was a door set into one of the walls. She pounded against the thick wood until the sound of Lou crumpling to the ground called her back to him.

"Penelope," Lou gasped, "you need to leave."

"Absolutely not," she hissed as she knelt on the ground next to him. "I'm not leaving you here." Her hands took the fabric of his shirt around the wound and tore it in two. She began tearing pieces of her underskirt to apply pressure to Lou's wound around the wooden shaft of the bolt. She knew better than to take it out without a way to close the wound.

Lou's eyes locked on hers as he grabbed her wrist with his bloodied hand. "Listen to me. They'll be here any moment and I will not allow them to get their hands on you. I'm no one, nothing. I'll be dead before they can get anything out of me, but they'll do untold things to you. *Please*," he begged, voice hoarse with pain, "please go."

A sob broke from Penny as she shook her head. “You aren’t *nothing* to me.” Lou’s hair caught the light of the torches held aloft by the group of men coming around the corner. His hand on her wrist tightened to the point of pain, but Penny hardly felt it in comparison with her terror.

“There’s the blasted fool who wrecked the warehouse!” One of the men shouted with a pointed finger toward Lou. The group took a collective step toward them.

Two shadows jumped down from above Penny to land between them and the threatening group.

The one with three heads growled menacingly as the other took a step forward into the light.

Penny’s entire being stilled with shock.

Amber Eyes drew the sword at his waist. “I would not take one step further if I were you.”

27

GHOSTS AND GLAMOURS

The man of Penny's dreams took a fearsome step toward The Cartographer's men as Penny held the cloth to Lou's abdomen. Spot bared his teeth and stalked toward the group. From behind, Penny could see the powerful aura Amber Eyes exuded, and her own fear crept down her spine. She hadn't seen much fae magic in action, but the magic rolling off of him was almost unnatural. As if he was made from shadow itself, the edges of him swathed in darkness. The men at the end of the alley stumbled back as Spot snapped his teeth.

"I would suggest you run." Amber Eyes' deep voice held the promise of pain. Spot barked in warning as well. With a roar from the golden-eyed warrior, the two lunged into a run at the men. The group let out several yelps and turned tail at the prodding of the fae and his fearsome dog, who gave chase back down the alley.

The sounds of pursuit continued until the only thing Penny could hear was the sound of her own pounding heart.

He'd come. Of course he did. He was a spy, just like Lou. They likely knew each other.

A groan turned Penny's attention back to Lou and she let out a small gasp. The veins of his arms ran black down his skin. Penny tore more fabric from her skirt as she saw the paleness of his face. Her eyes fastened on the base of his neck, the veins there taking on the tell of Lou's magic as well.

"Just hold on. Everything's going to be fine." Penny pushed down the sobs working up her throat and began shredding more fabric from her under clothing. She looked over to see Lou's usually shining eyes glazed in pain as he looked at her.

Go, he mouthed.

Her head shook violently. "I would never leave you here. You're my friend and I'm going to save you. I just need you to help me get you on your feet. On the count of three, I'm going to sit you up. Ready?" Penny counted "one" and pulled Lou away from the wall.

Lou's groaning swear broke a sob from Penny's tight control. Tears leaked down her cheeks as blood soaked into the already drenched cloth she held there.

How is he even alive? She prayed and prayed that he stayed that way until she got him help.

Grabbing the other strips, she wrapped them around his torso to hold the cloth in place and apply pressure to his wound around the bolt. From seeing injuries on the farm, she knew better than to take the bolt out herself without professional help and supplies.

"All right, now we have to get you to your feet. We can use the wall as support." Penny squatted down next to Lou and swung one of his black-streaked arms over her shoulder. Lou took several deep breaths before he let out a roar and stood using her help. She nearly lost her hold on him as he slumped from the drain of energy, but with the help of the alley's wall, he remained standing.

Penny's lungs huffed as she readjusted her grip on his side

to avoid aggravating his wound. "We just have to figure out how to get to the magic quarter. I have a friend there who can help us."

They both took a staggering step, then another, until they were at the mouth of the alley. She looked back and forth down the small road they came out on. Her eyes lifted toward the sky and she got a faint bearing on where they were. The market street was to the east of them, probably only a handful of blocks away. Which meant their destination was only a little further.

"Left," she whispered and turned in the direction of Farrah's shop.

Their steps dragged along the dust covered walkways. Penny did her best to keep Lou on his feet. They had to stop every couple of minutes so Penny could readjust her grip and Lou could take a break.

Time sluggishly passed. Sweat dripped down both of their faces and Penny couldn't differentiate between her shaking and his.

They made it to a larger road when Lou's body slackened and the full weight of him pressed against her.

No, no, no! The weight of his body brought her to her knees in the dirt. She did her best to take the brunt of his fall, but he still landed on the ground beside her with a thud.

"Lou," she whispered as she tried to pull him up.

He let out a small gasp of pain as he shifted, his face completely devoid of color and eyelids heavy. Sweat-plastered hair stuck to his cheeks and forehead. Glassy eyes looked at her and his chest fell in ragged breaths.

Penny's tears gushed at his suffering. "Lou, I'm sorry, but we aren't there yet. We have to keep moving." She brushed the damp hair off his cheeks and took his face in her hands. "We're almost there. Just a little farther."

Lou once again tried to stand up. Before he could even straighten his back, his amber eyes rolled back into his head and he crumpled to the dirt, completely unconscious.

"Lou!" Penny wrapped her arms under his and did her best to pull him off of the main road. His bottom half caught debris on the ground, making her arms strain in an effort to move him. A small alcove stood in the wall of the building next to them and she used what little strength she had left to drag him into the shadows.

With a small cry, she fell to the ground and cradled Lou's head in her lap. She laid a hand on his chest, barely feeling it move. Her fingers searched the side of his neck for his pulse and when she found the slow, sluggish beat, she broke. Tears fell from her eyes onto his tired face as she sobbed uncontrollably. Her shoulders shook in exhaustion and hopelessness as she watched the life leak from her friend.

Penny turned her face to the stars. "Great Gaia," her voice rasped, "please save this man." She looked down at the face she held in her lap and brushed his hair away from his closed eyes. "This world needs people like him— those who see the world for what it actually is. He helps those who truly deserve it. He's the closest friend I've ever had. I care about him. Please" —her voice broke— "*please,* don't take him from me..." Her words trailed off to the bright stars as her tears streaked through sweat and blood.

Her shoulders wracked with sobs as she cradled her friend's head in her arms. Lou had been right. She should have never agreed to all of this. If she hadn't been there... if he hadn't been there to try to save her, he would've been fine. He could have easily escaped without her.

Her forehead met his. She shouldn't have snuck out. She should have believed Mother about the people of this world. They only hurt the few good ones the Goddess gave them.

Penny didn't know how long she sat in that alcove, her brow against his. For all she knew, it could have been seconds or hours. What she did know was the ache in her chest and the trickle of blood she did her best to staunch. She hadn't noticed her teeth clattering until the sound drowned out the rushing of blood in her ears.

As she tried to slow her panicked gasps, she overheard a faint tinkling coming from around the corner. As it drew closer, Penny realized someone was coming down the alley next to them. Would it be wiser to hide or seek help? She looked down at Lou as if he would give her the answer, but his face remained blank. His chest continued to rise and fall under her hand, but the movements grew shallower by the second. Looking at the crossbow bolt, she made the decision.

With a kiss between his brows, she set Lou's head gently on the dirt beneath him and stood. A faint light glowed around the corner and Penny unsheathed one of her daggers. As the light grew brighter and she made out the sound of footsteps, she leaped from her hiding place.

"By the Goddess of the Four Courts!" The candle-holder yelped. Familiar white brows drew close over deep, brown eyes. "Penny?"

Penny fell to her knees at the sound of Farrah's familiar voice. Farrah knelt beside her and took her shoulders in her slim hands. "What's happened?"

Penny grabbed the fae's hands and dragged both of them to their feet. Without another word, she pulled Farrah toward Lou. "Please, Farrah, you have to help him."

Farrah stopped. "Stars," she breathed and nearly flung herself on top of Lou in her haste to look at his wound. "What happened? How long has he been like this? When you bound his wound, was there anything discolored?"

Penny sucked back her sobs and did her best to think back

to what she saw before she wrapped it. The image caused a twist in her gut, but she swallowed back her nausea. "I— I don't know. I couldn't see much in the light. I don't quite know how long it's been." Penny looked up at the moon and did some calculating in her head. "It can't have been more than an hour since he was hit."

"I'll need your help getting him back to the shop." Farrah waved a hand toward the rear of the alcove. A swirling mass of shadow writhed in a circle on the wall, growing until it was approximately Lou's height.

Penny stared at the darkness, a cold sweat breaking out all over her body. "What is that?" She could hear the fear in the shake of her voice.

"A portal." Farrah stood. "Quick. Grab his legs."

Penny couldn't move a muscle.

"Penny." Farrah cupped Penny's face in her hands to draw her eyes away from the dark spot. "I know the darkness has not always been kind to you, but I need you to help me get your friend through the portal. It's his only chance." Farrah moved to grab Lou under his arms. "Do not let him go."

Penny did her best to keep her breathing calm as she wrapped her hands under each of Lou's knees. She gripped his legs tight, though her hands slicked with sweat, as they got closer to the gaping mouth of nightmares. She took a deep breath as Farrah stepped through, holding Lou's shoulders above the ground. With a shudder, she allowed herself to be pulled into the waiting darkness.

Blindness. Complete and utter blindness engulfed her. Nothing lived within the portal, nothing shone within its space. Penny felt the screams leave her mouth, but no sound fell on her ears over the roaring of darkness rushing past. She still felt the fabric in her hands and the slight warmth of Lou's body through her fingers, but nothing else could tether her to the life outside of this place.

Echoes of yelling and screams not her own clanged through her head. Dark laughter and glass breaking. Curses and ripping fabric. She couldn't place the sounds, but they were ones her soul recognized.

Penny fell to one knee when the portal pushed her onto solid ground what felt like an eternity later. Her hold on Lou's knees slipped and his feet fell from her hands. She couldn't open her eyes, even as her magic connected with the earth around her. Flashes of life and color spread through Penny's awareness through her gift, but her mind was still trapped in the thundering darkness behind her.

She heard a groan and the tinkling of coins. Finally opening her eyes, she found Farrah hoisting Lou onto a cot, her fae strength giving her the ability to move him on her own. She likely hadn't actually needed Penny's help in the first place.

Penny gasped as she soaked in the new place they found themselves in. She would have believed the room to be a grove in a forest if she couldn't see the planks of painted wood peeking through the foliage around her. Trees grew along the walls, their leaves a canopy above their heads. Birds flitted through the branches where tiny lights lazily spun in the air. Lichen crawled up the edges of the room and coated legs of the tables standing about. Every available space was covered in books, glasses, and plants. Penny's magic buzzed and the glow spread from her palms to settle up her wrists. When she set a hand on the ground to push herself off her knees, a group of wildflowers instantly sprouted, making her jump.

"What is this place?"

"This is the back room of my shop," replied Farrah. "Now quit gawking and come help me get this out." Farrah ripped the entire front of Lou's shirt, revealing his torso. "By Danu, Mama would have a fit if she saw this."

Penny started toward Farrah and Lou. When her eyes landed on her friend, she noticed the black of his veins had receded and the coloring of his arms looked less pale. Her eyes trailed along the defined features of his abdomen and landed on the small spot of black just over his heart. Farrah got the last piece of wrapping off and hissed when she evaluated the wound.

Penny rushed to Lou's other side. "What can I do?"

Farrah looked at her as she used a cloth to wrap around the broken bolt. "When I pull this out, you are going to have to use the cloth sitting beside his head and apply pressure to the wound. It's probably going to be messy, but hopefully his healing will quicken once we get the ash wood and iron out. At least it should. I've only ever done this when Mama was there to help with the healing."

"It should?" Penny grabbed the cloth and looked at Farrah questioningly. "And what does the wood and iron have to do with his healing?"

Farrah stiffened and gazed back at Penny. "You don't know."

Penny stilled. "What don't I know?"

Farrah turned and counted to three before pulling the shaft cleanly from Lou's stomach. With a clatter, she threw it to the ground and Penny pushed her cloth to stop the bleeding. Farrah sat back for a moment before taking the cloth from Penny's hands. Farrah held it there for a moment longer before pulling the cloth back and looking at the wound. When she gestured for Penny to look, Penny found the wound nearly closed and the blood flow slowing to a small trickle.

Looking up, she found Farrah's eyes already on hers. "Penny, this man is *fae*— well, half."

Penny stared at Farrah then, slowly, her eyes returned to Lou. Her friend's face remained calm even as his body miraculously healed the trauma most people's bodies fought with for months. His face was still the easy going, mortal face she'd gotten to know. His ears still had the rounded look of a human. His coloring was not as vibrant or unusual as that of most fae Penny had come across. There was nothing otherworldly about him except for his kind spirit and golden eyes.

Penny turned back to Farrah. "He looks human."

"There are many gifts the fae— and even the water folk— wield. We are stronger, heal faster, can manipulate shadow or light— or water if you're from the Isles— grant gifts or cast curses. He's using a *glamour*. I don't know how he's able to hold it while he's unconscious, but his appearance is different than what you see here."

Penny's breaths shortened. "You mean he lied? He's been lying about what he actually looks like? Why? And how?" Fae — full fae— couldn't lie. The purer the fae blood, the more impossible it became. If Lou was half fae, lying should cause him a tremendous amount of pain.

Farrah shook her head. "That's not a question I can answer." She waved her hand once more and opened another portal. "I know your mother wouldn't be happy to find out you left the manor again. You should get back before the sun rises within the hour."

Penny shook her head and backed away from the swirling shadow. "I can't, Farrah. I can't go back in there. You know why. *Please*."

Farrah gave Penny an understanding look. "Penny, I know this will be difficult for you, but you have to go." Farrah once again waved her hand and a portal opened right behind Penny. She didn't have the chance to scream before it swallowed her whole.

28

AIR AND STONE

LIGHT BURNED AGAINST PENNY'S EYELIDS, BUT SHE COULDN'T WORK up the strength to open them and find the cause. Her ears caught on the sound of birdsong faintly trilling from far away and the sound of another person's breathing not far from where she was.

On the first attempt to open them, her eyes immediately teared up in the rays of light surrounding her. After a few tries, however, she was able to see she was lying in her own bed. Penny looked over and saw Sissy leaning forward in a chair, her head on the comforter next to Penny's hand. Penny gently reached over and brushed her fingers through her maid's sandy-blonde hair. At the touch, Sissy sat straight up and blinked at Penny.

"My lady? Are you awake? How long have you been awake? What time is it?" Sissy's head darted back and forth from Penny's face to the clock on the bedside table to Penny's hand laying on blankets once again.

Words caught in Penny's dry throat. Without a word, Sissy

immediately reached for the pitcher and glass sitting on the night table.

Penny sat up to take a few gulps and after Sissy placed the cup back, she was able to speak. “I haven’t been awake more than a few minutes. How long have you been here? How long have *I* been here?”

“It’s been several hours since your return. Nearly three o’clock. I’ve been here since you returned.”

She gave Penny a hard look. “What I would like to know is how you dropped from a shadowy, vortex thing, nearly unconscious, into the middle of your sitting room covered in blood. Especially after your cryptic request of the evening before. I thought you had just been going around calling off rebel meetings, not putting yourself in actual danger.”

The scenes from the night before shot through Penny’s mind. Her eyes watered. “Things certainly didn’t go as planned.” She looked at Sissy, at the concerned and confused gaze, and decided to tell her maid everything.

She told her about the night she was kidnapped, about how the man of her dreams had saved her. She talked about meeting Lou in Mother’s study and how they’d agreed to help one another. The entire story came out and when she reached the end, her face was sprinkled with tears.

“I don’t understand what happened, Sissy.” Penny shook with the weight of everything crashing down on her. “I should’ve believed Mother all of these years. I should’ve trusted her judgment and just been happy where I was.” She closed her eyes. “I’m such a fool.”

She should have seen it. Lou probably laughed at her every time she’d spoken to him.

Sissy took Penny’s hand firmly in her own. “I know you don’t believe all that, Lady Penny. You and I both know there is so much beauty to behold in this world. We know the Goddess is watching over us and we know She has a plan for all of us. If I were you, I would thank her for the opportunity you've received to help your people. To me, it sounds as if your mission was successful. You've done wonderful things and built yourself from the ground up. I think you must simply ask yourself... was it worth the sacrifices, and what are you actually mad about?"

Penny ruminated over the words for the whole rest of that day from her spot in bed. She'd gotten lucky. Sissy had used the excuse that Penny hadn't been feeling well earlier this morning and when Mother had come to check on her, Penny's obvious distress was convincing enough.

Had all of it been worth the sacrifice? Penny thought back over the last several months of training with Lou. The work had become something important. Of course her responsibilities in the orchards were important. People's livelihoods depended on their land and her gift, but Mother didn't really need her to accomplish any of it. If there were someone dedicated enough, the orchards would continue to prosper the way they had for the hundreds of years before Penny had even been born. Helping Lou fight against this rebellion had felt like something else, something life changing.

She'd actually begun helping people. Penny looked on her own heart. Helping Lou had helped her, and it was worth the sacrifices.

But what about the other question. What was she *truly* angry about? Of course not all men lied and the fae were not to blame for any of this. Had Lou's deception cut her so deeply? It was absolute nonsense. He was a spy. He didn't actually live the life of a common farmhand. Why should the fact that he was revealed to be fae change her mind about him?

"It shouldn't," she mumbled to herself. "Just because he hid something like that from me doesn't mean the other things weren't true. It doesn't negate our friendship— my friendship. I should give him the benefit of the doubt rather than paint him in the light Mother has colored the human male."

She simply needed to ask him why he withheld the truth. She would confront him when she next got the chance... if she got the chance.

"M'lady!" Aaron called as he rode toward her. Penny finally had the energy to get out of bed the next morning and needed to get into the orchard. Mother had left Sissy with a list for Penny of things that needed tending to and Penny had never been more grateful for the hard, diverting work.

"Good morning, Aaron," Penny replied with a real smile.

"Good mornin' to you. Yer mother asked me to take you back up to the house. Wanted to go o'er some numbers fer the harvest."

She plucked another late bloom and let it fall into the basket at her feet, joining the other blossoms that had opened too late for the season and the young pomegranates that had been attacked by pests or disease. "I would be happy to go back with you."

Aaron dismounted from his horse and began leading their small group back toward the manor. She'd been working in a field a little way off from the house. The walk back would give her the time to speak to one of the only men Mother ever trusted.

"Aaron, you haven't seen Lou around have you?"

"No, m'lady. I did get a note from him yesterday sayin' he wouldn't be back for a couple days. Said some family emergency come up and to dock him pay for the missed work. I don't have the mind to do so with him bein' such a good worker and all. Just hope it ain't nothin' serious."

"You find him to be such a trustworthy man?"

"I know a good man when I see 'em, Lady Penny." He gave her a wink that wiggled his bushy eyebrow. "You got yer gifts, and I got mine."

Penny couldn't help but smile. If it wasn't for the man's gruff accent, she would regularly forget he wasn't like most of the people in Olympia. Sireadh— Penny had heard them called "seekers" —were rare in their country and it wasn't often that people heard about them anymore. Most had left the continent after the Faerie Wars ended and the Mage Trials took up the fifty years after. Sireadh gifts were considered close to actual magic back then and many caravans were hunted down at the same time the Goddess-blessed were.

"Is that a Sireadh talent then? You're able to look a man in the eye and decide whether he is good or bad?"

"It ain't so black and white, m'lady. I din't learn many tricks from my caravan before settlin' here with my cousins, but what I did learn was to read a man's spirit. That'll tell you if a man will do wrong by you, not if he's good or evil. Seekers always know when best to bargain."

"And is Lou someone we can trust?"

Aaron nodded his head sagely. "That boy's gotta trustworthy heart if I ever saw one. Honorable to a fault. 'Tis why the Crown can trust him with a job like his."

Penny's heart jumped. "You know what he is?"

"How do you think he gotta job here? Boy came to me and asked if he could lay low in the fields while he does his work. Recognized me as seeker-folk and knew all the customs for makin' the deal. Been stayin' with me and Ada this whole time so I could keep an eye on him, but I found it wasn't needed after he started trainin' with you."

She gaped. "You knew this entire time? Why didn't you say anything?"

"I've known you for as long as you've been walkin', Lady Penny. I know you got a good head on your shoulders and yer ma taught you to be wary enough to protect yerself from heartbreak. I wasn't even worried 'bout him none 'til I watched you mope 'round the last couple days and it wasn't 'til I saw his note that my heart quit poundin'. I was worried he did somethin' ungentlemanly 'til he said he was comin' back." He gave Penny a smirk. "No man who breaks a lass's heart is dumb enough to come back to work for her."

Penny chuckled as tears gathered at her eyelashes. "I would hope not."

Aaron's expression grew serious. "Did he hurt you, m'lady?"

Penny shook her head. "No, nothing like that." She inhaled slowly and let it out even slower. She looked out over the fields, toward the town where she had left him. "More that I might have hurt him."

Aaron placed a comforting hand on her shoulder and she found his understanding eyes watching her. "'Tis sometimes hard to grow close to others. I watched you two off and on the fields and 'tis obvious you have grown fond of each other." He nudged her a little. "Maybe fonder than yer mother would like, eh?"

Penny let out a gasp and gave the man a little shove as he laughed.

"Why does your family seek to encourage my rebellion against my mother? Such treasonous acts from those we hold such confidence in." Not that she really minded. If Mother was stirring up rebellion, it would make sense that Penny was too.

The comment made Aaron laugh all the louder and Penny couldn't help but chuckle along with him.

"We all been 'round long enough to see how you differ from the duchess. She is the rock while yer the wind. She stays firm, steady. You fly through the air without lettin' anythin' get in yer way. Yer meant to play with fire and dance with snowflakes. We just wanna see you be who you are, not trying to be somethin' you ain't."

The tears Penny held back fell. Had it always been so obvious? Had everyone always known that she wasn't like Mother? Penny had seen the pictures of Mother in her youth. Their looks were nearly identical. If you placed an image of Mother alongside one of hers, Penny couldn't tell the difference except for the color of their eyes— and even then it was still close. She'd always been a cheap imitation of Mother, one who would never reach such heights as Mother had. She hadn't realized how opposite the two of them were.

"What if I don't want to be air? What if I want to be as solid and steady as a rock?"

"You can certainly try, but why try to be somethin' other than you? Just because you ain't steady don't mean you ain't fearsome. Don't ever think yer differences are weaknesses. Air can snuff out a blaze with a breath. The sea rages in the force of a storm. Trees can be completely uprooted by the tearin' of the wind. Sweet Gaia, if it tried hard enough, a gust could move a mountain. Strength isn't tryin' to mold ourselves into somethin' we ain't. It's changing the world with what the Goddess's already given us."

29

RELIEF AND REVELATION

The vision of gold against the late-summer sky had Penny rushing across the orchard. She couldn't care less if the other workers noted her haste or noticed the tears lining her eyes. It took a sharp look from Aaron to stop her from leaping into the vision's arms and looking over every inch of him to ensure his well-being.

"How are you feeling? Do you need a few more days of recovery? Does it still hurt? When did you get back?" She closed her mouth firmly against the tumult of questions she'd stored in her mind for his return.

Lou's smile lit up the orchard and melted a good number of the questions from Penny's list.

"I'm completely recovered, Lady Penelope. All thanks to you."

Aaron gave a little cough she knew he made to interrupt their reunion. Penny turned to look at him sharply, but as he tilted his head toward the small gathering of other workers, she understood his intention. She took a careful step away from Lou.

"Everyone here has been so worried about you. We're all happy to see you back on the orchard." With a slight nod, she took another step back. The group of five or six other farmhands all trotted over and gave their warm welcome to their peer— well, the man they believed to be their peer.

Penny lightly stepped back to where she'd been working, but her mind was far from the young pomegranates she reached out to with her gift.

The sun reached its zenith and Aaron called for lunch. Penny wiped her hands on her apron as she made her way through the trees. She heard the snap of a twig before a hand reached out to tentatively brush her shoulder.

"Lady Penelope."

Penny spun to find Lou in the shade of the trees. His eyes glowed with life so unlike when she'd left him with Farrah. Just his regular breathing made her want to kneel in the orchard right there and thank the Goddess.

"Lou. I can't tell you how relieved I am to see you up and moving." She swallowed. "I feared the worst until Farrah reached us."

Lou's eyes flashed with the pain of the memory. "I'm glad to know you keep such good friends. Without her help, neither of us would be looking at one another and I don't know if I would've enjoyed that very much."

He rubbed at the back of his neck. "Farrah told me she revealed my secret to you."

Penny's smile strained as questions pounded against her teeth. "Yes. She didn't give me any particulars, but she told me there was some sort of *glamour* on your person. That only fae are able to do such a thing."

Lou nodded. "She told me she said as much. Did she reveal how I was glamoured?"

Penny shook her head and he let out a short breath.

"I want you to know, Penelope, I wouldn't deceive you if I thought it wouldn't be for your own benefit. I knew if I showed up here as I am, that I wouldn't have been able to accomplish my mission. I couldn't have integrated myself in any rebel meetings if I'd allowed my heritage to show. If someone had seen you with me, they might have guessed we were up to something. I didn't want to put you in any danger."

Penny chuckled darkly. "I certainly didn't help you stay out of any."

Lou set a hand on her shoulder. "I'm very sorry about what happened in Eleusia, Penelope. I would never have let you come if I hadn't let my pride and my desire to spend more time with you cloud my judgment."

Penny's face warmed. He wanted to spend time with her? Her stomach fluttered. That was also the second time he'd called her by her given name during this conversation. She found she didn't mind it one bit.

"If anyone should be sorry, it's me. If you hadn't been trying to help me, that man would have never made that shot with the crossbow."

"None of the events of that night were your fault."

Penny nodded in acquiescence, even if she didn't yet believe it. His pale face and pained gasps still ran through her mind.

Lou gestured for her to follow him through the trees. They walked silently for a few minutes as she mulled over her feelings. Relief reigned supreme in her heart, but wariness still spread its tendrils through her mind.

She cleared her throat and their eyes met once again. "About the glamour… if it's not too impertinent, I'd like to see the real face of my friend."

Lou froze. Penny barely caught the myriad of emotions flash through his eyes. She wouldn't have seen the sparks of terror or longing if she hadn't been able to read him as well as she could now. He combed a hand through his hair and dug at the ground with the toe of his boot. He'd never looked so nervous.

"I don't think it will be anything as exciting as you may believe."

With the tips of his fingers, he tucked his shoulder length hair behind his ears. With a bob of his Adam's apple, he allowed the glamour to fade. Penny's eyes widened as his features changed.

The tips of his ears met at a point rather than rounded out like her own. His facial features sharpened so his jaw cut more sharply and his cheekbones slashed against the bronze of his skin. None of the changes were large, but the overall effect was certainly noticeable. Anyone would be able to see he was fae.

Penny let out a relieved breath. *Perhaps he wasn't as much a deceiver as I'd thought.* She should easily see how little he hid his real self and his reasoning behind it made complete sense.

She lightly brushed the edge of his cheek. "It's not as big of a difference as Farrah had led me to believe, but I can understand why you use it. I'm sure the rebels wouldn't allow you anywhere near them if you walked into their meetings looking like that."

Lou gave a small chuckle and his features shifted back to what Penny had come to know as normal— not that she would ever unsee what was under the glamour. His eyes still shimmered with something like regret as he looked at her.

"I'm surprised you wouldn't change the color of your eyes. They are quite remarkable." Her face heated as he smiled at her comment. "In fact, I've only ever seen one other person with eyes like yours. Say, you probably know him. He's a spy as well."

Lou's face blanched. "Yes I do know him. We must have

some sort of relation, but I don't know what." He pushed a smile onto his face. "I am glad you find the color so remarkable, but it's definitely something I would change if I could."

"You can't?"

Lou shook his head. "Glamours don't allow fae to mask the color of their eyes. The eyes are believed to be the windows to the soul and the fair folk can't completely cover up who they are, or it would be considered a lie. As pure fae are unable to lie, the magic compensates for it. It's the greatest tell of a glamour."

Penny's brows rose. "I never learned that in my fae studies. I only knew that purer fae can't lie without serious repercussions."

"It's not something most fae like to talk about. Some consider it to be a weakness and fae pride won't allow any of that to show if they can help it."

Her raised brow furrowed. "Farrah also mentioned you're half-fae. Why, then, can you lie?"

"We don't quite know." He shrugged. "Magic experts tested me when I was really young, but no one could come to any solid conclusions."

He looked up at the sun reaching beams through the leafy branches around them. "We should probably turn back toward the others. I wouldn't want you to skip lunch because I took up all of your time."

"I think asking after your health was as good excuse as any, thank you very much."

The feigned haughtiness had Lou's smile growing larger as they turned back to where the others had walked off to. "I appreciate the concern, my lady, but I don't think a lowly man such as myself deserves such attentions."

Penny stopped once more and looked at him seriously. "Lou, I consider you to be the exact opposite of a 'lowly man.'

You've become one of my closest confidantes and a wonderful friend. I would hope you'd expect me to ask after your well-being and be disappointed if I didn't. I care about you, Lou."

Lou's eyes flared with intensity. "As a friend?"

"Yes." Though Penny said the word, it caught in the back of her throat and tasted wrong on her tongue. She watched to see how Lou would react to the word himself, but the only thing that changed was the potency of his gaze. He answered in a small nod that twisted Penny's stomach.

Was it the wrong word?

As they continued walking, Penny's thoughts spun. Did she consider Lou simply to be her friend? It seemed such a small title for what the two of them had created with one another. They were beyond mentor and apprentice. Peer was too light of a term, but what would fit better? She couldn't call him a suitor. He'd never given any indication he thought of her like that— even if she wanted him to.

The word came to her.

"Partners."

"What?"

Penny looked up at Lou where he had stopped at the edge of the orchard. "We're more than friends, Lou. We've been *partners* on this crazy adventure. We've both been through too much together for mere friendship."

Lou stuck his hand out to her, and Penny took it. His eyes seared hers as he gazed at her in a way that caused her heart to race a bit more than a partner likely should. With a shake of their hands, the word cemented something between them.

Lou's lips quirked. "All right. Partners."

They had one week until Lou was to leave for the equinox and they'd still heard no new information on the rebels or The Cartographer. No new movement. No hints of any more rallies. Nothing.

"It doesn't make any sense," he huffed as Penny dodged his swing.

It had been like this for the last hour. The couple of mage-lights Penny had begun stashing out in the grove glowed along the edges of their sparring ring. The glint of steel reflected the lights as their blades met over and over.

Lou anxiously paced while sparring. It was quite the talent.

"Maybe they backed off," Penny replied as she tried to use the grass beneath his feet to entangle him, but he simply cut through the blades with his sword. It was always better to try to look for the good things that could be happening rather than just the bad. Mother always called her *Gaia's Advocate*.

At least, Penny hoped that was the case. She prayed that this would prove all of her fears were unfounded.

"Why would they? It's not as if that one man was holding the rebellion together. I know he was only a leader, not the head." At least that was what the rebel had claimed when Lou called him back from the dead. It made sense that he hadn't been The Cartographer. The rebel leader seemed smart enough not to publicize their involvement. It made the suspicions in the back of Penny's mind pound like a drum.

Lou tapped the fabric over her heart with his blade and they reset. "There are too many secrets, too many holes in the picture."

Penny thrust her blade at his torso and he easily dodged the blow while also landing a hit to her thigh with the flat of his blade.

That's going to bruise. "Maybe they are moving on from Eleusia? Would it be so hard to look at this on the bright side?"

He waved his long dagger at her distractedly. "My contacts in town said the men who were on their way to being recruited simply went underground. No more meetings, but they're all still there."

"What if they're planning a big party for the equinox and are giving all of the men time off?"

He gave her a flat look. "This is far from over, Lady Penelope. We've been trying to break up this rebellion since the Tyrant King died and his supporters were executed. If my suspicions are correct, they are simply lying low until they receive new orders."

His blade cut through her defenses and knocked one of the daggers out of her hand. He tilted his head toward where it landed and she ran to get it. When she turned back, he was actually pacing. Penny plopped herself on the ground by their water skins.

"You know, maybe this is a good thing. It gives us time to plan our next step."

His eyes never strayed toward her as he moved back and forth through the grass. Penny grew bored and began using her magic to shift the grass up and down in anticipation of his steps. He didn't even flinch when his foot met the tilled dirt instead of the soft tufts of greenery.

He finally stopped and turned in the direction Penny knew Eleusia lay. She stood and came to stand next to him. His face held the worry and confusion her own heart felt.

"What are they waiting for?"

Penny swallowed. What was *Mother* waiting for?

30

LOVE AND LETTERS

Dearest Penny,

Your last letter was seriously lacking in dramatic detail. You went on a secret mission, watched a building burst into flames, and saved the life of the super spy who has stolen your heart!

I NEED MORE THAN THREE SENTENCES!

We've finally made it to Autumn, and not a moment too soon. They have a two-week long celebration for the equinox and if we'd left any later we wouldn't have made it for the first of the festivities. The fae here have been very welcoming, if a bit strange. They find the strangest enjoyment in scaring the living daylights out of each other. I'd never heard Devan scream until we came across the werewolf in his wolf form pretending to chew on one of the house elves in our temporary home. It was as funny as it was terrifying. Apparently, it's part of the culture here.

I don't know how much Devan will be able to take.

I can't believe you got away with it without your mother finding out. I'm equally surprised she hasn't had you locked away in a tower by now. Or at least somewhere no men could ever reach you. She's always been terrified of anything happening to you and you were nearly killed going after a rebellion. Are you sure your mage gift is growing plants and not stupid luck? The Goddess must really want you to succeed in your efforts. I know the rest of us do.

I expect a much more detailed report of your outing in my next letter.

Your Very Exasperated Yet Supportive Friend,
Angelica

PENNY SAT DOWN NEXT TO MOTHER AT THE LARGE DINNER TABLE. IT was the first time in several days they'd sat down to a meal together. Mother had been working long hours in the fields as the young fruit on the trees needed tending to— not that Penny minded. While the initial cause of their disagreement had been months ago, the two of them still walked on eggshells around one another.

Lou had been a pacing nightmare the last couple of days and

had finally gone to Eleusia himself. He'd told her he would return before midnight for training. They were four days away from his departure. Four days until Penny would likely never see him again. What was she going to do when he left? Perhaps they could stay in contact. Maybe it was time to tell him that she thought about him as more than just a friend or even a partner.

"How many fields were you able to see to today?" Mother asked, breaking Penny from her thoughts.

It took Penny a moment before she was able to respond. "Four, if you count Star and Upper Left fields as one." The two combined were the same size as their largest field and sat right across the canal from one another.

"Good, good," Mother responded, nodding her head absently. She scooped another sip of soup into her spoon.

The lack of discussion resumed for a moment before Mother's spoon fell with a clang into her bowl. Penny jumped.

Mother frowned down at the utensil as if it had offended her. "I'm tired of the silence. I am tired of feeling more tension when I'm sitting down at the table for a meal than when I'm surrounded by piles of paperwork."

"Paperwork does always help you feel in control," Penny mumbled in reply.

Mother cleared her throat and smoothed out the tablecloth near her bowl, an indication that she actually wanted to slam her hands onto the tabletop. "I don't understand what's going on in that head of yours, Penny. Nothing has changed. I've always been direct with you and perfectly clear about the rules. It's nothing you have not lived without before."

"If you can even call it living." The words were less of a mumble than the last.

And perhaps things had changed. By the Goddess, there was a cursed rebellion in their lands.

Mother threw her hands up. "This is ridiculous! You run off

in the middle of the night, interrupt a rebel campaign meeting and now you think you know more about the world than your mother."

"I never said that. I simply said that I want to be more involved in the world. Not hidden away like I have some kind of plague."

"According to what this *Cartographer* is teaching, you do have some kind of plague. Fear like that will only turn to violence and it is my job to protect you from it."

"I'm not just talking about rebel meetings, Mother. I'm talking about *everything*. Even here, you've barely given me any more responsibilities since I came of age. Working in the fields and handling the workers' schedules is great and all, but how am I ever going to run this duchy if I never leave the shadow of the manor?"

"We go all over the duchy."

Penny scoffed. "Oh, yes. We stay on main streets, talk to the same people, and hide from anything that could be considered potentially harmful. We're so adventurous!"

"I don't know what you want from me, Penny. I will not allow you to come to harm if I have any say in it. I do what I do out of love for you and love for our land."

"You say that, but look around! Rebels are practically at our doorstep. Our people are committing treason. We've had crops and buildings burn down around us. We barely have enough people to work the orchards... Mother, it's all falling apart, and you won't even acknowledge it."

Mother shook her head. "You don't see the entire picture, Penny. You don't know how hard I'm working to fix everything. Why can't you just trust me?"

"Why can't you trust *me*?" Tears crowded Penny's eyes and she swiped at them so Mother wouldn't see. "Why can't you trust me to take the knowledge and wisdom you've given me and apply it? Why can't you see that I'm my own person and that I want different things than you? Why is it so hard for you to even let me help you?"

"I do trust you. You're a Barclay. You understand the things I do better than anyone. Our gift is sacred. We are sacred. I simply don't trust men not to try to take advantage of that."

"There you go again!" Penny rubbed her face with her palms. "It's all about evil men and their sinister plots. *Why?* Why do you hate every man who lives on this blasted planet?"

"You want to know why?" Mother slapped her hands on the table and loomed over the table at her. "Because *I married one.* I married a cursed scumbag who took advantage of me and every other woman he came across. From the moment I married him, I lived with a man who didn't care about anyone but himself and lived only for his next pleasure at the cost of everyone else around him."

Penny's heart dropped into her stomach.

Mother began pacing around the room. "The man I met at sixteen swept me off my feet. He was handsome and charismatic. He wrote me flowery letters packed with passion and desire. Filled my head with thoughts of true love and marriage and all the silly things little girls dream of. Being the second son of a business tycoon, I believed he would understand me, and from the things he told me, he did. I married him as soon as I turned eighteen. What I didn't realize was that it had all been a game to him."

"What kind of game?" Penny's voice came out so small Mother might not have heard.

Mother sank back down in her chair. "He played with girls' hearts until they gave him what he wanted. But instead of only wanting to take me to his bed, he wanted the title that came with my hand. We married with your grandfather's permission. What I didn't know was that both your grandparents would die only a few weeks later and leave me alone with a monster."

Penny's arms wrapped around her stomach and she shrank back in her chair. "Did he kill them?"

Mother shook her head. "No. An illness set in the house. We all caught it, but your grandparents were too frail to overcome it. They passed within hours of each other. It was after that when the rumors began circulating. People spoke of seeing the Duke of Eleusion in pubs or pleasure houses, chasing after every skirt he could find. He came home drunk more often than not. He came home angry those days as well. There were some nights I would wake up with so many bruises..."

Her hand came to her throat. "When you were three, I went to a meeting for something I can't even remember now. I came home a day earlier than I'd planned. I'd left you in Philomina's care, thinking the duke wouldn't be around. I" —she cleared her throat— "I was wrong. The duke had returned in a rage. I found the entire staff cowering in the stables." Mother drew a shaky breath. "Everyone, but Philomina. Her I found in the house, tied to the bed in the duke's chamber, with him sprawled out beside her in a drunken slumber."

Tears tracked down Penny's cheeks. *Oh, Philo.*

"She'd looked so broken, both in spirit and body, but the first thing she told me to do was find you. She'd mouthed the command and pointed at the bottles of pomegranate liquor we stored in the cellar your grandfather had built away from the house."

Mother stopped on the other side of the table. "Penny, I'd never been so terrified in my life. I found you unconscious, locked in that dark, dank cellar. Your tiny fists had been bleeding from you pounding on the door and you'd been so pale. Philomina said later that you'd been trapped down there since the night before and she was the only one who'd known. It had killed her to not be able to get to you.

"I saw you safely to the other servants when screams started coming from the house. I raced in with Rich behind me. We found the duke in his chamber, broken glass scattered around where Philomina now lay on the floor. He was screaming at her, spittle and curses flying from his mouth. He called her such terrible things. Told her she needed to leave before her lady came home and saw her in his chamber. Told her I would ruin her life because of what *she'd* done."

Mother's expression turned dark. "I didn't think. After seeing your bloody fists and Philomina's broken body, I couldn't. I grabbed the fire poker next to the fireplace in his room and I hit him. I hit him until his body stopped moving."

Penny couldn't breathe.

"Rich and I took his body back to that Goddess-forsaken cellar and threw him in. It only took a few minutes for the entire thing to set ablaze and collapse on top of itself. No one was able to dig out the body. We told everyone it was an accident. I used the earth to bury the cellar so far into the ground that no one would ever find trace of it again. We pretended to mourn that sorry excuse for a human being for the allotted time and then it was over. He was gone and I would never let anyone get that close to you ever again."

"Never?" The word escaped Penny in a whisper. She didn't even know why she said it.

Mother looked her in the eye. "Tell me, Penny, if a wife can't trust the safety of her family to her own husband, how is she to ever trust a single male ever again?"

Penny could do nothing but shake her head. Her father had been a horrible man. He'd beat his wife. He'd terrorized the people he had a responsibility over. He'd abused every good thing given to him.

And now he lay in a burnt pit in the ground.

Her attention focused on Mother. "Why didn't you tell me?"

Mother took a deep breath and sat in the chair across from her. "What good would that have done? What mother wants to tell her child that the man that should have been a father to her was instead a worthless pig? What child wants to grow up knowing her mother had to kill her father so they wouldn't have to live in fear for the rest of their lives? I didn't tell you because I was trying to protect you."

If Mother was willing to do that, what else was she willing to do without Penny's knowledge? While this situation had obviously been traumatic in the extreme, Mother could have told anyone. While his death had been at her hands, the things the duke had done wiped away any guilt in the eyes of the law. No one would have blamed her. But she hadn't told anyone. She'd allowed this anger, this pain to grow.

Was this what had driven her to fight against the Crown? Was it truly just about having complete control so no one could hurt her ever again?

And who else would Mother be willing to put down to do what she believed was right?

Mother's face blurred and more tears trickled onto Penny's cheeks. "But I would have understood. We could have talked about it. Come to something better than me living in ignorance—"

"What would that have done?"

"I wouldn't be floundering for a way to get you to understand what I need!" Penny's voice rose. "We could've made plans for me to do more around here. We could've worked together to keep each other safe. You wouldn't have been burdened with so much for so long." *You wouldn't have to hurt people because someone hurt you.*

"I am the duchess. I decide what burdens are mine and what are yours."

"But maybe I would've been able to help you!" Penny stood from her chair, sorrow and anger warring for dominance in her chest. "I could have done more. Maybe this rebellion wouldn't have taken root because we would've been on the same team when instead I've been trying to figure out what blasted game we've been playing this entire time."

"You're still going to fight me on this? After I just told you what kind of monsters live in this world? After I bare my soul —" Her words cut off. The emotion written all over her face disappeared and the Duchess of Eleusion came out.

"Fine." Mother mirrored Penny's stance. "Tomorrow, I leave for the capital. I was going to wait until after harvest, but since you've so vehemently demanded some more responsibility, I'll go now. I will not return until after the equinox and you will have full responsibility for the orchards while I'm gone. You will be running the entire operation here while I am away."

Mother leaned over the table toward Penny. Penny did her best to meet her eye. "This is your one chance. If anything— *anything*— goes awry while I'm away, it's on your head. You will take full responsibility for everything that goes on here. If there are any problems, there will be no more talk of leaving the duchy and no more of this defiant attitude. Am I understood?"

Without waiting for an answer, Mother rang for a servant. Philomina stepped through the door only a second after, her eyes red rimmed.

Mother pinched the bridge of her nose. "Tell Cook I'll take the rest of my dinner in my study. I have some preparations to make before morning." Her clipped steps rang through the dining room as she left.

Penny sagged back into her chair when the door shut.

Philomina remained in the room. Penny couldn't meet her eyes. "I'm so sorry, Philo."

Philomina's quiet steps swept across the room and took Penny's shaking shoulders into her arms. "Don't you ever apologize for what that monster did. He's gone and all of his vileness with him. You are here, bright and glorious for all the world to see."

She took in a deep breath. "I know Her Grace has taken her rules to the extreme. What she does, she does out of love. She wouldn't care so much, and you wouldn't feel so hurt otherwise." She pulled away and lifted Penny's chin. "You and I both know there are good men out there. We've seen them. I just don't know what kind of man it would take to ever change her mind."

Penny drifted toward the clearing, her mind still lingering on Mother's story and Philomina's tears. Perhaps she should tell Lou she wasn't willing to spar tonight. Or perhaps sparring would take away the pain in her chest for just a few moments.

Would she tell him what Mother had revealed to her? Would she voice her suspicions? Would she tell him everything or keep the gruesome details to herself? How would he look at her if he knew?

She shook her head. It didn't matter how he looked at her. She needed to tell him. If Mother was involved in the rebellion, they had to stop her.

Her steps slowed as she came upon the empty space, save the glowing magelight Lou usually left sitting on the other side. Her hand instantly went to the dagger at her hip as her eyes flicked through the shadows of the trees. She wouldn't be caught by surprise again if Lou decided to start a random attack exercise. Last time, she had to wear long sleeves for two weeks after it ended with a large bruise on her arm.

Penny stalked all the way across the clearing to where the magelight sat in its regular place. The difference this evening, however, was the folded sheet of paper tucked underneath the light.

Looking around once again, she crouched and pulled the piece of parchment out. After unfolding it, Lou's neat script stood as stark as his black veins against his skin.

Dearest Penelope,

I would have rather given this news to you in person. It pains me to know that I won't have the chance to see you one last time, but I'm not able to ignore the commands of the Crown Prince. I've been called back to the capital this very night as more pressing matters have come up in Olympia.

I leave you this note so you may know that I did wish to bid you farewell. I'll never forget the months we've had to grow together. I've learned more on this mission about myself than I ever had the privilege to before. Thank you for your friendship and for allowing me to see the world through your eyes.

Don't allow my absence to keep you from training. You have enough skill to take care of yourself. You never needed much of my help in that regard, but all the same, don't slack on your training just because I won't be there to watch.

Farewell. I hope the Goddess allows our paths to cross again.

Your Friend,

A small blotch of ink sat just below the closing of the letter, as if his quill had sat at the spot for a moment before deciding to leave it unsigned.

Penny's heart and body fell to the ground beneath her feet. The paper crinkled in her fingers as her hand fell limply into her lap.

He'd left.

The only man she'd ever trusted, the only man she'd let glimpse into her heart had left. Did this prove Mother was right? What was she going to do without him?

She shook her head. A tear landed on the paper laying in her lap. She swiped at her face and stood. "There has been enough crying tonight to last a lifetime," she chided herself. "Some silly rebels pop into my life, my mother may be helping them, I find out my father was a monster, and now I'm regularly reduced to tears?" She let out a wet laugh. "Pathetic."

She neatly folded the note and placed it in her satchel next to the picture of the missing fae boy. They would help her remember why she was doing this. With tears trailing down her cheeks, she checked both of her daggers and began working through the motions of *cumadh*.

Lou was a good man. He hadn't left her behind because she wasn't needed. He went to perform his duties. He was loyal.

And if he'd left her with orders to continue training, then she would. She would put all of her energy into honing the skills Lou had instilled in her with what little time they'd had. She wouldn't let him down, not in this. She would see her friend again and she would report that she'd done all he had asked of her.

She would make this work. She would get the evidence she needed. She would find out if her suspicions were correct.

Her lips moved in a prayer that the Goddess would see fit to bless their paths to cross again soon.

31

BLUE AND GOLD

MOTHER LEFT BEFORE THE SUN CRESTED OVER THE HORIZON. PENNY watched the carriage turn off the front drive and disappear into the orchards. Once the coach was completely out of sight and sound, Penny shut the front door and raced up the stairs toward her room. She needed to get to the study and begin searching. There was much to be done.

Penny strode into her rooms. The sound of humming swept through the space from her bedroom. She followed the noise to where Sissy sat, rummaging through her closet.

"Sissy? What are you doing up?"

Sissy's head popped out of the chest of boots Penny had sitting on the floor.

"I was looking for those nicer pair of work boots you got last month to set by your bed, but I can't seem to find them." Sissy returned to her digging.

Penny turned to where her boots hid under the small box by her desk. She'd ordered them from the capital right after she'd been given her daggers. They came with a built-in sheath for her blade and would make it easier to wear her weapon without it shifting around on her ankle. She hadn't wanted anyone to know about them and had taken to hiding them when they weren't on her feet. Apparently, Sissy had noticed.

"I think I left them just over here."

Penny raced over to her desk before Sissy could see and hid the daggers under the box. Sissy came out of the closet and Penny held up the boots, dangling from her hands by the laces. While she'd told Sissy about most of their interactions, the gifted daggers were something Penny didn't want to share with anyone but Lou.

"Sweet Gaia, I should've noticed them. This is why it's bad for me to be up this early." The statement was emphasized by a wide yawn breaking across her face a moment later.

Penny laughed and allowed the sleepy maid to help her get ready for the day. As Sissy made her way to the closet for Penny's hat, Penny tucked her blades into the sheathes in her boots.

Sissy sat Penny down at the vanity and began braiding Penny's reddish-brown locks into a crown. Penny caught her leg shaking more than twice while she sat there. Sissy pinned the strands into place and came around to Penny's side.

"I know you're nervous about today— by the Goddess, even I'm nervous. I brought you something that might bring some luck." Sissy reached into the pocket of her white apron and pulled out a small scrap of blue. She proudly held it up to the light. "This is my favorite ribbon. I wore it the day your mother interviewed me for the position as your maid. Every major event in my life, I've worn this ribbon. I figure something good must have rubbed off on it, so I thought to let you use it."

Sissy began to wrap the small, blue ribbon around Penny's left wrist. The smooth satin cooled Penny's skin. Sissy tied it off with a knot Penny would never be able to remove herself and tucked it under the cuff of her dress.

"I can't take your precious ribbon from you."

Sissy smiled and winked. "Consider it a loan then."

Penny smiled back and wrapped Sissy in a sisterly hug. She regularly forgot how much Sissy had been through with her. Memories of their years together brought small tears to Penny's eyes. She thought of Mother and Philomina now on their way to the capital and the tears slipped down her cheeks.

"I don't know what I'd do without you. Thank you."

After Sissy dubbed Penny ready, the two of them went to Mother's study. They parted ways at the door and Penny walked straight to Mother's chair. Stacks of paper sat on Mother's desk, all of it organized into categories like shift rotations, water schedules, business correspondence, and accounting ledgers.

"Sissy!" Penny hollered.

Sissy's smiling face popped into the study a moment later, telling Penny she hadn't wandered off too far. "You bellowed?"

Penny couldn't help the twitch her lips gave at the maid's chipper attitude.

"I was hoping I could send you down to Cook for the receipts."

Sissy looked at her with a furrowed brow. "Where's Rich?"

"He's performing duties in the village that my mother left him. He should be back by midday, but I wanted to get all of the accounting checked before going to the fields this morning." *And I need to find some sort of clue.*

Sissy gave Penny another cheerful smile. "I'll be just a moment then."

Sissy came and went faster than Penny had ever seen the girl move this early in the morning.

Penny began at the desk. She remembered Lou checking over crevices for hidden latches or false drawers. When that grew fruitless, she looked through the bookshelves, then the grandfather clock. Every nook and cranny in the space was run over by her fingertips. She even knocked on the wood planks of the floor until Sissy came up to tell her Aaron was waiting for her at the front of the house.

She would have to finish her search later.

The workday started with her riding Meli alongside Aaron as they went through the orchards and talked with the workers. Penny jotted down note after note to compare with the detailed numbers Mother had left her. They stopped at one of the fields and began to work their way through the trees, looking for disease and counting the ripening fruits. The bulbous fruits all showcased an array of pinks, yellows, and greens, not yet developing the deep, red color of mature pomegranates.

"It seems root rot isn't as prevalent this year," she remarked.

"Aye, m'lady. Trees are plenty healthy, and the fruit never looked so fine."

Aaron grabbed hold of one of the larger fruits and ripped it from the tree. With his hands, he opened the thick flesh to expose the innards of the fruit. Clear capsules of juice and seed stuck to the inside of the yellow skin. Those turned red when the fruit ripened.

"Might be the best harvest we've had in some time. You've been quite the little worker, m'lady."

Nothing could knock the smile off Penny's face after a compliment like that. She went through her day as if walking on air. Everything shone a little brighter after the dark fog caused by her suspicions of Mother. The green of the trees grew vibrant.

Everyone around her worked merrily as the sunshine rained down on them and the cool breeze took the sting of late summer away. The buzz of bees and the trill of the birds led Penny through the day, lifting her spirits in only the way Gaia's creations could.

The feeling lasted until the sun went down. Everyone went their separate ways and Penny found herself riding home alone. There had been very few times in the last six months when she'd been completely by herself. Either Mother had been hovering close by or Lou had accompanied her to the front drive of the manor. The quiet sounds of the night helped steady her, but the darkness crawled sinisterly toward her. Her leg rubbed against Meli's side and the hilt of her dagger brushed along her lower calf. The feel of the weapon eased the tightening of her chest enough for her to make it home without too many shadows chasing her. She thanked the Goddess for the light shining merrily out of the manor's windows that evening.

Dinner was a modest affair. Penny decided to take her food in the study so she could continue her search after she worked on her replies to the many letters on the desk. The window behind her stood open to allow the cool breeze to glide through the room and stoke the flames of the small fire providing the room with light. She meticulously pulled the pins out of her hair, allowing the auburn locks to fall in waves down her back. Her fingers massaged her scalp as a headache grew.

It took hours to go through everything to her satisfaction. Penny used a magelight on the desk as the fire burned low in the hearth. Her eyes grew heavy as she sat in Mother's chair and soon it was all she could do to keep her thoughts on the letter to Angelica before her.

"I hope you've continued your training."

Penny's head snapped up and she found Lou stoking the fire back into a roar. The smell of smoke tickled her nose.

"Lou," Penny gasped, "I'm so glad to see you. After I got your letter, I thought you were gone for good."

His eyes turned to hers. The gold reflected the heat of the fire as he gazed at her. He wore the same clothing he had when they'd met, his shoulder length hair spilling around his face.

"Me too," replied a voice from behind her.

Amber Eyes walked out of the shadows by the window. He sauntered over to stand next to Lou. Lou placed the poker back on the rack and stood next to him.

"What are you doing here?" Penny couldn't decide who the question was directed at, but both of them answered.

"I'm your friend, Penelope. I would never allow harm to come to you." Lou's voice was a balm to her soul.

"I remember you, just as you remember me." Amber Eyes' voice caused her heart to race.

Her eyes darted back and forth between the two of them. They stood next to one another in companionable silence.

"Do you two know one another?"

They looked at each other. Their expressions mirrored one another perfectly as they turned back to Penny.

"We've crossed paths before," replied Amber Eyes.

"You saved us in Eleusia," she responded. "How did you know we were there?"

Once again, they looked at one another then back to her.

"He always knows, Penny."

Penny's vision swam a bit as she stared at them, their forms combining in and out from one another. Penny coughed and waved a hand in front of her face. The smoke from the fireplace began to overwhelm her.

"We really" —her nostrils burned at the scent— "should fix the fire." She coughed over the words and walked toward the fireplace. The smell got worse and worse while the fireplace drew farther and farther away.

"Lady Penny!" Both of the men screamed and grabbed her arms. Penny thrashed in their grips as she tried to walk toward the fire. "*Lady Penny!*"

Penny jolted awake to find Sissy shaking her shoulders.

"Lady Penny! We have to leave. Everything is on fire!"

32

SMOKE AND SHADOW

Penny bolted to the open window of the study. The glow of hundreds of acres ablaze brought a cry to her throat.

Sissy grabbed her arm and pulled her toward the door.

“We don’t have much time.” Sissy’s voice held the urgency Penny tried so hard to instill in herself. “My father came as soon as he saw the first field lit. There’s hundreds of them.”

“Hundreds of what?”

“Rebels.”

Penny’s stomach dropped and her lungs seized.

The rebels had come to take revenge.

Sissy ushered Penny out the door of the study. Penny finally snapped out of her shock and kept pace with Sissy as they trotted through the halls. Through the windows, all of her family’s land was covered in the flames of anger she’d seen those men carry in their hearts. Those same men’s shadows rushed about through the flames, all running toward the manor.

Penny grabbed her maid’s hand and pulled her toward the stairs.

"Faster, Sissy."

Penny skidded to a halt at the top stair and pulled Sissy behind her. At the bottom step, three men stood with gauntlet clad hands holding a boy that could be no older than ten. His head hung down and a moan broke through his lips. The boy's clothing and hair were dirty, bedraggled. As Penny looked closer, she saw the tips of his pointed ears peek through the mess of mangy brown hair on his head.

She'd seen him before. Not in person, but on paper. He was one of the missing fae in Eleusia, the one who'd been missing since winter solstice. And the gauntlets clawing into his shoulders were covered in runes. From that distance, they were indistinguishable, but it wasn't hard to guess that they had some control over the boy and his magic or else he would have escaped.

"Penelope Barclay," one of the men shouted, drawing her attention. "You've been hereby charged with magecraft, consorting with the enemy, murder, and treason."

Her spine stiffened and she glared at the small boy's kidnappers. "Who dares charge me with such heinous crimes?" She took a single step down the stairs. "Who are you to come into my house throwing around accusations?"

"The Cartographer finds you guilty" —the man sneered— "and sentences you to death. May the Goddess purge this world of your stain."

All three men lifted their hands from the small boy. Instantly, the boy threw his head back and screamed. His hands flailed out to the side. They changed from the tan brown of a sun-kissed child to bright white of blinding light. Only members of the Day Court had magic over light. His face contorted in pure agony. Heat burst from his body and flames swallowed half of the stairway as well as the walls on the bottom floor.

Penny didn't take the chance to see what happened to the little boy as she pushed Sissy back toward the study.

"Move!"

Both their feet pounded down the hall as flames chased behind them. Penny ran just ahead of Sissy, her training with Lou giving her an edge over the slightly younger girl. The roar of the fire overwhelmed the thrum of blood in Penny's ears. Smoke wound its way into both her lungs as her home burned down around them.

Penny looked toward her friend. "Faster, Sissy. We have to move faster."

A crack sounded and Sissy's eyes widened as she looked up. "Penny, look out!"

Sissy shoved Penny forward, sending her flying into the carpet beneath their feet.

The sound of something heavy hit the ground behind her and sparks hit the exposed skin of her calves. Penny scrambled away from the scorching heat and turned around.

The ceiling of the hallway had buckled from the flames and a large pile of burning beams and stone took up half of the hallway, ending only a few feet from Penny.

Right where Sissy had been a moment before.

No.

No no no no no no no.

Screaming rang in Penny's ears. Tears fell on her cheeks and it wasn't until she realized they were coming from her that the screams turned into sobs. She crawled closer, but the searing heat stopped her from digging through the rubble for her friend.

There was no sign of her. Not a tendril of golden hair or flash of her light green serving dress. It was almost like this broken piece of Penny's home had eradicated Sissy's entire existence.

A shout sounded somewhere beyond the flames and Penny had to cover her mouth with her hands to muffle her cry.

A cry of fear.

Of fury.

Of anguish.

The flames on the walls grew higher and it took every ounce of Penny's will and Lou's training to drag herself off the floor and run in the other direction. Deep sobs shook her, broken by choking caused by the inhaling of smoke. Flames charged behind her, eating away everything in sight.

Penny made it to the door of Mother's study and opened it. She ran to the open window, following the smoke billowing out of it. The drop into the garden below was too high for her to make without serious injury. She tried to reach her magic out to any of the plants attached to the house. The vines choked in the smoke as she attempted to lengthen their branches. She worked on thickening the grass in the garden below to cushion her fall, but the blades caught the attention of the flames and burned to a crisp. Penny reached and reached with her magic, but nothing outside could help her.

Penny could see the flames slowly licking up the sides of the house as she looked out the window. She did her best to scream for help, but her voice rang raw into the blazing night. Her eyes fell once again on the entirety of her lands swathed in flame.

No one would be coming for her.

There had to be something she could use to rappel out the window. Her eyes landed on the small pot of ivy hanging from the ceiling and Penny reached out to it. The vines grew only for them to use up the water too quickly and reached a few feet out the window before flames caught on the ends. Penny tried to push it further, but the pot exploded, sending clay and soil over the floor near the flames at the window. Several pieces of dirt covered parchment scattered over the floor, catching on the flames.

Penny covered her mouth and reached out to grab a few that hadn't yet been touched by the flames or smudged by the soil from the pot.

Your mission was a success. The girl... really has no idea. ...time to focus on Eleusia's outskirts.

Chthonia is ripe for the taking. Send someone there to get things stirred up. We need all of the duchy under rebel control before we can move on to our bigger targets.

Keep eyes on him. ...work to get him out of the duchy, but don't let him suspect you... and I will be greater than any man who walks this earth.

Penny's thoughts spun. There was one more paper, now half eaten by flame. She blew out the ends as best she could, and a few spots of ash smudged over the words making large parts of it illegible.

...make sure you're gone from the house... Penelope has become a problem... you need to do something, or I will... Rich...

Penny's eyed burned, staring at the blocky handwriting meant to cover up someone's normal script.

She'd been right.

Mother had been involved all this time and now she had the proof. Why else would these notes be in the study? They even mentioned Rich, who had been at the rally in Chthonia. He followed Mother's orders like a loyal puppy. She had done this and as Penny suspected, it had all been a play for more control. Control not just over Penny's life or the lives of those living in the duchy, but everyone's.

Sick to her stomach, she stuffed the small scraps of paper into the pocket of her dress.

Penny turned toward the door. She needed to get out

before the fire found that part of the manor. She grabbed the handle. Searing heat met her skin and she instantly let go with a yelp. The crack of flames sounded from the other side and smoke billowed from the crack between the door and the hardwood floor.

She raced back to the window. Broken bones were better than losing consciousness from the smoke and dying by fire. She made it to the window, but before she could even stick her head outside to breath a sliver of air, a brick went sailing by her face. She stumbled back, tripping over the dirt and falling onto the floor.

The sound of men's laughter came from outside.

Staying low, she peeked over the edge of the windowsill. An entire mob stood below the window, brandishing anything even remotely resembling a weapon. If she went through the window, they would be on her in a heartbeat.

By the Goddess.

There was no escape from the study.

Penny scrambled to the fireplace, the only thing that wouldn't catch fire, and did her best to cover her face to keep from inhaling the toxic smoke.

Her tears made her skin ache.

Penny's mind began to fog as the smoke poisoned the air around her. Coughs wracked through her as her lungs attempted to dispel the smoke, but the black clouds continued to push their way back into her body. She watched Mother's study finally catch fire through tear-filled eyes. The smoke slithering across the floor.

Wait, not smoke.

Lines of black snaked along the ground. They wove through the flames, some winding around them to bring the blazes of orange and yellow down a few inches. They swarmed the room until one of them met the edge of her shoe in the fireplace. The next instant, the shadows receded like a wave on the beach and pounding began on the other side of the burning door.

After a few hits, the door buckled from the impact and Penny saw a pair of legs stride into the room. The nimble feet worked around the debris as the shadows smothered the brightness and heat of the flames. The legs bent and Lou's soot-covered face met hers.

"Thank the Goddess," Lou breathed, and reached to grab Penny's arms.

His hands were covered in ash the same color of the veins that wrapped around his forearms and up his neck. As Penny crawled out of the fireplace, her vision swam. She only stood for a moment before her knees buckled and she fell. Before she could hit the ground, Lou had her cradled in his arms and walked out of the study.

Smoke filled every inch of the hall. Penny saw the veins of Lou's neck blacken further as shadows pushed the smoke away from them and continued to smother the flames. Penny's attention split between Lou's weary face and the devastation around them.

He came back. He came back for me. She sucked in a relieved breath only for it to come out as a cough. The edges of her sight darkened. "How— how did you find me?"

The feeling of his lips against her hair brought clarity to her sight. "You're a light in the dark, Penelope. I'll always see you through the shadows."

Penny didn't know if her tears were from the searing heat of his words or the flames.

Lou raced her to her family rooms only to find the way blocked by blazing debris. Penny wracked her brain for another option, trying to banish the memory of her friend under another pile such as this. A thought struck and she pointed behind them.

"The servants' stairway is back around the corner."

Lou immediately turned around and strode toward the door.

She had to tell him what she'd found. Once she helped get them out of here, she would give him everything.

They made it to the stairs to find them crumbled into ash, the fire still raging along the walls around them. Lou's shadows curled around the flames, but the inferno seemed to be too much for them. Penny looked up to see the veins working up Lou's jaw. He looked down at her, frantic.

"Penelope, I never wanted you to know." His hands shook as he set her on her feet, but kept the arm around her waist to steady her. Penny couldn't take her attention away from the worry in Lou's golden gaze as he ran an ash-covered hand through his soot-stained hair. "I never wanted to deceive you, but I thought it would be better if you didn't know. I thought maybe in time, it could be different. I didn't know this would happen. I'm... I'm sorry."

One moment, Lou was standing in front of her. The next, the veins of black stretched up into his cheeks, changing the shape of his face. His golden skin turned fair and his ears pointed. The golden hair framing his face stopped reflecting the glow of the flames as it disappeared, and the shorter strands began soaking in the light as it darkened. His cheekbones grew sharp as well as the edge of his brow.

Lou no longer held her in his arms. Instead, the man from the ball, from her dreams, from those nights in Eleusia, stood in her friend's place. Penny blinked rapidly, attempting to clear the smoke and the vision of Amber Eyes. His face held a sadness not belonging to a face like his.

He'd fully deceived her. Everyone was lying to her. Was she

so blind that everyone around her had been able to fool her so completely?

Before she could speak, he once again lifted her into his arms. The shadows around them finally stifled the flames and Penny barely noticed when Amber Eyes' feet stepped into the open air of the stairway, and they fell through the open space. Penny didn't have the strength to hold tighter as the air swept past them and Amber Eyes landed on the bottom floor as if it were a two-foot drop. There were no more flames and the sole source of light came from the dying embers around them.

Penny coughed on the smoke left from the smothered fires. Her mind fogged as her lungs tried to take in more air than was available.

"We're almost out." The deep voice rumbled along her side. He'd even masked his voice somehow to make it less noticeable. Her competing emotions flailed as he carried her. His deception had been thorough. He'd saved her again.

She would never be able to trust him.

Her vision faded at the edges, but Penny did her best to stay conscious as she gave directions. It took all of her energy to point one way or another even though it seemed he knew where to go. Penny looked up again at the man.

"Is Lou even your name?" Penny's voice came out in a rasp even she barely heard, but he must have because he shook his head.

She coughed as more words caught in her throat. "In Eleusia?"

Penny knew her question was vague, but he answered the implication anyway. "I used a glamour of myself and Spot in the alleyway. I'm sure you noticed the edges were frayed. It was the only thing I could come up with at that moment to protect you."

Penny thought back and realized the shadowed aura the

glamour had exuded was simply the incompletion of it. Different fae had a number of varied abilities simply based on their own strength, much like the mages, though she didn't know the extent of such gifts. She sighed at her own incompetence, causing her to cough.

The entire walk, Penny saw no more evidence of flame and the shadows seemed to hold up the house around them. They finally made it to the kitchen and Amber Eyes kicked open the back door. The fresh air made Penny dizzy with relief and Amber Eyes staggered into the yard. Only the light from the flaming fields lit the ground around them. The manor stood filled with smoke and shadows.

Amber Eyes' walk slowed to nearly a crawl as he huffed down the front drive until it seemed they were far enough. He took a deep breath and the shadows inside the manor swept back to him, curling around his limbs and through his hair in a caress.

Without the stability of his magic, Barclay Manor fell into a smoldering heap.

"Aaron has everyone at the village. The rebels showed up at the manor right after he made it here to warn everyone. Most of the staff were in the kitchen and got out before the house was lit."

Penny's dry eyes once again watered. Her hand shook as she covered her mouth.

Sissy.

The sobs made their way up her throat until they burst from her. Her heart broke as the image of Barclay Manor crumbling with her friend inside beat over and over again through her mind. Anguish overtook her and Amber Eyes fell to his knees. He cradled her in his lap as he looked over every inch of her.

"What happened?" The absolute terror in his voice

reflected in Penny's heart. "Are you hurt? What's wrong? Penelope? *Penelope!*"

Her name on his lips followed her into the darkness.

33

ASHES AND MOURNERS

"I think she's comin' 'round."

The familiar voice brought Penny out of unconsciousness. The smell of straw and yeast mixed with the faint smell of smoke still caught in her nose. Everything sat in darkness and it took a few moments before she realized it was because her eyes remained closed. Her eyelids begged her not to move, but she overcame the urge to remain in the dark and opened them.

Above her, a lofted ceiling showed sturdy beams holding up a thick, wooden roof. The scratch of homespun fabric tickled her neck as she lay on a stiff mattress. Two heads hovered into view above her. Penny's eyes burned when they focused on the faces of Aaron and Ada. Soft sobs broke from her chest at the despairing faces of her friend's parents.

"Sissy."

The name was a cry in itself and both of their faces crumpled in grief as she spoke it. A soft hand smoothed the hair on top of Penny's head as tears fell down the sides of her face.

"She would've been happy you made it out," Ada said

soothingly. Penny could hear the tears in the back of the woman's throat.

"She protected me," Penny choked out.

Those were the only words she could release with the heaviness sitting in her chest. Aaron and Ada both shook with sobs as they took her hands in their own. The aching flesh of her hands barked at the contact, but Penny held them tighter. All three held each other's fingers as if they were the sole things keeping them grounded. At least, it was that way for Penny.

"Sissy would've done anythin' for you, m'lady." Aaron's voice clogged with sadness. "We all would. We're glad her sacrifice... that none of it was in vain."

Penny let out a moan and her sobs wracked her limbs. She couldn't tell how much time they sat there mourning together. It didn't take long for the exhaustion to sweep her into oblivion once again.

"How did she get here?"

The soft whisper of Mother's voice washed over her, and she woke once again. Her eyelids were more compliant than the last time and she focused on the ceiling above her smothered in night.

"One of the boys brought her from the house," Aaron replied.

"We'll have to make sure he's well compensated."

"Don't think you'll be able to repay him. Lad disappeared after he left her. Hasn't come back."

Penny blinked away the tears. She had no reason to cry over the disappearance of the man who had lied to her. At every turn, he'd made a fool out of her. They knew one another. They'd met and he hadn't had the decency to show her. What an idiot he probably thought she was.

"Very well. If he returns, let me know immediately. I'd hate to think what would have happened if he hadn't delivered her to your door."

Penny heard the grunt of Aaron's reply.

"I'm sorry for your loss, both of you. Sissy was a beam of sunshine in our household. She will not be forgotten."

"Thank you, Your Grace." Ada's voice held the sound of grief.

Penny decided she'd had enough and attempted to sit up. The room spun and she nearly fell back onto the mattress before strong hands held her up.

"Easy, m'lady."

Aaron's strong arms wrapped around her shoulders as he sat next to her on the bed. The mattress bowed slightly and Penny looked up to see Mother's figure sitting next to her legs. A small candle sat cradled in her hand until she placed it on the bedside table. Her sharp green eyes rimmed with tears as their gazes met and her chin wobbled slightly until her entire face crumpled.

"Oh, Penny."

Penny felt her own expression mirror Mother's. Aaron stood to allow Mother to tenderly wrap Penny in her arms. Their soft cries filled the space and Penny heard the bedroom door open and close. They held one another in the darkness of the room as they cried.

"Sissy, the orchards, the house. All of it's gone." Penny's cries reverberated through her bones and a deep weariness settled into her soul. Mother continued to smooth Penny's hair down her back. Tears fell on top of Penny's head.

"I know, my love. I know."

Did she? Penny couldn't trust her anymore. She couldn't trust Lou—

Amber Eyes.

Her heart broke all over again.

It took three days before Penny was deemed able to leave Aaron and Ada's house. Mother had snuck a doctor out of Eleusia under the rebels' noses and he'd been able to treat the few burns Penny had on her limbs and face as well as give them everything they would need to get to another doctor.

"I can't believe we have to leave," Penny said as Mother helped her lace her boots. Her hands had been wrapped the last few days, her skin still healing from the effects of the fire. It was worse than the sunburn she'd received when she had fallen asleep in the cottonwood grove at ten years old.

"It's not safe here," Mother responded. "The Cartographer has claimed the duchy as his own. While the mob here destroyed the orchards, the rebels in the towns struck. They went after every city official and law enforcer they hadn't converted to their cause. According to the letter I received from the bailiff after he escaped Eleusia, the rebels have already captured all of the gifted folk and loaded them on ships. Anyone caught defending those with powers is immediately arrested and thrown into the jailhouse under the bailiff's keep. They're slowly working their way through the duchy and will be upon us any day now."

Of course they were. Mother was feeding them information. She may have even been the cause of their house burning down.

Mother tightened the laces of Penny's boot. The ends had

frayed where the heat of the fire had singed them. Penny had both daggers tucked in the jacket Ada had let her borrow along with the dress that now draped over Penny's smaller form. It was the best they were able to procure on such short notice. Mother patted Penny's leg.

"The carriage is outside," said Mother. "Meli is tied to the back along with what little we were able to salvage from the manor."

"Did they find her?"

Mother was well aware of whom she was referring. "Not yet, sweetheart. I'm sure they will get through the rubble to her. She'll have a proper burial with or without her remains."

Penny sniffed, but didn't allow the tears to fall. There had been enough for today.

Mother helped her out of the chair in Ada's front room. As field master, Aaron had the largest house in the village. It stood at the end of the street, just in front of the small wood that sat along the river's edge. That same river was diverted into canals closer to the manor and fed all of the fields the Barclay's had ever tended. Alfie, their water mage, had likely already left the lands and the canals now ran of their own accord.

Penny and Mother walked onto the front porch of Aaron's house to find him and Ada both waiting for them. Ada held a basket out toward Mother, who took it in both hands as if it were made of gold.

"The neighbors made sure to contribute to the basket," Ada supplied. "It should easily get you to the capital with food to spare. We added extra bandages and a few extra water skins just in case." The woman turned to Penny. "We will be following you to the capital after Aggie and Thomas make it here this afternoon." Aggie was Aaron and Ada's older daughter who lived in Eleusia with her husband. One more person who had to mourn.

Mother wrapped one arm around Ada and whispered words Penny couldn't hear into the kind woman's ear. Tears sprang into Ada's eyes as her arms wrapped around her duchess. If only she knew Mother was the one who supported the men who had killed her daughter.

Penny walked up to them and offered her wrist. The blue satin had no lingering marks after having been safely tucked into the cuff of her sleeve during the fire.

"This was Sissy's favorite ribbon. I only have it because she allowed me to wear it the day of... the day my mother left. I can't remove it myself, but I knew you would want it."

Ada sniffled as Aaron wrapped his large hands around Penny's wrist.

"She'd want you to have it," Aaron stated. "You were her best friend, 'sides Aggie, and she would want nothin' more than fer you to carry it with you."

Tears dripped onto Penny's face as she wrapped both of Sissy's parents in her arms. She had no words to convey the depth of her grief or gratitude to these two people she had always been able to look up to. She broke away from them and strode toward the carriage, looking back and waving goodbye to the couple she'd always hoped she would one day have the opportunity to emulate.

Penny slumped into the carriage next to Philomina. Philomina's own eyes were red with grief as she tucked Penny under one of her arms.

"We're going to get through this," Philomina urged. "The Goddess has a plan for each of us and this is simply one small step that is going to lead to greater things than we could possibly imagine."

Penny could only nod as the door to the carriage closed and the driver urged the horses to carry them off. Her spirit raged within her. She couldn't come to terms with the fact that this was part of something greater. Shouldn't the Goddess prevent tragedies like this? What good could possibly come from such great sorrow?

Penny couldn't bear to watch the charred fields pass by out the window. Apparently, Mother couldn't either because she shut the curtains over the windows and sat back in her seat. The sole source of illumination came from the small lines of sunlight peeking through the edges of the heavy cloth. Mother simply stared at the floorboards of the carriage beneath their feet.

Could Mother have really done it? Penny couldn't quite believe she would burn down all of the work they had poured their souls into. Perhaps she was seeing the repercussions of her choices. Maybe this would help her see how wrong the rebellion was. Maybe she would change her mind about Prince Dion.

Mother shifted on the seat across from Penny. Her angry expression never wavered.

Philomina reached down and set a hand on Penny's knee. The ride to Olympia looked bleak.

34

SUMMONS AND TITLES

Penny gazed out the window of the small drawing room sitting at the front of the town house. For six days, Mother had sequestered them there while they tried to get their business in order. Deposits had to be returned, orders called off, and merchants reimbursed. The upstairs study had turned into a cyclone of business documents and correspondence. Penny had needed a moment to breathe after lunch before she could return to the chaos.

No one had come up with a plan to take back the duchy. Mother had sought out the council members who remained in the city the first night they'd arrived. The council had sent missive after missive to the people in the surrounding areas. The only thing anyone knew was that Eleusion had been taken and no one was getting inside.

Penny's burns had healed quickly with the salves the doctor had given her and the treatment she received from a healing mage. The itching as her skin repaired itself had been intense and she was grateful it had subsided. Her face glowed with new skin and the ends of her hair had been trimmed to cut away the burnt edges.

Someone walked onto their drive, distracting Penny from her blank staring. She got to her feet and swept toward the front door where Rich stood with his gloved hand on the handle.

"There's no need for you to answer, Lady Penny," said Rich.

"It's all right. I can handle this if you would see to my mother in the study."

Rich nodded in acquiescence and made his way to the stairs. Penny swung the door open to find a boy in the crown's blue and gold livery standing on the front step.

The boy startled when he saw her, his brows drawing in confusion until he cleared his throat. "Good afternoon, my lady. I come bearing a message for Duchess Dominique Barclay and her daughter Penelope."

"I'm Penelope. I will accept your message."

He hesitantly reached into his bag. "All right."

He pulled a folded envelope out of his satchel. He handed it over before giving a short bow and turning back the way he'd come. The royal seal in blue wax held the parchment together. Penny shouted her thanks to the retreating messenger and shut the front door. Penny turned it over to see Mother's name enshrined in black ink above her own.

"Who was that, Penny? Why didn't you let Rich open the door?"

Penny looked up to see Mother standing at the top of the stairs with the steward hovering just behind her. "It was a messenger from the palace."

Mother glided down the steps and took the envelope. She broke the pristine seal and glanced over the page before handing it over her shoulder to Rich. "It's a summons to the palace for an emergency council meeting."

"When are you to go?"

Mother's eyes caught Penny's. "*We* are to be there first thing in the morning. They've asked for us to give an account of what happened at the duchy."

Mother began discussing with Rich what documents she would need, and Penny darted up to her room. Her hands shook as she walked through the hallway. She didn't know if she was ready to talk about what happened with a group of strangers. She needed more time to collect evidence. The small pieces of paper hidden up in her room weren't enough.

Penny pushed out into the garden behind the house. Barclay House had extensive gardens with every type of flora. The earthy smell and the cool breeze soothed Penny's mind as she walked.

The sun was sitting just below the horizon, the light hanging on for its last few moments before the night finally smothered it.

Her thoughts carried her through the grassy paths. She used the plants beneath her feet to quiet her steps, making them almost silent. The small feat drained her faster than it did back home, the capital having less magic in the ground than the duchy. The stone and pure iron decorating the streets and houses of the city dampened the magic nearly as well as the magical wards. No wonder Mother hated coming here. It almost hurt to breathe.

Penny slipped into the patch of trees bordering the more formal garden. Birches, oaks, and ashes spread out before her, making her miss the cottonwood clearing at Barclay Manor.

She pressed herself against a particularly large oak and sat on the ground.

What was she going to do about tomorrow? Would she sit to the side and pretend she knew nothing? Would she accuse Mother of consorting with the enemy there in front of the entire council? Tears pricked the backs of her eyes just thinking about it.

A twig snapped behind her.

She didn't move. Her ears strained for any other noises and picked up on the quiet footsteps she hadn't heard moments before. A tall, cloaked figure slipped through the trees.

Penny waited until he'd slipped past her to follow him. His steps weren't silent, but she recognized the gait.

Rich stopped at the wall of the property. He removed a large stone from the wall.

A voice came from the other side. "Is it done?"

Penny stepped as close as she dared.

"It's done. Everything went according to plan. The fire brought the distraction we needed and gave her the perfect alibi for being in the capital."

"Excellent. Is Her Grace ready for phase two?"

Penny heard Rich's dark chuckle. "The Cartographer is ready."

Breakfast roiled in her stomach. She hadn't been able to eat more than two bites with Mother in the room.

She had to find him. She had to tell him what she'd heard. It didn't matter if she couldn't trust him to tell her the truth. He worked for the third prince. This was bigger than either of them.

Penny opened her door to find Philomina sitting in a chair in Penny's small sitting room with a needle and thread, surrounded by half a dozen dresses. The fire had made no exceptions for Penny's large wardrobe in the manor and they had to buy a few dresses to alter while they waited for the seamstress to restock Penny's closet.

"Philo, do you have any of the more formal gowns ready?"

Philomina set the light green dress in her hands aside and stood to walk with Penny toward her bedroom.

"I was able to alter one of your mother's older dresses in case something like this came up. It's a few seasons old, but with lace coming back into fashion, I only had to alter the sleeves and tuck in the waist to fit your slightly smaller size."

Philomina walked into the closet and pulled out the dress decorated in a dark green lace overlaying a beige colored satin. Three-quarter sleeves ended with a small bell at her elbow and the skirt fell to the floor. Luckily, Penny was the same size shoe as Mother and could raid her closet for matching slippers. Philomina did her best to help Penny into the dress quickly and the two of them set off toward Mother's rooms across the hall.

Mother stood in front of the mirror in an olive-green dress with a high collar and a cream belt. Philomina raced over to button up the back while Penny rummaged through Mother's shoe collection. There weren't nearly as many shoes here as there'd been in the manor, but Penny easily found a pair matching the dark emerald of the lace perfectly.

When both of them finished, Penny and Mother boarded the carriage Rich had waiting for them on the front drive. Penny's stomach swirled.

Keep it together. You just have to wait until you get to the palace. Then you can find him.

As the carriage took off down the drive, she recalled the last time she'd made this trip. Had it only been a year and a half ago? After the events of the last six months, it felt like a decade.

The front gates of the palace looked exactly the same. Thick iron curled into oak trees stood sentry along with the handful of guards. The armored men in royal colors checked over their carriage at the entrance. They were directed to pull up at the front steps leading into the large home of the royal family. This time, no lines of footmen stood waiting at attention and no glittering lights cast magic over the white facade of the palace.

Penny stepped out of the carriage onto the hard ground. One footman stood at the large door and closed it behind them as they all stepped inside.

"Are the others gathered?" Mother asked the servant.

"All but the princes themselves, Your Grace. Everyone else is in the council chamber."

"Then let's not keep them waiting."

Penny followed Mother through the large palace. She remembered the gilded filigree decorating the walls and the many pieces of artwork covering every surface. It wasn't long, however, before they turned down a path Penny had no familiarity with.

The hallways without windows were lightened with magelights housed in lanterns and chandeliers hanging above their heads. Courtiers began to pop out of thin air the closer they got to the council chamber. Noble ladies tittered behind fans as they passed and many of the men walked side by side down the hall in deep discussion. Penny's ears picked up the words "rebels," "fire," and "gifted" more than once as they maneuvered through the sparkling dresses and finely tailored suits.

"Here we are," announced the footman and knocked on the door. Another footman opened it from the other side. Penny straightened her posture and they entered the large council chamber. She needed to do her best to keep Mother's attention away from her.

Penny felt her mouth fall open. Mother's past descriptions didn't do the room justice. A humongous table stretched the length of the room, making a place for over thirty seats. A map of Olympia and the surrounding kingdoms took up a large portion of one wall. Banners decorated in the standards of all the noble houses draped from the ceiling surrounding a crystal chandelier dripping with magelights.

The multitude of people about the room stood decorated as much as their banners. Penny recognized most of them from Mother's lessons as well as business meetings she'd been privy to. Paulo and Lord Hermen were the first to make their way toward them.

"We're happy to see you both looking no worse for wear," remarked Lord Hermen. "We feared the worst when we heard about the devastation that took place in Eleusion."

"Thank you for your concern, Lord Hermen. As you can see, the fiends were not able to take us out of the equation so easily."

Penny wanted to shout.

Mother and Lord Hermen made their way to the table as Paulo sidled up next to Penny.

"I'm glad to see you're all right. I'm so sorry I..."

Penny set a hand on her friend's shoulder. "Paulo, I will never expect you to know everything. I could never blame you for what transpired. I know you have no control over what the Goddess allows you to see."

Paulo nodded and took the hand she had resting on his arm. He gave a short bow over it before standing and patting the top. The tips of his fingers met the soft satin ribbon still wrapped around her wrist.

"Regardless, I am sorry for the grief you've had to endure."

Penny's throat clogged and all she was able to offer was a nod in return. Paulo led her to stand beside Mother before shuffling toward his own chair.

Mother still spoke with Lord Hermen, but the two were interrupted as the doorman announced the arrival of the Crown Prince.

Prince Dion sauntered through the door, followed by a silent Prince Evan. Prince Dion called for everyone to rise from their bows and curtsies before his eyes landed on Penny and Mother. The pair made their way toward the two women as the gathered crowd scurried toward their chairs. Penny stood just behind the chair next to Mother's when the princes stopped next to them.

"Your Grace," Prince Dion began, "the news you've brought from Eleusion has brought great sorrow to our houses. We mourn with you over the losses your family and your people have endured. We assure you, it is our utmost priority to see everything set back to the way it was and your home returned to your caring hands."

Penny and Mother both curtsied.

"Thank you, Your Highness," Mother replied. "Your words are much appreciated."

"Anything you require, just let us know. We would be happy to help."

With the kind words, the two men walked to the head of the table. Prince Evan sat to the Crown Prince's right while the chair to the left remained empty.

"If we could all be seated," Prince Dion called across the room, "we can begin this council meeting."

The sounds of chairs in addition to the rustle of dozens of different fabrics echoed through the room.

"To start off, I'd like to turn the time over to Lady

Dominique Barclay as well as her daughter, Lady Penelope, to share with us what happened at their duchy."

Penny's chest stalled as Mother rose to speak.

"The rebels have taken over the whole of Eleusion."

The crowd murmured in response and Mother went into detail about the report from the bailiff in Eleusia. She gave an accounting of the acres of ruined farmland and the damage to the manor. All in attendance had their eyes riveted to Mother and the emotions on their faces ranged from shock to outrage. Mother answered every question calmly and eventually gestured to Penny.

"My daughter was in the house when the men set fire to it."

Penny took in the faces surrounding her once again before getting to her feet. Now was the time to finally decide. Did she tell them? Did she wait until she found Lou— or Amber Eyes or whoever he was? Her palms slicked. Her heartbeat picked up. She opened her mouth to speak and a side door burst open.

Everyone in their chairs started. All eyes shifted from her to the man striding into the room. Lou's golden eyes met Penny's across the large space as the rest of the council members stood. Silence greeted him as he sauntered toward the empty seat at the head of the table.

He was clad completely in black except for the gold of his belt buckle and the steel of his sword. His very presence demanded recognition and the aloof look of his face belied the fire burning in his amber eyes. His gaze never disengaged from Penny's even as he came up to the Crown Prince's side.

"Ah," sighed Prince Dion, "how good of you to join us, Prince Aiden."

EPILOGUE

AND THEN IT BEGAN

THE INTRUDER TOOK A DEEP BREATH OF THE SALTY, CITY AIR.

It smelled of pain. Heartache. Death.

Possibilities.

Returning to Olympia had always been part of the plan, but in all the many times the intruder had been there, the air had never buzzed under her skin as it did just then. It had never carried the foreboding of change.

A door in the alabaster wall across from her slid open silently into the courtyard where she hid in the boughs of a tall oak.

Waiting.

Watching.

Hair as dark as ink and skin as pale as moonlight slipped into the shadows. Amber eyes scanned the palace's formal gardens, but he didn't see the intruder perched in the tree above him like a griffin vulture. The boy prince stalked out into the night air, as the intruder recalled him doing when he felt cooped up in that gigantic castle of his. But he would not feel the bars of that gilded prison for long.

Soon, he would find himself in a different cage than the one he so wished to escape that night.

Soon, she would cast out all of the pests scurrying about the palace and those golden halls would be *hers*.

Green eyes sparkled as she watched the boy prince. This palace, this kingdom, all of it would be pulled out from under the unaware pretender, this child who thought he could play at being kingmaker.

He would find out what a *queenmaker* looked like soon enough.

But not yet.

The intruder smiled and melted back into the shadows. Her gleeful steps took her out of the palace gates. Even the lay of the street spoke of how high these people had come up in the world. She'd watched these sycophants kill her friends to put themselves up into these lofty houses.

The intruder's mouth twisted into a silent snarl. *It will be my greatest achievement when these boot-licking frauds burn within those walls.*

With a firm shake of her head, she kept walking. There was too much to do tonight— too much to prepare for. Her plans slowly took shape in her mind as she walked in the direction of the house dripping in ivy. Lights glowed through the windows, the entirety of Barclay Manor's displaced staff still settling in. Rich should be waiting for her out in the garden, away from the inhabitants of the house.

She would be meticulous. Discreet. There was too much riding on the fact no one knew she was the puppet master. The schemer. The Cartographer. If anyone figured it out before she was ready, her path would become difficult.

But she always left room for error. She'd learned to not underestimate the Crown Prince and his influence— especially over his youngest brother. By the Goddess, she would take everything from them. She stopped on the street and turned her eyes back to the glittering palace on the hill, imagining what it would be like to see the structure wreathed in flames. Turning away, she pulled the hood of her cloak down so low as to only show her deadly smile.

It was time to get to work.

AFTERWORD

As many of you may have noticed, a lot of this book has strong elements of Greek mythology. A lot of the stories within this book are direct references to the gods and goddesses of ancient times. The story of Artemis scaring off a potential suitor by disguising herself as a river monster is one. Another is Hermes pranking Apollo by making him believe his cows were diseased because they could walk backward. No, Persephone was never a pomegranate farmer, but Demeter was a rather overbearing mother. I did take creative liberties with some of the characters to match my story better—like the fact that I couldn't have Prince Dion be Penny's father because...well, ew. But the essence of the mythology is there if you look for it. There are so many tiny things that played a part in this story and really brought the mythology to life for me.

However, I think you will all be happily surprised with how this particular story ends.

ACKNOWLEDGMENTS

Wow, I seriously can't believe we're finally here! It's surreal! There are so many absolutely amazing people that played a role in bringing this story to life and I know for certain I am going to forget someone.

First off, I need to thank my family. Eric, my love, you are the kite to my string. I would never have seen the height I have without you riding the wind simply to see where it takes us. Thank you for teaching me how to dream. And to my girls, you beautiful, amazing daughters of mine, thank you. Thank you for being a part of this dream and for dreaming with me.

I want to thank my dad. Seriously, I would never have made it this far without your constant encouragement of me and your insistence that I join your writing group when I had that crazy dream that I thought would be a good story. David Haynie, Ben Bailey, Aimee Hall, Marci Johnson, you all have played such a big role in this book and in helping me build my craft. Thank you for letting me stay in the group even though I talk way too much.

A big portion of my thanks needs to go to Jeff Wheeler. It was completely divine intervention that put our paths together. Thank you for being the absolute best mentor in the world and for always encouraging me. Thank you Tyleah Merino, the best cousin/alpha reader/sound board of all time. You have been a constant support to these books and I can't believe I almost left you out of the acknowledgements because you have been such a humongous part of this book from the very beginning. Thank you Melissa Frain for helping me with the development of the story in its early stages.

I want to thank Tanya Anne Crosby for taking a chance on me. This book would have never gotten this far with you and the wonderful team at Oliver Heber Books. From the very bottom of my heart, thank you. To my editor, Kate Ward, you are a gem! You fixed so many problems that I had created for myself and made the book a hundred times better simply by looking at it. Thanks Inessa Sage for the beautiful cover art. I still drool every time I see it.

I also want to thank my amazingly talented fellow writers that have kept me aloft through plot holes and slogging manuscripts. Lindsay Hiller, you are my hero. Kelsey Brynn Larson, Bonnie Jo Pierson, HR Boyd, Marci Johnson (again), Kayla Beth Tillotson, Tarry Perry, Sally O'Keef, and Natalie Kraus, thank you for all of our Third Thursday Zoom calls and our outrageous text thread. You keep me alive most days.

Lastly, but most importantly, I need to thank my Heavenly Father. My gratitude will never be fully expressed in simple words, but thank You. You are the reason any of this was ever possible.

ALSO BY ALLISON ANDERSON

Children of Ash

Children of Ash

Son of Steel

The Cartographer's War

The Spring Maiden

The Shadow Lord

The Unseen King

The Unwanted Queen

The Cartographer's War: A Necessary Tragedy

The Seer's Assassin

The Fated Mage

ABOUT THE AUTHOR

Allison Anderson lives her best life as a wife, a mom, a dedicated member of The Church of Jesus Christ of Latter-Day Saints, and a fantasy writer. As a lifelong fantasy nerd, she finds it natural to create stories of her own and you can often find her jotting down new story ideas or talking about dragons. She's spent most of her life across the southwestern United States.

https://www.allisonandersonauthor.com/

www.ingramcontent.com/pod-product-compliance
Lightning Source LLC
Chambersburg PA
CBHW030241120726
47903CB00005B/1571
9781648394393